ONLY MY HUSBAND CALLS ME COOPER

Cali Kitsu

DDP

Winnipeg, Canada

koi no yokan
[ko-ee no yo-kan]

Noun:
The feeling upon first meeting someone
that you will inevitably fall in love with them.

For my husband, who knew instantly.

Thank you for reading *Only My Husband Calls Me Cooper*, the sequel to *You Can Call Me Cooper*.

This book can be read as a standalone but is best read after reading *You Can Call Me Cooper*.

A few quick notes, this version follows the Author's Cut of *You Can Call Me Cooper*, where the characters are a little older than they were in the YA version. I recognize that the situations in this book would not be entirely possible outside of a fictional world. This book contains mentions of surrogacy, adoption, and possible pregnancy complications. It is also mentioned that a completely off-page character in the past was found after an overdose, no further details are given.

Thank you for your support,
Cali <3

Table of Contents

Chapter 1: Puppies Can't Open Doors 1
Chapter 2: He Is The Wife 11
Chapter 3: Sweet Spumoni 24
Chapter 4: Can I Call You Daddy? 34
Chapter 5: Holy Cannoli 46
Chapter 6: Cocky Little Shit 54
Chapter 7: A Prick With Cute Features 60
Chapter 8: You Can Decide What Goes In My Mouth 64
Chapter 9: Only My Husband Calls Me Cooper 72
Chapter 10: The Nipple Fiasco 79
Chapter 11: Wine Tasting With Mom And Dad 98
Chapter 12: Kiss Like An Italian 111
Chapter 13: Sauce Slaps And Single People 119
Chapter 14: Ethan's Deep Love Of Cannoli 130
Chapter 15: What's That White Stuff On Your Face? 141
Chapter 16: Boo, Peter 151
Chapter 17: Shut Up, Cannoli Boys 164
Chapter 18: Not Without My Genie Costume 171
Chapter 19: That Bed Is Unusable 177
Chapter 20: What Are They Always Whispering About? 187
Chapter 21: Best Thing Ever 199
Chapter 22: He Is A Nice Guy, Though 204
Chapter 23: Home Sweet Home 213
Chapter 24: Unexpected News 219
Chapter 25: Sunbeams And Dragons 225
Chapter 26: Wicked Stepmother 232
Chapter 27: Pancakes With A Side Of Jealousy 242
Chapter 28: Naughty Puppy 258
Chapter 29: Gina Knows Best 264

Chapter 30: Is This A Date? 277

Chapter 31: Do We Know You? 288

Chapter 32: Don't You Dare Insult Anime 306

Chapter 33: How'd That Get Up There? 317

Chapter 34: That's How It's Supposed To Feel 332

Chapter 35: Take It Easy On The Cupcakes 341

Chapter 36: Not My King 361

Chapter 37: I Want To Kiss You Again 371

Chapter 38: My Pillow Smells Like You 389

Chapter 39: A Good Boy, A Greek God, & A Pool Man . 398

Chapter 40: Peacocking 410

Chapter 41: Flowers And Cannoli 417

Chapter 42: Your Everything Is Out 424

Chapter 43: The King And His Queen 430

Chapter 44: Let Me See It 440

Chapter 45: Sorry I Saw Your Schlong 451

Chapter 46: Arie In Waves 460

Epilogue 472

Chapter 1
Puppies Can't Open Doors

Following their intimate wedding, Coop and Ethan boarded a flight bound for their honeymoon in Tuscany, Italy, the next morning.

Ethan laid his head on his new husband's chest in his small plane seat, falling asleep quickly, while Coop practiced his Italian. He'd been studying for about three months but still wasn't completely confident in his ability to converse properly. Ethan spoke Italian fluently; both his grandmother and grandfather insisted upon him learning the language as a small child.

After a brief layover and a fifteen-hour flight, the two arrived safely. A taxi dropped them off at their resort shortly after landing. Ethan held Coop's hand as they walked toward the large glass entrance doors. "Mr. Morgan, this is gorgeous! I'm so impressed that you found it!"

Coop smiled and embraced Ethan. "Well, Mr. Morgan, I'm happy you like it. I've been practicing my Italian, too. I want to look good in front of your grandparents." He smooched Ethan's cheek.

"That's sweet, but you didn't need to do that. I told you they mostly speak English, anyway."

The two checked into their lavish honeymoon suite from Coop's phone. Ethan held the phone in front of the door, facing the lock. "Why isn't it working? It's an electronic key. We should be able to just"—he waved it again—"scan it and it should open."

Coop held his hand out. "Let me try it." He held the phone in front of the door, and it immediately unlocked.

Ethan's mouth dropped open. "What did you do that I didn't?"

"Puppies can't open doors," Coop said, pinching his chin. He gave Ethan a quick kiss and opened the door for him.

Ethan gasped at the stunning room. He ran over to the large glass French doors, eyes sparkling, looking out at the bright stars in the night sky. "Cooper, look at this, it's gorgeous!"

Coop dropped their carry-on bags down and walked across the room. Ethan grabbed his hand and opened the doors, pulling him outside. "Look there's a private garden, and a pool, and this sitting area is beautiful!"

Coop pulled Ethan in for a squeeze. "Come here, you're so cute. We have all these things at our new house; do you like this garden design better?"

Ethan hung his arms around Coop's neck and gave him a kiss. "Nah, our home is better." He looked around. "And our garden is bigger."

Coop smiled and picked him up, kissing the side of his neck, while Ethan wrapped his legs around him.

Ethan pulled his neck to the side, leaving Coop's mouth open. He looked at him in disbelief. "Already? We just got here. Our luggage hasn't even been dropped off yet."

Coop continued kissing his neck. "Mmm, yes, it has." He carried Ethan into the main living area; their luggage had indeed been placed in the room before they got there.

Ethan held Coop's face as he looked around. "Oh, great! They already brought it. That was fast! Oooh! Cooper, look there are so many roses here!" Ethan jumped down from Coop and walked across the room toward the large display of vibrant red flowers on the table. He picked up a small note from within the roses. *I love you, my puppy. I am yours and you are mine, forever. Love, Cooper.* He held the note near his heart and stuck his bottom lip out, then hugged Coop tightly. "Thank you, they're beautiful. This was so sweet and unexpected."

Coop moved in fast for a slow, wet kiss. Ethan pulled back after a few swirls of the tongue. "Mmm…we should shower, then let's try out the bed." He pulled Coop toward the bathroom.

Coop took the love note out of Ethan's hand. "There's a story behind this," he said.

Ethan walked into the large bathroom. There was a two-person clawfoot tub in the center that faced another private garden area. He pulled his mouth to the side. "I feel weird using a tub that other people have used."

"I knew you wouldn't want to use that. Upstairs is a large shower like ours, with a private sauna. Come on," Coop said, taking him by the hand.

"Oh, I forgot you said we had two floors. Is it just the bathroom up there?" The two walked up the spiral stairs together. Ethan gasped. "Cooper! This is better than the rooms downstairs."

"It better be. This is the main suite; downstairs is technically for any guests that we have."

Ethan scoffed. "Guests? Yeah, right. Who brings guests on their honeymoon? It's just you and me."

"Mmhmm. Just you and me, which means more beds for us to use."

Ethan pumped his eyebrows at Coop, then dashed inside the bathroom, while Coop unbuttoned his shirt and followed behind. "This is nice…" Ethan said, looking around the bathroom.

Coop tilted his head and held his arms wide. "You pumped at me. I thought you were telling me you were ready for sex?"

Ethan was a little late in his reaction to what Coop said earlier. "Yes, I did, and I am, but wait, what was the story behind the love note?"

"That was like ten minutes ago that I said that! Hurry up and take your clothes off."

Ethan squished his nose up and walked over to him. He pulled Coop's unbuttoned shirt off, sliding it off his shoulders, letting it fall to the floor.

Coop placed his hands on Ethan's waist. "I thought I could say everything in Italian, so I tried. The concierge kept repeating, 'No pets, no pets' I tried to explain that it was just what I call you, like a pet name, that confused her even more. I ended up needing a translator."

"That's so funny!" Ethan said. He felt a light air below his waist, and looked down. "What the? How did you get my clothes off? I didn't even realize you did that."

Coop squeezed Ethan's ass and pulled him inside the shower. "You're just so used to my hands on you. Now, get in here."

Ethan's cock instantly responded to his husband's command. He loved the way that Coop took charge when he was feeling particularly pent up, and since they hadn't had sex today, he knew that he was about to get it hard and fast.

Following a steamy warm-up in the shower, the two moved onto the bed. Coop pounded Ethan from behind. "Ethan—tell me—who do you belong to?"

"Fuck—I belong to you, my Cooper." Ethan's gold chain with Coop's baseball number on it, swung from his neck with each thrust. Ethan loved the feeling of Coop's thick hard cock sliding in and out of him. "Mmm…Cooper, I'm not gonna last much longer, if you get rough—"

Coop tightly gripped the sides of Ethan's ass. "You're mine Ethan Morgan—this sweet ass is mine forever…"

"My husband. Only yours, Cooper. Hah—hah."

Coop grinded in deep. "Call me your husband again. I'll make you come right now, baby."

"Mmm—I belong to you my husband—unh—my husband—make me come—"

Coop pounded harder, his breaths quickening as he hit Ethan's spot easily and rammed into it. "Unh—Ethan—fuck—unh—come for me."

Ethan moaned, clawing at the sheets, as he came. "Ahhh—unghh—Cooper, I'm coming—ungh—haah."

"Ungh—fuck—Ethan—haah—haah—mmm—"

After a quick cleanup, the two fell asleep upstairs for the night, wrapped in one another's embrace.

The alarm on Ethan's phone blared loudly at 6:00 am. He was tucked inside a spooning position and refused to move. "Nooo, it's not six already," he groaned.

Coop squeezed him tight and kissed him on the cheek. "Yep, it is. Come on, Puppy Morgan, it's time for our first workout as newlyweds.".

Ethan joked, "I think we've worked out plenty as newlyweds already."

Coop quickly turned Ethan onto his back, he pinned his hands above his head and got on top of him. "We could work out like that again, instead of trying out the gym… Is that what you want?" Ethan stuck his tongue out flat and wrapped his legs around, pulling Coop down. Coop stared down at him. "Gym tomorrow, you're too sexy. I need to be inside you, before we head out."

Following their morning workout in between the sheets, and a shower, Ethan dried Coop's hair with the hair dryer from the hotel bathroom. Coop smiled, sitting in a chair with a towel wrapped around his bottom half. Ethan ran his fingers through Coop's hair. "This is taking longer than normal. I guess this hair dryer isn't as strong as ours. I'm glad they had one, though."

Coop looked at his phone. "Yeah, me too. The gondola meet-up is at 9:30, let's grab breakfast from the hotel café and head over once we're dressed."

Ethan looked down at himself. "Can't I go in my towel?"

"No. Definitely not," Coop said, smacking him on the ass.

Coop and Ethan arrived at the gondola meeting spot along the Arno River. The red wooden boat had room for at least twelve people, but they booked it for themselves.

The English-speaking tour guide, an older woman with gray hair, greeted them, "Welcome, my husband and I"—she pointed to the boatman—"are happy to have you. We love newlyweds!" Her husband gave a nod from the back of the gondola where he stood with his long wooden pole.

Coop and Ethan sat close together in the middle of the boat, while the tour guide sat on the front facing them. It was a clear beautiful day, and the breeze off the river felt wonderful. The guide talked through the history of the buildings and gave them ideas of places to visit during their stay.

The two looked up in awe when they went beneath the Ponte Vecchio bridge. Coop pointed up at the buildings. "How can they feel comfortable in those shops? The buildings are hanging off the bridge!"

"Everyone asks that question," the guide said. "It's very secure, despite the way it looks. Now, tell me about yourselves. It's Mr. and Mr. Morgan, Cooper and Ethan, right?"

"Just Coop is fine, and the other Mr. Morgan here likes to be called Ethan or Mr. Morgan, don't know if he has a preference. Do you like one better than the other, baby?"

"Well, we're on our honeymoon, and I really like the sound of being called Mr. Morgan."

Coop whispered something in Ethan's ear, and Ethan elbowed him playfully. "Oh, you don't want that?" Coop asked.

The guide smiled brightly at the two and finally introduced herself as JoAnn. She explained that she and her husband, Ronnie, had five grown adult children, and several grandchildren. "Of course, Ronnie would rather be out here with me, just pushing the boat around, instead of listening to me gab on the phone to whichever adult child is having a meltdown."

Coop and Ethan's eyes widened. "Wow, five kids is a lot of kids," Ethan said.

"Yeah," her voice softened, "but they're all adults now. The time when they were kids passed by so fast. They were all angels; we had it very easy with them."

Ronnie scoffed. "Uh…I don't think so. I think you're talking about someone else's life!"

"Don't listen to him," JoAnn said. "The sun gets to him after a while. They were angels. Kids are such a wonderful blessing. Do you two want to have kids? One of our kids used a surrogate. My granddaughter looks just like my son. It's an amazing thing."

Coop and Ethan collectively bit their lips and looked down.

Ronnie remarked from the back, "JoAnn! Look what you did,

you made them uncomfortable. We're gonna get a bad review if you make people uncomfortable! You can't talk about stuff like that. I told you, just stick to the history of the buildings."

Ethan waved it off. "No. It's fine. We weren't uncomfortable because of that."

"Ha!" Ronnie shouted. "But you *were* uncomfortable! I told you, JoAnn!"

Coop smiled, rubbing Ethan's arm. "No, not really uncomfortable with the conversation, we're both a bit too jealous for that type of surrogacy."

"What do you mean jealous?" JoAnn asked. "Neither of you would have to sleep with the surrogate…I don't understand."

Coop and Ethan shared a quick smooch. Coop answered her, "I wouldn't want anyone to carry his child."

Ethan added, "I feel the same about him. Even though I think it's beautiful…and wonderful for other people, it's just not an option that we want to consider right now. Maybe we'll change our minds in the future."

Coop kissed Ethan's warm, smiling cheek, nuzzling his nose against it.

She tilted her head, looking at the two. "But you two are gorgeous, look at yourselves. Such beautiful features between the two of you. I think you should consider it. Some couples try for twins, and both are donors. You could do that… I know all about surrogacy. We just watched our son go through it…very lengthy process though."

Ronnie screamed playfully from the back, "JoAnn! Talk about something else, anything else, please? Two minutes of normal conversation is all that's needed at this point. The dock is right there!"

Coop and Ethan stepped off the boat, feeling happy that they chose this particular tour service. "Thank you very much," Coop said.

Ethan added, "We had a great time!"

JoAnn stood beside her husband, smiling brightly at them. "It was lovely meeting you both. Think about what I said."

"Terrible review, guaranteed. No doubt about it," Ronnie mumbled.

Coop pulled his phone out and checked the map. "The first museum is only a fifteen-minute walk from here. Come on, pup." He kissed Ethan's hand and held it.

Their private group tour of the museums included tickets to both the Uffizi and Accademia Galleries. Ethan was in awe of the beautiful paintings and sculptures. Coop embraced him from behind and propped his chin on his shoulder. "I love watching you look at art. If the people that made these pieces could've seen the way your eyes light up, they would've been very happy. Well, I guess some of them would…some were sculpted or painted from pain, so maybe not all of them."

Ethan was amazed at everything that surrounded him. "It's just so beautiful to create something that transcends time. I wish I could create something like that. But, no, my precious painting of us as kids tied…with a painting of a dog."

Earlier in the year, at the local art gallery, Ethan entered a competition through his college. The theme was separation. He submitted a newly made painting of himself and Coop at ten years old, showing the two facing one another on opposite baseball fields through chain link fences, each boy with tears in their eyes. It was a moving piece, and the emotions that the two boys felt at that time were palpable through Ethan's representation. He won first place in his category and tied for overall best, with a picture of a dog and its owner; the dog looking out of its front home window as its owner drove away.

Coop stuck his bottom lip out. "Aww, my puppy is still upset that he tied with a puppy."

"Well, yeah. I love dogs, you know that, but I mean, the dog was not even…no, that's not true. It was a good drawing. I'm not mad about the dog, but the guy was so snobby about sharing the win. Remember? He was so mean. I'll never forget that."

"Oh, I know you won't. So fiery."

"He kinda ruined the idea of ever getting a dog for me. I think I'll always imagine that guy now. I don't think I could do it."

"Yeah, I think I would, too. No dogs for us."

After a full day of sightseeing and street food, the two went back to their hotel room. Ethan reached into Coop's pocket enthusiastically, drawing a light grunt from him. He pulled Coop's phone out. "I'm gonna get the door open this time." He waved the phone in front of the handle several times, and the lock remained closed. He cursed in Italian and handed it back to Coop.

"I don't know that word, what does that mean?"

An older couple was walking by, so Ethan whispered it in Coop's ear. "Oh wow. I'll have to remember that one," Coop said.

Coop waved the phone once in front of the door lock, and it instantly opened.

Ethan gave up for the moment. "I'll get it open next time," he said.

Chapter 2
He Is The Wife

The next morning, Coop squeezed Ethan tightly and whined when the alarm sounded. "Baby, please, I don't want to go to the gym. I'm tired. Let me just hold you."

"Well, I'm not gonna force you to move. I love my big spoon. You want me to snooze it? Or turn it off?"

"Ugh," Coop groaned. "Let's snooze it for fifteen and then check out the gym."

Fifteen minutes later, the alarm sounded again. Coop nuzzled against Ethan's cheek, "You want to check out the gym?"

"Yeah, let's get dressed. That food yesterday probably sent our bodies into shock. We should try to stick to our regimen if we can."

Coop and Ethan, dressed in matching black track pants and white performance shirts, strolled through the atrium and down the long, quiet halls.

"How much further is it?" Ethan asked. "This place is huge! I don't even see a gym. I don't think we even need to run once we find it. We've been walking for like twenty minutes."

"The last sign pointed this way," Coop said. "We haven't even passed any employees to ask. Let's just go a little further."

Once they rounded the next corner, they finally reached the

gym. They peeked through the glass door before entering. It was a very small room, with two treadmills, two elliptical machines, one weight bench and a single exercise bike, all cramped inside.

Coop opened the door, and Ethan entered first.

"This looked much bigger online. Right, baby?" Coop asked.

"Yeah, but it's alright," Ethan said. "There's two treadmills and we can alternate with the weights. At least there isn't anyone else here, way too small for anything more than two people."

"Can we take the shirts off? I'm used to doing this chests-out, every morning. Helps me stay motivated." Coop winked at Ethan.

"Absolutely not." Ethan gestured toward the door. "What if someone comes in?"

"Maybe we can lock it. Is there a lock?" Coop walked over and inspected the door. "Ugh, no lock. Alright, fine. The shirts stay on." He stretched his arms and twisted. "So tight, though."

Ethan placed his phone on the treadmill control screen and turned their morning playlist on. They stepped on the treadmills, found their correct speed, and started their morning run. Coop sang aloud when their favorite song came on, while Ethan sounded out the electric guitar sounds.

The door opened, and the mirror-covered walls reflected a couple entering, holding hands. Ethan quickly turned the music off.

The girl rolled her eyes, as her partner tried to calm her about something.

Ethan and Coop tried not to listen, but with the size of the room, it was impossible not to hear the woman complaining about having to wait.

Ethan spoke politely while running, "Good morning, our run will be finished in another ten minutes."

She rolled her eyes again. Her huge diamond ring sparkled in the mirror reflection. She whispered loudly to her husband, "We're on our honeymoon, they're just two dudes, get them to leave. We don't have time to wait."

Her husband whispered back, "They're not just two dudes, they're huge. I don't want to piss them off. If they get mad, what do you think is gonna happen? I'm gonna get punched, not you."

Ethan and Coop looked at one another, they both clearly felt embarrassed for the husband. Coop would only punch someone if they truly upset Ethan, or if Ethan asked him to. The same went for Ethan.

The woman scoffed at her husband. "Don't be a wuss. Just tell them it's our honeymoon."

Her husband nervously spoke to Ethan, "Hey, man, thanks for the uh, heads up. We're um, on our honeymoon. We have a full day today; we were hoping to get in a walk before we head out."

"Yeah, we're on our honeymoon, too," Coop said. "This room is pretty small, we heard everything that you guys just said. Like my husband already told you, we'll be done shortly."

The husband gave his wife a look and shook his head in embarrassment.

She stepped closer toward their treadmills. "I'm sorry. I thought you guys were just working out on a business trip or something. I didn't think you were on your honeymoon."

Coop spoke to the woman in the mirror, "We don't really need to talk anymore. We'll be done soon."

She stood staring intently at them as they ran, while her husband was doing something on his phone. She spoke in a flirty voice while eyeing Ethan and Coop, "You guys are really…buff. So, are you like professional athletes, or models?"

Ethan was quickly slipping into spicy puppy mode. He was more than annoyed with the wife staring at Coop. He looked at her in the mirror, then raised his eyebrows at her husband and addressed him,

"Hey, does your wife always talk to married men in gyms? Feels weird trying to exercise with my husband and her just standing there staring at us."

The wife was unfazed and continued to stare. The husband walked near Coop's treadmill. "This is why you guys are lucky. It seems like you both agree on what should be said and shouldn't, probably since you're both guys. She doesn't ever know what makes me uncomfortable. We just got married and she's telling everyone that it's our honeymoon, expecting people to bow down or something. She just shouts out however she feels. It's been a crazy honeymoon so far."

Coop's eyes widened. "Whoa, you just said so many things."

"So many things," Ethan echoed. "We need you both to stop talking to us, please."

The woman put her hand on her hip with attitude and faced her husband. "See my mom told me you would be like this. She told me and I didn't listen. What did you even mean by that, 'you guys are lucky' comment? You don't feel lucky to be married to me?"

"Do you guys fight like this?" the husband asked Ethan. "I bet you don't."

Coop looked at the husband. "Hey, man, we have three minutes, could you just…not?"

The wife eyed Ethan from behind, checking him out, then moved her gaze to Coop. She whispered loudly to her husband, "I thought in most guy/guy relationships one is big and one is small. But they're both big. I'm confused. Isn't that a thing?"

Ethan's eyes widened, and he turned his treadmill off, with two minutes remaining. He'd had enough of this. Coop followed and turned his off, too. They stepped off the treadmills and wiped their faces with clean towels provided by the hotel.

The husband took several steps backwards.

The wife looked at Coop. "Oh, I see, yeah he's bigger."

Ethan cursed under his breath in Italian, while Coop gave the man a look of warning.

The husband put his hands up. "Don't hit me because of her. I can't fight, look at my arms, man." He lifted his sleeve and showed his thin linguini-like arm to Coop and Ethan.

"Neither of us is going to hit you," Coop said. "But what she said was not okay. Someone else might hit you, but not us, at least not today."

"Don't really want to end up in jail," Ethan added. "Supposed to visit my Nonna today. She wouldn't be too happy with that."

The wife squealed, "You have a Nonna? Me too! Aren't Nonna's the best? Mine makes the best sauce!"

Ethan whispered in Coop's ear; Coop chuckled loudly.

The wife pulled her husband over toward her. "We just got married at a theme park, we had a carriage and everything, my Nonna paid for it. It was so romantic. When he proposed, it was even more romantic."

Coop tilted his head. "How was the proposal more romantic than your wedding? I bet ours was better."

She excitedly described the proposal at a company dinner.

"That's really nice." Ethan gave her a fake smile. "Ours was better, though. We should go, didn't you say you were in a rush to exercise?"

"How was it better?" the husband asked. "I planned that for two years!"

"Two years? You already lost," Coop said. "What took you so long? I wanted to propose to him the day we got together. I only waited because I wanted him to have the perfect proposal."

Ethan held Coop's arm. "Yeah, we knew we were getting married from day one, can't compare the two. No contest."

The man folded his small arms across his chest. "Tell me the proposal story. Vanessa, use the treadmill if you want to."

Coop raised his eyebrows at Ethan. "See, this is why it was worth it to wait."

Ethan kissed Coop's cheek. "Everyone loves a good proposal story."

Coop explained the proposal, and the man snapped his fingers, pointing in excitement. "I saw that! I saw that! Oh man, I can't believe it's you two. My buddies and I watched that game!"

Vanessa's mouth dropped. "I knew you guys looked familiar! Oh wow, you're like famous for that."

The husband spoke excitedly to Ethan. "Yeah, man, when you stole home, it was crazy! My buddies and I were betting on what was going to happen." He pointed to Coop. "I thought you were gonna crank it out. One of my friends was like 'Nah number two on third base, just kissed his chain, he's gonna steal home.' I lost fifty bucks on that. It was worth it though. Wow, just wow!" The husband suddenly appeared at a loss looking at the two. "I wish there was something for you guys to sign for me. You're already famous college players. You guys will go pro soon, right? I'm gonna kick myself when we get home for not getting your autographs."

"You guys want to swap numbers with him?" the wife asked.

Ethan answered, "Sorry. We're really private people."

"Yeah, but good luck...with everything," Coop added.

Ethan and Coop headed back to their room, happy to finally be free of the very annoying newlyweds.

"It's crazy running into people from the states," Coop said. "People really are strange, though."

"Good thing you didn't take your shirt off before they got there."

"Me? I caught her staring at your ass. Didn't like that."

Ethan sighed. "Yeah, I was very uncomfortable with the whole interaction. I don't even know why they said half of the things they did."

Coop kissed his cheek. "People say the craziest shit to us. But I did like it when he talked about you stealing home. He brought up our chain kiss, which got him bonus points, too."

They reached the hotel room door, and Ethan held his hand out. "Let me try to open it again, I feel good. I'm loose, I can get it open." He rolled his neck in circles and jogged in place.

Coop passed him the phone. "Just one quick swipe, and it will open. Don't overthink it."

Ethan waved the phone in front of the door lock…nothing. He tried again, slower…nothing. He passed it back to Coop. "Just forget it. You do it. It's fine."

Coop waved it once, and it opened. Ethan shook his head. "I've been beaten by the door, again."

They removed their shirts once they stepped inside, then Ethan quickly headed for the fridge, grabbing two water bottles. He tossed one to Coop, who caught it against his chest, then followed Ethan upstairs to the shower. Coop drank from the bottle, and Ethan watched him, thirstily, as the water dripped slowly down Coop's chest.

Coop raised his eyebrows at him. "You want a taste?"

Ethan nodded silently and kissed him with force, grabbing his face with both hands. He pulled Coop's track pants down, and stroked his sweaty, hard cock.

Coop gripped Ethan's sides and slid his hands inside the back of his pants squeezing his ass. Ethan quickly stepped out of his pants and into the shower. He dropped to his knees and greedily slurped and sucked his husband's massive cock, which he'd grown quite accustomed to pleasing.

He pulled Coop's cock out of his mouth and held it near his lips.

"Mmm. This is mine." He stuck his tongue out flat, licking the entire length, then took it back into his mouth.

Coop rubbed Ethan's wet hair and gripped it, looking down at him. "Baby, where do you want it? Do you want me to fuck you? Or do you want me to finish?"

Ethan didn't answer with words, he sucked Coop harder, and massaged his balls, while looking up at him.

Coop gripped Ethan's hair tight as he came in his mouth. "Mmm—ungh—fuck—Ethan."

Ethan stroked him, milking out every drop of Coop's cum. "Mmm. I'll never get tired of that. I love the taste of my husband."

Coop picked Ethan's naked body up, and Ethan wrapped his legs around him. "It's your turn, Mr. Morgan," he said while walking him toward the large bed.

A couple of hours later, the two walked around the city, with plans to visit Ethan's grandparents in the afternoon. They found a nice café with outdoor seating, and decided they'd grab some brunch. A server greeted them quickly in Italian and gestured to a small two-person table. He placed two menus down and walked away toward the kitchen.

Coop and Ethan sat down in the black iron chairs, which felt a bit small for both of them.

Coop already knew what would happen once they ordered food. He would order something unhealthy since they were on vacation, and Ethan would try to stick with something somewhat healthy. Ethan would take one bite, and Coop would end up giving him his food. It happened nearly every time they went out for a meal together. Even when they would eat with the team, Ethan did the same thing. "I'm gonna get the banana pancakes and sausage. Do you want the same?" he asked Ethan.

"Hmm," Ethan said, reading the menu over. "No, I think I'll get the spinach omelet with a side of fruit and focaccia toast."

Coop dropped an eyebrow down. "Are you sure? You don't want the pancakes, too? We're on vacation, and pancakes are your favorite on cheat days."

"Nah, I think the omelet sounds good."

They shared a quick smooch just as a server came over. He was polite and to the point. He wrote down their order quickly, with minimal conversation and sped off to the next table, then into the kitchen.

After just a few minutes, the server returned with their food. He spoke in Italian, "Alright pancakes for the big guy," he said placing the plate in front of Coop. "And an omelet for the baby face," he said, placing Ethan's plate down.

Ethan's mouth hung open as the man walked away.

Coop's eyebrows squished together as he spoke to Ethan, "Hey, I didn't understand all of that. Was he being rude? I think I'm having trouble with inflection."

"No. It's fine. He wasn't purposely being rude. Just said something about you being a big guy and me having a baby face. I guess it's just what people see when we're together. It's fine. Don't worry."

Coop tilted his head and held up three fingers. "Three things: first, whenever you say you're fine, or it's fine, you're not fine. Second, you do have a handsome baby face. Third, I will go beat him up if you want me to."

"Oof, you know me too well. I just think it's weird that people are always sizing us up. That woman this morning was just ridiculous.

'One guy is always smaller than the other.' She was so out of line. Now this guy."

Coop looked at Ethan softly. "Baby, you are perfect. Don't let other people bother you. Of course, they size us up, they have nothing else to talk about, they're bored. You are literally the only person in the world that I want to talk to. It's just you and me." He leaned forward across the small table and kissed Ethan on the mouth quickly, earning a big smile from his husband.

"Just you and me, forever," Ethan said, staring into Coop's eyes.

Coop pushed Ethan's plate toward him. "Now, take a bite of the omelet that we both know I'll be eating, so I can give you my pancakes, or just pass the plate over."

Ethan tried a bite of the omelet. Coop watched as he struggled to swallow it. "Oh, that is not good. Don't eat it, Cooper. I can just eat the fruit and toast."

Coop swapped plates with him. "Every time. You never learn. It's the cutest thing. This is why I always order pancakes when we go out for breakfast. You did this the first time we went out, remember? At Fregi's?"

Ethan cupped his face in his hands. "Oh my God, this really does happen all the time. I'm sorry."

Coop fed Ethan a bite of the pancakes and smiled. "Don't be sorry. I love it. It's adorable. I mean it."

Ethan dug into the pancakes while Coop ate the omelet and bread. They finished their meals and quickly paid for their food.

After their brunch, Ethan and Coop were immediately drawn in as they came upon a children's home. The building was obviously very old, and looked incredibly dilapidated. Ethan couldn't help but wonder what the conditions inside were like. He tugged on Coop's shirt. "Cooper, we have so much money, how can we help? We can't see this and do nothing."

There was a worker outside near the entrance, and the two decided to approach him to see if they could possibly learn more about the home. The language barrier was unfortunately a little too strong for Coop at this particular establishment. The man they spoke with could only speak Italian; he seemed to understand some English, but said he couldn't speak it. Ethan spoke to him in Italian; he explained that they were a wealthy married couple that wanted to help in whatever way they could. The man looked very confused, upon hearing they were married. Ethan decided he would have a little fun with it and repeated himself, but this time, he told the man that Cooper was his wife, and they were well-known wealthy Americans.

Coop's eyes slightly widened as Ethan spoke, he tilted his head at Ethan. "What did you just say to him?"

Ethan smiled and waved his question off.

The man repeated what Ethan said back to him in Italian. He pointed at Coop while speaking to Ethan. "You are saying that you are married, and he is your wife, and you are the husband, yes?"

Ethan answered him in Italian. "Yes, exactly." He held Coop's arm. "My wife."

The man scoffed. "It's not possible. He is the man, you are the wife. You are saying it wrong."

Coop seemed to find the whole situation hilarious; Ethan watched as he tried not to react by biting his lip. He knew Coop's Italian had gotten better, but he was pretty sure that Coop didn't know what he told the man.

"Did you understand him?" Ethan asked.

Coop didn't answer. He kissed Ethan's cheek and looked down at the ground.

Ethan placed one hand on his hip and spoke to the man, "I'm not saying it wrong. I'm a man too. He is the wife."

The man was adamant. "No, no it's not possible, you are the wife." The man imitated Ethan's hand on his hip, and shook his head, then pointed to Coop. "This is the man."

Ethan grabbed Coop's hand and stormed off.

"Do you want me to go back there and try to find someone else to talk to?" Coop asked.

"Forget it," Ethan said, feeling flustered. "Damn it, now we're late for our taxi."

"I got it," Coop said. He called the hotel, and they arranged for another car to meet them upon arrival.

Ethan pouted as they walked. "Stupid guy. What does he know?" He'd never felt so small. Three times already, different people pointed out their difference in size. Compared to almost any other man, Ethan would be considered a big guy. At six feet tall, every piece of his body was perfectly toned. Coop, who stood only an inch taller, was not over muscular either, but his shoulders were a bit broader. Ethan truly couldn't understand it; why did people feel the need to point out their size difference? He wondered if every person they met sized them up like this.

He folded his arms and stopped walking. "What do you see when you look at me, Cooper?"

"I see the love of my life, my delicious husband and my spicy little puppy." Coop quickly pulled him into a firm embrace. "You are really upset, huh? How can I make it better, baby?"

Ethan tucked his face against him, inhaling his scent. He kissed the side of Coop's neck softly, melting in his warm embrace. Whenever Coop held him like this, everything around them seemed less important. "It's okay. Your hug made it better, just like it always does."

Coop squeezed him tighter. "Mmm. I love you, Ethan. But don't kiss my neck when we're already late. Especially not when we're trying to get to your grandparent's house."

Chapter 3
Sweet Spumoni

A taxi dropped them off at Ethan's grandparent's house about thirty minutes later. Ethan and Coop held hands as they walked up the steep driveway. "Yeah, they moved to New York in 1970, when they were both twenty," Ethan said. "They had my mom and Aunt Tina, raised them there and moved back here in 2010. They used to visit the states often. I'm sure they'll be impressed with your Italian, but don't worry about it too much. You can speak English; they won't care either way."

Ethan knocked on the door. A woman's voice responded, "Come in!"

Coop pulled his head back and looked at Ethan. "Do they just let anyone in who knocks?"

"Probably," Ethan said while opening the door. "Meanwhile we have a security guard, and a gated entrance. It's funny, right?"

Ethan's Nonna was inside the kitchen, cooking up a big pot of gravy. Coop and Ethan inhaled deeply as they walked inside.

"Smells like your mom's gravy," Coop said.

"Mmmhmm. So good. I love this smell."

Ethan's Nonna smiled brightly, and hurriedly wiped her hands on her red apron, while they walked toward her. Her voice sounded very much like Ethan's mom's, but with a bit more Italian. With her arms extended, she greeted them, "Patatino! And you must be Coop! It is so nice to meet you! Nipote, come here, hug Nonna." She gave Ethan a very big hug, twisting him around. "You look good, sweetheart."

She held her hand out to Coop. "I'm Diane, but you can call me Nonna. Now, Gigi already told me that you don't like to be hugged, but maybe I can get you to hug me later. A handshake feels so impersonal, all business, no love."

"I don't mind if you hug me," Coop said, opening his arms.

She wrapped her arms around his waist and squeezed tight. "Oh, thank goodness. You *are* solid. Gigi always exaggerates so I wasn't too sure what to expect. Now, I don't have to worry about Patatino. She took awful pictures of the wedding; I could barely tell what was what. It's too hard to see which of you is the bigger man on a phone. Now I can tell." She smiled and released him from the hug.

Ethan's mouth fell open, and he shook his head.

"What's that face about?" his Nonna asked. "Are you hungry or tired?"

Coop smiled and wrapped his arm around Ethan's shoulder. Ethan couldn't believe this was happening again. The comfort he felt just a few minutes ago was gone, replaced with insecurity and agitation. He gestured to his own body and then Coop's. "Nonna, we wear almost the same size clothes. Cooper is literally one inch taller than me."

"Yeah, so? By definition, doesn't that make him the bigger man physically, or not?"

Ethan sighed. "Yeah. I guess it does. Where's Pop Pop?"

"He's outside, probably watching birds. It's his new favorite thing."

Ethan and Coop walked around to the back of the home. Coop

pulled Ethan aside before opening the door. "Are you okay? What has you so upset? Were you that mad that your Nonna said I was bigger than you?"

Ethan tilted his head and looked at the floor. He felt embarrassed for feeling the way he did, but he couldn't lie. "Kind of. I'm not used to people acting like I'm small. It's happened three or four times on this trip already."

Coop stuck his lip out and looked into Ethan's eyes. "Hey, I love you. You *are* strong, and you're not small. Everything about you is perfect." Coop gave him a quick kiss and squeezed him tightly.

"Do you think the guys on the team think the same things about us?"

Coop ruffled Ethan's hair. "The guys on the team probably don't think that, since half of them are shorter than you. Besides, none of them have ever said anything like that to me."

Ethan slid the door open, and they walked outside into the large backyard. The smell of fabric softener floated in the air as a warm breeze blew through the clothes drying on the clothesline. Ethan's Pop Pop was sitting in an old brown rocking chair on the far side of the yard; he was indeed looking at birds.

"Pop Pop, you're too young to be sitting outside bird watching!" Ethan called out.

Pop Pop's very thick, salt-and-pepper eyebrows raised. "Patatino! You're late. Had me worried." He stood and embraced Ethan, then extended his hand to Coop. "Name is Frank, but you can call me Pop Pop, like Ethan does."

"It's great to meet you. I'm Coop," he said, shaking his hand.

Pop Pop took a step back and looked the two over. "You guys are two handsome fellas. No wonder your mom and Tina are always going crazy about Coop! Have you two looked at yourselves in a mirror? It's almost unfair looking at the both of you. When I was your age, I could've had anyone I wanted, but like you two, I found my heart early on. Stuck to her like glue. The rest is history."

Coop kissed Ethan on the cheek and rubbed Ethan's shoulder.

Pop Pop smiled. "That's nice, I can see how much you love my grandson."

Coop held Ethan's hand. "He is my whole world."

"That's exactly right," Pop Pop said. "Marriage is for life. He is your whole world; you got that right."

Ethan kissed Coop on the cheek.

"You two are gonna give old Pop Pop a cavity," he said, opening the door and stepping inside.

Coop walked into the house behind Ethan.

From inside the kitchen, Nonna called out, "Frank, is he still pouting?"

"They're inside too, honey," he answered, wiping his feet.

She giggled. "Whoops. Patatino, are you still pouting?"

Pop Pop nudged Ethan and spoke to him in Italian, "Why is she saying you're pouting? What happened? You don't seem upset."

Ethan replied in Italian, "No, I'm not upset. I'm fine."

Coop couldn't pretend that he didn't understand any longer. He felt far too guilty and refused to let Ethan suffer in silence. He put his hand on Ethan's shoulder, and spoke in perfect Italian, to Pop Pop. "He was upset earlier because Nonna said he was smaller than me. It started this morning with a few different people. We just left a children's home with an impossible man, who really got under his skin. Ethan called me his wife, and the man gave him a terrible time about it. He told Ethan that he was smaller, so he was the wife, and I was the husband. Guy was a moron."

Coop awaited Ethan's reaction, hoping he wouldn't be too upset.

He'd yet to make Ethan mad at him, in the time they'd been together, and that was something he definitely didn't want to do.

Ethan's mouth hung open, while Nonna joined him with wide meatball eyes. Ethan covered his face with his hand and hung his head.

Pop Pop's caterpillar-like eyebrows raised. "You speak Italian? That's fantastic. Sounded natural."

Nonna wiped her hands on her apron. "Patatino, Nonna is sorry. I didn't know you had a complex about this. You are a big man, honey. You really are. Who says one of you has to be the wife, anyway?"

Coop could see that Ethan was beyond embarrassed. He stared silently, red-faced at Coop, while Coop pulled him into a hug. He whispered into Ethan's his ear, "Sorry, you were so cute earlier. I just wanted you to let you have fun with it." He smooched Ethan quickly on the mouth.

Ethan playfully pinched both of Coop's cheeks. "Cooper, you knew the whole time what he was saying? I'm so embarrassed," he said with a bright smile.

That smile was what Coop was waiting for. Ethan's expression made him feel so much better. "Don't be embarrassed. No one is going to call you my wife if you don't like it, baby."

Ethan gave a nod and kissed him in agreement.

Following a knock on the front door, both Nonna and Pop Pop called out, "Come in!"

"I guess they do tell everyone to come in," Ethan said.

An older woman came in with a very pregnant younger woman. The older woman was distressed; she spoke animatedly in a dialect that Coop had trouble following.

Nonna spoke to the women, while Pop Pop led Coop and Ethan into a guest room. Pop Pop put his hands on his hips. "Here's the deal with those two, the mother is furious because the daughter is pregnant with a son. The family is poor, and the daughter doesn't want the baby. Her mother, Miriam, is refusing to care for the child, once he's born."

Ethan and Coop were stunned. Ethan spoke softly, "But…but why? Italians are all about family. Why wouldn't she want to care for her own grandson and why doesn't the daughter want him?" Coop held Ethan's hand and squeezed it.

Pop Pop shook his head and answered, "The daughter has some kind of a condition, who knows whether she'll survive the birth, or pass away before then."

"Wouldn't she want to care for her daughter's son if something happened to her?" Coop asked. "Wait, what about the father?"

Pop Pop shook his head. "She doesn't know who the father is. And like I said, the family is very poor. Who knows who he is. No one will claim that child."

Ethan gave Coop a look, one that he instantly understood. He got this look whenever he wanted to help someone. It was one of Coop's favorite things about him. But right now, Coop was feeling a bit nervous at the timing of this particular expression.

Ethan put a hand on his forehead and grabbed the doorknob. "Pop Pop, can you give Cooper and I a few minutes to talk. I'm a little tired from today. I just need a few minutes alone with my husband."

"Of course," Pop Pop said. "You guys take all the time you need. I should warn you, though, if you're trying to avoid Miriam and Bianca, it won't work. I'm sure they're staying for dinner. They probably smelled Nonna's gravy and came over for that very reason."

"I'm not trying to avoid them." Ethan sighed, shaking his head. "We'll be out in a few minutes and introduce ourselves properly."

Pop Pop left the room, and Ethan leaned against the door with his eyes closed.

Coop sat on the bed and patted his thigh. "Come here, pup."

Ethan sat on his lap and was quickly wrapped in an embrace from behind. "Ethan, I know what you're thinking," Coop said softly, as he perched his chin on his shoulder and kissed his cheek.

Ethan leaned his head against Coop's. "I'm sure you do."

The two sat there in silence for a few minutes. Ethan stood up and looked at Coop with concern in his eyes. "Wait, what if you don't know what I'm thinking?"

Coop tilted his head. "Baby, look at me. I'm thinking the same thing, one hundred percent. But we just don't know enough yet. Let's go talk to them, and be sure we understand their situation, before we get carried away with our thoughts."

Ethan nodded, and the two shared a quick smooch on the lips.

After a few hours of getting to know each other, Ethan led Coop back into the guest room. "Cooper, would you want to adopt him? Could it actually work?"

Coop pulled Ethan in and squeezed him tight. "Ethan, you already know that I want a baby as much as you do. A little guy running around would be so much fun, but we have to be very careful. There has to be so much that needs to be done."

Ethan's eyes were tearful staring at Coop. Coop pinched his chin. "Puppy, don't look at me like that. I just don't want either of us to get our hopes up. Let's call my dad and have him talk to our lawyer. But just don't look at me like that, okay?"

Ethan kissed him. "Okay, I'll try."

Coop called his dad and his husband Levi to talk it over. They were floored at Coop's request.

His dad spoke to their family attorney in the background, while Levi talked to Coop. "Coop, listen," Levi said. "I really do understand how you two feel. When your dad and I were younger, we wanted kids, and we knew we wouldn't be able to have them. Obviously, our circumstances were different, but we can both relate to wanting to raise a child together. We need to get a lot of things straight, though. My first concerns would be, what is wrong with Bianca? Is her illness something that can be passed on to the baby? If her illness doesn't prove terminal, would she want her rights back, maybe not now, but what if you two pay her a lot of money, and she decides she wants the child back?"

"We understand, Levi," Coop said. "We both share those concerns, they're completely valid. Tell my dad to give me a call when he wraps up with Dan, okay? Also, do me a favor and tell him that Dan can just call me. We'll cover the international charge if Dan's worried about it."

With his head on Coop's shoulder, Ethan's words were broken by sobs, "Cooper, I can't take it….I don't understand…"

Coop squeezed him in tight. "Shh, it's gonna be okay. Don't cry. We're on our honeymoon." Ethan nodded through tears. Coop kissed his forehead. "I know…it's so terrible…We'll do whatever we can. I promise, baby."

Nonna knocked on the partially open door. "Ethan, Coop, can I come in?"

"Of course," Ethan answered.

She entered the room and sighed. "It's a difficult thing to watch people suffer. Am I understanding what I'm seeing here? Are you two thinking that you want to adopt the baby when he's born?"

Ethan sniffed and looked at her with red, watery eyes. "Yes, Nonna. We want to take care of him. We can save him."

Coop held Ethan and rubbed his shoulder. He looked at Ethan's grandmother. "Nonna, we won't ever be able to have a child on our own. We would have to go through surrogacy or adoption, there is really no other option. For the two of us right now, seeing someone suffer and knowing that a little boy will be born and not—" His voice briefly cracked. He cleared his throat and added, "We can't just leave him alone."

She tilted her head. "Guys, listen, this is all very touching, but do you have any idea how much money something like this would cost?"

Coop bit his lip and remained silent.

"Nonna, we have more than enough money," Ethan said.

She spoke to Ethan softly, "Patatino, I don't think you understand. I mean a lot of money."

Ethan pulled his phone out of his pocket and quickly navigated to their banking account. He held the phone out to Nonna. She looked at the screen and squinted. "What are you showing me?"

"Do you see that big number?" Ethan asked. "Count from the zeroes. That's our checking account. We can show you the savings if you want, it's even bigger."

Her eyes widened, and she sat down on the bed next to the two. "How can two people have so much money? Is this real? What bank is this?"

Ethan held his hand out and took the phone back, he navigated to the savings account and passed it back to her.

Nonna looked down at the phone and stood straight up. "Sweet spumoni! I have never seen so much money in all my life."

Ethan smiled. "We paid cash for our new house, too. It was not cheap."

She looked at him confused. "I am…there are…I…how?"

Coop always felt awkward talking about money but felt the need to explain based on how shocked she was. "I've saved up a lot over the years, and Ethan's been saving, too. We make a good amount of money. We have one more year, and then we'll most likely get signed by pro teams, and that will make more zeroes." He winked at Ethan and kissed his cheek.

Nonna's eyes went meatball again. "Where can any more zeroes go? There are no more zeroes!" She tried to calm herself. "Alright, alright. Dinner will be ready soon. Listen, you guys, money aside, it will not be easy for a lot of other reasons. I don't even know how it could be possible."

"Nonna, I am not leaving this country without him," Ethan said, standing up.

Coop's eyes widened. "Well, he won't be born for a while so, we'll definitely need to go home and get some—" Ethan looked at him with tears in his eyes. Coop was accustomed to giving him anything he wanted; he lived for Ethan's happiness and couldn't stand his little puppy pout. Coop started over. "We are not leaving this country without a plan to bring him home, or at least one to help. And if possible, bring him home."

Nonna nearly dropped Coop's phone as it rang in her hand. "Ahh, oop, hot patata," she said, as she passed the phone back to him. She wiped Ethan's tears, and whispered, "I love you, sweetie. Just try to be calm, okay? I've never seen you like this. Things take time." She opened the door and left, to rejoin her guests and Pop Pop.

Coop answered the phone, "Hey, Dad, what did Dan say?"

Chapter 4
Can I Call You Daddy?

Coop's dad replied, "We have a full house right now on the line, Coop. Dan is on, Levi is here with me on speaker, and we have our friend Madeline Parson on, she's also a lawyer."

Coop's eyes widened. "Okay. Well, hi, everyone, let me put you on speaker, so Ethan can hear too."

Madeline took control, speaking quickly, "Hi, I'm Madeline, I'm a defense attorney with experience in family law and international relations. Dan and I have worked together on the odd case here and there."

Before Coop and Ethan could reply, Dan spoke up, "Hi, guys, listen, I'm going to just be here in the background, Maddie is way more experienced with this than I am."

"Hi, Madeline," Ethan said. "Do you prefer Maddie or Madeline?"

"Depends on what you look like, honey!" she replied.

Levi scolded her, "Maddie! Get it together, they're newlyweds!"

"Oh, Levi, calm down," Madeline said. "I know that. Ethan, you can call me whatever you want; Maddie or Madeline, either is fine. Coop, I'm a big fan, you can call me Maddie if I can call you daddy. Hahaha… Kidding, I'm kidding!"

Levi yelled, "Maddie! This is serious!"

Coop and Ethan looked at one another and sighed.

"Jeez…alright, just trying to ease the tension," she said. "Guys, you have about a million problems that I can think of right off the bat. First of all, you're supposed to be married or cohabitating for at least three years, I know you don't meet that requirement. Next, do you know how many children have been granted international adoption to the US from Italy in the past… let's say six-ish years? I just looked into it. Take a guess."

Coop answered, "No idea."

She replied, "One, just one. That's one child in all of Italy to go to the US by means of adoption. Adoption won't work, we need to consider this to be a surrogacy agreement, I think I can swing it that way. I know you aren't worried about money, so that's one thing you've got going for you. Next, what's the health condition that she has?"

"It's a rare condition with the placenta," Ethan replied. "I think she may have gestational diabetes, too."

Madeline sighed. "Okay, well, neither of those things… Well, one of those things… Okay, actually, neither of those things are great, but the baby should be fine if we can make sure she's getting proper care. Do you know if she's been receiving prenatal care?"

"She goes to a free clinic," Ethan said. "But I don't know how often."

Coop spoke up, "Madeline, we like to play by the rules, but we also like to play ball, so who do we need to get to play ball with us to get this through? She's due in two months.

"What? Two months?" Madeline sighed. "With gestational diabetes and a placental condition and who knows what else, you'll be lucky if she doesn't go into labor in a month. Who do we need to play ball? A lot of people. I'm going to need to make you two look very good, very fast. Thankfully, my father has some friends at the embassy that owe him a few favors, and you two do a lot of charity work involving children, as does your father. I'm thinking I may be able to use those things to my advantage."

"Madeline, I'm really worried about her living conditions," Ethan said, "they're terrible according to my grandparents. Our honeymoon ends in five days… We can't just leave."

Madeline sighed into the phone. "Alright, see. You got me on your side already, but I can see smoke in the distance. Coop, listen to me. I figure people out easily, it's why I'm good at my job; your dynamic is already obvious. You're going to have to be firm with Ethan. You two will provide a nice place for her to live, you will pay for her food, you will make sure she goes to a proper doctor's office, and you will also pay for that. You have to treat this as a surrogate transaction going forward. Coop, I mean it, this is going to be dependent on you. Ethan is probably crying already, if I've got him figured out."

Ethan was indeed softly crying. Coop spoke up, while rubbing his back. "Well, he's only crying because it sounds kind of harsh, she is a person, and we didn't even know her five hours ago. She's been carrying him for seven months."

Tom said, "Maddie, hush for a minute. Coop, listen to me; you *are* going to have to be firm here. There is only so much that can be done. You two have to focus on the things you can control."

Ethan dabbed his eyes with his finger as he spoke through sobs, "We just want to help. I can't stand this. We have enough money to give him a good life and to help her get what she needs. Who cares about anything else?"

Coop held Ethan in close and kissed his cheek.

"Oh boy," Madeline said. "Listen, you're six hours ahead of us, take some time to talk it over and be sure this is what you want, and

I'll start working on my end. This next part is very important, if she brings up money or payment, I want you to call me immediately. It's acceptable for you to pay for a room for her or buy groceries, but you absolutely do not give her money until we get this figured out. You call me. Do you both understand?"

Ethan and Coop answered, "Yes, we understand."

"Alright, your trip ends what day?" Madeline asked. "When will you be stateside?"

Ethan spoke up, "I am not leaving—"

Madeline interrupted him, "Stop. Yes. Yes, you are leaving without him. I already know what ridiculous thing you're trying to say. He won't be born for another two months. You most certainly will leave without him. Do one more thing for me, come up with a name for him and give it to me tomorrow. I'll call you guys in the morning. Everyone on this call good with that?" Everyone agreed, and Madeline hung up, as did the other parties.

Ethan stood in front of Coop who was sitting on the bed. He inhaled, then exhaled deeply, "Cooper, I'm sorry...I feel like I'm getting carried away, but I just can't help it. I want to do whatever is best for everyone."

Coop held his hands. "I understand how you feel. Never doubt that."

"I won't," Ethan said.

Coop stood and gave him a nice deep kiss, pulling his body close. He whispered in Ethan's ear, "Listen, we need to get back to the hotel soon. It's been too long since you've felt it." He ran a finger down the outside of Ethan's ass. "After this, we'll go back to the hotel, order room service, and your husband will make it all better."

Ethan grabbed onto the back of Coop's hair and dove back into his mouth; he pushed him down onto the guest bed and straddled him.

Ethan's ringtone sounded. He hopped off Coop and sat on the bed next to him. The two looked at the screen: *Mom calling.* Ethan's eyes widened, and he turned to Coop. "I don't feel like doing this with her. I was just about to take your pants off."

Coop knew Ethan wasn't kidding. If Gina hadn't called, he was sure to have been stripped clean by now. "Naughty pup. Just answer it. We know she won't stop once she starts."

Ethan reluctantly answered, "Hi, Mom."

"Hi, Mimmo, sweetie. Are you okay?"

Ethan rubbed Coop's hair. "Yes, of course. Why wouldn't I be?"

"Well, Levi just called me and said that you two are trying to adopt an unborn baby or adopt a sick woman's baby. He wasn't very clear. I tried to call Nonna, but she didn't answer. What's going on?"

Ethan recapped the day's events. Gina was silent. "Mom, I'm okay. I'll do what's right. You know I will. I'm not going to jump into anything."

She broke her silence. "Coop, can you hear me?"

"Yeah, I can hear you." Coop winced.

"Okay, good. Does he not realize that he's already jumped in? Headfirst, no less? I'm so confused. Had you two even considered having a baby before? You just got married, you should be on your honeymoon, you know, not dealing with any drama. This is a lot of drama. He's sensitive but he's not usually… Never mind. You don't need me to explain. I just want to be sure you two understand what you're getting into. Having a baby is hard enough on its own, and Levi explained that there will be a lot of legal hurdles. Just take care of Mimmo. I don't know what else to say."

Coop replied, rubbing Ethan's cheek, "I will always take care of him, but his little puppy pout is making it hard for me, right now. And we've definitely talked about having kids. It was one of the first things we talked about after we got engaged."

"His puppy pout, oh you two!" She sighed and continued in a softer tone, "It's almost five there, so I'm sure dinner will be ready soon. Please just take it one step at a time. Follow your hearts and trust in one another. I love you both."

Nonna called from outside the door, "Was that Gigi?"

Coop smiled as he held Ethan's hand and walked to the door. The two left the room, and Ethan pulled his Nonna aside, while Coop headed for Miriam and Bianca.

Coop sat on the stiff, floral couch across from Miriam and Pop Pop, who were on a matching loveseat. Bianca sat on an old-style recliner, off to his left.

The girl's mother, Miriam, addressed Coop, she spoke quickly in Italian, "You and your wife partner want the baby?"

Coop understood her, but since the dialect was a bit tricky, he looked at Pop Pop to be sure he understood her correctly. He gave Coop a look indicating he shouldn't bother correcting her. Coop leaned back into the cushion and looked up. His large body was far too big on the small old-style couch. It was also very hot, and he was starting to feel a bit overwhelmed.

He looked at Miriam, then spoke to Bianca in Italian, "My husband and I do want to adopt him. We also want to make sure that you get the care that you need. We can take care of everything."

Bianca rolled her eyes and spoke in Italian, "Why, it's just a baby? You don't even know me, or the father."

Coop furrowed his brow; he looked at Pop Pop and repeated what he thought she said to him in English.

Pop Pop confirmed, "Yep, that's what she said."

Coop nodded slowly, as Ethan came into the room from the hall with Nonna.

Ethan sat next to Coop on the couch. "These are the same couches you guys had when I was little!" He patted the seat and lightly bounced on the cushion, smiling at Pop Pop, while Miriam gave him a proper stare down.

"What happened?" Ethan asked Coop. "Why are they looking at me like that?" Coop quickly caught him up to speed, and Ethan took control of the conversation. He turned to Bianca. "We won't be able to have a baby by ourselves. Surrogacy in this form is our best option."

Neither Bianca nor Miriam gave any reaction.

Coop rubbed his back, and Ethan started again, "We're very wealthy, and we don't like seeing people hurt. I believe that fate brought you here today."

Bianca rolled her eyes, then spoke in Italian, "No. Gravy brought me here today."

Coop and Ethan found that hilarious. That was the first bit of favorable personality Bianca had shown since she arrived, and they welcomed it. Being two sarcastic men, any child of theirs, would surely be used to sarcasm at a young age.

Bianca shifted uncomfortably in her chair. "I don't understand why you want him. I don't even know who the father is. If you are rich, can't you buy a baby in America?"

Ethan and Coop looked at one another confused; they looked at Pop Pop for confirmation.

"Yep, she said that," Pop Pop confirmed, while shaking his head.

Her mother Miriam took a different approach, she asked, "How much money?"

Coop patted Ethan's thigh and leaned forward speaking, "We are working on that right now. Within the next few days, we will try and secure a new residence for Bianca, as well as food and medical care. Our attorney will help us in the morning."

Bianca crossed her arms. "How much money for the baby?"

Coop could see that Ethan was feeling a little heated. He rubbed his arm to calm him. "Don't…shh, baby. You don't want to make them upset. The translation probably just makes it sound worse."

"Nope," Pop Pop said, shaking his head. "It's not the translation, they're only interested in the money."

Coop looked at Ethan, concerned. "What do you want me to do, baby? I can't give them a number. I have no idea. I could say something too high or too low. We shouldn't give them a number. Madeline just told us to call her if they brought up money."

Nonna spoke in Italian, calling from the kitchen, "Time to eat."

The six sat down to a boisterous meal, with Pop Pop and Nonna telling stories of Ethan as a small boy. Bianca and her mother were not at all interested in the conversation. Ethan watched as Bianca shoved the pasta and sausage in, clearing her plate at record speed. Nonna scooped more onto Bianca's plate, and she finished the second plate quickly as well.

Ethan whispered to Coop, "This is making me nervous. Is she starving, or is that how much a pregnant woman eats?"

"Shh. Probably both, baby."

After dinner, Nonna placed a tray with homemade cannoli in the middle of the table. "These are Patatino's favorite. I made them fresh this morning!"

Ethan covered his mouth watching Bianca shovel three large cannoli into her mouth, one after the other. He whispered to Coop, "That is so unhealthy, so much sugar."

Coop nodded slowly and rubbed his back. "They haven't agreed to anything yet. You can't say anything to her. Plus, you really shouldn't say anything to a pregnant woman about how much she eats."

After they finished their dessert, Coop and Ethan stood near the front door facing Miriam and Bianca. "We'll come back tomorrow after we speak to our attorney," Coop said. "Hopefully, we can get into specifics and reach an agreement."

Miriam held her hand out, palm facing up. Coop was confused. "Why is she holding her hand out?"

Pop Pop shook his head. "Euros, boys. She is waiting for euros."

"Euros for what, though?" Ethan asked.

Nonna intervened speaking in Italian to Miriam, then translated to Coop and Ethan, "She wants the money for the baby."

Coop pulled his phone from his pocket. He knew it was time for him to call Madeline. "We can't give her money for the agreement now. Doesn't she understand that?" he asked Nonna.

Miriam didn't understand English, she raised her chin at Coop and spoke in Italian, "No money, no baby."

Coop sighed and walked into the guest bedroom, while calling Madeline, with Ethan following behind. They sat on the bed, holding hands.

The phone rang a few times before Madeline answered, "Yeah, hello? Why are you calling me already?"

"I'm sorry for calling so soon," Coop said. "We were on our way out and the mother just brought up money. She even held her hand out."

Madeline sighed. A man's voice could be heard in the background, "Who is that? Your dog isn't calling you right now, is he?"

Madeline replied to the voice, "Shh, shut up, no."

"Maybe that's her husband?" Ethan whispered.

Coop shrugged and covered the phone. "I have no idea, but he sounds like a jerk."

Madeline spoke, "Damn it. Money already, huh?"

They conversed for several minutes and by the end of their

conversation, Madeline sounded extremely frustrated. "Guys, I think I'm going to have to go there. Damn it…"

The man's voice spoke again in the background, "Go where? We took the day off."

"Get your naked ass back in bed. I'm not talking about right this minute," Madeline said.

Ethan's mouth turned down, and he pulled his head back.

Coop could tell what Ethan was thinking, the thought of talking to someone on the phone with a naked person in their bed seemed pretty disgusting to him, too. But he pressed on. "So, what should we do?" Coop asked. "She literally said the words, 'No money, no baby.'"

"No money, no baby? She shouldn't have said that. Listen, this is a long shot and its definitely not legal and won't hold up in court, but go ahead and…wait, how much money do you have on you?"

Coop pulled his wallet out. "On me, we have 4,000 euros."

"What are you stupid? Why are you carrying around so much? Loaded or not, that's a dumb thing to do. Alright, well, you said they were poor, this will definitely come up later and I'm going to have to answer for it. Give her 2,000 euros and tell her it's for the surrogacy agreement. Tell her you are going to record her, have Ethan's grandmother speak to her instead of you and take a video of the transaction. She and the mother need to both accept the payment and state the reason for it. This isn't even going to hold up…Why am I even? No, do it. That's what I want you to do. I'll call you in the morning." She ended the call.

Ethan shrugged his shoulders. "Do we do it or not?"

Coop sighed while massaging his own temples. "I don't know. This feels gross, paying them like this. It's a human being we're talking about."

"Yeah, but we're paying her so she can take care of herself. We're not paying for the baby, even though that's how Miriam and Bianca said it. But we can wait until the morning if you're uncomfortable. I'm calm now. She's not going to just walk away when she knows we have money."

"I'm sure you're right," Coop said. "We should probably do what Madeline told us to, though. If there's a way that she can flip it and use this for us, then we need to take a shot."

They walked back into the family room and recorded the exchange. Miriam put her hands on Bianca's shoulders and lightly nudged her toward Ethan and Coop. She thanked them both, while rolling her eyes.

Coop looked at Ethan and whispered, "You know, she's kind of rude for a twenty-year-old."

Ethan nodded in agreement.

A few hours later, the taxi dropped Coop and Ethan off in front of their hotel. "I'm so exhausted from this day," Ethan said, leaning his head against Coop's shoulder.

Coop came around the front of him, and Ethan hopped right onto his back. He lifted Ethan up, while people walking by watching them. "Now, Mr. Morgan, we're just going to relax tonight," Coop said. "First thing tomorrow, we'll figure everything out. No more stress until then."

Ethan kissed the back of his neck softly, then laid his head down, squeezing him lightly, with his arms draped around his neck. He inhaled. "Your smell always calms me. I love you so much, Cooper."

"I love you, too, but your smell does the opposite to me. It gets me all worked up."

They approached their hotel room door. "Let me try it," Ethan said, as he reached his right hand for Coop's phone. Since he was still on Coop's back, he used his left hand to stabilize himself while trying to scan the phone in front of the door. Coop tilted him closer with the same result. Ethan gave up, he hopped down and passed Coop the phone. Coop waved it, and with just one swipe, the door opened.

They walked upstairs hand in hand. Coop threw his phone and wallet down onto the dresser and pulled his collared shirt off his head. Ethan stared at him in lust. "Mmm…you really are the sexiest man in the world."

Coop looked down at his chest and lightly flexed his arms downward, pumping his eyebrows at Ethan.

Ethan raised his chin. "Very hot, but take off the pants."

Coop unbuttoned as he laid on the bed, then slid his pants off, and Ethan quickly joined him. The two had a passionate, sweet lovemaking session, that lasted for almost two hours.

Ethan rubbed Coop's chest lying beside him. "I love that sex lasts longer if we're sweet. When we're rough it's like fifteen minutes."

Coop pulled an eyebrow down. "If you want it to last longer, I can always make it last longer…but yes, you are correct."

Chapter 5
Holy Cannoli

The next morning, the two awoke to a mix of texts and voicemails. They listened to the messages on speaker while sitting in bed. Ethan held his hand over his mouth in disbelief. Apparently, Madeline, Levi, and Tom were going to head to Italy, on a flight leaving tonight and arriving early tomorrow morning.

Coop rubbed his temples. "Okay, so they're all coming here. How do you feel, today? I mean about the baby. Not about all these people, crashing our honeymoon."

"I still want to bring him home, but I understand that this is going to take time."

Coop gave him a quick kiss on the cheek. "I still want to bring him home, too. But, baby, we can't stay here for two months. Financially, we could, but would you really want to do that?"

Ethan leaned against Coop's shoulder. "I don't know. As long as I'm with you, I don't care where I am. I just want to be sure that he's going to be okay."

"Don't worry, puppy. We obviously have a very dedicated attorney behind us. I wasn't a huge fan of the way she talked, but she did sound like she knew what she was doing."

"Why are they all coming here, though? No one explained that part in the message. I feel like we have so much to do right now."

"We can't do anything else until we know what we're dealing with. Let's call your grandparents and meet with them tomorrow instead. Meeting with Miriam and Bianca today isn't going to help anything. Now, let's go downstairs and order breakfast. I'm starving and I guess we're not doing the gym at this point."

Ethan called his Nonna but was still a little stressed at the thought of everyone joining their honeymoon. He walked over to smell the roses on the counter. "Cooper, I just want to lay around, eat cannoli and have sex before everyone gets here."

"Hmm, that gives me an idea," Coop said. Ethan watched as he picked the phone up and called the concierge. Coop spoke to them in Italian, "Yes, we'll take six cannoli, please. Thank you."

"Six? I can't eat six."

"I only got two for you to eat. The rest are for—come here." Ethan approached and leaned down. Coop whispered in his ear.

"Oof. Yes!" Ethan said enthusiastically. "Yes please, let's do that as soon as we get them."

Levi and Tom boarded a flight to Italy, while Madeline and her companion boarded behind them.

Levi slid his body in front of Tom. "I don't want the window, Tommy. Can I have the aisle, please?"

Tom smiled, backing up, letting Levi have his way. Levi sat in the outside seat, while Tom stood beside him and reached overhead. His strong bicep peeked out of his short sleeve shirt and his package was right next to Levi's face, as he placed their bags in the overhead bin. Levi's eyes widened; he lifted his elbow and rubbed it lightly against Tom's dick. Tom looked down, still trying to make the bags fit.

Levi looked up at him. "Are you doing this on purpose? It's right in my ear, Tommy."

"You like it, shush."

Tom gave a few extra shoves up top, forcing his bulge to graze Levi's cheek two or three times. Levi covered his mouth and closed his eyes. "Oh God…Tommy, stop, this is a long flight. I won't make it."

Tom leaned down and kissed Levi's cheek. He sat next to him and tried to lean back. "These seats are so small," he complained while wiggling from side to side.

Once Tom was settled, Levi laid his head against his chest. "I really don't know what to do here, Tommy. I know why we're going but it just seems wrong. It's their life, if this is what they want, and can somehow make it happen, why should we—"

Tom rubbed Levi's hair. "Shh. I know, but we need to see the situation ourselves. We'll try not to interfere."

Levi closed his eyes. "I don't want to make either of them upset. We were younger than them when we had kids. Besides, I learned my lesson from Luke when I tried to stop him and Kory from getting Toby." He sighed. "We have stubborn sons."

"Yeah, but mostly your son is the stubborn one. I'm not even sure Kory wanted the puppy at first, but once you told them they should think about it, Luke wouldn't back down. I can't think of a time that Coop has been stubborn since he's been with Ethan. Now, before that, is a different story."

At the other end of the row, Madeline sat next to the window in her seat, she pulled her phone out and quickly sent one more email. She leaned her head on her blonde-haired, male companion's shoulder. "I always wanted kids, you know?"

The man pulled the lollipop out of his mouth and stroked her curly hair. "We could have kids, who would stop us?"

She lightly smacked him and closed her eyes.

"You still taste like cannoli, Cooper," Ethan said, then sucked Coop's tongue in another aggressive kiss, inside the hot shower.

"Mmm," Coop moaned and pulled back. He held Ethan's soapy shoulders firmly. "Baby, you sucked all the cannoli off, there is no more. I can order more for later, but there is no more in my mouth. I promise. He looked down at his own clean body. "There is no more down there either."

Ethan rinsed his hair in the shower, savoring the taste and the mental images from their food play a few minutes ago. He let out a light moan, leaning his head under the water.

Coop closed his eyes and plugged his ears. "I already know what you're doing. You're such a tease. I don't even need to see you to know what's happening. You said you wanted to go check out the garden, so I'm getting out now." Coop chuckled. He stepped out of the shower grinning, and Ethan followed behind.

After they got dressed, they headed off to the local rose garden. The flowers were in full bloom, and the park was full of people. Coop bent down to smell a rose, and Ethan took a picture of him beside the bright pink flowers. "Look at you. You're so perfect. You'd never know your face was covered with cannoli thirty minutes ago."

Coop stood and shook his head at him. "Don't bring that up right now, Ethan. Gonna get my brain remembering things. You said you wanted to sightsee, if you make me start thinking about sex, we're not gonna do anything else for the rest of the day."

"Yeah, I know, and part of me does want to just do that, but—" Ethan looked to the side. "I really wish I could draw here. It's so nice that they let people just lounge around on the grass. It would be nice to paint in a space like this."

Coop pulled his phone out. "We should be able to find the stuff you need, right? The downtown area might have a place with art supplies. Do you want to paint or draw, you said both, which one are you feeling today?"

Ethan looked around in thought. *He made sure we had a nice garden area outside our room. I should just paint there.* "Hmm, I think I'd like to paint today, but I can do it at the hotel."

Coop took him by the hand. "My phone shows an art supply place nearby. Let's go. Are you hungry? We can grab something on the way, if you want."

Ethan put a hand on his stomach and shook his head. "I'm still full from all the cannoli."

"Same. Good thing our dinner reservation isn't until later. If it was now, I don't think I could eat."

After a quick walk, the two reached the art shop. Coop held the door open, and Ethan walked inside. They held hands and looked around at the large space, packed wall to wall with art supplies. Ethan was having a hard time keeping the baby and Bianca out of his thoughts while he looked at all the brightly colored paints. He frowned at Coop and leaned his head on his shoulder. "I feel bad. I want to make sure she's getting the care she needs, but we haven't done anything to help. I feel guilty for some reason."

Coop pulled him into a hug. "You're too cute. We gave them basically $2,000 last night, and whether they realize it or not, there's more to come. We can't do anything else right now. Let's just have fun. Tomorrow we'll have a lot to deal with." He gave Ethan a quick smooch and rubbed his shoulders.

Ethan's eyes widened at the display in front of him. "Cooper!

Look at these! The colors are perfect." He picked up a box of soft colored acrylic paints and showed them to him.

"Ooh! I like the colors. Are those good paints?" Coop pointed at the rack. "Do you want all of them?"

"Really good paints. But, no, I just need this box and..." He grabbed a large canvas and foldable easel and smiled at Coop. "Maybe this stuff, too?"

Coop took the easel from him. "We can get all of it, but we won't be able to take this on the plane, and the canvas will be too big for carry on. I'm sure we could mail it, though."

Ethan nodded and grabbed a few new specialty brushes and pencils. He looked down at everything bundled in his arms. "Maybe I should just get a new sketchbook? I could just draw instead."

"I want you to get whatever makes you the happiest."

Ethan gave him a quick kiss. "You make me the happiest."

The cashier wasn't friendly at first but lightened up after both Coop and Ethan spoke in Italian. Ethan explained that his grandparents lived nearby and that they were on their honeymoon. The man's forehead creased as he looked at the two, studying them as they paid. After taking their payment, he awkwardly complimented their muscles and good looks.

Ethan felt relieved once they walked outside. "Whoo, I thought he was gonna say it for sure. Did you see how he looked at us?"

Coop held the easel under his arm. "It's weird when strangers talk about our looks. I would never do that to anyone but you."

Ethan leaned the canvas against the wall near the bed upstairs. He grabbed a towel from the bathroom and laid it on the floor, then sat on it, close to the canvas. "There, that's better. Sometimes I like working on the floor. It's more comfortable," he said.

"You sure you don't want to paint in the garden?" Coop asked.

"Nah, it was pretty hot on the walk over. It won't be good to paint outside in this heat. Plus, it will be dark soon. I'm good right here."

Coop ruffled his hair, then stretched out on the bed. "Can't wait to see what you paint."

Ethan studied the canvas silently for a long while, contemplating what to paint. He finally decided and started to sketch with his pencil. He called out, "Our reservation is at eight tonight, right?" There was no answer. "Cooper? Are you asleep?" He stood up and sure enough, Coop was fast asleep on the bed. Ethan rubbed his cheek and sat back down on the floor.

He continued his outline deep into the night.

"Ethan, baby, it's 1:00 am, what happened?" Coop asked in a sleepy voice.

Ethan turned to face him. "Oof, I didn't realize it was that late. I'm sorry. I should call it a night."

They quickly changed into their new matching couple pajamas. Both pairs were black, with their initials embroidered in white. They wore them for only a moment or two, before both found them too uncomfortable. "I can't sleep with this long-sleeved shirt on," Coop said, as he unbuttoned it.

Ethan shook his head. "Nope. Too uncomfortable." Ethan pulled his shirt off too.

They brushed their teeth, then snuggled up spoon style, shirtless in bed. A few minutes later, Ethan was awoken by Coop jolting straight up. His eyes shot open, and he lazily reached for Coop's back. "Whoa, what is happening?" he mumbled. "Lie back down."

"Wait, we had reservations. I ruined dinner. I'm so sorry, pup." Coop snuggled back behind Ethan and kissed his shoulders.

Ethan reached up and patted his head. "Don't worry. It's okay.

Love you." Ethan wanted to ask him if he was hungry but fell asleep before he could get the words out.

Chapter 6
Cocky Little Shit

Early the next morning, Tom, Levi, Madeline, and her companion stood in the hallway between their hotel rooms, discussing their plans to head to Coop and Ethan in a few hours. Madeline was already in business mode. "We can't waste time, Levi, don't screw around. You either, Tom. I know how tired men your age get, don't do anything stupid. You're here for a reason."

Levi's mouth hung open; his left hand was on his hip. He sassed her right back, "Maddie, we are not that much older than you. Just because you have this boy toy here with you"—Levi gestured to her blonde companion, who was sucking on a lollipop—"that doesn't make you any younger."

The man pulled the lollipop out and pointed it at her. "Ha! He just called you old."

Tom tugged Levi away. "Alright, Maddie, we get it. We'll meet back in the lobby. You schedule the taxi in case we fall asleep."

Madeline and her companion settled into their room. The man undressed and headed for the bathroom. "What the hell is this tiny shower? Maddie what kind of a hotel is this?"

"Have you never been to Italy?" she asked him. "Most bathrooms are like this. Very small, with just the curtain for the shower."

He looked down. "There's no separation between the shower and the floor. This is so weird."

"You were the one who wanted to come."

He pulled her in behind the curtain with him. "I still do."

The phone in the honeymoon suite rang loudly. Ethan covered his face with a pillow. He and Coop both knew who was calling and collectively groaned at the sound. While they wanted to reach a surrogacy agreement, they didn't feel like dealing with Tom and Levi, and, quite honestly, they weren't looking forward to meeting Madeline, either.

Coop stuck his head under the pillow with him. "If we ignore the phone, will they go back home?"

"No, I don't think so."

The ringing stopped, and Coop's face brightened. "It worked." Coop's phone rang again. "I still don't hear anything," he said.

Ethan finally answered the call. "Good morning, are you guys already here?"

"Yes, we've been in the lobby for ten minutes," Tom said. The concierge said they also called your room phone a few times. Are you guys ready?"

Coop took the phone from him. "Hey, Dad, we're not ready yet, you guys can just come to the room."

A few minutes later, the group arrived at the honeymoon suite. Levi and Tom entered first, followed by Madeline. She walked quickly through the room toward the roses. "Oh, wow, these are beautiful, Coop. What a nice thing to do for Ethan on your honeymoon. I'm Madeline by the way."

Ethan dropped an eyebrow at her. "Why did you assume he sent me the flowers? Why not assume I sent them to him? Also, hello, nice to meet you."

Before Coop could say anything, Madeline's companion slowly sauntered in, with a lollipop in his mouth, wearing a casual black suit. His blonde shoulder length hair was down, apart from his bangs, which were pulled tightly back in a small elastic. His dark brown eyes searched the room.

Ethan instantly felt a strong sense of annoyance at his demeanor.

Her companion answered Ethan's question, "She said that because you wouldn't send flowers to him, he would send them to you."

Levi bit his lip, then said, "He is gonna be a problem."

Coop stood in front of Ethan. "Normally when you walk in a room, you introduce your—"

"I'm Liam," the man interrupted. His eyes still searched the room, while he walked. He tossed his empty lollipop stick in the trash and gave Ethan and Coop a false smile.

Tom spoke, "Liam is a lawyer too."

Ethan whispered to Coop, "I told you I wanted you to beat people up that piss me off if I'm not allowed to go spicy puppy."

Coop kissed him on the cheek, then held his hand.

Madeline turned from the flowers. "Ethan, you have a complex because he's bigger than you?"

Ethan's mouth dropped open.

She sighed and rolled her eyes. "Let's start over. I'm Madeline, I speak plainly and honestly. I don't play games, and I'm not interested in people's feelings. I'm here to help you with a surrogacy agreement, not to be your friend. It's easier for me if I separate clients from friends. If you have a complex, that's too bad for you. You're both hot, but your husband is probably an inch taller than you, he's also a bit bigger in the chest. Do I need to spell the rest out? Ethan, people will make assumptions for the rest of your life, who cares? You want to raise a child with him, and you're worried about who I think sent the flowers? He sent them, there's no question about it. Get over it."

Coop turned to face Madeline. "Are you always so rude when you meet people though? I don't like you talking to him like that."

"Let's go. I'm over it," Liam said. "They have no idea who you are. Just forget it. This is a lost cause anyway." He pulled another lollipop out of his pocket and stuck it in his mouth, then placed the wrapper in his pocket.

"Enough," Levi said pointing at Liam. "Listen, kid, I don't know where you keep pulling these damn pops out of, but they really add to the whole *I'm a cocky little shit* vibe that you have going for you. Those two are paying you, as are we, if you aren't here to help then shut up."

Liam held his hands up. "Alright, alright."

"Why are you paying them?" Coop asked his dad. "I don't even know who he is. I know you guys said Madeline was the best, but why should we pay him? And, again, why are *you* paying him?"

Madeline whistled loudly, drawing their attention then spoke frankly. "You guys want the baby or not? If not, I'll take Liam, and head out."

Coop rubbed Ethan's shoulders. "You want to do this with them, or not? My dad and Levi trust her, but we can find someone else if you want."

Madeline interjected, "I wouldn't recommend that. No one is going to take this case." She pointed at Levi and continued. "Why do you think the missus over there agreed that they would pitch in? I'm worth your whole bank account."

"She'll take it all too," Liam said. "Ruthless."

The standoff eventually ended with them coming to terms.

Madeline sat at the dining table drinking an espresso, while Liam wandered upstairs.

Coop held his left hand out gesturing toward the stairs. "Your son is kind of rude."

Madeline choked on her drink, holding her pointer finger up.

Liam called excitedly from the stairs, "Maddie, they have a normal bathroom, they even have a sauna!"

Ethan got a vibe from the two that Coop didn't pick up on. "Cooper, I don't think that's their situation," he whispered.

Coop furrowed his brow at Ethan, then looked back to Madeline. "Wait, he's not your son?"

Liam stuck his head around the side of the stairs. "Nope, I'm her daddy."

Madeline dropped her head back and screamed, "Oh my God. Why did I bring you?"

Liam shouted playfully, "'Cause you like me so much!"

Ethan made a disgusted face and asked, "Since you're all about not sparing feelings, Madeline, Isn't he much younger than you?"

Liam sauntered back down the stairs.

Madeline replied bluntly, "Yes, Ethan, he is, but what can I say? He's great in bed."

Liam's eyes widened in excitement, and his mouth hung open. He pulled his phone out of his pocket. "Say that again, I want to record it."

Ethan's phone rang and he answered it quickly, "Hi, Nonna." He spoke to her in Italian, venting a bit of his frustration about both Madeline and Liam, then caught her up on their situation, and they made their plans for the day.

"Ethan that was amazing!" Levi said. "I had no idea you were fluent. So beautiful."

Coop whispered in Ethan's ear. Ethan playfully patted the front of Coop's pants, in response.

Coop called the concierge and requested two taxis, and a few minutes later, the group headed to Nonna and Pop Pop's.

Chapter 7
A Prick With Cute Features

The taxis arrived one behind the other, at Ethan's grandparents' home. Walking up the steep driveway, Levi held Tom's arm. "I can't do it. I can't tell them not to go through with it. I'm weak, Tommy."

Coop whispered to Ethan, "So that's why there here. I guess Levi really just doesn't know how to whisper."

Madeline and Liam walked beside Tom and Levi. Madeline obviously found something that Liam did funny. She sounded almost giddy. "Stop, no more. I'll make you stay in the car, Liam."

Liam pulled the lollipop out of his mouth and pointed with it. "You can't make me stay in the car; the driver already left."

Ethan stepped around the others and knocked on the door.

"Come in!" Nonna shouted.

Liam was obviously shocked by Nonna's invitation. "What? These people don't even ask who's at the door? I don't even see a camera, Maddie."

After introductions, the large group sat at the long-oval dining room table along with Bianca and her mother. The table had more room today, since Nonna added the extra leaf portion, making space for more chairs.

From the moment the group walked in, Bianca's eyes were glued to Liam.

Madeline whispered to Ethan, while casually pointing at Bianca, "Well maybe the dad is good looking. She's checking Liam out. He's a prick but he has cute features. That should give you hope."

"How?" Ethan asked, turning his palms upward on the table.

Ethan controlled the conversation, translating for the others who didn't understand. Bianca's mother, Miriam, asked why they brought such a bright haired, bossy woman with them. Ethan didn't translate that. He just shook his head.

As far as Bianca and Miriam were concerned the arrangement was already complete. Miriam explained that they accepted the money and didn't need anything else.

Madeline listened to Ethan as he relayed that, then exhaled loudly. "This is going to be a problem, guys."

"Why?" Tom asked. "She's saying it's a done deal. I didn't even know you told them to do that. Seems like a stupid thing to do, Maddie."

"It was not a stupid thing to do," Liam argued. "They gave her money; they recorded her giving up her rights, agreeing to be their surrogate. It's actually quite brilliant. Probably won't hold up, but it was still very smart."

Levi cocked his head to the side at Liam. "How? How could paying them money without an official contract be smart?"

Liam pulled a lollipop out of his pocket.

Levi threw his hands up. "Another one?"

Liam slid the wrapper off and shrugged at Levi. "Yeah, they calm me. I've always liked them"—he popped the pink lollipop in his mouth—"Levi, listen, it was smart because they obviously don't care about the baby. They were only interested in money. It makes these two look better and those two look worse."

Madeline looked at her phone, and she spoke quickly, "We have to head to the office. Liam, go call for two taxis. Use the same service, please."

Liam saluted her and headed outside.

Madeline continued, "Ethan, tell her mother that the bossy lady with the bright hair figured out a way to win this thing." She stood up and walked quickly outside to join Liam.

Levi looked confused at Tom. "What did she say? Bright-haired, bossy lady. What does that mean?"

Tom shrugged in response. "No idea."

Ethan slid a hand down his face looking at Coop. "Wait, so she..." Ethan said.

Pop Pop confirmed Ethan's realization, "Yep, she understands Italian. Couldn't you tell? Smart girl, she was following everything. I'm surprised you two didn't notice that. What a shark! You guys are in good hands."

Nonna squealed with laughter. "Wait till I tell Gigi!"

Ethan spoke to Miriam; he explained that they would be in touch soon. Miriam smiled and thanked him; she was much nicer to both him and Coop today.

They said their goodbyes to Ethan's grandparents, and headed out the front door, with Tom and Levi following behind. "Oh, this is why Madeline left in the middle of the conversation," Ethan said. "I didn't even notice that Bianca followed Liam outside."

Madeline stood between Liam and Bianca and shouted in Italian at her, "What are you doing trying to pick up a guy? You're pregnant!"

Bianca crossed her arms, resting them on her large baby bump.

Liam held a translator app open that loudly repeated everything in English.

Bianca rolled her eyes at Madeline. "He is a very hot man. I am already pregnant. There's no risk here."

Ethan, Coop, and Liam's jaws collectively dropped.

Madeline was livid, she spoke very quickly in Italian, "You are not allowed to sleep with other men. You are carrying their son, right? You agreed to that. I'm going right now to get papers filed. You already signed them. There is a contingency that prohibits you from engaging in intercourse. Also,"—she pointed to Liam—"he is with me."

Liam grinned widely. He turned and spoke quietly into his phone translator, then held it up. The phone voice spoke in Italian, "Yes, she is my mother."

Madeline smacked him on the arm. She spoke to Bianca again, a bit softer, "With your condition you could harm their son. Not only that, but you could harm yourself."

Bianca waved Madeline off and continued staring at Liam.

Ethan made a pouty face and looked at Coop, tugging on his arm.

"Yeah, this is uncomfortable," Coop said. He rubbed Ethan's back. "I hadn't considered she would do that."

"Not that. Cooper, she called him *our* son."

Coop smiled and gave him a smooch, pulling him in tight.

Once Madeline was certain that Bianca understood, the group got into their taxis.

Chapter 8
You Can Decide What Goes In My Mouth

After a short ride, the group stood outside the agency building, near a large waterway. Madeline and Liam planned to file the surrogacy agreement on Coop & Ethan's behalf, but hadn't really explained much of the process to them.

Madeline looked at her phone, then spoke to Coop and Ethan. "I don't know how long this is going to take, but you don't have to come in for this part. I'll let you know if we need you." She turned and motioned for Liam to follow her.

Liam held a file in his hand and raised his eyebrows at Madeline. "You really think you got this?"

She nodded. "No doubt about it. Let's go."

Coop rubbed Ethan's arms and kissed him on the forehead. "She said she's sure she can get it done. Maybe she really is worth all the money we're paying her."

Ethan smiled at him. "If we can have a baby and help Bianca, too, I'm pretty sure there's no amount I wouldn't pay."

Coop loved so many things about Ethan, but the fact that Bianca was quite honestly so rude to the two of them, and Ethan still wanted to help her, was something that Coop found exceptionally adorable. It wasn't just about adopting a child together for Ethan, it was the fact that he saw someone in need and refused to look the other way.

Coop held Ethan's face in his hands and stared into his eyes. "How did I get so lucky? I love your heart, Ethan. We're gonna do our best to help, pup. I promise."

Tom looked at the two of them and spoke softly, "You guys, I really can't believe you're doing this. We came here to try and talk some sense into you both."

"Tommy, don't," Levi said.

Coop held Ethan's hand and squeezed it.

Tom started again, "I guess there's no point, right? Let's just see what Maddie comes back with."

Levi's phone started to ring. "Ah, the stubborn son is calling," he said, looking at Tom. "Hi, Luke, how's it going? Sorry we stole your boss for a few days."

Coop and Ethan looked at one another. "I guess she must be the boss at his firm," Coop said. "I had no idea."

Ethan tilted his head. "I thought Kory was Luke's boss, though."

Tom joined their conversation, "Maddie is the boss, her dad is the CEO, but he's retired. Kory is a Junior Partner. Get it?"

They both nodded in understanding.

Levi continued speaking, "Well, no, we haven't hit any vineyards yet. Hopefully tomorrow. Yeah, I don't think Ethan and Coop are big fans of Maddie, but this little shit with her is even more annoying. Lollipop in his mouth every five minutes… Hello, Luke? Hello…?" Levi looked at the phone and shrugged. "I guess we lost the signal. I'm sure he'll call back."

The four walked around the downtown area while Madeline and Liam remained inside the building.

Ethan pointed at a small outdoor stand. "Giovanni's Gelato, can we stop for some?"

Coop ruffled his hair and pulled him toward the stand. "Of course."

Levi's eyes widened. "Ooh, yes! You know what I want, Tommy. I'll grab a table."

Coop ordered a strawberry cup, and Ethan ordered vanilla. They sat on a small iron bench next to one another, across from Tom and Levi. The red and white table umbrella blocked the harsh afternoon sunlight.

Ethan took a bite of his gelato. "Hmm…this is good." Coop tilted his head and looked at him. Ethan took another bite. "Maybe it's just because of all the cannoli yesterday, but it tastes kind of…"

Coop slid his cup over to him and pulled Ethan's over. "No, it's fine," Ethan said. "You have the one you ordered." Coop stuck the spoon in the strawberry cup that was now in front of Ethan and fed him a bite. Ethan's eyes lit up. "Mmm. That is so good!"

"Baby, I told you, just order what I order." Coop kissed him on the cheek. "You always like whatever I have better."

Ethan smooched him on the mouth. "I'll remember next time. Or maybe I just shouldn't be allowed to order? You can decide what goes in my mouth."

Coop whispered for several moments in Ethan's ear, then kissed him softly on the cheek. Ethan's eyes were wide with excitement looking at Coop, as he took a large bite of the strawberry gelato.

"Oh my gosh, this mint chocolate chip is heaven," Levi said. He fed Tom a bite. "Tommy, do you think we'll be able to see a vineyard tomorrow?"

The group's attention turned at the sight of Liam and Madeline walking out of the building. Madeline's hands and hair were flailing around, as she spoke on her phone. Liam stood in front of her, obviously amused, based on the giant grin on his face.

Ethan pulled an eyebrow down. "Look at her posture. She's

pissed, but not at him. He thinks whatever she's mad about is funny. They're a strange couple."

Levi stood and waved. "Maddie, over here!"

Liam walked in front of her, while she continued her conversation. He approached the gelato stand and loudly ordered two strawberry cups, then carried them over to the table and stood beside Coop. "She's talking to my brother," he said after he took a bite.

Madeline's whole face was red, and she shot Levi a nasty look.

Liam pointed at Levi. "This is your fault."

"My fault?" Levi pointed at himself. "What did I do?"

Liam raised his eyebrows as Madeline ended the call. He sat beside Coop and held the other cup of gelato towards Madeline. "Showtime," he said.

Coop scooted a little closer to Ethan.

Madeline grabbed the gelato and took a bite, staring Levi down.

Levi stuck his spoon in his cup and threw his hands up. "What? Why are you staring at me? What did I do?"

She shook her head in annoyance. "Give me a minute, Levi." She took a few more bites and handed a very thick file to Ethan and Coop.

"What is this?" Ethan asked, as Coop opened the file.

She rolled her eyes. "What is it? Just read it. You have to sign about five hundred pages; we need to bring it back tomorrow. Looks good so far, though. Major hurdles going forward will be making sure she takes care of herself properly until the delivery and just hoping she doesn't run off somewhere. They'll also need to interview you both, see the home, and some other stuff, but you can read about all that yourselves."

Ethan and Coop started reading through the massive file. Ethan looked up at her. "So, are they going to pass it through?"

"The specifics are in there," she said. "Messy and ugly, but it's going to work. Of course, if you two"—she pointed to Tom and Levi—"wanted to give me a little extra money, to make up for Levi's tremendous blunder, I wouldn't be opposed."

Levi finished his gelato and shouted across the small table, "What did I do?"

Madeline took another bite and forcefully stuck her spoon into her gelato, leaving it there. She rubbed her temples looking at Liam. "I can't believe I even have to explain this."

"Don't explain it." Liam shrugged. "Who cares? They don't care."

Madeline exhaled. "Liam is Kory's brother."

Levi's mouth dropped open. "What? This little shit is my son's brother-in-law?"

Liam grinned proudly. "The one and only."

Coop's eyes were wide looking at Ethan. "I had no idea," Coop whispered.

Levi stood up from his seat, then sat back down. He stood back up and looked down at the bench. "Damn it, this bench doesn't allow for a dramatic walk off." He sat down again and shook his head. "Maddie, how could you not have told us this?"

Liam cocked his head to the side. "Why is it really your concern?"

"I think it's time for another lollipop, kid," Tom said.

"See, this is why she doesn't want to tell anyone about us," Liam said. "It's been this way for the last three months; everyone always brings up my age. So stupid."

Ethan leaned forward looking at Liam. "If I could just say something. It's not really your age, it's just that you're kind of a..."

"A dick," Coop finished Ethan's sentence.

"So, who cares if I am? I'm a year older than you two. I don't hear people calling you two kids. You're about to adopt a baby from some girl that you don't even know, after being around her for what, five minutes? Everyone hopped on a plane here to fix everything for you guys, right? But me? I'm a lawyer, I work hard, I study, I do things for myself, and my damn girlfriend won't even call me her boyfriend in public because I'm younger than her."

Coop winced while speaking, "Madeline, you said you didn't want to be friends with us, and this feels like personal friend talk."

Ethan shook his head and looked at her. "So unprofessional," he added, with a smile.

"No. You two will not win me over," Madeline said. "Luke is my best friend. I'm not your friend. I'm your attorney."

Levi rolled his eyes across the table. "Luke is your best friend? Funny, he's never said that to me."

"He hasn't said it to her either," Liam said. "It's a one-sided friendship."

The group finished their gelato and walked through the downtown area, with Coop and Ethan at the front of the group. After a few blocks, Coop stopped and squatted down in front of Ethan, Ethan hopped on his back, holding onto the file.

The six decided to eat at a gorgeous rooftop restaurant that overlooked the Arno River. A waiter walked them to a large open table with a stunning view.

Ethan and Coop looked through the file as the other four held conversations that they weren't interested in. Ethan pointed to an empty spot on one of the forms. "This seems weird, but we need to give him a name, like Madeline said the other day. I guess we can change it once he's born, but they need one for the agreement."

"Yeah, let's do that when we get back to the room. I don't want any suggestions from these guys."

Ethan looked at him softly. "Cooper, Is this real?"

Coop turned his body to block Ethan's face and moved in for a kiss. He only allowed a momentary swirl of the tongue, but it was enough to make Ethan moan lightly.

The other four were too engrossed in their conversation about tomorrow's plans to notice.

Coop pressed his forehead to Ethan's. "Puppy, it's real, we're gonna have a son." Ethan smiled brightly and gave Coop a quick smooch.

Madeline spoke up, "Hey, lover boys, did you get to the page where it shows how much you'll be paying for until she gives birth?"

She reached across the table, stretching in front of Liam. Liam covered his mouth. "Uh, hello, Maddie, don't bend across the table like that."

She pulled the file back and whacked him with it. "They're all gay, they don't care about me bending over a table."

"Not them, I'm talking about them." He pointed to the seats behind their table. They were filled with people who were smiling and staring over.

She gave a quick smile and sat down. "Now, see, I'm here with my boyfriend and people are checking me out. If I was by myself, no one would pay attention to me."

Liam's face brightened. "You said it! You called me your boyfriend. Ahh, finally."

Madeline didn't pay any attention to him; she thumbed through the file and pulled out the stack showing Coop and Ethan's financial agreements. "Here, put this stack on top and review it when you get back to your hotel."

Ethan and Coop arrived back at their hotel shortly after dinner. Ethan had lost all confidence after being beaten by the door lock, so many times. "Cooper, don't even pass me the phone. I'm not even gonna try to open it." Coop held the phone in Ethan's hand and slid it together with him. The door opened immediately.

Coop comforted him. "See? Just like everything else, it works if we do it together, puppy." He kissed Ethan on the cheek.

Ethan sat inside on the bed and pulled the financial stack out again. He looked at the numbers intently, while Coop sat beside him. "Alright, so, Madeline is gonna set all this up? We just have to pay for it?"

"Yeah, she said that everything would be taken care of."

Ethan passed Coop the file and laid flat on the bed. "What do we do now? Do we just go home in a few days?"

Coop placed the file on the nightstand and laid beside him. "Well, I guess so. We're not going to stay and watch her until she gives birth. We can add your Nonna as our local representative. She can go to the appointments and fill us in afterwards, and, yeah, Madeline said they would take care of everything. I don't think there's anything else we can do. Plus, we need to get ready for him at home. We don't have any baby stuff. It will probably take time to get everything ready."

"Yeah, you're right. Plus, I do miss our bed," Ethan said as he laid his head on Coop's chest.

Chapter 9
Only My Husband Calls Me Cooper

The next morning, Coop, Ethan, Liam, and Madeline had a hearing at the family affairs office. While they were inside, Levi and Tom waited outside for them. Levi was feeling more than a little anxious over everything. "How is this even happening? Can it really be this easy?" Levi asked Tom.

"Not in a million years. I have no idea how she's gonna pull it off. Magic, I guess. Just don't question it."

Levi's phone rang; he answered it excitedly. "Hi, Luke, I lost you yesterday, sorry about that."

"No, Dad. I hung up. I can't believe you didn't know that Liam was Kory's brother. I'm still in shock, and I'm not sure if Kory will ever recover."

"Well, how should I have known? He didn't use his last name when he introduced himself. Maddie didn't tell us until after you hung up on me."

"Riiight, but, Dad, don't you see the resemblance between Kory and Liam? Actually, hang on Kory wants to talk to you."

"Hi, Levi, how are you? Are you guys enjoying Italy?"

Levi replied, "Well, I'm happy you're calling me Levi, finally. There are too many Mr. Morgans at this point. Haha, four of us now! But, honestly, I'm a bit stressed out. I'm thrilled that Maddie thinks she can get this through, but I'm nervous and afraid for the boys. Also, still a little embarrassed that I didn't realize Liam was your brother."

"Don't worry about that. He's such a little jerk; I'd be more embarrassed if you'd made the connection. If he gives you any trouble, just slap him around. As far as the surrogacy situation is concerned, I would be nervous, too. Then again, I'm not a fan of babies."

Ethan and Coop sat in front of a row of three Italian lawyers, and a few other men in suits, while Madeline and Liam sat beside them. A lawyer who spoke English from the other side looked at the four of them. "Has the temporary residence been secured for the carrier?"

Liam answered politely, "Yes, sir, we have secured that as of this morning."

The lawyer questioned further, "Have you inspected the property to be sure it's satisfactory?"

Liam scoffed. "With the amount of money our clients are paying, it better be."

"You didn't answer my question," the lawyer retorted. "Are you saying you have not personally inspected it? The carrier is set to move in within forty-eight hours, correct?"

Madeline asserted control. "We will inspect the property at the conclusion of this meeting, which better be soon. You people are asking such ridiculous questions. Our clients are married, wealthy men, do you think they'll approve a residence for the carrier of their son, if it's less than perfect? Surely, you don't."

A different lawyer from the other side agreed. "No, I surely don't. We will interview the carrier one final time tomorrow, after she approves the residence, which, as you stated, I am sure is more than acceptable." He looked at Coop and Ethan. "We will also need to conduct an in-home visit of your actual home within the next thirty days. Be appreciative of that, normally we wouldn't even entertain such a thing, especially not within such a small window of time."

"Yes, thank you. We appreciate your help," Coop said.

"We're extremely grateful for your understanding," Ethan added.

The meeting concluded, and Liam, Coop, and Ethan walked toward the exit. Madeline stopped for a moment to talk to the English-speaking lawyer. She acted more than friendly, flirting loudly and even put her hand on the man's shoulder. The man seemed very pleased and whispered something in her ear. Liam watched intently, as he pulled a lollipop out of his pocket and stuck it in his mouth. He spoke quietly to Coop and Ethan, "She's always like this. Unbelievable. A pregnant girl hits on me, and I swear she had fire coming out of her ears. I didn't hear the end of that yesterday. But here she is, doing that." He gestured to Madeline, who was currently whispering something in the lawyer's ear but covering her mouth with a file.

Coop and Ethan smiled uncomfortably, then walked outside, leaving Liam and Madeline behind. "I don't want to get in the middle of that," Ethan said.

"Me neither," Coop said, taking Ethan by the hand. "Let's go find my dad and Levi."

Levi and Tom were sitting at the same Gelato stand as yesterday. "Good news?" Levi asked.

"Yep. A few things still have to be done," Coop said. "But, yeah, everything seems like it's gonna work out."

Tom stood up and pulled him in for a hug. "What are you hugging me for, Dad?"

Tom patted his back and released him. "I'm just proud of you. That's all."

"I guess Liam already found a house for Bianca, so we're supposed to check that out," Ethan said. "Then a couple more interviews, with one at our home in Florida within thirty days."

Coop ruffled Ethan's hair and turned toward the Gelato stand. "I'm getting us some gelato and we're both getting strawberry."

Ethan pulled on Coop's arm. "No, wait, I really want choc—"

Coop tilted his chin down and lowered his eyebrows.

Ethan remembered his promise, seeing Coop's expression. "Never mind. I'll have whatever you're having. Thank you."

While Coop grabbed the gelato, Ethan sat across from Tom and Levi. He noticed that Liam looked even more irritated than normal, as he and Madeline walked over and joined the group. Coop sat beside Ethan, and Madeline passed the file she was holding to him. "I'm not a fan of calling you Coop, by the way. Seems so frat boy," she said.

Coop took the file. "Well, I don't pay you to like my name, right? Only my husband calls me Cooper."

"That's annoying," Liam said under his breath.

Ethan was pretty sure he was the only one who heard him. He furrowed his brow at Liam's comment but decided to just ignore it.

Madeline looked at Coop and said, "You are kind of nasty…I like it though."

Liam grabbed Madeline by the waist and pulled her close. He took the lollipop out of his mouth and whispered something in her ear. She rolled her eyes, seeming not to care about whatever he said and addressed the group quickly, "Alright, we need to check out the residence that Liam picked. I'll text everyone the address. Let's meet there at 2:00 pm. Levi, it's near a vineyard, so maybe we can check that out after."

Levi's face lit up. "Oh my gosh, yes! I've been dying to visit one with Tommy since we got here! I'm craving an authentic, full-bodied red."

Liam, still visibly aggravated, said to Coop and Ethan, "We can play some ball, too, so wear clothes that you want to run in."

The couples headed back to their hotel rooms. Ethan and Coop were quickly entangled upstairs. Coop pulled one of Ethan's legs up and threw it over his shoulder. "No soft stuff, not enough time, baby." He lubed Ethan up quickly and shoved his cock inside.

Ethan grasped at the sheets; he loved when Coop allowed it to hurt just a little. "Fuck, yes. It's so hot when you take me like this." He moaned in pleasure, begging for more. "Unh—mmm—harder—fuck me harder—mmm—"

Coop bit the side of Ethan's calf. "Mmm—yeah, you like it when your husband works your tight little ass—so naughty—unh—" He pounded harder, grunting with each thrust.

Ethan pulled Coop's face in for a kiss, lifting his head to meet his mouth.

"Down," Coop commanded and licked across his mouth.

"Ahhh—unhh—Cooper—" Ethan tugged on a chunk of Coop's hair, attempting to kiss him again.

Coop avoided his mouth, instead leaning down to bite one of Ethan's nipples, drawing louder moans from his husband, as his cock drove even further inside. "Mmm—make me come, Cooper. I need to—"

Coop slowed his pace and readjusted his posture. He spoke softly, looking down at Ethan, "You want to come, baby?"

Ethan nodded, scratching down Coop's chest. "Yes—please—hah—I'm so fucking close."

Coop leaned down, going extra deep and achingly slow, pulling back every time he grazed Ethan's spot. He whispered in Ethan's ear, "Say it, say what I want to hear, and I'll do it… Make me come, too…"

Ethan begged, knowing exactly what Coop wanted to hear, "Io appartengo a te, marito mio. Vieni per me. Ti prego."

Coop ground quickly into Ethan's spot, as Ethan writhed beneath him, his come shot out between their bodies. "Yes—unngh—Cooper—unngh—haah—haah—I'm coming."

Coop buried himself deeper, releasing inside. "Fuck—ungh—haah—haah—" His body fully relaxed on top of Ethan's. "Mine," he murmured, tucking his face into Ethan's neck.

Ethan loved these moments. He was always the one collapsing into Cooper, and when Cooper allowed himself to fall onto him, it was in these moments that Ethan felt the closest to him.

After a quick shower, Ethan ordered room service. He was really craving a white pizza, something that Coop didn't realize was actually called pizza bianca, since he'd never tried it. Coop brought the trays into the bed with them. He chuckled a bit looking down at everything they ordered. "Our bodies must be so confused with all this food we're eating."

Ethan smiled. "Yeah, but I'm pretty sure that honeymoon calories don't count." He took a bite of fried ravioli, then grabbed a piece of white pizza and put it on a plate in front of Coop. "You're gonna love it, I promise," he said, as Coop looked strangely at the slice.

"Whoa, this is actually delicious," Coop said, as he finished his first bite. "I think like it better without the sauce."

"I know. It's so good!" Ethan said, taking a bite of his own slice.

"How long is it before babies can have pizza?"

Ethan chuckled. "A long time, I think at least a year, but maybe longer? Definitely needs teeth for that."

"Well, let's give him white pizza, as soon as he can have it. Maybe we'll give him white pizza before he tries regular pizza. He should only have the best things."

"Deal," Ethan said, as he grabbed another slice. He looked at the time, realizing they needed to leave soon. "We don't have our gear with us; do you think the lollipop guy has gloves and bats? I'm sure he doesn't have a mitt for me."

"Let's find out. I'll text him," Coop said, pulling his phone out of his pocket.

Ethan put his hand on Coop's phone. "Two things: First, you're not allowed to text other men like lollipop guy about non-work or non-surrogacy related things. I don't want him thinking we're friends with him. Second, they seemed like they might be fighting, so let's just text Madeline and ask her."

Coop's eyes widened excitedly. "Puppy, that sounded almost possessive. I loved it." He smooched Ethan on the cheek, then texted Madeline.

"Of course I'm possessive over you. You're mine. I'm still considering that leash my Aunt Tina told me I should get for you."

"You're the puppy here. If anyone needs a leash it's you," he said, ruffling Ethan's hair.

A few moments later, Coop received a reply from Madeline. "Nope, she says we don't need to bring anything. So, we should head over now."

Chapter 10
The Nipple Fiasco

Coop and Ethan arrived at the residence for Bianca, ten minutes later than they were supposed to. The residence was a charming, stone covered, two-bedroom villa, with a large backyard, a pool, and a private gated entrance. Liam, Madeline, Levi, and Tom were waiting in the driveway, beside a blue Ferrari.

"You guys are late!" Madeline shouted. "I don't like to be kept waiting. First time you've done that to me. Better be the last, too."

"Sorry," Ethan said. "It was my fault. I tried to—"

Coop stopped Ethan's apology. "No," he said, quickly kissing him on the cheek. "She works for us, don't let her fool you, baby."

Liam mocked her, "Hahaha. He's not afraid of you. This must be difficult for you, Maddie."

The group entered the home together. Coop and Ethan were in the back of the group. They walked slowly, taking everything in.

"This is nice and cozy," Levi said. "Terribly decorated, but I don't think she'll mind. Liam, you picked this out?"

Liam pulled a lollipop out of his gym shorts and stuck it in his mouth. "Yep. Maddie said to pick something nice, but not too nice."

Levi tilted his head at him. "Even have them in your gym shorts, huh?"

Liam smiled and pulled a red lollipop out of his pocket. "Here, just try it."

"Thanks, but I don't want to offend my palate," Levi said. "We're going to the winery after this."

Liam stuck it back in his pocket. "I'm going too, who cares? What's the big deal with your palate? Oh, wait, Luke told me you're like a wine taster or something."

Coop winced, seeing Levi's eyes widen.

"Oh shit," Tom said loudly while grabbing Levi's hand.

Levi stuck his other hand on his hip, with sass. "Excuse me? Is that what my son said? A wine taster? A wine taster?!"

Liam scoffed. "I don't know. I wasn't really interested. He's kind of annoying, honestly. Why would I care what my brother in law's dad does?"

Levi dropped an eyebrow. "Riiight—"

Liam interrupted him, pulling his lollipop out and pointing it at him. "See that, that too! You both do that all the time, 'Riiight'. So annoying."

Ethan imitated Madeline to the best of his ability, speaking to Liam, "So, if I'm reading this right, you're jealous of Luke, because Madeline considers him to be her best friend? Who cares, Liam? Who cares who she likes better, she's sleeping with you, not Luke. Get over it."

Liam put his lollipop back in his mouth and pointed at Ethan. "Touche."

"Let it go," Tom whispered, putting his arm around Levi's waist.

After the tour of the inside, the group walked into the large yard. Liam pointed toward the left entrance. "Well, there will also be a private security guard stationed at the gate entrance, he doesn't start until tomorrow, though."

Tom looked at Liam and Madeline. "Is that really necessary?"

"That's a stupid question," Madeline replied. "Of course, it's necessary. This is an expensive property, rented normally by wealthy tourists. Not to mention, we need to be sure she isn't letting men come in and out. We paid security extra for that. Well, you guys did." She pointed to Coop and Ethan.

Liam jogged around to the front of the home, opening the trunk of the Ferrari.

"I always forget Ferrari's have trunks in the front instead of the back," Ethan said. "I thought he was gonna start working on the car for a minute. Wait, did he drive that here?"

Madeline giggled. "Yep, he just rented it. You two are paying for it of course."

Tom patted Ethan and Coop's shoulders. "Good thing you boys are loaded."

"I swear, Maddie," Levi rolled his eyes, "you are genuinely an awful person, and he is equally horrible."

"Oh, shut up, Levi, I'm paying for the wine tasting."

Levi cocked his head to the side and clapped sarcastically at her.

The group watched as Liam jogged back, holding a soccer ball and four orange cones. Coop felt disappointed. He nudged Ethan. "He didn't mean baseball…he meant soccer."

Liam pulled the plastic wrapping off the cones and looked up. "What? Baseball? Why would you think I meant baseball?"

"We all play baseball," Coop said. "Of course, we would assume that."

Ethan chimed in, "Yeah, Liam, you said we would play ball, isn't that what you said?"

"Yeah, I did. Oh well, you guys aren't afraid of kicking a ball, are you?" Liam teased, as he quickly set up two sets of mock goal zones.

Madeline grabbed Levi's arm. "Come help me get the other stuff out of the car."

"Can anything else even fit in that tiny frunk?" Levi asked, as Madeline pulled him toward the car.

"Don't worry, it's big enough for wine, a blanket, and glasses that we brought from the hotel. There's a small cooler with water, too."

Tom pointed, looking at Ethan. "Ethan's the fastest one here, I'm taking him on my team."

"No, Dad." Coop pulled Ethan in front of him. "This is my husband. He stays with me. You get Liam."

Coop wrapped his arms around Ethan's waist from behind and rested his chin on his shoulder. Ethan gave him a quick smooch. "Yeah, we're a team, you get Liam."

Liam jogged over with the ball. "What are you guys talking about?"

Tom kicked at the ground, pouting. "Teams."

Madeline and Levi had already set themselves up nearby, on a blanket with a bottle of wine and glasses. Liam glanced over at them. "Well, those two are gonna just sit on their little blanket and drink wine, I guess."

Levi shouted, "Tommy, are you good? I'm gonna catch up with Maddie, okay? I'm not playing soccer."

Tom waved, then turned to Liam. "Are you any good?"

Liam took the ball with his feet, showing off, juggling. He flipped it around easily, demonstrating complete control. He then kicked it across the yard, in between the goal cones and smiled. "All-star, baby."

"Well, alright, I'm with you then," Tom said.

Liam shook his head. "Nope."

"What do you mean, nope?" Tom threw his hands up. "There's only four of us."

Liam smirked. "We flip for it, then."

Coop was annoyed instantly with Liam's suggestion. "Come on, we're on our honeymoon, man."

"We're all guys here, I don't give a shit about your honeymoon. I want to win. I want you with me," Liam said to Coop.

"Not happening, little man."

Liam kicked the ball in between the goal cones again, showing off with speed in front of Coop. "You like that? If you're with me, we'll win."

Coop held his arms wide. "Kick it all you want. I'm on a team with my husband, or I don't play."

Liam rolled his eyes at Coop, jogging away to get the ball. "Fine," he called out. "But we switch after two goals, how about that?"

"What's wrong with me?" Tom asked Liam. "I was an All-star in baseball. Could have been drafted."

Liam juggled the ball on his knees. "Alright, let's go, Tom. You can be the goalie. I'm a striker."

"Oh, I get it," Tom said. "You didn't want to go up against Coop because he's bigger than you."

"You really don't know anything about soccer, huh?" Liam asked.

"Of course, I do, my daughter's been playing soccer since she was six. I know how to play."

Coop walked Ethan over into the goal area on their side. "I'm not really comfortable with you being the goalie. He kicks pretty hard, baby."

"Are you serious? Cooper, do you see the pitches that fly at me? They come in at a hundred miles per hour sometimes. He didn't kick that hard."

Coop *was* serious, and genuinely worried. He held Ethan's face. "You have a mask and gear on, though. Right now, there's nothing protecting you."

From across the field, Liam yelled, "What's taking you guys so long?"

Coop shouted back, "I don't want you guys kicking a ball at my husband's face!"

Levi called out from the blanket, "Coop, he's a catcher! He'll be fine. The pitches in baseball are way more dangerous than a hit from a soccer ball!"

Ethan had a small smile, holding Coop's hands. "Hey, look at me, it's not gonna hit my face. I can block anyth—" Ethan stopped talking, while staring across the field, as Liam tied his hair in a tiny bun at the back of his neck.

Coop waved in front of Ethan's face. "Hello, where'd you go, baby? You zoned out."

Ethan pointed to Liam. "His hair."

Coop pulled his head back, he looked at Liam, then at Ethan. "Are you checking him out right now?"

"Dumbest question you've ever asked me. You know I wasn't. I was just remembering something Kai said about that kind of bun."

Coop pulled his T-shirt off. "I don't like it when you look at other men, Mr. Morgan."

"Put your shirt back on. It's a terrible hairstyle. At the time, I asked Kai what that would mean if you did it. It was during my hair training camp."

Coop looked back at Liam and dropped an eyebrow. "That low bun? I would never have…"

Ethan put his hands on Coop's bare shoulders. "I know. It is terrible. That's what Kai said, and that's what I think, too. I am married to the sexiest man alive. Do you really think I was checking him out?"

Coop gave him a quick smooch. "Nope. Not even for a second.

Just wanted to take my shirt off for you," Coop said as he started walking backwards.

Ethan shouted, "Cooper, put your shirt back on. I'm serious!"

Coop shook his head and stuck his tongue all the way out, while continuing to walk backwards.

Ethan pulled his own shirt off and tossed it in the grass. He raised his chin and smiled.

Coop's mouth dropped open, and he jogged quickly back to Ethan. "Puppy, put your shirt back on!" he shouted.

Tom took his shirt off and tossed it near Levi.

"You show 'em, Tommy!" Levi cheered.

Liam looked at Tom's chest. "Whoa, you're jacked too, huh? Shit. All three of you took your shirts off. You leave me no choice." He pulled his shirt off and tossed it near Madeline.

Madeline clapped, and shouted, "Yeah, owww!"

"Liam put the bird chest away!" Levi yelled. "You're not in the same league as those three. Don't listen to your girlfriend. The visual is awful from over here. Terrible."

Liam's mouth hung open at Levi's comment.

Tom looked Liam over. "You have good muscle definition. You look good. Don't worry about it."

Liam tried to think of something rude to say, but came up empty. He had no problem being rude to Ethan and Cooper, or even Levi, but for some reason with Tom, it never felt right to give him attitude.

Tom yelled, "Coop, Ethan, come on. Levi and Maddie are already halfway through a bottle."

Liam held the soccer ball under his arm and turned to Tom. "Can I ask you something?"

Tom raised his eyebrows and lifted his chin. "What's up?"

Liam started, "Were you ever mad…well, I guess it probably wouldn't make sense for me to ask you. Never mind." Liam juggled the ball on his knees.

"What is it?" Tom prodded. "Just ask. Neither of them are going to move until one puts their shirt back on…probably."

"Taking your own relationship aside, were you ever upset that Coop was gay?" Liam asked.

"No. Why would I be?"

Liam kicked the ball around on the ground. "What do you think of parents who aren't supportive of their kids when it comes to that?"

"Well, I'm probably the wrong person to ask, since I am married to a man."

"Yeah, but you were married to a woman, and you had two kids," Liam said, continuing to kick the ball while avoiding eye contact.

"Well, yes, but that was not what I would have chosen for myself. I love my life now and I love my kids, but I would have given anything to marry Levi right out of high school. Unfortunately, with my parents, Levi was just too worried and left me. I wouldn't want to see anyone go through what I did. It's not right. There are so many other things for people to get upset about. What gender your kid prefers, or how they identify shouldn't matter. A parent should be concerned with their child's safety and happiness. If someone is in a loving, healthy relationship, why should it matter?"

Liam took it all in and stayed quiet. Ethan and Coop were laughing loudly at the other end of the yard about something, both still shirtless.

"I know your dad was the state attorney, was he not supportive of your brother? Is that why you're asking me this?"

Liam rolled the ball with his foot, staring at the ground.

"Nah…I mean, how could he be, when my mom's death was really Kory's fault."

Levi and Madeline were deep in their own intense conversation.

Levi looked at Madeline as he swirled his wine. "But, Maddie, how did you end up with Liam? And how did Kory not notice it?"

"Honestly, it just happened one night, and it kept happening. But, I don't know… Kory works a lot and he and Liam don't really get along. Liam blames Kory for everything; his mom's death, Collie's heart attack, gas prices, anything. They just aren't close enough for Kory to have noticed."

"What happened with the mom? Luke said she passed away when Kory was a teenager. How could that have been Kory's fault?"

Madeline looked at him softly. "It definitely wasn't his fault, but you won't like it if I tell you. Wait…are you a sad drunk or a happy drunk?"

Levi scoffed. "I'm not drunk, and I don't know, I'm probably a bit of both. With my career, it takes a lot to get me drunk."

"Alright," Madeline sighed. "I'll tell you, but you better not tell my best friend."

"Agreed."

She finished her wine and placed the glass down. "Kory had a friend that he played soccer with, they hung out every day. Well, I guess the family, minus the friend and Kory, assumed Kory was coming over so much, because he was into the boy's sister. So, Kory and his friend used that to their advantage. Kory played up liking her, pretending that he was interested, so he could be invited to family dinners, parties etc."

Levi interrupted, "Wait, wait stop. Did the friend know he wasn't into the sister?"

"Yes, of course. Stupid idea as it was. He and Kory came up with it together. The parents were the type that took a lot of family trips. They came up with the idea before a ski trip. Kory laid it on real thick with the parents and the sister. So, the parents invited him to come along. Well, boy, was that a bad idea. The first night of the trip, they found Kory and the son, making out in one of the bedrooms."

Levi's mouth hung open.

Madeline nodded, eyebrows raised. "So, a big fight took place, the parents were screaming at Kory and the son, the daughter was devastated. The father was a big shot local politician, he called Kory's dad, who at that time was the state attorney, with a bad attitude like Liam. Kory's mom, dad, and Liam left that same night and headed to the Tennessee mountains to pick Kory up. Another big fight happened at the resort when Kory's family got there. Both dads were screaming about their reputations, both shouting at their sons, and also yelling at each other. Kory was devastated…just a dumb kid, you know? Brace yourself now…once they got back home, the friend's father called to say their family was moving away. He warned Collie that Kory was not to try and contact their son, or he'd ruin Collie's career. I have no idea what he had on Collie, but something, and it had to have been bigger than two teenagers kissing. Two days later, Mom was found unresponsive from an overdose."

Levi covered his mouth with both hands.

Maddie shook her head. "I know. So, Collie went crazy on a mission to bring anyone ever associated with drugs down, hard and fast. He became known for showing no mercy. Kory ended up hating him, and you know… here we are."

Levi poured a full glass of wine; a few tears escaped his eyes. "Wait, so what happened to the friend? Did Kory ever talk to him again?"

"Yeah, they went out on a single date in college. Kory said it was terrible. They had nothing in common. Kory was not interested at all. I've actually never seen him really interested in anyone besides Luke, honestly. He's a good husband; he loves Luke very much. I have a lot of fun working with both of them."

Liam ran past Coop, kicking the ball outside the field of play. Coop chased him down. "Liam, what happens now? Do I get possession since it went out?"

Liam grabbed the ball and jogged back. "Hey, now that we're away from your dad and your husband…you know you have scratches and hickeys, everywhere, right?"

"Yeah…and?"

Liam nodded slowly. "Why do you wear a number two"—he pointed to Coop's chain—"and he wears number one? Are those your baseball numbers? I would've thought you were one and he was two."

Coop hung his head backwards in annoyance. "Ethan's number *is* two, mine *is* one, we wear each other's numbers. He is mine and I am his…get it?"

"Wow. I hate you guys, but I kind of like your dad. This is what happens by the way." He dropped the ball and kicked it towards the goal at Ethan.

Ethan stopped the ball, catching it against his bare chest.

"Nice!" Coop clapped. "Good job, baby!"

Ethan raised his hand up and smiled with a bit of a wince, while rubbing his chest.

Coop jogged over quickly. "What's up? Did that hurt? I told you it would hurt if he hit you with it. Let me see, move your hand."

"No, I'm fine, really." Ethan covered the right side of his chest.

Liam walked over and stood in front of Ethan. "That was a nice save. Did it knock the wind out of you or something?"

Ethan shook his head. "No, I'm fine."

Coop tried to pry Ethan's hand from his chest. "Baby, I'm serious. Move your hand."

Ethan sighed, keeping his hand pressed tightly against his chest. "You're not gonna be happy if I do. Please, just leave it. I'm fine."

Coop whispered in his ear. Ethan's eyes widened; he moved his hand away immediately. Coop gasped. "Oh my God! Puppy, your nipple!" He turned to Liam. "I'll kill you."

Liam jumped back from Coop and looked around at Ethan. He yelled, "What are you gonna kill me for? It's scratched from the ball, but his damn nipple has a hickey on it! That's not from the ball! What the hell, are you guys animals?"

Tom jogged over to them. "What happened, did Ethan get hurt?"

Liam pointed at Coop. "Ask your son! He said he was gonna kill me, but it's not my fault!"

Coop was holding his hand over Ethan's nipple. He knew he needed to calm down. Even though he was pissed that Ethan got hurt, he knew it wasn't really that bad. "It's nothing, Dad, the ball scratched him, he's alright. It's just a scrape."

"Yeah, right!" Liam shouted. "His nipple looks like it was attacked by an animal! He must have caught the ball against it, so it's making that big-ass hickey look worse."

Tom closed his eyes and shook his head. He headed over to Madeline and Levi, with Liam following behind.

Coop grabbed Ethan's shirt off the grass and shook it out. He held the neck open and slid it over Ethan's head, while he stretched his arms through the sleeves. Coop kissed his injured nipple through his shirt, then held his face.

Ethan kissed him softly. "I love you. Can't believe you threatened me with that."

"I love you, too." Ethan shook Coop's shirt out and slipped it over his head. Once his shirt was on, Coop teased him, "You really liked the cannoli the other day, huh? You caved instantly for it. Such a naughty puppy."

"Mmhmm…can't wait to do it again," Ethan said, pulling his husband in by the waist.

Coop gave him a quick smooch and lightly squeezed his ass.

Maddie passed Liam a water bottle from the cooler. "Hey, you looked good out there." Liam purposely let some water drip down his chest, as he drank it. Madeline eyed him. "Mmm, pour it down from the back, your ass is better than your chest!"

Liam spit his water out. "Maddie, that's so mean!"

Levi pointed at Coop and Ethan who were making their way over. "Liam, look, they put their shirts on, now's your chance. Put it back on."

Liam shook his head and knelt on the blanket in front of Maddie. "I'm not putting it back on until Tom does. I don't care what those other two do." He took a sip of Maddie's wine, then brought his face in front of hers, moving in for a kiss.

She pulled her head back. "No… Don't even try it. Those two have enough PDA for the whole damn world." She playfully shoved his face back. Liam stood up and jogged over toward Coop and Ethan without saying anything else.

"He's not so bad, Maddie," Tom said, looking down at her.

Levi's mouth dropped open. "What? What do you mean he's not so bad?"

Tom leaned down on the blanket and invaded Levi's mouth quickly with his tongue. "Mmm…Tommy," Levi moaned as Tom pulled back.

Tom stood and smiled. "If you're too afraid to kiss him in front of people, I think you should probably think about why that is, Maddie. I kiss Levi all the time. Who cares who's watching? Liam's kind of sensitive. You're gonna end up hurting him if you aren't careful."

Levi and Maddie both looked at one another confused, then back up to Tom.

Maddie crossed her arms. "What do you mean he's sensitive? What the hell were you guys talking about earlier?"

Tom looked over at Liam. "Some people don't like PDA and that's fine, everyone needs to do what's comfortable for them. I'm not judging. I'm saying that he needs affection, he's begging for it."

"Yeah, I know." She sipped her wine. "It's just hard for me. He's all over the place."

Ethan watched Liam jogging over. He felt like there'd been a strange shift in Liam's behavior in the past few minutes. "I feel like something changed after he talked to your dad. That's weird, right?"

"Really weird," Coop agreed. "I'm gonna ask him about it."

Once Liam reached them, Coop said, "Earlier, you said that you liked my dad, but you hated us. Why did you say that? More specifically, why did you say you like my dad?"

"Your dad is cool," Liam said looking over at Tom, while tightening his bun. "He's a good dad. You two, you're just annoying."

Ethan cocked an eyebrow. "I feel like you use annoying the wrong way, you know that? I've heard you do it probably four times. Whenever you say something is annoying, it seems like you think the opposite."

"Yeah, I probably should've gone to therapy when I was younger...and right now, my girlfriend is just stressing me out. Shut up, we aren't friends. You guys are seriously annoying." He took the ball and jogged over to Tom, who was making his way back toward the group. Yelling over his shoulder, he added, "And I mean annoying. I know how to use the word!"

Tom shouted over, "You guys ready to play some more?"

Liam held the ball under his arm, walking beside Tom. "Oh yeah, Coop, it's time to switch, right?"

Ethan couldn't hold back any longer. This was no less than the third time he tried to get Coop on a team with him, and Ethan was getting close to going into spicy puppy mode. He held his arms wide. "Hey, why do you want to be on a team with my husband so bad?"

"I told you guys earlier; I want to win. He's the biggest one here, he can block anything that gets past me."

"No." Coop shook his head. "And you said we would switch if someone scored two goals. Nobody scored."

Liam dropped the ball and quickly kicked it in between the two cones. "One."

Ethan's mouth dropped open. He jogged in between the cones and grabbed the ball. "Wow, what a cheater. Cooper, I'm staying in here. He needs to score on both of us, which will never happen." Ethan held the ball and kicked it high.

Liam smiled and ran for it, with Coop right next to him. Tom ran in between the cones on the other side. Coop beat Liam to the ball and kicked it toward his dad. Tom ran out and kicked it far down the field. Liam called out, "Nice, Tom! That was a good clearance."

Ethan grabbed the ball and looked at Coop, he raised his eyebrows, then kicked it high. Coop flew down the field, but Liam was speedy, he put his body right in Coop's path. Coop decided on a different tactic. "Hey seriously, what happened with my dad?" Coop continued looking at Liam but ran around kicking the ball. Liam looked up for just a second to answer, and Coop kicked the ball past Tom.

"Ha! Goal, baby!" Coop shouted and ran over to Ethan, they high fived, and Coop picked him up. Ethan wrapped his legs around him and whispered in his ear. Coop nodded enthusiastically. "Guys we're skipping the wine thing. We have something to do."

Ethan, being carried in his favorite position like a koala, called a taxi service.

"You're gonna score once and then leave?" Liam rolled his eyes. "You guys really do suck." He grabbed his shirt off the ground and tossed Tom his, too.

Ethan hopped down from Coop, in front of Levi and Maddie. Liam and Tom walked over to join the group. Levi looked up and asked, "You guys are leaving?"

Coop wrapped Ethan in a hug. "Mmmhmm."

"Well, it is your honeymoon, and you better get it while you can," Levi said. "Once the baby comes, they'll be no time for that."

Coop and Ethan smirked at Levi's comment. Coop pulled an eyebrow down. "I don't know about that."

Liam chuckled. "Baby is gonna be crying and screaming… mostly because it has you two for dads…but also because babies are hella annoying."

Tom pulled Levi up and gave him a quick kiss on the cheek. Levi held his own forehead. "Whoops. I got up too fast," he said. Tom held his arm around his waist, to keep him steady.

Madeline lifted the empty wine bottle. "We drank this whole thing, and I feel fine. What kind of wine is this?" She squinted at the label.

Liam sat down beside her on the blanket. She smiled at him and laid her head on his shoulder, in a rare show of affection, and mumbled, looking up at him, "Oh, hi, Lee."

Liam's eyes lit up. He held the top of her head. "Yeah, she's drunk. She only calls me Lee in bed, so I'm not sure about the wine tasting."

Maddie's head shot up. "I'm not drunk. But you need a shower. You smell like outside."

"You just called me Lee; you definitely are drunk. And we're outside, so of course I smell like outside."

Levi leaned against Tom's shoulder. "That wine had very little alcohol in it, she really shouldn't be drunk. She drank more than that last night, and she was fine."

"She is though," Liam said.

"Maddie, what do you think?" Tom pulled his phone out. "Levi and I are going to call a cab and stop back at our room, then head over to the tasting."

She raised her head from Liam's shoulder, looking confused. "When did you both put your shirts on?"

Liam smirked. "Told you so."

"Let's just do it…tomorrow…just reschedule it." Maddie said in a low voice. "This one says he wants to take…a cooking class anyway…maybe we can do…both things together."

"Tommy, I don't want to cancel." Levi pouted. "Let them cancel. We can still go."

Tom kissed Levi's cheek, then looked at Liam. "Did she say you want to take a cooking class, Liam? Or was she talking about you, Coop?"

Liam didn't answer.

"Well, we have a cooking class scheduled for tomorrow afternoon, but I didn't tell her about it," Coop said.

Ethan was so excited for their cooking class. It was one of the things he and Coop were most looking forward to. He squeezed Coop's hand. "Do you think we'll be able to make it?"

"I think so, pup."

Liam asked, looking up from his phone, "Is it a private class, or a group one?"

"It's kind of both," Coop answered. "It's a couple's cooking class, but there will be other couples there."

Levi tugged on Tom's elbow. "Oh, how fun! I wonder if there are any spots left."

"Hey," Liam said to Coop. "You guys can take the Ferrari. The four of us can take the cab." He tossed Coop the key.

"What? No, I'm not taking it. I didn't rent it." Coop threw the key gently on the blanket.

"I'm not being nice here," Liam said. "I need you guys to take it. She throws up when she gets like this. I'm not playing." He threw the key to Ethan this time.

Ethan tilted his head and looked at Coop. "I don't understand why it needs to be us. If it's just because she might puke, your dad or Levi can just drive it, they're staying at the same hotel."

"Yeah, I'll drive it, toss me the key." Tom held his hands open.

Coop covered Ethan's hand, stopping the throw. He looked at Liam. "Wait, she said that we were paying for it anyway, right?"

Liam nodded. "Yep. So just take it. If she pukes in the car, it's gonna cost you even more."

Maddie squinted, opening then closing her eyes. "I don't feel great…Liam, let's go."

The taxi that Ethan called pulled in front of the house. Coop rubbed Ethan's back. "What does my puppy think? You want to take it?"

Liam furrowed his brow, watching for Ethan's answer. Ethan smiled. "Yeah, let's do it. Our insurance will cover us."

Coop opened the passenger door of the Ferrari for Ethan and

closed it once he sat inside. He waved goodbye to the group and got into the driver's seat.

Ethan coughed. "Oof, her perfume is strong in here." He leaned back into the seat. "It feels like we're laying down. It's so low."

Coop started the car. "I haven't driven a Ferrari in a long time. My dad was going to buy one about two years ago, but he ended up passing on it. This is a brand-new model, it's nice."

Ethan entered the address for their hotel into his phone, and they sped off, revving the engine as they drove away.

Chapter 11
Wine Tasting With Mom And Dad

Levi and Tom picked up the bags, glasses, and trash from the blanket beside Maddie. Liam looked at Maddie softly. "Hey, come on. You gotta get up." Maddie dropped her head on his lap, without opening her eyes.

Levi looked down at Liam. "You need help getting her to the taxi?"

"You guys are all such jerks," Liam said. "Would you ask Coop if he needed help carrying Ethan?"

Levi's mouth dropped open, and he screeched. "Such a little shit, you are! No. I wouldn't, because we've all seen Coop carry Ethan on many occasions, he literally did it ten minutes ago!"

Liam scooped Maddie up from the side and stood up, carrying her. He started walking toward the taxi. "I don't need help carrying my girlfriend."

"Shhh," Maddie whispered. "Don't call me your girlfriend. Someone will hear you."

Liam gave Tom and Levi a cocky grin. "Remind me, which one of you said she wasn't drunk?"

They opened the doors to the taxi; Tom sat in the front and the rest in the back. The taxi driver seemed to not like the look of three men getting in the car with a woman who was passed out. Liam put Maddie in the car next to Levi, then sat on her right and closed the door. He tilted her head so it would lean on his shoulder.

The driver shook his head, no, and yelled, crossing his arms. The three men looked at each other confused. Liam pressed his translator app and spoke into it. He explained the situation to the man.

The man looked at Liam, then Tom, speaking Italian, he said, "I thought this big guy here was the boss and you two had taken advantage of the other two. They are married, really?"

Tom, Levi, and Liam looked at each other as the translation came through. Liam spoke to both Tom and Levi, "Let's nod and smile. Who knows how accurate the app is. Didn't even make sense, but he's fine, so just smile." The driver took them to the hotel, without further delay.

Liam pulled Maddie out of the taxi and carried her toward their suite. Tom opened the room door for Liam, who was trying to maneuver the handle and keep a grip on Maddie. "I could've opened it myself," he said, placing Maddie on the bed.

Levi turned Tom's body back toward the door. "Let's go, he doesn't want our help, and we need to change and head out in a few, for the tasting."

"Hey, you're gonna miss the wine tasting," Liam whispered.

Maddie winced at the light, as she partly opened her eyes. "No… you go. I'm staying here."

Liam grabbed a lollipop from a bag on the nightstand and popped one in his mouth. He called out, "Wait, hold up, she doesn't want to go, do you guys mind if I go with you?"

Levi threw a hand up. "That's where the stash is. How are your teeth so white? You should have a ton of cavities!"

"I've never had a cavity." Liam showed off his pearly white teeth, smiling wide. "So, can I ride with you guys? I'm gonna go either way, I should tell you that."

Levi's head shook side to side. "No. Why? Why would you want to? Your girlfriend is passed out on the bed. You're just going to leave her here?"

Liam pulled the lollipop out of his mouth. "Maddie, do you care if I go to the wine tasting and leave you here while you puke or sleep?"

Maddie waved her hand lazily, and Liam put his pop back in his mouth. "See, she doesn't care. She's gonna sleep…trust me. Not my first time bringing her back drunk from somewhere."

Tom looked at Levi. "Up to you. I don't care if he rides with us."

Levi sassed, "Well, I do, he's been rude this whole trip and now he wants to hang out with us, because Maddie's out? Coop and Ethan aren't even going with us. I thought it would be romantic, Tommy."

Tom whispered in Levi's ear.

Levi cocked his head to the side and rolled his eyes at Liam. "Fine. You can come. We're leaving in thirty minutes; you call the car service."

Liam smiled. "Great, but"—he pulled his pop back out and gestured with it towards them—"why do all of you always whisper shit to one another? Everyone always says I'm rude, but that's a pretty rude thing to do."

Levi looked at Tom and quickly threw a hand up. "See, now we get to deal with that for two hours." Tom opened the door, and guided Levi out by the hips, closing the door behind them.

While Ethan and Coop were tongue deep in the cannoli covered ecstasy of one another's bodies, the other three men headed off to the wine tasting.

Liam wore a dark navy suit, while Tom dressed in a light brown suit with a baby blue button down, and Levi wore a white dress shirt, brown dress pants, and a navy-blue cardigan tied and draped around his shoulders.

Liam sat in the back seat next to a window with Tom in the middle, and Levi against the other window. He sucked his lollipop happily and looked at the people outside.

Levi was annoyed, they were quite cramped with three men in the backseat. Levi leaned forward, looking to the right. "Why didn't you sit in the front? Don't kids like to sit in the front seat?"

"Go ahead, be mean to me," Liam urged him. "I don't care. Maddie's not here. I don't care if you call me a kid."

Tom patted Levi's thigh.

The drive was short, and they were quickly dropped off at the front door of the quaint, brown stone-covered building. Tom and Levi locked arms, with Levi clutching the inside of Tom's elbow.

The host spoke English, much to the relief of the group. He looked down at his computer screen, with an uncomfortable frown. "I'm sorry but we're going to have to reschedule your group. I apologize for the inconvenience."

Levi's mouth dropped open. Tom laid on the CEO charm that he was known for. "Good evening, sir, my name is Tom Morgan." He smiled brightly and continued speaking to the host. Five minutes later, Tom was still chatting him up. "Yes! And now they're going to adopt a baby, so I'm going to be a grandfather! Can you believe it, at forty years old? A grandfather!"

The man's eyes sparkled as he leaned on his elbow talking to Tom across the counter. "Oh, but you are too young! I can't imagine!

What a lucky woman to have grabbed you at a young age! Where is your wife?"

Levi with sass, slapped his hand on the counter. "*I* am his wife! Thank you. Now, you have stood there drooling over *my* husband, which I have allowed, because I am an Enologist, and I have been dying to try an authentic full-bodied, red. But if you don't stop flirting with my husband and let us pass, I'd be happy to smack whatever you have lying around, right against your—"

Tom pressed his lips quickly against Levi's, cutting off his rant.

Liam whistled and raised his eyebrows.

The host appeared to be in shock, either from the berating, the news that Levi was Tom's wife, or the fact that he had front row seats to the two of them making out voraciously in front of him.

Liam leaned toward the host. "My mom really doesn't like it when people hit on my dad. So can we go through, or did you still need to reschedule us?"

The man stared a little longer at Levi and Tom's intense kissing session, adjusting the glasses on his reddened face. "No, you can go on ahead and they'll seat you inside. The group before you just cancelled at the last minute."

Levi and Tom continued kissing. Liam cleared his throat. "Ahem…ahem…Mom, Dad. Let's go."

Levi pulled his head back from the kiss. "Sorry, son, your father tastes like lollipops."

Liam shook his head and walked through the draped red curtain, lifting it behind for Tom and Levi. "Disgusting. No shame, you two."

Levi shot the host one more nasty look, as Tom held his waist and pressed him through the curtain first.

The woman inside greeted them, she spoke English, as per the request on their reservation. She was young, tall, and thin, appearing to be in her twenties, with chin-length black hair. She greeted them quickly, "Welcome. Here is the first selection we have for you." She placed three wine glasses down and showed the wine to the men, then poured it, walking away immediately after.

Levi's phone rang; he pulled it out of his pocket and showed the screen to Tom who looked concerned. "You should answer it."

Liam sipped his wine and made a sour face.

Levi answered the call, "Hi, Gina, Is something wrong? We're at a wine tasting right now."

"Who is Gina?" Liam whispered to Tom.

"Ethan's mom."

Levi tilted his head and looked at Liam across the table. "Gina, I'm looking at him right now, that's not going to help with anything. Trust me."

Liam pointed at himself. "Me?"

Levi gestured for him to put a lollipop in his mouth, which Liam misunderstood as him telling to go suck something other than a lollipop. His mouth hung open as he looked at Levi, who continued talking. Liam carefully considered what had just happened. He instinctively reached for a lollipop. "Ohhhh, you were telling me to put a lollipop in my mouth! That did not look the way you thought it did," he said.

Levi ended his call, rolling his eyes.

Tom asked, "What did she want with Liam?"

"Yeah," Liam said. "How am I involved in whatever is going on? I don't even know Ethan's mom."

Levi huffed. "Gina's mother told her all about Bianca's attempt with you. Gina is convinced that she'll be able to deduce what the baby's father looks like if she sees you. She wanted to get on a plane; I got her to settle for a picture. So, smile."

"No way." Liam waved his hands. "Maddie will be pissed if you send a picture of me to another woman. I'm not playing around."

Tom took a sip of his wine. "How would this even prove anything?"

Levi shrugged as he finished his glass. "Blech, fruity…you don't start with fruity."

"You're a snob, huh?" Liam asked.

Levi looked at him and quickly took a picture. Liam's mouth dropped open. "Don't, seriously. You have no idea how much trouble I'll be in."

Before Levi could try and convince Liam to let him send it, the waitress came around with the next wine. "Next we have a delightful white for you," she showed them the bottle and poured it into their glasses.

Liam took a drink of his wine. "Ugh, this is even worse than the last."

Levi's phone rang loudly. "Gina again," he said, shaking his head.

Liam held his hand out toward Levi. "Let me talk to her, please?"

Levi answered, "Hi, Gina, the man whose appearance you desperately seek would like a word." He passed Liam the phone across the table.

Liam took the phone, he spoke in a charming manner, "Hello, my name is Liam Collins, to whom do I have the pleasure of speaking with?"

Levi's mouth dropped open, and he smacked himself lightly on both cheeks.

Tom chuckled. "He's like a different person."

Liam's face lit up when talking to Gina. He was genuinely flattered by what she said. "Thank you, Gina. Yes, I have been told so by many women. None that sound as beautiful as you, though."

Tom tapped his finger on the table, drawing Liam's attention. Liam covered the phone. "What?"

Tom leaned in. "That is Ethan's mother. He will literally kill you, strangle you probably. You don't know Ethan. Maybe you think he's nice, and he is, but he has a fiery temper."

"Spicy puppy mode is not a joke," Levi added.

Liam turned his attention back to his phone call. "Oh, forgive me, Gina. My companions tonight are overdramatic. Yes, yes, I'm sure you know that all too well." Liam covered the phone. "She really does sound hot though, is she?"

Tom pulled his phone out and scrolled to Ethan's name. He held one finger up to Liam. "One more time and I press it. He'll be even madder, because I'm sure we'll be interrupting whatever X-rated thing the two of them are doing… Also, she is married."

Liam heeded the warning from Tom and rushed to finish the phone call. "Yes, I understand. That's fine. I'll have Levi send a picture. Yes, it was an absolute delight speaking with you. Rest assured, your son and your future grandson are in good hands."

He handed Levi his phone back. "Alright, Levi, take my pic. Let me just hold my wine." Liam held his wine and gave a sexy stare into Levi's camera phone.

Levi shook his head. "Can't unsee that."

"What is with you and older women?" Tom asked.

Liam shrugged. "I don't know. They're all so bossy. I like it."

The waitress came around with the next wine, this time, she just poured it into each glass and left without saying anything.

Levi huffed. "What kind of a wine tasting is this? She hasn't taken the time to explain anything. This is terrible." He sniffed his wine. "Ick, no. Don't want that." He pushed his glass forward and folded his arms.

Liam sipped the wine. "Oh, I actually like this one."

"You would," Levi said. "It's a cheap wine."

"I don't really like wine at all," Liam clarified. "I just didn't want to be puked on."

Tom looked at Levi softly and rubbed his arm. "Hey, we'll go to a better one before we leave. Maddie picked this one. I'll find a better one tomorrow. I promise." He kissed the wedding band on Levi's finger.

"Okay," Levi said, with a smile. He leaned in for a quick kiss.

Liam looked down at his phone. "Hey, there's a wine tour tomorrow, that's rated five stars. A driver takes you around in a van to a few different vineyards, they pick-up and drop-off at the hotel. You guys want to do that? Maddie's going to be upset that she missed this. I can book this one for all of us, it's a van so we'll have room to spread out. Coop and Ethan could fit, and we'd still have room." He looked up at Tom and Levi. "Yes, or no? Kind of a lucky break that they have a van available. It's not until five o'clock, but that's good; Maddie and I have something else to do for lunch, anyway."

Tom deferred to Levi. "Up to you, what do you think? I know you wanted it to be romantic, that may be hard with everyone around."

"As long as I'm with you, I don't care who else is there. Let's do it."

Tom leaned in and gave Levi a kiss on the cheek. Levi swayed his head along with the music that was playing. "Do you like this guy's voice, Tommy?"

"Yeah, I do. Way before our time but, the romantic crooning seems especially fitting here in Italy."

Liam rolled his eyes at the two and groaned while he reserved the group van, then placed his phone back in his pocket. "Can I ask you both something?"

Tom looked at him. "Go right ahead."

"Are you guys and the other two, legit? I mean, are you just this happy all the time? The other two are all over each other, and I really did think Coop was going to kill me earlier with the whole nipple fiasco. I just don't understand. Luke and Kory are the same, just always happy, lovey, and kissing… How is that real?"

Tom answered him, "Yeah, we're all just really happy, Liam. What else can I say? All relationships look different, there's no right or wrong, but as far as the three couples you mentioned, we're all fiercely in love with our partners."

Liam pulled an eyebrow down, playing with his napkin. "Why do you call yourself his wife, Levi? That makes Ethan mad if someone says it, but you don't seem to mind."

"Sometimes I'm his wife, sometimes his husband, depends on my mood," Levi said with a giggle.

Liam tilted his head. "I guess I don't understand that."

Levi shrugged. "No one asked you to. Personally, I don't really care what people call me, as long as it isn't derogatory."

"I didn't mean to offend you, if I did," Liam said. "I want to try and understand people better, but I just can't seem to."

"Sometimes it's more important to respect people than it is to understand them," Levi said softly.

Tom added, "Sometimes your husband also asks you to disrespect him, which is a whole different thing." He winked at Levi.

Liam shook his head at the two. "Too much information."

Levi tilted his head, looking at Liam. "Are you happy with Maddie?"

Liam nodded and twisted his napkin. "Sometimes… It's just hard. We don't fight a lot; she just yells a lot. Having to keep everything a secret is my biggest problem. I should thank you, by the way. We've been sneaking around for three months… Now at least my brother knows."

"Three months is a long time to keep a relationship a secret," Tom said. "What's the end game? Will there be a point where you guys tell people that you're together? Like a set amount of time?"

"I don't really have any say, honestly. Maddie's basically a celebrity in our field."

Levi's phone chimed; he looked down at the screen. "Gina says she feels better about the father now. Says you're very cute."

Liam pumped his eyebrows. "Give me her number." Tom kicked him under the table. "Ouch, I was kidding. You guys are so annoying. You keep correcting me and yelling at me like actual parents."

The three wrapped up their very bland wine tasting around eight o'clock. All three were only lightly buzzed, no one was fully drunk. They decided to head back to their hotel and call it a night.

As they stood outside the doors to their rooms, Liam pulled the lollipop out of his mouth and spoke to Tom and Levi. "Thank you both for letting me crash your date…and for… Never mind. I'll see you guys tomorrow for the tour."

He opened the door and went inside to find Maddie still asleep on top of the covers where he left her. He placed his phone on the nightstand and walked over to her suitcase beside the bed, quickly grabbing out a cotton pajama set for her. "Maddie," he whispered beside her ear, "I'm gonna put your PJs on you, okay? Or do you want to do it yourself?"

She rolled onto her back and raised her arms over her head. "Just do it for me. My head hurts, Lee."

"Always calling me Lee when you're being nice." He dressed her in her pajamas and tucked the covers around her.

After a quick shower, Liam stared into the bathroom mirror at his reflection. *Is this really the type of relationship I want?* Levi's words from earlier echoed in his mind. *Are you happy with Maddie?* He stood in the doorway of the bathroom and said quietly, "Maddie…I think we should break up." Maddie, of course, didn't reply. Liam climbed into bed and turned to the opposite side.

Maddie sniffled. "Did you mean that?"

Liam stayed on his side facing the opposite direction. "I didn't know you were awake." He felt the bed shake along with the sound of soft sobs. "Maddie, let's talk about it tomorrow."

"Yeah, okay," she replied. A few hours later, Maddie snuggled up tight behind him. Liam took her hand off his side, gently placing it onto the bed and scooted further away.

Maddie spoke softly, "So, I didn't imagine that…you really said you wanted to break up with me. But why?"

"What do you mean why? Maddie, we're around two couples who are really in love with one another. How do you think it makes me feel knowing that I'll never have that?"

Maddie sat up and looked at him. "Who says you don't already?"

"How can it be the same? We've kept this a secret from everyone. Kory and Luke only know because of Levi, otherwise literally no other human beings would know, aside from the two of us. Does that sound the same?" Liam asked, sitting up.

Maddie shook her head. "I'm sorry. I really didn't consider that it was hurting you. I don't like it when people talk about us. I'm older than you…Lee…people say things, and I worry about that. You're just… You're my… What do I even say to make you understand?"

Liam kicked the sheets off in frustration and stood up. His hand instinctively reached for the bag of lollipops on the dresser, and his posture softened. He spoke gently, "Maddie, listen, I don't care about your age or about what people say. What I care about is feeling like I'm the only one invested in this relationship. I don't want to hide it. Three months is a long time. In all that time, I never once asked you how long you planned to hide me away. I'm asking you now. If we stay together, when will our relationship not be a secret? When can

I tell people? I want you to meet my friends. I want to introduce you as my girlfriend. I don't want to feel like I'm the only one who cares. I knelt down to kiss you today, and you shoved my face back. It was so embarrassing, everyone was watching."

Maddie stood up with fire. "You know what? You want to break up with me? Fine. Do it. You care so much about what other people think… I'm with you, why isn't that enough? What the hell happened to you today? You obviously talked to Tom and Levi, since you're suddenly worried about this." Not getting a reaction, she antagonized him further, "Do it, go ahead. Say it again, say you want to break up with me."

Liam looked at her with both hands on his hips, taking it all in. He grabbed a lollipop out of the bag, slowly pulling the wrapper off. He walked across the room to the furthest trash can, thinking, *She doesn't realize that I can see right through her. This is the same tactic she uses in court. She's scared… Do I really want to break up with her?*

Chapter 12
Kiss Like An Italian

Coop and Ethan stared at their cooking class reservation on Coop's phone. Ethan pointed animatedly. "That is definitely him, that's the same guy! You know it is! Look at his face!" The phone reflected a picture and biography of the class teacher. It appeared to be the same man from the children's home that they met earlier in the trip.

Coop read the biography, then sighed. "Yeah, it says he does a lot of charity work. It's definitely the same guy. He made you so upset the other day. Do you want to reschedule, or try to find another place?"

Ethan shook his head. "No, absolutely not. We're gonna go. You've been looking forward to this. I'm fine; don't worry. I can keep it together." Ethan stood up and looked through their clothes that hung in the closet. He mumbled to himself, "Gotta find the black polo, that one is tight on my arms and chest..." He thumbed through until he found it, then grabbed a pair of slim fit jeans and walked into the bedroom.

"What were you saying in there?" Coop asked. "Something about a tight shirt?"

Ethan smiled at him and started undressing. "Maybe..."

Coop stood up and walked into the closet. "Hey, how about we have fun with this guy? I have a few ideas, if you're up for messing with him." He pulled out a white button-down shirt, and rust-colored pants, then grabbed a matching belt and loafers. Once they both got dressed, they headed toward the class location in the Ferrari.

Ethan rubbed his hands on the steering wheel as he reversed out of the hotel. "Oooh, this is so smooth. There's no room for a car seat though."

Coop looked at him from the passenger seat. "No, but we could still get one, if you want it. We could use it for date nights, or whenever he's with our parents."

"We just traded everything out. Would you want to get rid of one of the new ones? The little guy can only ride in the Cayenne. Do we really want another car that has no backseat?"

"Probably not, but whatever my husband wants, he gets." He rubbed Ethan's cheek softly.

"I already have everything I want. I'm married to you and now we're gonna have a baby." Ethan kept his eyes forward and continued, "Still surreal to think about. I'm so happy, though. Do you think most expectant parents are nervous like this? I'm just starting to get worried about her health, and how it could affect him."

Coop put his hand on Ethan's thigh. "Don't worry. Maddie set things up so that all of Bianca's meals are being premade and delivered, she won't even have to make anything. She'll just toss it in the oven or microwave. Couldn't be easier. Your Nonna is here to make sure she goes to her appointments, and we can check in whenever we want. The time is gonna pass by quick. He'll be here before we know it."

"Yeah, you're right. You always know how to make me feel better." Ethan pulled in front of the large blue "P" sign and parked the car. "I'm glad we beat the rain. Looks like it's gonna pour soon."

The storefront window read *Cook Like a Chef, Kiss Like an*

Italian. There were flags of all types represented, which made them both smile. Ethan pulled Coop in by the back of the head, he parted his lips with his tongue forcefully. The two shared a deep passionate kiss on the outside of the building. Ethan pulled back. "That's how you kiss like an Italian."

Coop rubbed his thumb across Ethan's bottom lip. "Mmm…I love it, Mr. Morgan."

Ethan placed his hand on the door handle. Coop stopped before walking in and looked at him. "I'm gonna do it, okay? If you want me to stop, just give me a signal…whimper like a puppy or something."

Ethan reminded Coop again, "I'm not asking you to do it, though. I just want to have fun with you."

Ethan held the door open, and Coop walked inside first. The two held hands while scanning the room for the man from the children's home. The classroom was gorgeous. There were a total of four white granite-topped cooking stations, each with its own stainless-steel oven, mounted behind it. Above each station hung utensils, pots, and pans from silver racks.

A young man greeted them in Italian.

Ethan replied in Italian, "We requested an English-speaking chef, I can follow Italian well, but my wife has a bit of trouble with it."

Coop smiled and nodded. He spoke in Italian to the man, "Yes, my husband is right. My Italian is passable, but not perfect like his."

The man didn't flinch, he smiled and switched quickly to English. "Yes, of course. I apologize, we have two other couples today, two requested English and one didn't specify. I wasn't sure which couple you were." He looked down at a paper on the counter. "Ah, you must be the newlyweds, The Morgans." He paused, looking down at the paper, then back up at them. "That's strange. Did you make two reservations?"

"No. I'm sure I didn't," Coop said.

The man looked at the paper confused. "Can't find good help these days. Well, since you two are the first ones here, pick whichever station you like."

Coop asked, "Are all of the ovens the same?"

"Ah, you're the chef half of the couple," the man said. "The oven at the far-right station is the best."

Ethan and Coop walked over to the station with the best oven. Ethan wiped his hand on the smooth granite. He was still confused by the two reservations question. "What do you think that was about?"

Coop shook his head. "I have no idea. I definitely didn't make two reservations." He opened the drawers of the station and looked up at the hanging kitchenware, he pointed up. "Do you like this, baby? I think it would look good in the kitchen."

Ethan looked up. "Yeah, I think it would too, let's order one." They continued looking upward while discussing colors and shapes for the design they wanted to order.

The door to the room opened, and the man greeted the next couple. Coop and Ethan dropped their heads forward, hearing a familiar voice. Tom's smile shined brightly, while he held Levi's hand and walked over to them. "Hey, boys! I didn't know this was the class you guys were taking! Looks like we'll be cooking together."

The host looked at his paper then back up to Tom and Levi and clapped his hands. "Ahh! I understand, you are also the Morgan's! Family! How wonderful!"

Levi giggled. "Yes, well, this is a happy coincidence, this was the only class with any availability last minute. How lucky!"

The host said to Levi, "If you would like to use this table across from Mr. and Mrs. Morgan, you'll be able to face one another. Some families prefer that, or you can use the one beside them, to allow more privacy. We're waiting for one more couple that signed up yesterday afternoon. You should choose your station before they get here."

Levi furrowed his brow. "I'm sorry, sir, did you refer to them as Mr. and Mrs. Morgan? I am the only Mrs. Morgan here. I can understand the confusion, but the other Mr. Morgan really doesn't like it."

The man looked perplexed and headed toward Coop and Ethan. He approached them cautiously and spoke quietly, "I apologize, did I misunderstand you earlier? I would like to refer to you as respectfully as possible."

Coop spoke quietly, "No, sir. You understood correctly. I am Mrs. Morgan; I would appreciate you referring to me by that name."

The man smiled and looked both Ethan and Coop over, slowly. Ethan stuck his chest out a bit more, and using his left hand he pulled his right elbow across his body, stretching to show off his muscle.

Tom and Levi watched from a few feet away. Levi looked on in confusion. "What's the puppy flexing for?" he asked loudly.

The host walked back to Tom and Levi. "I apologize, but the Mrs. Morgan over there would also like to be called Mrs. Morgan. The other teacher that works here is running late, normally there are two of us. When he gets here it will be easier, but it may get a little confusing. I apologize in advance. With two Mr. Morgans, and two Mrs. Morgans, I hope it won't be too troublesome."

"Which one of them told you to call him Mrs. Morgan?" Tom asked.

The host answered him, "I don't think it's for me to say."

Another employee came from the back room; she held a pack of blank name stickers and a black marker. The man ripped off two stickers and passed them to Levi and Tom. "This should help me keep everything moving smoothly."

Levi read the sticker aloud, "Ciao mi chiamo."

The host explained, "It says hello my name is, you add your name right there." He pointed to the bottom of the sticker.

Levi wrote: *Mrs. Levi Morgan.* He passed the marker to Tom, who wrote: *Tom.*

"Fantastic," the host said. "Tom and Mrs. Levi Morgan."

Next, he walked over to Coop and Ethan, passing them two stickers and the marker. Ethan looked at Coop and shook his head. Coop raised his eyebrows. "I'm gonna do it."

Ethan turned to the host. "I'm sorry, sir, could we have just a moment of privacy, please? I'll bring the marker back to you, as soon as we're done."

Ethan held the marker tight, giggling. "Cooper, don't. We were only going to do it so I wouldn't look bad in front of the guy from the children's home, and he isn't even here."

Coop pulled the marker out of his hand. "Come on, who cares? You heard Levi getting bent out of shape about being the only Mrs. Morgan. That's an added bonus."

"Oh, I agree. Watching Levi in diva mode is the best."

Coop held the capped marker and tapped it onto the nametag. "Do it or not? I really want to."

Ethan crossed his arms, thinking.

"If you're a good pup and play along, we can do *that* again tonight."

"Do what again? Be more specific."

Coop whispered in his ear, "Cannoli...covered...cock."

Ethan pulled the cap off the marker. "Do it."

Coop wrote *Mrs. Coop Morgan* and proudly stuck the sticker on his chest. He kissed Ethan on the cheek. "Cannoli gets you every time, baby."

Ethan took the marker and wrote: *Mr. Ethan Morgan.*

Coop peeled the sticker off and stuck it on Ethan's chest. "I love seeing your name. It makes me so happy."

Ethan pulled Coop's face in and gave him a smooch on the mouth. "I love you, my Cooper. I love my new name, too." He looked back up at the hanging kitchen rack. "I think black would probably be better. I would like one similar to this, with the lights on the sides."

"Me too," Coop said. "I think that sounds perfect."

Levi and Tom walked over. Tom asked, pointing up, "You guys thinking of that for the kitchen?"

"Yeah, Dad. We're thinking a flat black maybe, with lights."

Tom looked at Coop's name tag and winced. He elbowed Levi, who was considering color options for the hanging rack aloud, even though no one asked him to. Levi flinched. "What? Why are you elbowing me, Tommy?"

Tom raised his chin toward Coop. "I don't think Mrs. Morgan asked you for your opinion."

Coop and Ethan both eagerly awaited Levi's reaction. Levi blinked his eyes dramatically several times. "What the hell is that? Your name tag says Mrs. Coop Morgan! That's why he said that earlier! Did you do that just to get me all worked up?"

"Thirty percent was for you, seventy percent was for this other guy that isn't here."

Levi cocked his head to the side. "What does that mean? The other couple?"

Coop rubbed Ethan's back. "No, the guy who started this whole thing from the children's home a few days ago. Coop explained what happened as Ethan leaned on the cooking station with his face in his hands.

"I don't know which part is funnier, that you understood him Coop, or that the guy kept arguing about it!" Levi giggled.

Coop mocked the man, "Guy was relentless. 'No, it's not possible, he is the husband.' He just kept repeating himself."

Levi made a pouty face. "So, you wanted to be Mrs. Morgan today, so Ethan wouldn't look bad in front of the guy?"

Coop smiled and ruffled Ethan's hair. "Of course, I'd do anything for him. Plus, I really wanted to dig into that jerk, but I guess I won't be able to."

Levi rested his head against Tom's shoulder and looked at Ethan and Coop softly. "Tommy, I really love the way these two support each other."

"Yeah, they're going to be great parents," Tom said with a smile.

The host came back around; Ethan passed him the marker and thanked him. The host explained that the other couple was running a few minutes behind. He asked if they would mind waiting, which they all agreed was fine.

Levi cocked his head to the side, staring at the wall with the slogan shown. He read it aloud, "Cook Like a Chef, Kiss Like an Italian." He turned toward Ethan. "But do Italians really kiss different, Ethan?"

Coop stood in front of Ethan. "Don't ask him that! Don't look at him like that either!"

Levi rolled his eyes.

"Ah, this must be the couple we're waiting for," the host said.

The door opened, and the four looked up.

Chapter 13
Sauce Slaps And Single People

In walked Maddie and Liam, neither looking the least bit surprised to see the group. Levi shouted across the room, "Maddie, Liam! You two are the other couple?" The host quickly greeted them and gave them name stickers.

The host walked over to Levi. "Mrs. Morgan, are you also acquainted with this couple?"

"Yes, the four of us are here in Italy together. We came to help the newlyweds with something. I didn't know they were the ones you were waiting for."

Tom nudged Levi. "Remember yesterday Maddie said he wanted to take a cooking class today. I guess she was talking about Liam."

The two filled out their nametags; Liam wrote *Liam,* while Maddie wrote *Single?* and placed the marker down. Liam looked at her annoyed and pulled his lollipop out of his mouth. "Are you serious? You're not even gonna write your name?"

The host looked at Liam and then at Madeline. He inhaled, then slowly exhaled. "I apologize, I don't want to offend, but the purpose of the tag is so that I can address you properly. Is that how you would like to be addressed?"

Maddie was obviously in a bad mood. She spoke quickly, "Are you saying that my name can't be what I've written? I could have been named anything by my parents, could have renamed myself, could change my name as many times as I want. Yes, I want you to call me Single. That's my name today, until he decides otherwise." She pointed at Liam, who was shaking his head looking at the floor.

Looking thoroughly defeated, the host headed for the back room without a reply.

Liam walked over to Coop and Ethan, while Maddie walked over to Tom and Levi.

Liam pointed at their nametags. "What's the joke? I don't get it." He held a hand up. "Actually, you know what? I take that back. Levi said I need to respect, not understand. Sorry, Coop."

Coop and Ethan looked at each other. Ethan whispered in Coop's ear.

Liam's eyes shifted between the two and he sucked his lollipop. He asked, "When is this class gonna start? We're late and it hasn't even started."

Ethan could feel the tension between Maddie and Liam, and after the whole nametag thing, he was too curious not to ask. "Hey, you seem to be in a weird kind of mood. Did something happen? What was the deal with Madeline's nametag?"

Liam yelled over, "Maddie! Ethan and Coop want to know what you wrote on your nametag!"

Maddie stuck her middle finger up at him. She shouted, "Single?" and shrugged her shoulders.

Coop and Ethan's eyes widened. Liam waved it off. "We didn't break up per se. It's kind of a boss-level fight for dominance at this point."

Liam walked over to Tom and Levi, with Maddie standing across from him. "You shouldn't flip people off, Single, it's very rude."

Maddie looked at Liam and pulled her already low-cut shirt down lower. "Fine. I wonder if the host is interested, maybe he was upset about my nametag because he was just confused about our relationship. You know, since this is a couple's class that I signed up for with my boyfriend yesterday. Even though he claims he didn't know how I felt about him, despite the fact that I signed up for a couple's cooking class with him in Italy."

Levi and Tom walked around to the other side of the cooking counter. "Oh, Tommy, it's raining now." He pointed outside and gave a pout. "I hope it clears up before later. We won't be able to tour the vineyard if it doesn't."

"I'm sure it will clear up by then," Tom said. "This is supposed to take a few hours anyway."

Liam and Maddie situated themselves on the cooking counter that faced Coop and Ethan's, with Tom and Levi choosing the counter to the left of Ethan and Coop.

"This should be interesting," Coop whispered to Ethan.

"Mmmhmm, lunch and a show."

Maddie yelled across the cooking station, "Why does your nametag say Mrs. Coop Morgan? You never asked me to write that on your paperwork."

Ethan chimed in, "Well I don't remember hiring a lawyer named Single, either."

Liam teased Maddie, "Oh my God, hahaha. Neither of them is afraid of you. I thought it was just Coop, but Ethan isn't afraid either!"

The host finally came out to join them. After working his way through several instructions, the group began to prepare a crust for each of their pizzas.

Coop and Ethan worked together to knead and roll the dough. Ethan proudly rubbed flour on Coop's hands. "I know about this, this makes your hands not stick to the dough! I know something about cooking!"

Coop smooched him while rolling the dough. "Oooh, it worked! Thanks, pup."

Ethan and Coop looked over, noticing that Maddie and Liam were working surprisingly well together. They flirted and whispered with Liam wrapping his arms around her from behind and even showing her how to use the rolling pin properly. They seemed like a completely different couple than they were a few minutes earlier.

Levi watched entranced as Tom rolled the dough. "Mmm… roll it, Tommy." Levi's phone rang, and he answered it excitedly, "Hi, Gina, what's going on? We're making pizza in a couples' cooking class." He listened as Gina gave her reason for calling. "Oh, that's great. Yeah, I'll let them know. No, they're here too, so are Liam and Maddie." He nodded. "Okay, I'll put you on speaker, go ahead."

Gina's voice sounded loud inside the room, "Mimmo, Coop! Hi, boys, I just called to tell you that Nonna said they viewed the house with Bianca, and it went great. She and her mother are happy as clams with it."

"That's great, thanks, Mom." Ethan gave Coop a kiss on the cheek. "It's all gonna work out. Just like you said."

Gina asked giggling, "Did Levi say that sweet little cutie, Liam was there? I want to say hi to him."

Maddie looked at Liam, standing beside her. "Why the hell is his mother asking to talk to you? And why did she call you cute?"

Ethan saw only red looking at Liam. "Answer her. Quickly." He wiped his hands on the white cloth on the counter.

"Oh shit…," Coop said. He put his hands on Ethan's shoulders. "Wait, she's probably just messing around. It's your mom. Give it a minute, baby."

Levi spoke, "Uh, Gina, Liam is busy right now."

Gina unknowingly added fuel to the fire. "Well, I can wait for him. I showed his picture to Tina. I texted it to her and she said—"

Maddie forcefully chucked a handful of flour across Liam's face.

"That's not enough," Ethan said. "I'll kill him."

Coop wrapped his arms around Ethan's chest and squeezed tight from behind.

From the back room, the man from the children's home entered the fray, his name tag said *Lorenzo*. "Whoa, whoa!" Lorenzo spoke in Italian, so only Ethan, Coop, and Maddie understood, as well as Gina, who remained on the speaker. In Italian he screamed at Maddie, "What have you done? There's flour everywhere!"

Liam still hadn't spoken since before the flour slap. Maddie stood enraged, stepping closer to him. "Look at me, why does his mother have a picture of you? Why is she calling you cute?"

Levi walked over while holding the phone, and Tom followed behind.

Gina spoke, "Levi are you there? I can't hear what's happening."

Coop squeezed Ethan, still holding him from behind, arms locked around his chest.

Levi tried to explain the picture situation to Maddie and Ethan.

Gina, didn't help matters, adding, "That's right, I asked for it for that reason, but he was just so charming and suave, and the picture was just sexy. You know Tina, my sister, she's single and—"

Tom grabbed the phone out of Levi's hand and hung up.

"Thanks, Dad," Coop yelled over.

Levi looked at his phone. "Why didn't I do that?"

Tom shook his head at him. "Everyone here is asking the same thing."

Liam still hadn't moved; his face and hair were covered in flour. Maddie stuck her whole hand in the bowl of bright red sauce and scooped a handful out, then chucked the sauce across Liam's face.

Liam, now covered in sauce and flour, stood unmoving as the thin sauce dripped down his face.

"Holy shit!" Tom screamed. "Maddie, you can't slap him!"

Maddie rolled her eyes. "Shut up, Tom. I didn't slap him either time, the flour slapped his face and so did the sauce."

Ethan was still seething, while Coop tried to calm him, arms still around Ethan's chest locked tight. "See, it was just some dumb thing, baby. Seems kind of weird though. Don't understand what his looks have to do with our son, but you know your mom. She's always trying to set people up."

Ethan nodded his head and tried to turn his body around toward Coop.

Coop squeezed him tighter, refusing to let him turn. "Nuh-uh…not happening. Now the guy from the children's home is here. I don't want you to lose it. When you're not going to kill Liam or blow up on that guy, I'll let go."

"I promise I won't, Cooper. Just hold me, let me turn."

Coop peeked around at his face. "Hmmm."

Ethan whimpered softly, with puppy eyes.

Coop was a sucker for the puppy whimper, he turned him immediately, locking his arms around his waist in an embrace.

Ethan tucked his face into Coop's neck and inhaled his scent. "Mmm, much better. Thank you." Ethan reached down and swapped their nametags, placing the *Mrs. Coop Morgan* tag on himself.

Maddie screamed at Liam, "No wonder you wanted to break up with me. You got your ex calling you, his mom calling you, the aunt is somehow involved and even the carrier is trying to sleep with you."

Lorenzo looked around, and spoke in Italian to Maddie, "He seems to deserve it, but you can't throw food. You've made a mess. We have another class this afternoon. Now you're all behind schedule."

Liam finally grabbed a cloth and wiped his face. He spoke calmly, "I don't know what he just said, but I can't believe you just did that to me, Madeline."

Madeline pulled him in quickly by his shirt and said loudly, "Ha! You just called me Madeline. You wouldn't have said that without meaning you wanted sex. Do you admit defeat?"

The rest of the group all made uncomfortable faces.

Ethan still tucked in Coop's embrace, rubbed his back. "I can't believe this is happening during our cooking class. I'm sorry, Cooper. We can take another one, maybe tomorrow? I know how much you were looking forward to it."

Coop chuckled. "I could never be upset when you're with me. I just don't understand what's happening. Did they break up, or not? Liam said it was like a boss battle, was he being serious?"

Liam remained silent. He removed Maddie's hand from his shirt, pulled his wallet out and handed Lorenzo five hundred euros. The man looked at him in confusion accepting it.

Liam shouted across the cooking station to Coop and Ethan, as the man counted the money. "Hey, can one of you tell him the money is for this?"

Coop dropped an eyebrow down. "For what?"

Liam took the bowl of sauce and dumped it all over Maddie's head!

"Pfftt." Maddie spit the sauce out and wiped her face using her hand.

"Oof," Coop said.

"Oof is right," Ethan agreed. "Can't believe he just did that!" He shouted to Lorenzo, "The euro he just gave you is to cover the cost of dumping the sauce on her head."

Lorenzo counted the money again and said in Italian toward Liam, "For this amount, you can spill whatever you want."

Ethan called out, "He says you're all good, Liam. Doesn't care that you dumped sauce on her head."

Levi interjected, "Not to get in the middle here, but your outfits are going to be ruined. If there's any hope of saving—"

Maddie wiped one hand down her face and held the other to Levi, telling him to stop. She pointed to Tom and Levi. "You. You two, this is your fault. He was fine until he talked to you two morons!"

Tom's mouth dropped open. "What?!"

Levi's head cocked to the side with sass. "If you treated him better, he wouldn't have needed to talk to us. Don't blame your problems on other people, *Single.*"

Lorenzo walked over to Coop and Ethan, happily holding the five hundred euros. He pointed at the two speaking in Italian. "Ah perfection! I remember you two! See, the nametag is correct! I told you that you were saying it wrong the other day!"

Ethan smiled at him. "Yes. I said it wrong."

Lorenzo gave a thumbs up and walked into the back room.

Coop tilted his head looking at the Mrs. Coop Morgan sticker on Ethan's chest. "That's why you switched it earlier. Are you sure? You don't have to wear a nametag that says Mrs. I could also just go beat him up. Whichever you prefer."

Ethan grabbed Coop's face with both hands and gave him a big smooch on the mouth. "Thank you. I'm leaning towards beating him up, though. Honestly, I feel like it's fine if someone says I'm your wife. I don't particularly like it, but as long as they know that we're married, I guess I don't really care…actually never mind, yeah, let's beat him up."

Coop smiled, ruffled his hair, and gave him a quick smooch. "Stay, puppy." He walked toward the employee entrance and knocked on the door.

Ethan shouted, "Cooper don't really beat him up!"

Coop walked into the back entrance after Lorenzo opened the door and allowed him inside.

Ethan remained at his station and watched the verbal smackdown that was taking place at the station across from him. *I hope Cooper comes back soon. I wonder what he's doing?* he thought.

Maddie, covered in sauce, threw her arms up at Levi, yelling, "You told him to respect and not to try and understand people? That was a stupid thing to say. Should I respect a murderer's decision to murder? Or a thief who steals? What about a dictator?"

Levi with extreme sass shouted, "Oh no! You did not. You took that way out of context. I simply explained that when it came to people in our community, that in my eyes, in my view, I would rather be respected than understood. He said he didn't understand me being both a wife and a husband, do I need him to understand that? No. I don't, Maddie. Much like I don't need to understand how you think it's appropriate to be in a relationship with someone younger than you, whose father you were engaged to! Do you need me to understand it? Do you need anyone else aside from the two of you, to understand it? No! You don't! What you need is for people to shut up and let you live your damn life! And if that includes him, then great, and if it doesn't then let the guy go…he's obviously got many other options." He panted, out of breath, staring her down, while Tom rubbed his back.

Maddie didn't respond. She grabbed Liam by the shirt and pulled him outside by the storefront. It was still pouring outside, but the overhang seemed to block some of the rain from them.

Ethan looked toward the employee door as it opened. Lorenzo walked out with Coop behind him; Coop wore a new sticker that read *Mr. Coop Morgan.*

Lorenzo handed Ethan a sticker that said: *Mr. Ethan Morgan,* written in Coop's handwriting, along with a cannoli on a plate.

Ethan removed the Mrs. Coop Morgan sticker from his shirt and replaced it with the new one.

Lorenzo said in Italian, "Please, accept my apology. I shouldn't have made a judgement based on your husband's muscles. I really thought you were saying it incorrectly. I truly did not mean to offend. He told me you love cannoli; this is a family recipe, you'll love it."

"Well, my husband does know of my deep, deeeep love of cannoli."

Coop whistled and smiled, then gave Ethan a kiss on the cheek.

Bam! The group looked forward at the sound. Maddie's drenched red hair was pushed against the storefront window and Liam was kissing her. The two were entangled like this momentarily, before Liam stuck his head inside the door. "Hey guys, we're gonna take a taxi back to the hotel." He looked at Lorenzo. "If there are any additional charges, one of the annoying Morgans can pay for it." He smiled and waved. He and Maddie embraced one another outside while waiting for a taxi.

Ethan and Coop looked at the door, then each other. Coop tilted his head. "I don't even care how they ended up out there. But why does he think he can spend our money?"

Ethan was confused as well. "I honestly have no idea. Who told him he could?"

"What taxi is going to pick them up? Look at Maddie she's covered in sauce!" Levi said.

"No idea," Tom said. "But the rain is washing some of it off, though."

Levi stood beside Tom and looked side to side through the window. "Let's see how long it takes, before a taxi stops."

Lorenzo returned to the employee door. Before opening it, he said in Italian, "I'll be back in a few minutes, and we'll continue the class. I'm just waiting for help."

Coop and Ethan nodded at him.

Ethan held the cannoli to Coop's mouth. "You get to try it first, for being the sweetest husband ever. I can't believe you did that. I love you so much."

Coop opened his mouth wide, tongue slightly sticking out and took a soft bite as Ethan held the cannoli. "Mmmm. Oh my God, puppy! Eat it. Right now. It's so good."

Ethan took a bite of the cannoli; his eyes almost fell out of his head. He looked at Coop, then at the cannoli. The only thing better than cannoli was cannoli mixed with Cooper. He held the cannoli back to Coop's mouth and nodded.

Coop in tacit understanding, licked the cannoli filling, sticking his tongue deep inside of it as Ethan held it, watching him.

Ethan opened his mouth and pressed his lips against Coop's and licked the cannoli cream off his tongue. Ethan moaned. "Mmmm, delicious. I wonder if he has any more that we can buy?"

Coop licked his lips and smiled. "Such a naughty pup. Getting me all worked up. We haven't even finished making the pizza yet."

Ethan moved in for another kiss, hanging his arms around Coop's neck. "Just one more taste."

Chapter 14
Ethan's Deep Love Of Cannoli

Ethan heard Tom and Levi talking, but didn't want to pull back from Coop's mouth just yet.

"Aww, I feel bad, Levi. They came here for a romantic afternoon and then the four of us showed up. Look at them. They're so in love."

"Yeah, they are. I feel bad, too. Let's go bother them, anyway."

Ethan broke the kiss and looked over to see Levi leading Tom toward their station. He noticed a cab stopped in front of the building and watched Maddie and Liam hop inside.

"Hey, boys," Levi said. "What's the deal with your nametags— no, wait, what is that half empty thing on your plate?"

"It's just an empty cannoli shell. We shared the filling," Ethan said, with a wink toward Coop.

Levi pulled an eyebrow down, eyeing the empty cannoli. "Is the outside not good, it looks like you took just a bite of it, then sucked it all out or something."

Coop covered his own mouth. "Please stop asking questions."

Levi put a hand on his hip. "What? I'm starving and I've never seen a cannoli before. I was just wondering what it was. What did I say wrong?"

Ethan truly couldn't control himself. Once he started teasing

Coop, he could rarely stop once he got a reaction from him. "No, the shell is good, we just didn't want it today. We like licking the filling out better. It's really sweet. If it's made right, it's nice and *thick*…it's a perfect dessert, my favorite."

Coop still covered his own mouth.

Ethan, the insufferable tease, explained further, "Yeah, Levi, sometimes you can suck all the cream out, like fast or slow…the mouth feel is amazing and it's just really…*thick*. If you're like us, and you don't want the shell, you can spread it on other things, or you can just stick your tongue right in and suck—"

Coop covered Ethan's mouth, then whispered in his ear.

Ethan's eyes widened, and he pretended to zip his own mouth closed.

Levi with his hand still on his hip, said, "That sounded very sexual."

Tom started pulling Levi toward their own station. "Don't think about it anymore. Coop said no more questions."

Levi looked over his shoulder. "Why did you pull me away? They had new nametags on, I didn't even get to ask when that happened."

Coop lightly smacked Ethan on his ass. Ethan giggled, but was afraid of losing out on the cannoli play that he was promised. "I'm sorry. But really, Cooper, we can't let Levi ask Lorenzo for the cannoli. We need them for tonight, they're better than the ones at the hotel."

Lorenzo and the host from earlier entered from the employee door, along with two young children. The man from earlier now wore a nametag, showing that his name was Angelo. The two little ones clung to him, one on each leg. Angelo walked in between both stations and apologized for the lack of professionalism during their class.

"Hardly any fault of yours," Levi said. "The troublemakers are gone now."

Angelo held the top of the children's heads. "Yes, well these two are my troublemakers, Massimo and Mila, they're twins. They had to leave school early today because of an issue at their preschool. I had to run there and pick them up. I was lucky Lorenzo got here when he did." Angelo looked at Maddie and Liam's destroyed station and rolled his eyes. Massimo and Mila both held large white cleaning cloths, they ran over to the messy station and started to clean it. "They love to help when they're here," Angelo said.

Lorenzo approached Coop and Ethan, he looked at the cannoli shell, then up at Ethan. He spoke in Italian, "You didn't like it, Mr. Ethan?"

Ethan answered, without smiling. "It was the best cannoli filling I've ever had. I was really impressed with the consistency and flavor of the filling."

"Do you have any that we can buy?" Coop asked.

Lorenzo nodded. "Yes, of course. Remind me at the end of class. Now, let's get back to preparing. I just need to grab something quickly." He hurried into the employee room.

Coop dropped an eyebrow at Ethan. "You didn't like the shell, huh? You purposely left the shell out of your compliment."

"Mmhmm, I don't forgive him for the other day. He knows it. He's Italian...he gets it. I love the filling, but I'll never forgive him."

Angelo emerged from the back room and gave instructions for the rest of the pizza making lesson.

Coop interrupted him, "Excuse me, can we make ours a white pizza? I just had it for the first time ever, last night."

"Yes, of course, we have some ricotta in the back, go ahead and brush your crust with olive oil and use the garlic that you minced. I'll grab the ricotta and the other cheeses."

Tom and Levi looked at one another. "Do you want white pizza, too?" Tom asked.

Levi shrugged. "How should I know? I've never had it. I don't know what it tastes like." He purposely spoke louder, even though Coop and Ethan could already hear everything he was saying. "I'm not asking Ethan; his food descriptions are way too sexual for me."

"You definitely shouldn't," Tom said. "We'll just stick with the regular way."

Angelo came back with ricotta, pecorino, parmesan, and mozzarella cheeses. He gave some cheese to Tom and Levi, then brought the rest to Ethan and Coop.

Mila and Massimo had begun to fight and were smacking each other, while crying.

Angelo cursed under his breath in Italian standing next to Coop.

Coop smiled and his face lit up, he looked at Ethan. "I know that word! You taught me that the other day!"

Ethan rubbed his back. "I'm so proud."

Angelo walked over to the kids, and they stopped hitting each other. He lifted Mila on his hip, while Massimo teased her. Mila stuck her tongue out at him behind her father's back. Angelo guided Massimo into the back room, while carrying Mila. He briefly stuck his head out of the door. "After you all finish with the cheeses, stick the pie in the oven, set the timer on your station for thirteen minutes. I'll be right back."

Both groups finished prep and stuck their pizzas in the ovens. Coop set their timer for eleven minutes, he looked at Ethan and shook his head. "He told us our oven gets hotter, he's probably just not paying attention because of the kids. Ours will need less time if it gets hotter."

Angelo came back out, his clothes were a mess, his shirt half untucked, and his hair looked like it had been tugged on. He peeked through the window of Levi and Tom's oven. "Looks good, Mr. and Mrs. Morgan."

He walked over to Ethan and Coop and peeked through the glass at their pizza. "I should have told you to set the time for two minutes less, this oven gets hotter."

Coop smiled. "You told us that when we came in. I set it for eleven minutes. We're good."

Angelo looked at the nametags, he seemed confused, but pressed on, "Well, Mr. and Mr. Morgan, I'm glad you two have such good memories. My kids have zapped my brain. You two are newlyweds, so let me give you a piece of advice. Don't do it. Don't have kids."

Tom and Levi heard him and walked over. Tom put his hand on Coop's shoulder, and said, "I think kids are wonderful, Angelo. They're all unique and different. They're a lot of fun."

Angelo rolled his eyes. "Yeah, a lot of fun. I had to leave work early to pick them up because they were fighting, and the teacher couldn't separate them. I got one biting, one pulling my hair, they're always eating, running, or screaming. They jump on my furniture; they destroy all things. One of them spilled juice all over the backseat yesterday, took me an hour to clean it up and you know what? The car stinks today. Yeah…kids are wonderful."

Levi winced. "Well, these two are expecting a baby within two months, so we're all pretty excited about that."

Angelo held his forehead. "I apologize, that was very rude of me. It's been a long week. Kids are wonderful and they're a lot of fun."

"You don't have to lie," Ethan said. "We're not worried about it."

Coop hung his arm around Ethan's shoulder. "Yeah, you already said all those things, you can't take them back."

Tom added, "You guys will only have one, so it will be different anyway. Angelo, you have twins, that's a whole different battle."

Angelo looked at Ethan and Coop, he spoke facetiously, "Yes, one will be a walk in the park. Easiest thing in the world, raising a child."

Coop and Ethan's timer beeped, and Coop pulled the pizza out of the oven.

Angelo clapped. "Yes, beautiful! Perfectly made! Let it cool for two minutes, then enjoy!"

A few minutes later, Tom and Levi's pizza was done. Angelo inspected it. "Yes, very nice. Well done. Same applies to you, let it cool, then enjoy. I'll be back in a few minutes."

Coop called his dad over and asked if he would take a picture of him and Ethan with their pizza. The two smiled brightly, cheeks pressed together for the photo. Both couples enjoyed their lunch, leaving no slices behind.

Angelo came out from the back room. "Would both couples like dessert? The class includes homemade cannoli with an espresso."

Ethan was afraid there might not be any cannoli left to bring back with them. He nudged Coop.

Coop asked, "We mentioned to Lorenzo that we would like to buy some cannoli to bring back to the hotel with us. Did he already let you know that?"

Angelo answered, "No. He didn't, but that's fine. We make it fresh here. We make a big"—he held his arms to represent large shape—"tub of it every morning. Then we fill the shells, as people finish the class."

Ethan's mouth dropped open. "Could we—"

Coop put a hand on Ethan's chest and interjected, "How much of that tub can we buy?"

"Without the shells? You just want the filling?"

Coop nodded. "Yes, we want to buy as much as you'll sell us."

Angelo thought for a moment, then responded, "Give me a

minute, let me see what I can do." He walked into the employee room.

Levi threw his hands up and dropped them on the counter. "So it *was* sexual."

Ethan and Coop ignored him, they were too busy talking about how much cannoli filling he would sell them.

Tom leaned over his counter facing them on the right. "What are you going to do if he comes back and says a ridiculous number? Like five thousand euros?"

Coop and Ethan looked at each other, then at Tom. "Worth it," they said at the same time.

Angelo came through the door carrying a large, sealed glass container filled with cannoli cream. Ethan and Coop's eyes lit up, watching as their prize approached them. Angelo placed the container on the counter. "This is three quarts of cannoli, made fresh this morning. I can sell it to you for 150 Euro."

Coop nodded and pulled his wallet out. He happily exchanged the euros for the cannoli and shook Angelo's hand. "Thanks for everything. This was really fun."

Ethan added, "Yeah, we had a great time and thank you again for the cannoli."

Coop picked the container up and pulled Ethan by the hand quickly past Tom and Levi's table. "Bye, guys, we're going back to the hotel," Coop said.

"Bye, Tom and Levi," Ethan shouted, while Coop pulled him outside the door.

Ethan handed Coop the keys and took the container of cannoli. "You drive, I'll hold this."

Coop opened the passenger door for him, then quickly got into the driver's seat and headed for the hotel.

Ethan tapped the top of the container. "This is a lot of cannoli, Mr. Morgan."

"Mmmhmm…well, my husband has a *deep* love of cannoli."

Ethan chuckled in reply, "Did you see Levi's face when I said all that other stuff? It was hilarious. He was so confused."

"No, I was trying to not get hard, you were waking him up with all your dirty talk. He reacts so easily to everything you say or do, especially when it comes to our food play."

Ethan eyed Coop's dick. "That's mine. He knows it."

"See, you're doing it to him again," Coop said, shifting in his seat.

Ethan decided to pause the teasing. "Alright, we can't do anything in this rental car, anyway. Wait, when does this need to go back? He didn't even tell us."

"I have no idea. He didn't ask for it today, I assume just because they were covered in food."

Ethan looked in between the seats for any paperwork. "We really should have checked the papers before we drove it. What would we do if we got pulled over?"

Coop pulled his mouth to the side. "I have no idea. I don't want to call them."

"No, we're definitely not calling them. We finally just escaped everyone."

Ethan's phone rang.

Coop raised his eyebrows. "Is that really him calling?"

"No, it's Sal," he said as he answered the call. "Hey Sal, what's going on?"

Sal, Ethan and Coop's security guard at their new home, called to let him know that they had a false alarm at the house about thirty minutes earlier. He explained that the thunder from a strong storm that passed through shook one of the windows, setting off a sensor.

Ethan was confused. "I understand what you're saying, but those are impact windows, they shouldn't be shaking from thunder."

Coop spoke loudly, "Sal, call the window guys and have them check that window. Ethan's right, they're rated for 175 mph winds. Definitely shouldn't shake to the point of the alarm going off."

Sal answered, "You got it guys. What time do you get back tomorrow?"

"We don't," Ethan replied. "Tomorrow is our last full day here. We leave early the following morning."

Coop added, "Don't try to rush us home, Sal."

"Alright," Sal said. "I'll see you guys when you get back. I'll call the window company."

Ethan ended the call and looked at Coop. "Hey, who do you think wins in a fight? Your dad's security guard or ours? Tony or Sal?"

Coop replied, "Sal. I've seen it happen."

"Really? The little brother beat the older one up? When did that happen?"

"Yeah, it was when I was younger, and they both worked for my dad. I think I was eleven. At the time, my dad used Tony at the gate and Sal was responsible for the inside of the estate. One day, some teenagers, snuck in and were having themselves some fun in the pool."

Ethan winced making a disgusted face. "Uh?"

Coop patted Ethan's thigh. "No, not that kind of fun. They were just jumping in the pool, taking pictures by the grotto. That kind of fun."

"Oh, okay. So, whose fault was that? What happened?"

Coop gave Ethan's thigh a squeeze, then put his hand back on the steering wheel. "Well, Sal saw them on the monitors in his office and called Tony. The estate lights flipped on, and the whole place lit up. Alarms started blaring. It was around 1:00 am. Tony and Sal headed over, and my dad ran downstairs. Back then, my room was in the main estate, so I snuck out behind him."

Ethan's mouth dropped open. "You could've gotten hurt…or worse if they weren't teenagers. Wait, your dad didn't notice you?"

"Nah, he was like a superhero flying out the door. It almost looked like he had a cape on, his robe fluttered when he ran outside. I remember it looking really cool. He was always very protective. I wasn't afraid at all."

"Your dad in a cape?" Ethan tried to picture it. "Levi maybe, but I can't see your dad in one."

"It probably didn't look that cool in reality, either. Just a thirty-year-old guy in his house robe. Anyway, I hid around a tall hedge in the garden. Tony and Sal were screaming at each other, and the two teenage boys were just sitting off to the side. My dad threw his hands up yelling at both Sal and Tony, while pointing at the kids. Tony said it was Sal's fault, Sal said it was Tony's fault. My dad looked at the kids, asked them how they got in, they didn't reply. They just looked at each other and remained silent. You should have seen these two, they were in their board shorts, even brought their own towels."

"Really? So, I guess they planned it. Wasn't a spur of the moment decision, then."

"Nope. My dad squatted down, told them he'd let them go if they explained how they got inside. He told them if they didn't, he would let the security guards handle it. Tony and Sal were big guys then, too. So, one of the kids explained that it was just a prank for their senior year. The other remained silent. They wouldn't say how they got inside. My dad looked at the two of them for a minute, then stood back up. He told the kids to get off the property. He said they were lucky that they reminded them of someone. The kids ran off, towards the front gate. He looked at both Tony and Sal, and told them he was going to check the security footage himself. Dad turned to walk back inside and—"

Ethan interrupted him as the pulled into the hotel, "What are all these people doing in the parking lot?"

Coop drove slowly through the crowded parking area. "I have no idea, maybe it's a special event or something. I didn't see anything when we booked, though."

Several minutes later, the two held hands and walked into their hotel room. Ethan placed the large cannoli container on the nightstand near the downstairs bed. "You want to do this down here? Or upstairs?"

Coop placed the car key down and took his shirt off. "Here's good. Now lay down. You've teased me all day, Mr. Morgan."

Chapter 15
What's That White Stuff On Your Face?

Meanwhile, Maddie sat beside a shirtless Liam in their hotel room bed. Liam sucked on a lollipop, while they both stared at their laptops. Maddie peeked at Liam's screen. "What are you working on? I'm sure I didn't miss anything."

Liam scrolled through search results for Ethan and Coop. "I'm making sure there's nothing that's going to come up at their home interview. These two are squeaky clean though. No social media except for the stuff from the Foundation and whatever charity work they do. Other than that, it's just baseball stuff. Hey, did you see that they wear chains with each other's number on them?"

Maddie pulled an eyebrow down. "How would I see that? I noticed their chains, but I didn't see what was on them. That's cute, though." She continued looking at the screen while Liam scrolled.

"It's annoying," Liam said.

She pulled her head back and looked at him. "How is that annoying?"

Liam's eyes widened looking at his screen. "Here's something, this is their proposal clip, want to see it?"

Maddie and Liam watched as Ethan kissed his chain, then stole home. They watched the proposal, and Maddie clapped. "That was amazing! I didn't know this existed. Now, I think the chain thing is even cuter. The camera even panned to Coop kissing his chain. They're like one in the same person, those two."

Liam smiled. "Yeah, both jerks…can't stand them."

"You like them. Give it up. I know you rented that car so they could have it. That's why you haven't asked for it back. You're not fooling me."

Liam rolled his eyes, and said, "Gimme a break. You would've puked everywhere in that thing."

Maddie pointed at the screen. "What's *Separation*? Click that."

An article showing Ethan and Coop holding Ethan's painting of the two when they were younger popped up. Maddie read it aloud, while Liam scrolled through it. They enlarged the picture, and both stared at it after reading the story behind it. Maddie and Liam both looked at each other softly.

"Alright, I can't say anything bad about this," Liam said.

Maddie eyes wide, said, "I can. How the hell did that tie with a dog? Let me see the painting of the dog, pull it up."

Liam scrolled through the article and found the painting. Maddie tilted her head. "Really? See this is cute, but I think Ethan should have taken that. No tie in my eyes."

Liam stared at it for a minute then went back to the painting of Coop and Ethan. He looked at it silently, then said, "Separation, separation…" Liam's head suddenly snapped up, he tossed the laptop down and jumped out of bed. "Shit! Maddie, Shit! We forgot something! What time does the family affairs office close?"

Maddie jumped up with him. "I think it closes in two hours. What's wrong? Why are you saying separation? Those two won't ever separate, that's just the name of the painting. What did we forget?"

He threw his clothes on, grabbed the laptop, a few lollipops, and a file, then quickly called a cab to pick them up.

Back in the honeymoon suite, Coop was slowly licking cannoli off Ethan's thick cock. His phone rang several times; of course, both men ignored it.

Ethan moaned, holding onto Coop's hair. "Mmm, come on, I'm ready. I won't be able to hold out much longer. Fuck me, or I'm gonna come."

Coop looked up at him. "No. You have to wait. You were too much of a tease today. You don't get to come yet."

Ethan's phone started ringing.

Coop looked up at him, he gripped Ethan's dick firmly. "I'm not stopping. Not for that phone and not for your begging." He rubbed his face back in between Ethan's legs and resumed licking and sucking his cannoli covered balls.

Their phones continued ringing for several minutes.

Ethan whined, "Mmm—Cooper—please. Fuck me." The hotel phone started ringing loudly, and he leaned up on his elbows.

Coop looked up at him. "Do you want me to stop, baby?"

"Mmm. No, don't stop. I just want the phones to stop." Ethan shoved Coop's face back down and closed his eyes. "Mmm— definitely don't stop—your mouth feels so good—mmm."

Coop rolled his tongue firmly around the head of Ethan's cock. "Have to get all this cannoli off, then I can fuck you."

Loud knocking and banging came from the hotel room door. They both jumped. Coop wiped the cannoli off his mouth and chin. "What the fuck is that? Is someone really banging on our door?"

Ethan was equally frustrated. "Damn it! Who the hell would be banging on our door?"

They both stood up, and Coop started walking toward the door.

Ethan screamed, "Don't open the door, you're naked!"

"I know that! I'm just gonna look through the peep hole."

Ethan grabbed both phones and saw several missed calls from Maddie and Liam.

Coop looked through the door and saw Liam holding a stack of papers, with a lollipop in his mouth.

Liam knocked on the door again. "Guys, I don't care what you're doing! This is an emergency!"

Coop and Ethan both looked at one another.

Coop called through the door, "Liam, what the hell, man? We're in the middle of something. What's the emergency?"

Liam hung his head forward. "Just open the door, I'm not playing. Hurry up!"

Coop and Ethan grabbed the white hotel robes from the downstairs bathroom and put them on.

The phone rang again, and Ethan answered it, while Coop headed for the door. "Hello, Madeline, what's wrong?"

Madeline screamed, "We've been calling you for twenty minutes! There's no time to explain. Just sign the papers Liam has, fast. He's outside your door, and I'm in the parking lot." She ended the call.

Coop opened the door, and Liam came inside. He wasted no time placing a stack of papers on the side table along with a black pen. "Guys, sign these papers, right now. You'll thank me for it later, but I can't explain. The office closes soon."

Coop looked down at the papers, along with Ethan. They tried to read them quickly, and Liam screamed, "Guys, trust me, please! I would not screw you over. Just fucking sign them!"

Ethan stammered looking at Coop. "I, I, I don't know? What

the hell are we signing? Madeline just called and yelled the same thing."

Coop asked, "Why can't you just explain?"

"I really won't make it in time." He pushed the pen in Coop's hand onto the paper.

Coop sighed and looked at Ethan.

"Think of it this way," Liam said. "I have all of your personal information, and I rented that car in your names. Do you think I need your signatures to screw you over?"

Ethan and Coop nodded at one another and signed. Liam tossed his lollipop stick in the trash and ran out of the door with the signed papers.

Ethan wiped Coop's face with his thumb. "Your face is a mess, cannoli everywhere. I don't think he noticed, though."

"I don't think he did. We should probably call Madeline and ask what we just signed."

"Yeah…we should."

Coop pulled Ethan's robe off and tossed his naked body over his shoulder. "After. We'll call them after." He smacked Ethan's ass.

Madeline waited anxiously in the back of the taxi. She called Liam's phone and hung up, just as Liam came around, running full speed. Liam got in beside her, and the driver headed for the family affairs office.

Liam, out of breath, said, "Holy shit. Those two…You should…call them and explain…they almost didn't sign them."

Madeline looked at him. "They're coming on the vineyard tour later, right? We can explain then. I'm pissed at them for not answering their phones. Ignoring me, who do they think they are?"

Liam still panted as he shook his head. "No…they were

definitely…Coop had some white stuff on both sides of his face… they were probably just…you know what I'm saying. Don't make me say it."

Maddie tilted her head. "Ohhhh, okay. Wait, what kind of white stuff?"

Liam shook his head. "Don't think about it…not what you're thinking, though. I mean it could've been but…I don't know, why does it matter?"

Maddie and Liam hurried inside the family affairs office with the stack of papers. They filed the addendum to the surrogacy agreement successfully. Liam embraced Maddie, as the officer stamped it with the seal. She looked up at him. "That was a really amazing thing you just did. I didn't even think of that."

Liam gave her a quick kiss. "Well, something just clicked. I saw the word separation, and I know those two wouldn't be able to handle it, just based on the past few days with them. Hopefully it won't come into play but with the health conditions, it's better we did that."

Maddie smiled. "Let's head back, it's almost time for the van to pick us up. I still need to change clothes, and I haven't even checked on Tom and Levi; they better not be late."

Levi and Tom stood near the bed in their hotel room, getting ready for the tour of the vineyard. Levi opened the bag from their trip to a specialty costume store that they stopped at after the cooking class. He placed a pack of three flat hair clips down and pulled out the sexy costume that he and Tom purchased. He rubbed the black see through material and gold accent coins.

"Try it on," Tom urged him. "I want to see it."

Levi held it up. "Okay, but no funny business, we have to get ready soon."

"No promises," Tom said. As Levi walked into the bathroom, Tom looked at the pack of hair clips on the bed and noticed that one was missing.

Levi came out a few minutes later and stood in the doorway facing Tom.

Eyes wide, Tom said, "You are the sexiest genie I've ever seen. Come over here."

Levi approached, the front of his hair was swept to the side in a small braid, secured with his new flat hair clip. Tom took in the sight; the costume was two pieces, the black see-through pants hung low, with slits on the side. There were gold coins and beads strung along the front of the waist. The top was also black with gold accents, it was a halter style, that showed off Levi's smooth shoulders. Tom grabbed him by the waist and pulled him close.

Levi wrapped his arms around his neck. "Later I'll grant you one wish."

Tom gave him a deep, wet kiss.

Levi's phone rang, Tom held his face in place through the kiss and the ringing. He wasn't going to stop for any phone call.

Then, Tom's phone rang, and Levi returned the favor, holding his face in place through the ringing.

Once the ringing stopped, Tom and Levi continued their quickly escalating passionate kiss onto the bed.

Levi's phone rang again, this time he and Tom separated their lips. Levi reached for the phone, while Tom held Levi's waist in place, not letting him move. "Ugh, it's Maddie."

Tom grabbed the phone, he spoke frustrated, "What, Maddie? We were in the middle of something."

"What is with you men?" she replied. "It's 3:30 in the afternoon."

Tom sighed. "I know what time it is. Why are you calling us?"

"Liam just pulled off a great save for Coop and Ethan. They were in the middle of something too, I guess. I was wondering if they're coming on the tour with us, do you know if they are?"

Tom put his hand on his forehead. "No, we forgot to mention it to them. We didn't even know if you two were still going."

"Well, I'm not calling them again. I'm tired of all of you not answering your phones…plus Liam said Coop had…never mind that. I'm not calling though"—her voice dropped to a whisper—"I think Liam would be really happy if they go. He won't say it, but he likes hanging out with them." She ended the call.

Levi crossed his arms. "That Liam is a hard one to figure out."

Tom was growing pretty fond of Liam. He gave Levi a smile. "Nah, he's easy to read, just look closer."

Levi took the phone back from Tom. "Well, we got interrupted and so should they."

"Let's just text them," Tom said shaking his head. "Give them all the details, if they want to go, they'll text us back."

Levi patted the side of his hair and frowned. "Oh, Tommy! My braid fell out, can you fix it?"

Tom kissed Levi's forehead and took the clip from his loosened braid. "Of course. You text them and I'll braid."

Following their cannoli play and late afternoon sex, Coop washed Ethan's hair in the shower.

Ethan leaned back as Coop massaged his scalp, moaning in pleasure. "Mmm, that feels so good…yes…"

Coop warned him, "Don't start something you can't finish, pup."

Ethan turned and looked at him. "I know, but your fingers are like magic, when they massage and rub, it's just, mmm…so good."

Coop pointed down at his dick. "You're doing it again. He's waking back up. Such a tease."

"No, no, stop. I'll stop. I'll be good," Ethan said.

The two finished showering and walked out of the bathroom, their bottom halves wrapped in towels.

Coop's phone chimed loudly with notifications. He walked across the room and picked it up, reading the text and then passing it to Ethan.

Ethan read the text from Levi and looked at Coop. "Hmm. Do we want to do that?"

Coop pulled his mouth to the side. "Well, tomorrow is our last day here and we didn't get to go to any vineyards. It would be fun if it were just us, but—" He was far too attracted to Ethan's wet body wrapped in a towel. He rubbed his eyes. "I can't think straight, you need to put a shirt on, baby."

"Me?" Ethan pointed to himself. "You need to put a shirt on. I can't concentrate. Let me read the text again."

Coop sat on the side of the bed, and Ethan stood in front of him, reading the message. "I still have questions," Ethan said.

Coop nodded. "Yeah, me too. Starting with why you're standing directly in front of me, still in a towel. I'll give you three minutes to make up your mind on the vineyards, then I pull that towel off."

Ethan backed up a few feet. "I'd rather just stay here with you, but it would be fun to go. The next time we come back, we'll be bringing the baby home. I don't think we'll be going to any vineyards then."

Coop smiled and stood up, then embraced Ethan tight. "We're gonna have a baby, puppy." He kissed Ethan's cheek and rubbed his back, while squeezing him. Earlier in the year when they'd talked about having a baby someday, the idea seemed so far away, and they had no idea how it would work out, but now that everything was falling into place so easily, he felt incredibly happy.

Ethan smooched Coop back and smiled. "I'm so excited, Cooper."

Coop rubbed Ethan's arms and said, "Text Levi and tell him we'll meet them at their hotel at five o'clock. I'll grab us some water."

Coop walked into the kitchen, while Ethan texted Levi. Ethan placed the phone down and walked near the kitchen. He tilted his head and teased him. "Cooper, I thought you said I had three minutes and then you were gonna—aaahh!"

Coop grabbed Ethan's towel off and chased him quickly up the stairs. "You're gonna get it now, you little tease."

Chapter 16
Boo, Peter

Tom and Levi stood in the lobby waiting for the rest of the group. Tom watched as Levi checked his hair clip, sliding his fingers down the braid that Tom put in for him.

"Is my braid okay, Tommy?"

Tom kissed his cheek. "Perfect." He held Levi's hand and walked toward Maddie and Liam who were also holding hands.

"Hi, guys!" Maddie said. "Cute braid, Levi. I like the barrette, too."

Liam pulled his lollipop out of his mouth. "I have nothing to say about the braid or the barrette."

Levi tilted his head, looking at them. "Well, you both look nice…nicer than this afternoon. Did you clear up your little problem, Single?"

Maddie held their clasped hands up and rolled her eyes. "Would I be holding his hand if we didn't?"

Tom noticed Liam looking around and remembered what Maddie said earlier. He didn't want to embarrass Liam and point out that they would be there soon. Instead, he asked Levi, "Boys said they would be here at five, right?"

"Yep, they said five o'clock."

Liam looked down at the ground and lightly kicked a pebble. Tom saw a small smile on his face.

Maddie teased him, "See, your buddies are coming. We're going to have a great time, even though you hate wine."

Liam pulled her face in, and gave her a big kiss, which she didn't fight or pull back from.

Coop and Ethan came around the corner. They both made disgusted faces at the sight of the two kissing. Ethan whispered, "Is this how people feel when we do that?"

Coop kissed him on the cheek. "Who knows? I only care about your feelings."

Levi called out, "Hey, guys! Right on time! There's the van!"

Coop and Ethan smiled, then made a quick turn and speed-walked to the van. Ethan whispered, "Why are we walking so fast?"

Coop squeezed his hand. "I want the backseat. Come on."

They stepped inside the van, and the driver greeted them. The driver saw Ethan and said, "Oh, big guy, hello, welcome."

Coop ducked in behind him. The driver said, "Oh, wow, another big guy, hello, welcome."

Ethan and Coop successfully claimed the back seat and high-fived.

Maddie and Liam came next, the driver said, "Oh, pretty lady, hello, welcome."

"And tall guy with a lollipop, hello, welcome."

Maddie and Liam sat in the second row.

Coop and Ethan were already enjoying themselves. Ethan chuckled. "I guess he just says what he sees. This is gonna be so much fun."

Levi entered next. The driver greeted him, "Cute one with a braid, welcome."

Levi smiled. "Oh, hello. Thank you."

Tom entered last and sat beside Levi in the front row. The driver said, "Model man, face of a boss, welcome."

The driver looked in the rearview mirror. "Welcome again to all of you, I'm Larry, the youngest in my family. We've been running these vineyard tours for ten years. We have seven vans that operate on a daily basis. We aim to please. You're all very lucky to have me as your driver. Let me tell you—if you would've gotten my brother, Peter, yuck. You would've hated him. He's no fun." The group collectively laughed. He continued, "Alright, you laughed, that's great. Now I know what I'm working with. Everyone say: Boooo, Peter!"

Ethan and Coop looked at each other, the other couples also exchanged confused glances.

Levi said, "Boooo, Peter!"

The rest of the group followed, shouting out the same.

Larry clapped and put the van into gear. "Alright. Thank you. We hate Peter here. Peter is responsible for all the bad things on this tour. Just remember that."

Levi leaned forward. "What kind of bad things should we expect?"

Larry answered, "Anything. Always be ready for anything, but I'm talking about red lights, traffic, grannies crossing the street, bad wine… All of that, you just yell out 'boo, Peter,' and you'll feel better. Trust me."

Coop laughed and wrapped his arm around Ethan. "He's funny. He made me hate Peter and I don't even know him."

"Me too!" Ethan said.

Larry said, "Now, I can't look at you, of course, since I'm driving, but everyone go ahead and introduce yourselves.

Levi introduced himself first, "I'm Levi Morgan, this is my husband, Tom Morgan."

Larry answered, "Very nice, welcome, Levi and Tom. Who's next?"

Coop shouted from the back, "I'm Coop Morgan and this is my husband Ethan Morgan, we're here on our honeymoon."

Larry called back, "Welcome, Coop and Ethan. Congratulations on your marriage. Two couples from the Morgan family, very nice."

Liam spoke up, "I'm Liam Collins and this is my girlfriend, Maddie Parson."

Larry answered, "Welcome, Liam and Maddie. You better put a ring on that one soon, too pretty to be called someone's girlfriend."

"A ring? She just agreed to let me call her my girlfriend this afternoon. She definitely isn't gonna let me put a ring on her."

"That's right, so don't even ask," Maddie said.

Larry shouted, "Boo, Peter!"

Maddie's jaw dropped. "Did you just 'boo, Peter,' me?"

Larry nodded his head. "Yes, ma'am. I call it like I see it. You told him he shouldn't even ask, but that's not what you were thinking, was it? Hahaha. You get a 'boo, Peter' for that."

Coop whispered to Ethan, "Does that mean she wants him to ask?"

Ethan nodded. "I guess so. She didn't correct him."

Larry asked, "So what have the newlyweds been up to on their honeymoon?"

Levi answered before Coop could get a word in. "Well, they bought three quarts of cannoli for their hotel room. I can say that much."

Larry looked in the rearview mirror. "That's a lot of cannoli. Shells too or just the cream?"

"Just the cream, in a huge container," Levi answered.

Liam snapped his fingers, nodding at Maddie.

"Yep, that's probably what you saw on his face!" Maddie said.

Coop and Ethan's mouths hung open.

Liam tried unsuccessfully to stop Maddie from saying anything else by covering her mouth with his hand. Maddie pulled his hand off and shouted, "Liam noticed earlier that Coop had white stuff on the sides of his face. I guess it was cannoli cream!"

Larry yelled back, "Well, you're newlyweds and I hate to do this to you, but boo, Peter!"

Coop asked, "Why do I get a 'boo Peter'?"

"Yeah, why is he getting a 'boo Peter'?" Ethan asked. "Liam came into our hotel room, it's not like Cooper walked outside with cannoli cream on his face."

Larry answered, "You both get a 'boo, Peter'. Three quarts of cannoli and you didn't bring any for anyone else? You could've bought some shells and brought some along. Also, I've never heard of anyone doing that with cannoli, so you know what? Boo, Peter, for the rest of us who haven't tried it."

They arrived at the first vineyard and Larry parked the van. "Alright, everybody, you have thirty minutes here, then we'll head to the next one. Have fun!"

The group was greeted by an older man named Francis. He introduced himself as a tour guide and long-time employee of the vineyard. He started off the tour by showing them the beautiful rows of Sangiovese grapes.

Maddie asked, "When can we try the wine that comes from these?"

"So uncultured." Levi scoffed. "Look at these grapes, Maddie. They're perfect."

Coop and Ethan lagged behind the rest of the group and took selfies together. They weren't too interested in the history of the grapes.

Francis brought the group to a nice covered outdoor area. The long black table was covered with two platters of cold cuts, cheeses and bruschetta.

Maddie and Liam sat on one side while Tom and Levi sat on the other. Ethan and Coop leaned against the fence, after all the cannoli, neither were very hungry.

Francis brought out a nice, white wine and poured it into six glasses.

Levi raised his eyebrows at Maddie. "You remember what happened yesterday, right?"

Maddie took a sip, looking at Levi. "I'm fine, you worry about yourself."

Ethan and Coop walked over and grabbed their wine without sitting down. Ethan looked at Coop and swirled his wine. "I don't know if I want to drink, honestly. I just thought it would be fun to see everything."

Coop felt the same. "I'm not drinking either.

Ethan gestured with his wine glass toward the table. "Should we give our wine to one of them?"

"I don't think so," Coop said. "Let's just put the glasses over here. If they want them, they'll grab them." They put both their glasses on the far end of the table, and Coop grabbed Ethan's hand. "Let's go ask Liam what we signed earlier. He isn't drinking."

Coop sat to the left of Tom, and Ethan sat on Coop's left. They looked across the table at Liam and Maddie. Liam raised his chin at Coop and Ethan. "Where have you guys been?"

Coop winked playfully at Liam and answered, "Ethan was making sure there was no more cannoli on my face."

Ethan asked, "Hey, really, what did you have us sign earlier?"

That question drew the interest of the entire group.

Liam sighed. "It's a long story. I just realized there might be something you guys wouldn't be able to handle."

"Don't say it like that." Maddie elbowed him. "I'll explain it if you don't want to."

Tom pointed at Coop and Ethan with his thumb over his shoulder. "You realized something these two couldn't handle? What could that be? They've literally been inseparable since they got together. I don't think there's anything they can't handle together."

Liam nodded. "You just said it."

"I'll explain," Maddie said, patting Liam's arm. "Liam was looking online to see if there was anything negative that might come up during your at-home interviews."

Coop interrupted her, "There definitely isn't but continue."

"Yes, like I said, he was looking but didn't find anything. What he did find was your proposal video, which was very moving, by the way. I like the necklace kiss that you guys do when you're playing together. Anyway, that led to us finding the picture you painted, *Separation*, and we read about that. I almost cried, really. Very sweet. Liam liked it, too. You shouldn't have tied with that dog, by the way, but that's beside the point. Anyway, Liam realized after seeing *Separation* and reading the story behind it, that you two couldn't survive if you were separated."

Ethan and Coop asked at the same time, "And?"

Liam took over, "Well, I was thinking about the carrier's condition and what would happen if she went into preterm labor. Hopefully it doesn't happen, but if so, the baby would most likely end up in the NICU, meaning he would need special care until he was ready to go home. That would be a problem for you two because traditionally only one parent can be in the NICU at a time, especially overnight, at least in the States. Not only that, but if that happens and you guys aren't here, I needed to be sure you guys signed off on all of your parents and Ethan's grandparents as temporary guardians until you two get to the hospital. I needed to be sure that in a worst-case scenario, where the carrier doesn't make it, that he would be in the care of your family, not accidentally end up with the carrier's mother. So, I took care of a lot of problems all at once today. Now, if something happens, you'll both be granted immediate access to the NICU, together for as long as he's there, which again, hopefully he won't be. You're welcome."

Maddie said, "He left some stuff out. We had to run to a printer, you guys wouldn't answer your phone, but yeah, he got it done. This was all him."

Coop and Ethan were speechless.

Tom and Levi both thanked Liam and Maddie.

Coop started to speak as he squeezed Ethan in tight, with his left arm wrapped around him. "Liam...we...just... get up, follow us for a minute." Coop and Ethan stood, holding hands.

Liam stuck a lollipop in his mouth and followed behind them away from the group.

Liam leaned next to the side of the wooden pavilion, standing across from Ethan and Coop. He pulled his lollipop out of his mouth. "What's up? What did you pull me over here for?"

Ethan started, "I don't even know where to begin. I'm just really thankful...but this also just brought up a lot of possibilities that... I...we—" Coop kissed Ethan's cheek and rubbed his shoulder with his arm wrapped around him.

Liam put his lollipop back in his mouth. "It's alright, I get it. You want to thank me."

"We do," Coop said. "But I'm not really good with other people's feelings. I just want to thank you for what you did. I don't know what you saw when you looked at the painting or the proposal that made you think of it, but I can speak for both of us and say we're truly grateful. My spicy puppy here doesn't usually like people once he decides he doesn't, so he's probably dealing with some inner turmoil."

Ethan nodded. "Accurate." He kissed Coop's cheek, then looked at Liam. "Thank you for what you did…really. We'd never thought of those things. I'm really happy that my painting and our proposal moved you in that way. It means a lot to me, to both of us."

Liam put his lollipop back in his mouth. "So, you guys like me now?"

Coop and Ethan looked at each other. "Too soon," Ethan said, "way too soon."

Liam threw his hands up and walked back to the table, grabbing Ethan and Coop's still-full glasses for himself and Maddie.

Ethan and Coop stayed behind. "Cooper, I just didn't even think about that. What are we gonna do if that happens? We'll be so far away."

Coop rubbed Ethan's shoulders, then hugged him. "We'll get through it, together. We shouldn't worry. She has an appointment this week, we'll see what the doctor says. Really lucky he thought of that, though. I hope they didn't miss anything else."

Ethan rested his head on Coop's shoulder and inhaled. "I really mean this, your smell is magic. Your words too, but the smell is just so calming." Coop gave him a quick smooch, and they headed for the table.

Francis approached the group and advised them that their tour time at this location was over. He thanked them and walked the group to the van.

The group piled in the van single file starting with Ethan and

Coop. Larry started talking as soon as the entire group was seated. He turned his body to face the group. "Boo, Peter, right? This is the most boring stop on the trip. One glass of Pinot Grigio, so cheap, right?"

Levi clapped. "Yes, boooo, Peter! Are the two other stops better, Larry?"

Larry turned back in his seat and reversed out of the gravel parking lot. "Yes, this one always is the worst," he said. "It's beautiful and the scenery is gorgeous, but if you went there for the wine, then what do we say, gang?"

The group yelled, "Boo Peter!"

Larry nodded. "Exactly. It's all Peter's fault. Little bastard."

Levi spoke loudly to the group from the front seat, "I still can't believe Liam thought of that. Sounds like something Kory would've done."

"Kory?" Maddie scoffed. "No. Kory doesn't like kids, he wouldn't have thought of that. You should've seen Liam watching the video and studying the painting. I thought he was going to cry, but he just popped out of bed. Flew around the room like a superhero."

Liam was obviously quite proud of himself; he smiled and sucked a lollipop while Maddie bragged.

Ethan's face lit up looking at Coop. "Superhero! Your dad's cape, you never finished your story about Sal and Tony."

Levi turned and asked Coop, "I'm sorry, when did your father have a cape? More importantly, what color was it?"

Tom leaned his head back on the seat embarrassed, while Levi faced the group behind them.

Coop corrected him, "No, it wasn't a cape it was his house robe. I was telling Ethan a story about some kids that got into the estate once."

Tom said, "Oh, When Tony—"

"Don't steal my story!" Coop shouted. "I just got to the good part. I'll tell it."

Larry looked in the mirror and said, "Yeah, tell the story loud, so I can hear it up here, too. Don't make me 'boo, Peter' you, newlywed."

Coop sat up straight as the whole group turned to face him in the van. "Alright, so, we had two security guards, Tony and Sal. One was responsible for the gate, the other was responsible for the inside of the estate. One night, some teenagers snuck in. The two of them argued about whose fault it was. Now, these are two very big men."

Larry interrupted, "Bigger than you?"

Coop pulled his head back. "Bigger than me, when? Then? Yes, since I was eleven, now no. Well, they're stocky guys though, not athletic guys. In good shape but not the same."

Larry nodded. "Understood."

Coop started again, "Well, the two teenagers wouldn't talk, wouldn't say how they got in. My dad let them go, then told Sal and Tony that he would check the cameras himself to see whose fault it was. I hid behind a hedge when he went back inside. Sal looked at Tony, and pointed in his face, blaming him. Tony mumbled something and, bam, Sal punched him right in the side of the face!"

"Holy shit!" Liam yelled, enthralled at Coop's retelling.

"Oh, so, they're brothers," Larry said.

Coop raised his chin. "Yes, but how do you know that? I didn't even say it."

Larry answered while stopped at a red light, "Sounds like Peter and me, that's how."

Ethan looked at Coop and asked, "Then what happened?"

Coop raised his eyebrows. "Then it got serious. They started really pounding on each other. Sal worked Tony's face pretty good. Tony was just trying to get a shot in."

Tom spoke from the front seat, "My turn. So, I was downstairs in the security room looking at earlier footage and what did I see? Aside from the kids sneaking in over the back portion of the gate, I saw Coop, hiding behind a hedge, watching the fight like he was watching a movie, his mouth was open, head bobbing around."

Liam pulled his lollipop out and asked, "So which guard was responsible, Tom?"

Larry yelled, "Peter, whichever brother is Peter, that's who was responsible!"

"Well, it was really both of their faults," Tom said. "Out of respect for Tony, who I'd known longer and was also the older brother, I placed more of the blame on Sal."

Larry, who was stopped at another red light, pointed in the rearview mirror at Tom, saying, "Boo, Peter! Boo, Peter!"

Tom shrugged and asked, "What? They didn't come in through the gate by the guardhouse. It was technically Sal's fault."

Maddie chimed in, "Mmm. I don't think so. You said that Tony was responsible for the gate, then you said they came over the gate. So, that makes it his fault."

Liam agreed with her, as did Levi.

Larry shook his head in the driver's seat.

"It was years ago. He works for Coop and Ethan, now. All water under the bridge," Tom said.

Larry said, "Everyone, you know what to do!"

They group said in unison to Tom, "Boo, Peter!"

"Don't 'boo, Peter' me," Tom said to Levi. "I was being nice that night. I let those kids go because they reminded me of us. Remember that time we snuck into the country club pool, after dark? Then we showed up in front of Paul, Gina, and the rest of the crew, barefoot? Those kids and Sal both got off easy because of that."

Ethan whispered to Coop, "I don't think it was Sal's fault either. I feel better that we have him instead of Tony."

Coop agreed, "Me too." The two shared a quick smooch.

Larry looked in the rearview mirror and saw the quick kiss. He called back, "Newlyweds, no fooling around in the backseat. I forgot to warn you of that. I will slam on the brakes and 'boo, Peter,' you both."

"Don't worry, we're not animals," Coop said.

"Yeah, right," Liam said. "Tell that to the hickey on Ethan's nipple!"

Larry's eyes widened.

Tom shook his head and whispered, "Again with the nipple."

"Well," Larry started. "I should 'boo, Peter' you for that, too. My wife won't touch my nipples. Says they smell like onions."

Levi winced. "Now that's too much information, Larry."

Chapter 17
Shut Up, Cannoli Boys

Larry parked at the next vineyard. "Alright, everyone, you know the drill. Try to remember my name is Larry when you get back. I can already tell which of you will forget it."

The group was greeted by their new tour guide, Amelia. She briefly gestured to the rows of grapes, then led them inside to the lower level. They walked down a staircase that led underground. Behind the large wooden doors was a huge cave, full of wine barrels. Amelia went over the history of the property and talked about all the ways that wine tastes can be affected during production.

Levi pulled on Tom's arm. "I love this. This is so fun, Tommy!"

Tom gave him a kiss on the cheek.

Coop and Ethan were in the back of the group, snapping more pictures of one another.

Liam turned around, he pulled a lollipop out of his pocket and stuck it in his mouth.

Maddie looked down at her phone, uninterested in whatever Liam was doing.

Liam sauntered over to Coop, and Ethan and asked, "Do you guys like wine? I noticed you didn't drink it at the last place."

Ethan whispered to Coop and Coop nodded.

"We don't hate it," Ethan said. "I just don't feel like making a fool out of myself."

Liam asked, "Oh, do you get stupid when you're drunk?"

"Yeah, something like that," Ethan said.

Coop pulled Ethan closer, squeezing his hand. "When we drink, we just prefer it to be at home."

Liam walked back next to Maddie and wrapped his arm around her. He whispered in her ear, then looked back at Coop and Ethan, who weren't paying attention. He threw his hands up. "Damn it, I whispered to show you guys how it feels, you weren't even paying attention!"

Maddie looked at him confused. "Why did you just say, 'pss pss pss' in my ear?"

The tour guide handed them all a full glass of a bold Viognier. Levi swirled and sniffed, then sipped. "Oh, this is nice. Do you like this, Tommy?"

Tom sipped his wine and answered, "I do. I tasted peaches, and maybe tangerine. Am I right?"

"Yes!" Levi said, rubbing his back. "Also notes of honeysuckle, and if I'm not mistaken a hint of vanilla. Delicious, nice full body."

Liam and Maddie sniffed their wines. Liam took a big drink and looked at Maddie. "Oh, shit, that *is* good."

Maddie sipped her wine, then brought the glass back to her mouth and guzzled the rest down. Liam's eyes widened. She turned around to Coop and Ethan who were holding their full glasses. She held her hand out. "Give it," she said to Ethan.

Liam downed the rest of his glass and joined her, holding his hand out to Coop, he mocked Maddie. "Give it." Coop and Ethan passed them their untouched glasses. They took them without thanks and walked away, quickly placing their empty glasses on top of a brown wooden refuse tray while they drank from the new ones.

Tom and Levi continued walking through the cave with the tour guide, leading the group from the front. They finished their wine and placed it on the next open refuse tray. Tom abruptly squished Levi's face in his hand. "You're so beautiful," he said before kissing Levi's squished mouth.

After the kiss, Levi moved his jaw side to side. "Are you feeling it already, Tommy?"

Tom smiled, and his words came slowly, but not overly so, "No… I'm just…in love with you. I'm so lucky…"

Levi brought his face close to Tom's and looked into his eyes. "How many of me do you see?"

Tom spoke at a normal pace, "Stop it. I'm fine. Don't be silly." Levi took him by the hand, and they continued following behind the guide.

The guide stopped at the next wine station and handed them all a glass of pink Rosato. "Mmm," Levi said as he sniffed it.

Maddie and Liam had already finished the two glasses that Coop and Ethan gave them just a few minutes earlier. They happily accepted the new wine and drank it.

Ethan and Coop placed their full glasses on the refuse tray and left them behind quickly.

After downing their wine, Maddie and Liam then turned to Ethan and Coop, who both held their hands out, showing no glasses. Maddie turned around and nudged Liam. "Hurry up. Go get them," she said.

Tom and Levi finished their wine and placed the empties down. Tom was getting very clingy, he pulled on Levi's shirt. "Stay close to me. Don't go too far. I don't trust the guide."

The guide walked the group back to their van and thanked them for their business.

The group allowed Ethan and Coop to get in first, since they sat in the back. Ethan ducked inside. Larry said, "If I'm right, at least three of you are drunk."

Coop followed behind Ethan and smiled looking at Larry. "Not the two of us, not sure about the others."

Maddie came in next, laughing very loudly at something that Liam said.

Larry, who was turned sideways in his seat, looked at Coop and Ethan, he put up one finger and pointed at Maddie.

Liam came in next and sat beside her, he leaned his head on her shoulder. Her curly red hair covered his face.

Larry raised his eyebrows and held up two fingers to Coop and Ethan. "Now, this next one is a toss-up, not sure which one it will be," Larry said, as Tom entered.

Tom sat in the seat and sighed. "That was a long walk." He looked to the left and didn't see Levi, then looked to the right to see him stepping into the van. Tom held his right arm out and reached for Levi. "Angel, come here, sit next to me."

Larry put up three fingers and said to Coop and Ethan. "That's three! I told you! You guys want to see another trick?"

"Yeah, go ahead," Ethan said.

Coop encouraged him, too, "Let's see it."

Larry reversed after Levi was settled in. "Do you remember what I said earlier, newlyweds?"

Liam and Maddie shouted, "Boo, Peter!"

"Yes, always 'boo, Peter,'" Larry said, "but, no, not that."

Ethan whispered to Coop, "I think he's talking about someone forgetting his name."

Coop shouted out, "Alright, we remember. Who is it?"

Larry called over his shoulder, "Hey, dad of the newlywed."

Levi and Tom both looked up. Larry looked at them in the

rearview mirror. "You, with the braid, don't answer." He looked at Tom and asked, "What's my name?"

Levi looked at Tom and smiled, while Tom leaned his head on his shoulder. "What is his name? I don't remember."

"Boom!" Larry said. "I Win! 'Boo, Peter' to you, rich dad."

Coop and Ethan laughed.

Levi sassed, "Well, you don't remember his name, *Larry*, why should he remember yours?"

Tom lifted his head. "Larry, your name is Larry!"

"Doesn't count," Larry said, shaking his head.

Maddie and Liam were in the midst of a discussion about engagement, which was probably a bad idea given their current state. They both spoke loudly, not in anger, just due to all the wine.

Liam said to Maddie, "You're saying whoever decides to marry you would have to ask your dad's permission first?"

"Yes, it's my dad's company, do you think I have any choice? If he doesn't accept them…"

"Hahaha," Tom said. "Screw your dad. Screw all dads."

Larry's eyes widened in the rearview mirror.

"Shh, you're a dad," Levi said, rubbing Tom's shoulder. "What are you saying?"

Coop and Ethan giggled to themselves. "I've never seen him full-on drunk," Coop whispered. "Just buzzed. This is fantastic."

Ethan nodded in agreement.

"What?" Liam asked. "Screw all dads? She didn't say anything about screwing anyone."

Tom stammered, "Well, you know…you know…what I say? Do what I did to my dad. That will teach him."

Levi covered Tom's mouth. "Shh… Tommy, don't."

Tom bit him playfully. "Don't bite me," Levi said, pulling his hand back.

Coop was interested, he leaned forward in his seat. "What did you do to grandpa? What's he talking about, Levi? He doesn't even talk to my grandpa."

Levi shook his head. "No. I will never speak of it. Nope."

Coop and Ethan shouted, "Boo, Peter!"

Levi put his hands up. "I don't care. I will not say it."

"I'll say it," Tom said. "Liam, listen…my dad was the reason that my little angel here…left me… So, I called him when…when we got back together."

Levi said, "Yep, that's it, that's the end of the story."

Tom sat up straight, well, as straight as he could, and spoke loudly, "No. That's not it… I had Levi bent over and smacked his ass with the old man on the phone. Let him hear Levi beg for it. I told him…what we were doing, let him know…he couldn't stop love…"

Coop and Ethan's mouths hung open in shock.

Liam's eyes widened, while Maddie cackled beside him, hiccupping loudly.

"Wow," Larry said. "That was quite unexpected. Savage… I respect that, though. Boo, Peter, to your dad."

Liam turned and looked at Coop. "No wonder he's never phased by the stuff you two do!"

Levi looked at Tom, in a mix of embarrassment and laughter. "Do you feel better now? That was too much to tell people. Coop and Ethan are in the back seat!"

Tom blew raspberries. "Coop doesn't care. He hates that old smelly man, too."

Coop shouted from the back, "Coop does care! Coop doesn't want to hear about that!"

Ethan added, "Ethan doesn't either!"

Levi cocked his head to the side and turned around. "You two cannoli boys, shut up, or I'll come back there and smack you both."

Larry pulled into a parking spot at the final vineyard. "Alright everyone, this is the last stop, they're going to finish you off with a nice red, and some more food. Anyone staying in the van, or is everyone getting out?"

Levi looked at Tom who was half asleep with his head on his shoulder. He whined, "Tommy, I've been dying for the red this whole trip. I don't want to miss it!"

"We'll go in with you," Coop said to Levi. "But you should probably leave my dad here."

Tom picked his head up. "No. Levi's not leaving me. Ever." He clutched Levi's body tight, then laid his head on his lap.

Levi smiled down at him and rubbed his face. "No. I'm never going to leave you."

Ethan said, "Liam, Madeline this is the last stop, do you guys—"

Madeline told him to be quiet with her hand, as she waved him off, shaking her head.

"I guess we can just go back to the hotel, Larry," Coop said.

Larry saluted him. "You got it.".

Levi mumbled about his disappointment but rubbed Tom's face softly.

Chapter 18
Not Without My Genie Costume

There was a huge parking jam when they arrived at the hotel. Cars were everywhere, people were arguing. It was a picture of chaos as Larry pulled in. "What the heck is going on here?" Larry asked.

Coop and Ethan looked around. "This looks like our hotel earlier," Ethan said. "Is there something big that people are visiting for, Larry?"

Larry shook his head. "No. It's tourist season, but this must be something really big."

People were shoving their suitcases in their trunks and appeared to be yelling at one another outside. The line to drop off was so backed up that Larry couldn't even move the van.

Maddie looked outside. "What is going on?"

"Let me go ask that officer over there," Levi said. "You can't move anyway, Larry. Is it okay if I get out?"

Larry nodded. "Yeah, if your husband doesn't wake up swinging."

Levi placed Tom's head gently on the seat and whispered to him, "I'll be right back." He gave him a quick kiss on the cheek and got out. The group watched him walk over toward the officer. Levi threw his hands up in frustration after a minute or two of conversation and pulled out his phone.

Coop's phone rang. He answered, "What's going on, Levi?"

Levi yelled through the phone, "He can't understand me! He doesn't speak English! Can one of you please come out here?"

Coop and Ethan got out together. Ethan spoke politely to the officer and asked him to explain the situation. The officer explained that the hotel was closed due to an emergency with the hotel's air quality. He also stated that no one would be permitted to retrieve their belongings or return to their rooms until tomorrow. Ethan translated after he understood everything.

Levi bolted and ran toward the hotel. He yelled backwards, "I'm not leaving that! I'll be right back!"

The officer looked at Coop and Ethan and rolled his eyes. Coop spoke in Italian, he asked the officer if Levi would be arrested for running past the barricades.

The officer shrugged. "Maybe yes, maybe no."

Levi was fast, running through the parking lot. Coop and Ethan watched as he skirted in between cars, barricades, and officers. They headed back to the van, so they could fill the others in. Tom was still lying on his side across the front seat when they entered.

"What did he go running for?" Larry asked.

Coop explained the situation, and Maddie and Liam laughed. Coop said, "What are you guys laughing about? You won't be able to get your stuff until tomorrow. You have no hotel tonight. You have nowhere to sleep."

They continued laughing.

"Do you guys understand what's happening?" Ethan asked.

"Yeah," Liam said. "We just don't care."

Maddie turned in her seat to face Ethan. "Wait, what did you say about the hotel?"

Ethan explained everything again, slowly.

Maddie looked at Liam. "You need to get our stuff. I have nothing with me. We can't leave our laptops there."

Larry's van still hadn't moved from its original spot. Coop patted the back of the seat to get Liam's attention. "Hey, Levi just ran to go get something, maybe you can too. The officer said maybe he would get arrested, but maybe he wouldn't."

"Levi is so clumsy," Maddie said, "he probably fell somewhere by now."

She started to get up, and Liam put a hand on her shoulder. "No, you stay here. I'll need you to bail me out if I get in trouble. Levi might need you, too." Liam shuffled out of the van, and the group watched as he walked over to the officer and handed him a lollipop. The officer gave him a big smile and let him pass.

"How did he do that?" Coop asked., "He doesn't even speak Italian."

"You two don't realize how charming he can be," Maddie said. "He doesn't need words. It's in the eyes."

Larry's phone rang. "Oh no. It's Peter." Larry answered the phone, "What, Peter?" He held a conversation with him for several minutes, then hung up. He shook his head. "We're going to be stuck here for a while. Peter says his van is on the other side of the drop off zone and hasn't moved."

Levi came running back toward the van. He held only one small thing in his hand. He flung the door open and got inside. "Oh wow! That was crazy," he said loudly, while panting.

Tom sat up and looked at him, confused.

"Levi, where is your luggage?" Coop asked. "What did you grab?"

Levi held up a black and gold bundle. And placed it back on his lap. "We just bought this, and I didn't even get to wear it properly."

Tom tilted his head, and asked through half-lidded eyes, "What's that, the genie costume?"

Maddie leaned forward saying, "Oooh, let me see it!"

Levi held it up one piece at a time, smiling. Maddie admired it. "That's beautiful, Levi."

Ethan could tell that Levi didn't have a firm grasp on the situation they were in. He tried to help him understand. "Levi, you guys have no hotel tonight, and you left all your stuff in your room. All your stuff. You were in your room, and you left all your stuff."

Coop held his arms up. "What were you thinking?"

Levi looked at the outfit and dropped his head. "Do I have time to try and run back, Larry?"

"At this rate you'll be sleeping in the van, so go ahead."

Levi placed the outfit on Tom's lap and leaned Tom's body against the window on the left. "I'm going back in!" he said, as he jumped out of the van.

Coop hung his head against the seat. "Wait, we have to get the Ferrari, the valet parked it somewhere."

"Nope, that's where Peter is," Larry said. "Valets are running around crazy. It's deadlocked over there, too."

Ethan laid his head on Coop's shoulder. "What are your dad, Levi, Madeline, and Liam gonna do? There are probably no hotels with open rooms. It's already late…do we let them…?"

Coop turned his mouth down, shaking his head. "Oh no, baby, please, no."

"Alright, it's up to you. If you feel comfortable leaving them out on the street."

Larry yelled back, "We're all gonna be sleeping in this van, anyway!"

"Nope, that's not happening, "Coop said. "We'll walk to the Ferrari and sleep in that before we sleep in here."

"That's a thought," Ethan said. "We could give Maddie and Liam the car to sleep in, then your dad and Levi could stay downstairs."

"No, Liam and Maddie are drunk, what if they try and drive somewhere?"

Maddie turned backwards and asked, "Have you two been there the whole time? Where's Liam?"

Larry warned, "Don't give her any keys!"

Liam came back dragging two large suitcases and holding a large carry-on bag. Larry hopped out of the van and opened the rear doors; he helped Liam place the bags inside, then they both got back into the van.

Liam was out of breath. "Damn. I think I got everything."

Levi came slightly into view; it was too hard to tell what he was carrying or dragging. Coop and Ethan decided to help him. They got out of the van, jogged across the lot, and were shocked to see all the barricades and obstacles that Levi made it through.

"I think his baseball days came back to him," Ethan said. "He was always really fast. He had a lot of skills."

Levi saw the two and smiled brightly. He had two large suitcases beside him and held two carry-on bags. Together, they got everything back to the van. There wasn't too much room behind the backseat, but they were able to squish everything inside.

Ethan laid his head on Coop's lap and whispered to him. "I really don't want to stay in this van anymore. Can we walk to the hotel?"

Coop rubbed Ethan's hair softly. "Just close your eyes, as soon as we move, I'll wake you up. If I see an opening, we'll get out of here."

Two hours later, Coop and Ethan jumped at the sound of the door closing. Ethan sat up and leaned into Coop's body. He pouted as Coop held him. "Cooper, we're still here? Are we gonna live here now?"

Coop gave him a smooch. He knew how to make Ethan calm down, and was definitely willing to do it, especially with the rest of the van passed out or drunk. The two exchanged a look. Ethan shook his head and Coop nodded. Ethan scooted to the other side of the seat and shook his head again. Coop patted the spot next to him, and Ethan scooted back beside him.

Larry got back into the van, he whispered softly, "Hey, he says it will be just a few more minutes, they've started moving up front. Valet is out, though. They said anyone with a car in valet has to come back tomorrow. They locked up all the keys."

Coop's eyes widened. "That's a $300,000 car. I hope nothing happens to it."

"I got you guys the extra theft insurance," Liam said. "It will only cost you a hundred euros if someone steals it."

Ethan asked, "Hey, Larry, can you take us all to our hotel? They can just stay with us. We'll pay you extra."

They gave Larry the name of the hotel, and he agreed to drive them there. Finally, at 10:30 pm, they were out of the parking lot and on their way.

Tom sat up and looked around, holding Levi with his right arm. "Where are we going? It's late and dark."

"We're going to Coop and Ethan's," Levi said, "there was a problem at the hotel."

Chapter 19
That Bed Is Unusable

The group finally got out of the van. Coop gave Larry an extra five hundred euros and thanked him. Each couple grabbed their bags and followed Coop and Ethan to their room. Ethan yelled back, "The room is a mess, don't judge us."

Coop opened the door, and everyone shuffled inside. Coop sighed, remembering that the cannoli play from earlier made quite a mess. "Alright, there are two spare rooms, one is unusable. Don't ask. One couple can take the good spare room, and the others can use the living area, it has a pull-out bed inside the couch. There are blankets and spare linens that housekeeping left this morning right here." He patted the stack of towels and sheets.

Levi raised his hand. "Can I use the spare sheets to make the unusable bed usable? I won't judge."

Ethan and Coop looked at each other. Ethan winced. "Ugh. We'll just fix the bed. Just wait a minute."

Liam and Maddie headed toward the other bedroom. "We're gonna get set up in other room, guys," Liam said.

Maddie sniffed the flowers as she walked by. "They still smell fresh," she said.

Tom and Levi sat on the couch, while Ethan and Coop tidied

up the room for them. Levi rubbed Tom's shoulder. "I don't feel great about sleeping in a bed that they've, you know, done that in, Tommy. Not sure how you feel about it. Not like we have a choice, though."

Tom rubbed his temples. "I'm still not even sure what the hell is happening. Why are you holding your genie costume?"

Levi patted Tom's lap. "Don't worry about it. I can't explain it all over again. It's too exhausting. What a long, crazy day." Tom kissed him on the cheek, and the two leaned back on the couch.

Coop stretched the corner of a clean fitted sheet over the left side as Ethan pulled the opposite corner. "Well, this is definitely not what I expected we'd be doing tonight," Ethan said.

Coop shook his head and tucked the other corner. "No, definitely not. We're lucky, though. If we hadn't gone with them, odds are we would've been here, dicks deep in cannoli, and they would've been banging at the door again."

"Oof, well at least Liam caught that stuff earlier," Ethan said. "I was not a fan of the interruption, but I'm really thankful for what he did."

Coop passed Ethan a corner of the fluffy white blanket. "Yeah, me too. Do we like him?" Coop asked.

Ethan pulled his mouth to the side in thought.

Coop added, "I'm torn because he did all that stuff for us, and said nice things about your art, and the proposal, but he's still pretty rude."

Ethan looked around the room. "Yeah, I'm not too sure either. Whenever I consider what he did, I just feel a lot of different emotions. On one hand, I'm grateful that he thought to add those stipulations. But when I consider that, it makes me more nervous than anything. On the other hand, yeah, he's said some pretty rude stuff to us, but I think he really just wants to be our friend. So, I'm still deciding, I guess."

Coop came around and fluffed the pillows on Ethan's side and gave him a quick smooch on the mouth. "Well, I like who you like, and I hate who you hate, so it could go either way for me. I've never seen you change your mind on someone though, so he may be on the right track, unlike Lorenzo."

Ethan shook his head. "Lorenzo can never be redeemed, forget it. Liam, eh, he's got a chance."

The two stood side by side inspecting the room, with their eyes. "I think we got it all," Ethan said.

Coop walked over to the nightstand. "Yeah, I don't see any more cannoli cream. Weird that they're gonna sleep in here though."

Ethan shrugged. "It is, but what choice do they have? Their plane leaves tomorrow, this will be their last night sleeping in a bed before they leave. It's better than a couch bed."

Coop pointed up at the fan. "Is that?"

Ethan squinted, looking up. "How the hell did we get it up there?"

Coop grabbed one of the disinfectant wipes from the container they brought in. He wiped the blade down. "I don't know, but I can only imagine how much is on the fan in the upstairs room. This was just foreplay." They inspected the room one more time, then walked out into the living area.

Levi, Tom, and Liam were looking at Ethan's canvas sketch, which Liam held in his hands. Ethan's eyes widened. "Oh, I forgot I left that on the bed in there. I didn't want to get cannoli on it, so we moved it."

Liam shook his head. "No shame. Any of you. At all."

Ethan took the canvas and looked at it. Levi asked, "What's wrong Ethan? You can't imagine the baby's face yet?"

Coop shook his head and rested his chin on Ethan's shoulder.

"Nope. He stopped the other night and hasn't picked it back up. Says he can't picture him."

Ethan sighed. "Just hard to imagine what he'll look like. I sketch whatever I'm thinking about, and us bringing him home was what I was picturing."

Liam elbowed Ethan. "You must have a lot of sketches of X-rated cannoli activities then, right?"

"No, not really," Coop said. "Cannoli was a new thing for us. Frosting, now that's a different story."

Ethan gave Coop a quick smooch.

Liam snapped his fingers, realizing something. "Wait, I know what you can do. No, that might not work. Let me look into something. I'll be back in a minute, well, longer than a minute if Maddie's awake." He walked into the bedroom and closed the door.

Coop looked at Ethan and asked. "What do you think that was about?"

Ethan shrugged. "I have no idea."

Tom walked over to the black hotel phone on the side table. "I'm going to order room service"—he opened the table drawer—"do you guys have a menu?"

Ethan shook his head. "Nope. They'll make whatever you ask them to."

Tom pulled an eyebrow down. "I find that hard to believe."

Coop scoffed at him. "Well, I find it hard to believe that you told everyone what happened with grandpa, but you did."

Levi winced and bit his lip, looking down at the floor.

Tom pulled his head back in confusion, and looked at Levi, then back to Coop. "What did I say about that old sack of crap?"

"Nope." Coop shook his head. "Not gonna repeat that. Out of respect for Levi."

Tom looked at Levi. Levi closed his eyes and nodded slowly at him. Tom's mouth dropped, "No… I wouldn't have." He pulled Levi into his arms. "You must have been so embarrassed. I'm sorry. How did that even come up?"

Levi gave him a kiss. "Don't get upset about it, Tommy. Been awhile since I've seen you sloshed anyway."

Coop pulled Ethan over to the stairs, he whispered, "Do you want to order with them or just do our own thing? It's already late."

Ethan leaned against the staircase. "I'm really hungry. I'll eat whatever you want. Let's just order a bunch of stuff for everyone."

Around thirty minutes later, room service arrived with several carts of food. Coop gave them a big tip and thanked them. "Food's here, everyone," Ethan called down the hall.

Coop and Ethan made a big plate of food for themselves to share and went outside to the sitting area. The stars were especially bright, and there was a nice warm breeze, making an extremely beautiful setting. Ethan poked a toasted ravioli with his fork. "Here, try this, Cooper. You didn't have any the other day."

Coop opened his mouth, and Ethan fed him the ravioli. "Mmm, so good. I'm gonna miss this food."

"Same. But we're really gonna have to be sure to go to the gym in the morning."

Coop finished a few more pieces of ravioli, while Ethan twirled pasta around his fork. "I can't believe they're all sleeping over," Coop said.

Ethan nodded. "I know. So weird. Now we can't have sex."

Coop pulled his head back. "Says who?"

"Says me. We can't do that with everyone downstairs!"

Coop raised his eyebrows and looked around, surveying the landscape. He stood up and held his hand out to Ethan. "Come with me."

"Nuh-uh, I know what you're gonna do. You're gonna pull me

behind one of these hedges and do it. No. I can't, there's too many people inside."

Coop opened and closed his extended hand and looked at it. "You're gonna leave my hand open? You're not gonna hold it?"

Ethan tilted his head and placed his cloth napkin on the iron bistro table. He stood up and held Coop's hand, smiling. "You didn't deny what I said."

Coop brought their clasped hands to his mouth and kissed Ethan's hand. "No, I'm not gonna deny my intentions. I'm not thinking of a hedge or a bush, though."

"Well, whatever it is, we can't do it. Someone could come outside."

Coop bent down and rolled Ethan's pant legs up, slightly, then did the same to himself. They walked over to the small private pool and sat down on the edge. Coop pulled Ethan onto his lap, then embraced him from behind as the two placed their feet in the water.

"This is nice, the water is so warm," Ethan said.

Coop kissed his cheek. "Mmmhmm. So warm. We haven't even used this yet. It was so hard to find a room with its own private pool, too."

Ethan leaned back into Coop's firm embrace. Coop's right hand started slowly making its way toward Ethan's zipper. Ethan leaned back further to allow him access. Just as Coop gripped the zipper in between his thumb and forefinger, he heard the sound of the garden doors opening.

"Oh, there you guys are!" Liam shouted. "I thought you went up to your room already."

Coop gave Ethan's hardened dick a pat through his pants. "Later," he whispered in Ethan's ear.

Liam walked around the pool and sat on the other side. He swung his legs and feet in the water. He was wearing shorts now, so his legs were deeper in the water than Coop and Ethan's. He looked around and said, "Wow, this is really nice. I haven't seen a hotel room that had its own private pool. I thought everyone just used the resort pools." He pulled a lollipop out of his pocket and stuck it in his mouth.

Coop wrapped his arms tighter around Ethan from behind and looked at Liam over Ethan's shoulder. "Yeah, it was hard to find. I thought we'd use it, but this is the first time in the whole trip."

"We came out here the first day and looked around, "Ethan said. "Then I thought I'd paint over there by the garden, but it was too hot."

Liam snapped his fingers. "I remember what I came out here for. You said that you were having trouble imagining what your son's face was going to look like, so I looked some stuff up. You can request that the carrier has a 3D or 4D ultrasound done. That will give you a good look at his face. Then maybe you can finish your sketch and paint it."

Ethan and Coop looked at one another confused. Liam explained what a 3D ultrasound was, and what he'd just learned from an article online.

"I had no idea such a thing was possible," Ethan said. "I've only heard of regular ultrasounds."

Coop shook his head. "Me neither."

"I did something good for you guys again," Liam said. "You're welcome."

Ethan and Coop smiled and thanked him.

Liam laid back on the hard concrete surface, his legs still dangling in the water. "Do you guys think Maddie really wants me to propose to her?"

"Oof," Ethan said. "Well, it's hard to say. We haven't known either of you for very long. The way she was tonight, I'd say she does. The way she was the past few days, I don't know."

Coop nodded. "I agree. Larry did too, so maybe she really does. He was a stranger and called her out. He even gave her a 'boo, Peter', remember?"

Liam stared up at the stars and asked, "How did you guys know you wanted to get married?"

"Because Ethan is the only one that my heart has ever wanted."

Ethan gave Coop a quick kiss on the mouth, then said, "Because he let me call him Cooper."

Liam sat up. "Yeah, why is that? Even your paperwork says Coop, but Ethan calls you Cooper."

"It's special when he says it. The first time he said it to me, I knew we'd be together forever. I've always hated people saying it, but not Ethan. When he said it, everything just fell into place."

Ethan added, "We've been inseparable ever since. Haven't spent a single day apart."

Coop smooched his cheek. "And we never will."

Liam's phone dinged. "Ah, it's Maddie," he said, looking down. He hopped up and shook his legs off. "Alright, guys, thanks. This was fun and thanks for letting us stay the night. The hotel thing was just unbelievable. Can't be what you both had in mind for tonight."

Ethan stood up first and pulled Coop up by the hand, "Come on, my Cooper. I'm tired. Let's go to bed."

Coop held his hand and followed him inside. The hotel room was quiet as the two walked upstairs into the bathroom. Ethan headed straight inside the shower, leaving his clothes on the floor. Coop entered behind him and undressed. Ethan pointed at him through the glass shower door. "Seriously. I'm too uncomfortable with everyone down there. Both of you"—he pointed to Coop's face and dick—"need to behave if you come in here."

Coop looked down and spoke to his cock, "Did you hear him? He said there's no playtime tonight. Stay down." Coop slid the door open and got inside with Ethan.

No more than five minutes later, Coop was giving it to him hard from behind, while Ethan was bent over in the shower. He thrusted deep and whispered, "I thought you said you didn't want it? Yet here we are, couldn't resist my cock, isn't that right, Mr. Morgan?"

Ethan held a hand over his mouth and nodded.

Coop thrusted harder, as Ethan softly moaned. Coop whispered while slowing his pace, "Do you want me to put you in bed, or do you want to stay in here? It's hard for me to fuck you quietly with the echo in the bathroom, baby."

Ethan begged between thrusts, "Bed—please—mmm—fuck me—in bed."

Coop pulled out and licked Ethan's hole, then lightly smacked his ass. "Damn, baby, I just want to eat you out."

"Cooper, fuck. I'm not gonna be able to be quiet if you use your tongue like that." Ethan stood up straight and hung his arms around Coop's neck. Coop lifted him easily, and Ethan wrapped his legs around him tight, while Coop carried him to bed.

"Ride me," Coop said, passing Ethan the lube from the nightstand.

Ethan knelt beside him on the bed and squeezed some lube into his hand, then stroked Coop's cock. Coop loved the feeling of Ethan pumping him, but he loved the feeling of being inside him even more. He grabbed the lube and coated his fingers with it, reaching around and rubbing Ethan's already loose hole. "Mmm, baby, I can't wait anymore. Your ass is ready. Get on top of me."

Ethan climbed on top and moaned as Coop pushed deep into him from underneath. "Mmm—Cooper—it's too deep."

"Shh, if you don't want anyone to hear. I'll go slow." Coop held

Ethan's ass in his hands controlling the speed, moaning, while savoring the feeling of Ethan's warm hole gripping his cock. "Nice and slow, baby. Just like that. Mmm."

Ethan shook his head, riding him faster, bouncing harder. "Mmm—ungh—I'm gonna come—I—can't hold it."

"Do it. Come on me, I want you to. It's so fucking hot when you do it." He gripped Ethan's ass with one hand and stroked him quickly with the other, as Ethan moved up and down on his thick shaft. "Do it—Ethan—come all over your husband."

Ethan moaned, "Ungh—ungh—" His girthy piece exploded all over Coop's rock-hard chest. "Haah—haah—My Cooper."

Coop looked down at his chest. He swiped his fingers in Ethan's cum, bringing them to his mouth and tasting it. "Mmm—so good. You came so good for me, baby. Bounce a few more times for me, I'm right there, too."

Ethan leaned his head back in pleasure and rode Coop harder, and Coop came quickly and fiercely inside him. "Ungh—fuck—Ethan—hah—hah—"

Ethan stood up and grabbed two washcloths from the bathroom, he wiped himself off with one, then cleaned Coop's chest with the other. Coop smiled at him with his hands behind his head.

"I accept full responsibility for what just happened," Ethan said.

Coop nodded. "That's right, my little tease."

They rinsed off together in the shower quickly, put on their comfies and got into bed for the night.

Chapter 20
What Are They Always Whispering About?

Tom's voice whispered, "Coop, Coop, wake up."

Coop who was spooning Ethan, as per their normal sleeping position, looked up. "Dad? What the hell?" he whispered.

"Shhh," his dad said. "You'll wake everyone up. It's 5:00, you guys want to hit the gym?"

Coop blinked a few times. "What? No. Dad, we workout at six, not five."

"Since when? It's always been five."

Coop turned back over and spooned tight around Ethan, ignoring him.

Ethan answered, "Not since we got together, a few days after that we moved it to six."

Tom stood with his hands on his hips. "Well, I didn't know that. Can't you guys just go with me, now? I don't know where the gym is, and you probably need a key for the door."

"No, and no, you don't. Just follow the signs."

Tom scratched his head and looked down at the two. "Boys, I haven't worked out with you together. Come on, who knows when we'll have another chance to do it?"

Coop rolled over and looked up. "The gym is really small. It's barely big enough for two people."

Tom's posture dropped and he whined, "Come on, would you guys just get up?"

Ethan turned over and looked at Coop. "Maybe we should just go."

Coop groaned, "Ughhhh fiiine…we'll meet you downstairs in a few minutes."

Tom smiled and went back downstairs.

Coop kissed Ethan's cheek. "Good morning, baby. Sorry about him."

Ethan kissed him back. "Good morning. No, don't be sorry. It's cute that he wants to go with us. He looked like a little kid begging."

They got up and changed into their matching gray track pants, with gray compression shirts. Ethan looked Coop over and fanned himself. "Oof. You're making me hard at 5:30 in the morning, gonna be a long run."

Coop's mouth dropped open. "Again? Again, with the teasing? You never learn." He gave Ethan a crisp smack on the ass.

Ethan's phone chimed. "What? Who would even text us at this hour?" Coop asked.

Ethan grabbed the phone from the nightstand and shook his head. "It's Liam."

"What does he want at 5:30 in the morning?"

Ethan and Coop walked downstairs; Ethan held Coop's hand from behind. Tom and Liam were both waiting by the door. Coop shook his head them. "I told my dad, and I'll tell you, too. The gym is small. We're gonna be right on top of each other."

Liam shrugged. "I don't care. I think it'll be fun. I want to see how much you guys can lift."

The group walked through the quiet hotel to the gym. Ethan

peeked through the door once they rounded the corner. "Good, there's no one else here."

Coop held the door open for Ethan, and the rest of the group piled in behind him. "See," Coop said, gesturing to the small space, "told you guys. There's barely any room."

Liam walked over to the weight bench. "Alright, Coop, let's go. Show me what you can do."

Ethan put his hand on Coop's shoulder. "As much as I can't wait to see him do that, we need to run first."

Coop and Ethan got on the treadmills and started their run. Tom walked over to one of the elliptical machines. "I guess this is me, today," he said as he stepped onto the pedals.

Liam decided to use the elliptical machine next to Tom.

Once their individual warmups were done, the group made their way over to the weight bench.

Coop stared at Ethan, as Ethan briefly lifted his shirt to cool himself. *Such a little tease*, Coop thought. He walked over and whispered into Ethan's ear. Ethan's eyes widened.

Liam patted the stack of weights. "Alright, out of the three of you, who can lift the most? Has to be you, right?" He pointed to Coop.

"You insult me," Tom said. "Unbelievable, you insult me right to my face."

"Oh no. Cooper, listen to me, if you get hurt because of this, that means no sex. I'm just gonna throw that out there. Don't let them goad you," Ethan warned.

Coop rolled his eyes. "Like I'd let that happen."

Tom walked over to the weights and started piling them on both sides of the bar. Liam counted, then said, "Three hundred pounds?"

Tom lay under the bar, and Ethan stood above to spot him.

Coop chuckled. "Come on, Dad, three hundred pounds and my husband has to spot you? You're getting old."

Tom easily did ten reps and sat up. He patted Coop on the shoulder and said, "Come on, superstar, your turn."

Coop laid on the bench and looked up at Ethan. "We can't be here with him all morning. He's gonna try to go up in increments of twenty. Forget that."

Liam raised his eyebrows and asked, "How much do you want me to add?"

Coop waved him off. "None. Ethan will get them. He knows how much to add."

Ethan bent down and kissed Coop's forehead, then walked over to the weights. He came back with two fifty-pound weights, one in each hand and placed them on opposite ends of the bar.

Liam was in shock. "Ethan, you just carried fifty pounds in each hand like it was nothing! Hang on a minute, I gotta see something." He walked over to the weights stacked on the display and tried to lift a fifty-pound weight with one hand. "Holy shit! I can't do it. How strong are your hands, Ethan?"

Tom rolled his eyes and walked next to Liam. He easily lifted the fifty-pound weight with one hand. "Okay, that was unnecessary," Liam said. "I already said I couldn't do it. Didn't need to rub it in, Tom."

Tom playfully pushed Liam.

Ethan stood over Coop and looked down. "Cooper, listen to me; I don't want you going to your max, okay? Just stop at four hundred. For me?"

Coop nodded and smiled. "Okay, I promise."

"Is he saying that your max isn't four hundred?" Tom asked, walking over. "It was three-fifty the last time we worked out."

"Yeah, and when was that?" Coop asked. "My max is not four

hundred. I hit four hundred when Ethan and I got together, but recently I've gotten to four-forty."

Ethan smiled at Liam and Tom, whose jaws hung open.

"Bullshit," Tom said. "No way."

Coop looked up at Ethan and asked, "Do you still have the video, pup?"

Ethan pulled his phone out and showed both Tom and Liam a video of Coop at home in their new gym, lifting four hundred forty pounds.

Tom held his hand over his mouth. "What a monster you are. Wait till I tell Levi. He's gonna flip out."

Liam agreed, "Maddie too."

Tom waved Coop off. "Don't even bother lifting, I concede. I saw the video. I can get to three-fifty, that's my best."

"Oh, come on," Liam pleaded. "Just do a few, Coop. I've never seen anyone lift that much in-person."

Ethan patted Liam on the shoulder. "I'm gonna have him do something better. You want to see something cooler than weights, or are you just interested in the four hundred pounds?"

"Cooler," Liam said. "Definitely interested in something cooler, but what could be cooler?"

Coop sat up on the weight bench and looked at Ethan. "You're gonna let him see it?"

Ethan nodded as he placed a clean towel from the linen basket on the carpet covered floor. "Alright," Coop said as he laid down.

"I'm only letting him do two reps, or else he'll get carried away," Ethan said. "We joke about not being animals, but he really is one."

Coop held his arms up, and Ethan laid across his hands. Coop easily lifted Ethan once, then twice, fully extending up and back down, both times. Ethan smiled as he jumped up and pulled Coop into a standing position with his hand.

Liam stood in disbelief. "You just lifted a human being! That is a human! Your husband is a big guy, too! How much do you weigh, Ethan?

"Two-ten. Coop is two-twenty."

"Very impressive, son. That will come in handy when you're holding a crying baby all night." Tom and Liam chuckled together.

The four walked back toward the hotel room at a leisurely pace. Ethan and Coop held hands in front of Liam and Tom, who followed behind.

Coop whispered in Ethan's ear. Ethan said enthusiastically, "Yeah! Let's do that!"

Liam shook his head, and spoke to Tom, "I always wonder what they whisper about, do you?"

Tom furrowed his brow and pointed to Coop and Ethan while they walked. "Those two? No. I don't wonder. Use context clues, you're a lawyer. Nine times out of ten, they're either talking shit about someone, or it's sexual."

Ethan and Coop both gave a thumbs up over their shoulders with their free hands.

"Yeah, but who's to say which one that was?" Liam asked.

"Sexual." Ethan said.

"Hey, guys, I don't want to be rude, but I really don't want to take a bath after the gym. Can I use the shower upstairs?" Liam asked.

Coop looked behind at him. "How do you know we have a shower upstairs?"

Liam answered facetiously, "I snuck into your room last night, while you guys were asleep and found the shower."

Coop and Ethan stopped walking and turned around to face him.

Liam put his hands up and waved them side to side. "Come on,

I'm playing. I went up there the first day I met you guys, don't you remember?"

Ethan and Coop looked at each other. Ethan whispered in Coop's ear. Coop nodded and raised his eyebrows. "Ohhh, yeah."

Liam smiled, as the two turned back around, and started walking again.

"What are you smiling at them for?" Tom asked. "What did we just talk about?"

Liam thought for a second, then raised his eyebrows. "So that whisper was them talking shit about me?"

Coop and Ethan gave him a thumbs up over their shoulders. Ethan called backwards, "To be more accurate we were talking shit about the version of you that we met that day."

"That makes me feel better for some reason," Liam said.

They finally reached their room and stood in front of Ethan's honeymoon nemesis, the hotel room door. Coop held his phone toward Ethan. "Together, or you wanna try it solo? You can do it; I know you can."

Liam and Tom looked confused. Tom waved Liam off. "Don't bother asking, let's just wait."

Ethan jogged in place for a moment then shook his arms around and rolled his neck.

Coop moved Ethan's body to face the door and stood behind him. He placed his hands on Ethan's shoulders and rubbed. "Come on, baby. You can do it, just one swipe."

Ethan nodded. "Just one swipe, that's it."

Coop said loudly, "Wait, I know! Think of it"—he brought his mouth to Ethan's ear and whispered—"like a really quick, smooth lick on my cock."

Ethan waved the phone once, and the door opened immediately. "I finally did it! That worked!"

Coop clapped. "You did it, puppy! Only took a dirty metaphor to get it done. I'm so proud." The two shared a quick smooch, then walked inside with Tom and Liam behind them.

Liam shook his head. "Well, that whisper was definitely sexual. Hey, wait, so can I use the shower or not?"

Coop turned to face Liam. "Yeah, go ahead. Just don't touch any of our stuff. We'll be out here for a bit, make sure you lock the bathroom door."

Ethan grabbed four towels and passed one to Tom, one to Liam and kept two for himself and Coop, then he and Coop walked over to the outside door.

Liam nodded. "I will. Do you guys have body wash and shampoo I can use? I left that stuff at the hotel."

"Yeah," Ethan said. "You can use whatever is in there. The hotel brand stuff is still on the counter, we haven't used that."

Liam started walking up the stairs.

"Wait," Coop called out.

Liam stopped and turned around. "What?"

"This should go without saying, but don't use our bath poufs, man. There are washcloths in the basket near the sink."

Liam made a sour face. "That did not need to be said. Why would I do that?"

"I don't know," Coop said. "I just felt like I needed to say it."

Ethan opened the door, with Coop following behind him. They headed toward the pool, holding hands. "Ah, it's so nice and dark out here," Ethan said. "The sun isn't even up."

Tom stuck his head outside. "Hey, are you guys going in the pool?"

Coop hung his head back in annoyance. "Yeah. Just gonna cool down."

"Alright. I'm going to use the bathtub. Should've asked for the shower before Liam." He pulled his head inside and closed the door.

Ethan looked down at their bottom halves, then back to Coop. "We can't go in the pool with our track pants on."

Coop pumped his eyebrows at him. "I wasn't planning on it." He started to pull his pants down, but Ethan stopped him.

"Cooper, we cannot skinny dip with four other people inside the hotel."

Coop pulled an eyebrow down and looked at him. "Can't skinny dip like how we couldn't have sex with anyone in the suite, but did, last night? Or do you really mean it?"

Ethan looked around, feeling nervous. "What if someone comes out? We haven't seen Madeline or Levi yet, what if one of them comes outside? Levi would run back in, but I can't stand the thought of Madeline seeing that. No. Forget it."

Coop looked at Ethan and ruffled his hair. "Here, go stand by the door and tell me what you see."

Ethan jogged over to the door, and Coop stripped down to his tight black boxer briefs. He got into the water and stood facing Ethan in the pool, he asked, "Alright, baby, what can you see?"

"Just your shoulders and your chest," Ethan said, standing on his tippy toes. "But back up and let me see what it looks like if you're on the other side."

Coop shook his head. "No, just come over here. We'll stay right here on this side, and I'll face this way. Then we don't have to worry."

Ethan still felt a bit nervous, but knowing that Coop was in the pool, wearing nothing but his underwear, gave him the courage to strip. He quickly pulled his shirt and pants off and got into the pool. Coop held him tight as Ethan wrapped around him and kissed him on the cheek. "What time do we have to bring the Ferrari back? It's probably going to be a mess at the hotel. I can't even imagine how many people will be there, screaming at the valet."

Coop sighed. "Yeah, I don't know. We'll have to ask Liam. What do you think about the ultrasound idea by the way? We didn't touch on that again last night. Should we get that done?"

Ethan nuzzled his face next to Coop's neck and laid his head down, without a response.

Coop gave him a light bounce, while squeezing his ass. "You okay? What's wrong? We don't have to do that if you don't want to."

Ethan sighed, and lifted his head, looking at Coop. "I want to. I really do. But part of me thinks we should just wait and be surprised. I guess I can't explain it. It must sound crazy."

Coop gave him a smooch on the mouth and said, "It doesn't sound crazy to me. Let's skip it, then. She probably wouldn't want to do it anyway."

"Yeah, it will be a surprise when we get to see him. I'll just finish the picture then."

Coop's eyes widened as he looked at the door. He whispered, "Don't move, baby."

Liam walked outside, he'd barely taken a step before Coop yelled over, "No. Liam, go back inside."

Ethan shook his head against Coop's shoulder. "I knew this was going to happen."

"I need to tell you guys something," Liam said, as he took a few steps closer.

"Stop, Liam!" Coop shouted.

Liam's mouth fell open, and he snapped his fingers. "No! Are you guys having sex? In the pool? The sun is up for crying out loud!"

Ethan looked backwards over his shoulder. "Don't be stupid. We're in our underwear. We're not having sex!"

"Oh, okay, who cares then?" Liam asked. "I'm not interested in your underwear. We're all guys."

Coop shook his head. "No. It's not the same. Go inside, we'll be there in a minute."

Liam put his hands up and headed back towards the door. "Okay, fine," he said, then walked inside.

Ethan was still wrapped around Coop tightly. Coop squeezed his ass and bounced him a few times, grinding against him. "Let's go inside," Ethan whispered. "They'll be leaving soon anyway." He could tell Coop was disappointed, but with the sun out, and their company roaming around the inside of their hotel, he couldn't have sex with him in the pool, at least not while their company was here.

Coop bounced him a few more times, and Ethan held his face in return. "I love you, my Cooper. I love you so much."

Coop tilted his head and brought his mouth near Ethan's. "I love you, Ethan. I always will." He pressed their lips together and gave Ethan a quick swirl of his tongue. Ethan kissed him back then unwrapped himself from Coop's embrace.

They walked out of the pool and noticed matching hard situations pressed against each other's briefs. Ethan winced and passed Coop a towel. "Here, wrap up tight and just stay behind me."

Coop pointed at Ethan's dick. "Me? What about you?"

"I can play it off, just stick him really close behind me, get in nice and tight and go in fast."

Coop shook his head. "Your words! Your words, puppy... Seriously."

"What did I say?"

"Oh, you don't know, huh?"

They wrapped their bottom halves in towels and headed inside, with Coop following closely behind Ethan. They looked around and didn't see anyone, so they quickly dashed up the stairs before anyone saw them.

Liam called up the stairs, "Are you guys dressed, can I come up?"

Coop's mouth dropped and he shook his head, still wrapped in his towel.

Ethan shouted downstairs, "No, we're getting dressed! We'll be down in a few minutes!"

Chapter 21
Best Thing Ever

Liam was standing at the base of the stairs when Levi and Tom came out of the guest bedroom. "Good morning, Liam," Levi said. "Heard you guys had fun at the gym this morning."

Liam nodded. "Yeah, but they're back to being jerks again. I wanted to tell them something."

Madeline joined the group from the opposite side. "What are you all standing around for? We should pack up and head out. I just saw on the news that there are a bunch of delayed flights. Where are Ethan and Coop? I need to go over a few things with them."

Liam pointed upstairs. Madeline yelled, "Hey! We're leaving soon, I need to go over some things with you guys!"

Coop and Ethan walked downstairs. Coop held his hands up. "What are you yelling for? You probably just woke the people across the hall up."

Ethan shook his head. "So loud."

Madeline flared her nostrils and walked into the bedroom that she and Liam used last night.

"Good news, guys," Liam said. "I called the rental car place. They have a twenty-four-hour line. I told them about what happened at the hotel, which they already knew from a few other renters. They said they'd pick the car up, because they have other cars there in the same situation. So, you guys don't need to worry about bringing it back."

Ethan and Coop nodded, they both smiled and thanked him.

Liam whispered, "One more thing, but don't get mad. I wouldn't recommend doing that 3D ultrasound, it gave me a weird feeling for some reason. But, also, the baby kind of looks like an alien made out of cheese, well at least the ones I saw online did. I wouldn't do it."

Ethan dropped an eyebrow. "Made out of cheese…what?"

Coop put a hand on Ethan's shoulder. "Cheese or no cheese, we already decided that we weren't going to do it. Ethan and I would rather be surprised."

Levi from across the room added, "Yeah, I wouldn't do that, either."

Madeline brought her laptop out and pulled up the surrogacy documents. They went over everything again, quickly. "So, I'm still your attorney, but I won't have much to do as long as things go smoothly from here on out. Now, if something should not go as planned, or if you need anything. You just call me."

Liam looked disappointed as he crossed his arms and looked at Maddie. She held her palms out toward him. "What is with you today? You've been running around crazy for the last thirty minutes. We didn't forget anything. What is your deal?"

"No, it's nothing," Liam said. "I'm sure we didn't leave anything out."

Maddie raised her eyebrows and looked up at Liam. "Of course we didn't."

Liam's arms remained crossed, while he looked over her shoulder at the computer. She swatted at him. "Stop it, don't hover over me like that. What is wrong with you today?"

Coop whispered in Ethan's ear, and Ethan whispered back through laughter.

Liam stood next to Maddie and took control of the computer, scrolling through the documents and nodding. After a few moments of silently searching, he said, "You guys should probably make two reservations for when you come to pick him up. One for the week before the due date and one for a month before…no, that doesn't make sense…well, you could get vacation insurance that allows you to move the dates, but that could be bad too. I'm sure we'll know more after her next appointment. Who knows what kind of a doctor she's been seeing. We need to make sure that your Nonna asks all the questions that you guys have, so make sure you write them down. Well, the doctor is supposed to call you both after the appointment anyway, so she really doesn't need to even ask for you, I guess."

The entire group stared speechless at Liam. He'd been rambling on for several minutes without any input from the group.

Maddie looked at him seriously and asked, "Are you okay?"

Levi said, "Yeah, Liam, they're just really annoying, right?"

Liam smiled at Coop and Ethan. "Guys, you can call me too. I'll always be around to help."

The group said their goodbyes and brought their luggage to the door.

As the group started to leave, Ethan whispered to Coop and Coop nodded. "Okay, pup, but just this once. No one else, ever again. Ever, okay?"

Ethan nodded in understanding.

Coop called out, "Liam, hold up, come here for a minute."

Liam walked over and lifted his chin. "What's up?"

Coop stood on Liam's left side and Ethan stood on Liam's right. They nodded at one another over his head, then both brought their faces close to Liam's ear on the side they each stood on.

Liam's face lit up between them. "Oh my God. Is this happening? Are you guys gonna whisper to me?!"

Ethan whispered, "This is a secret, we don't like Madeline."

Coop whispered, "We think she's terrible." They both patted him on each shoulder and smiled.

Liam smiled big. "I am so happy right now. I don't even care that you just insulted my girlfriend. That was so great. Best thing ever."

They both shook his hand and thanked him for everything he'd done.

Coop leaned against the door after the group finally made its way out. Ethan sank into the couch. "Oof, I am dreading the thought of the airport tomorrow morning. But I'll be happy when we're back in our home."

Coop nodded and walked over to him. "Me too," he said, as he sat beside him. He kissed him on the cheek. "Alright, it's the last day of our honeymoon. What should we do?"

"Whatever you want. I'm so tired," Ethan said, laying his head against Coop's shoulder.

Coop ruffled Ethan's hair and kissed the top of his head. "Maybe we can just relax for a bit and go out later. Is there anything that you wanted to do that we didn't get to?"

"Nope, but if there's something you want to do, let's do it."

Coop's phone rang, interrupting their planning. "Oh, look its Kai. I told him not to call until we were back."

Ethan smiled at him. "Just put it on speaker."

"Hey, Kai, we're still in Italy, what's up?"

"Well, yeah," Kai said. "But you're leaving in like an hour or two, so you're probably just sitting at the airport. I want to hear how the trip was."

Coop corrected him, "No, we leave tomorrow."

"What day is today?" Kai asked. "It's Saturday, right?"

"Yeah, it's Saturday the…" His eyes almost fell out of his head. "Oh my God, Ethan!"

Ethan pulled his phone out of his pocket and looked at their tickets. "Cooper! Our flight leaves in an hour!"

Chapter 22
He Is A Nice Guy, Though

Ethan hopped off the couch, and Coop hung up on Kai in a panic. "Okay, we can do this, baby…we just need to pack everything really fast," Coop said.

They ran up the stairs and threw their clothes and various souvenirs in their suitcases. Ethan looked under the bed, then popped back up. "Maddie did say there were delays this morning. Maybe we'll make it."

"Do you think they're on the same flight?" Coop asked.

Ethan shrugged and tucked his canvas sketch inside his suitcase, wrapping a few shirts around it.

Coop called the concierge and pleaded for the next available taxi. The concierge assured them that there were several on standby for the airport and stated that she would personally make sure one was available.

Ethan called Tom, while Coop did a lap around upstairs, checking for any forgotten items. Tom answered, "Hey, Ethan, what's going on? Did we forget something?"

"No. What's your flight number?"

Coop pulled both large suitcases downstairs, while Ethan followed and dragged the rolling carry-on bag.

Tom replied, "Flight 0419, why? You sound out of breath is everything okay?"

Ethan passed Coop the phone and did a quick search of the downstairs rooms. Coop shouted, "Dad, we're on the same flight as you guys! We're leaving for the airport in two minutes, just doing a quick once over!"

Levi and Tom shouted, "What?!"

"We screwed our days up. I have no idea what we were thinking. How is it there? Maddie said there were delays, right? Please tell me our flight is one of those."

Levi shouted from the background, "It's delayed but only by twenty-five minutes!"

Ethan ran out of the bedroom. "We're good, that's everything! Let's go! Bye, Tom."

Coop asked, "Are you sure that's everything? What about your canvas?"

Ethan pushed Coop out the door. "I wrapped it in some shirts. Come on, we gotta go."

They ran quickly through the outdoor walkways and found a taxi driver standing in wait. The taxi driver pointed at them, then opened the trunk with a smile. They tossed their luggage in, just as rain began to fall. Once inside, they laid their heads back on the seats and high-fived.

Tom answered a call from Coop while staring at the flight boards beside Levi.

"Hey, Coop, are you on the way?"

"Dad...we're in the taxi...what's the situation there?" he asked between breaths.

"Are you actually out of breath?"

"Dad, shut up, you're on speaker…yes…I can't believe this is… happening. We just packed…everything in, like…ten seconds."

Tom looked at the large flight boards and found their flight. "You guys are good. It's raining here. It still says delayed twenty-five minutes."

Ethan asked, "Tom, are you guys reading it correctly? Neither of you speak Italian."

"Yes, Maddie taught us what it said as soon as we got here, so we wouldn't bother her while she fights with Liam."

"Why is she fighting with Liam?" Ethan asked.

Tom looked at Maddie and Liam who sat arguing in a pair of seats away from where he and Levi stood. "I have no idea, I think Maddie just likes to fight, honestly."

"What about your easel?" Coop asked Ethan. "You left it. Maybe I can call the hotel and have them ship it to us."

"No, that's very sweet, but don't worry about it. I have three different easels at home. Maybe we can ask them to donate it to the children's home… Oh! That's something we haven't thought about before. Remind me when we get home to look into getting easels for the kids at the children's home."

Tom chimed in, "That's a great idea!"

"I forgot you were still on, Dad. Just don't let that plane leave without us. Do whatever you have to do. We'll be there soon."

Tom placed his phone in his pocket and walked over to Levi. "Boys say they're on the way. They'll be here soon. Coop told me to do whatever we can to make sure the plane doesn't leave without them."

Levi walked near the large window and looked at the planes taking off and landing. "Well, it's raining, so that helps them. How did they get their days mixed up?"

Tom shook his head. "I have no idea. Maybe the baby stuff threw them off."

Levi stared at Maddie and Liam with his arms crossed, he bit his bottom lip.

"What are you thinking about," Tom asked.

Levi pulled his mouth to the side. "Just thinking of an emergency plan if they don't make it in time."

"Well, out of the four of us here, my angel definitely has the most dramatic flair." Tom rubbed his cheek softly.

"Yes, well, I can't deny that." He dropped an eyebrow at Tom. "You're calling me angel again, Tommy. What's going on? Did you grab a toddy when I wasn't looking?"

Tom pulled his head back. "What the hell is a toddy?"

"A toddy… like a drink…you've never heard anyone say that?"

"No, when did you hear it? Who even says that?"

Levi shrugged. "I don't know. A lot of people I work with."

"That's funny. No, I didn't have a toddy."

Liam and Maddie were locked in a loud argument sitting in the far row of seats. Maddie shouted, "It doesn't matter! You're supposed to stick up for me, no matter what!"

Liam threw his hands up. "How many times do we have to go over this? You expect that I should know automatically how to respond in every situation. Maddie, we were dating in secret for months, forgive me if I don't always react the way you want me to."

"No, I don't expect that, but if someone said something rude about you, I would put them in their place."

"You would not. You're always telling people that I'm a prick, or a jerk, or a little shit…come on, Maddie, be serious. If you're going to fight with me about some dumb security guard that we'll never see again, at least admit that you don't always stick up for me."

Tom shook his head at Levi, while the two watched their

argument. "Security is gonna come over here if Maddie doesn't calm down," Tom said. "Should we say something?"

"Nah," Levi said. "It's not our place."

"That was before we were dating in public!" Maddie shouted. "I haven't done that since then."

"So, since yesterday?" Liam argued. "It's new, Maddie. I'm not mad that you don't. I'd rather people think those things about me. I don't want people thinking I'm a nice guy, anyway."

"Good, because you aren't a nice guy, Liam. It's one of the things I like about you. You start being too nice, and people will take advantage of you."

Liam threw a hand up in frustration and shook his head. "You make no sense. Literally." He alternated hands, arguing conflicting views. "You want me to be a jerk, but you want me to stick up for you. Which one is it? A jerk can't stick up for his girlfriend. Maddie, just tell me what you want from me."

Maddie abruptly stood up and covered her mouth. "Stop! I'm gonna throw up." She ran toward the bathroom with Liam chasing behind.

Levi and Tom quickly walked after them.

Liam stood against the wall opposite the women's bathroom entrance, with his eyes closed.

"Hey, kid, what's wrong?" Tom asked.

Liam patted his pockets. "Damn it!"

"Are you okay?" Levi asked. "You guys have been arguing since we got here."

"I'm good. She said she felt like she was gonna puke and ran in there."

Levi's mouth turned down. "Maybe she ate something bad?"

"I don't know, she was in the bathroom for a while this morning, too. I think her stomach has just been bothering her. She's also been mean all morning. More than usual."

Tom patted his shoulder. "You guys were together, but also not together for a long time It's just going to take some getting used to."

"That's what I told her! It was probably that way for you two, right? You were apart for a long time, I'm sure it took a while before you got used to being around each other all the time."

Levi and Tom looked at each other and shook their heads.

"No," Levi said. "Not really, but our situation was far from comparable. We were essentially waiting for each other for over twenty-one years. Everything fell into place when we got back together."

Tom kissed Levi on the cheek. "Yeah, it really did. But, Liam, don't compare other relationships to your own. Everyone is different. Each relationship is unique. Just because we don't argue or fight doesn't mean that people that do shouldn't be together."

"It's just been an eye-opening trip, being around the four of you," Liam said. "I think that's the kind of relationship I want. I don't like fighting with her. Everyone else, I love fighting with. It's one of the reasons I became a lawyer. I love screaming about being right, and convincing other people to believe me, but with Maddie its just—"

"Annoying?" Levi asked.

Liam shook his head. "It's not annoying. It's frustrating."

Tom and Levi shared a look of understanding.

Tom stood silent, considering if it was his place to say anything. He really liked Liam and hated seeing him so upset.

Levi swung his carry-on bag side-to-side lightly and looked at Liam. "Riiight, but you really like her, so I'm sure it will work out."

Tom wasn't so sure about that.

Maddie walked out of the bathroom. Her face was pale, and her hair was a mess. She saw the three and rolled her eyes. "Three guys standing outside of a women's bathroom, looks a little weird. Someone's going to call the cops on you. You look like bunch of perverts standing there."

Deciding to forgo a reply, Tom and Levi walked back toward the waiting area and sat in two open seats. Tom exhaled and looked at Levi. "Liam just said frustrating, not annoying."

Levi nodded. "Yeah. I picked up on that." He looked around the concourse from his seat, then stood up, placing his carry-on bag on Tom's lap. "Tommy, hold this for me, I'll be right back."

Tom watched as Levi walked quickly over to one of the many snack shops in the airport. He saw a few women turn to stare at him. Tom thought, *He's so cute. I could never fight with him. I don't know if Liam and Maddie are going to make it. Wait, what the hell is he buying?*

Levi walked back, smiling brightly at Tom, while swinging a small plastic bag on his wrist. He sat in the seat beside him and quickly kissed his cheek. "Are Liam and Maddie still by the bathrooms? I don't see them."

"Me neither. Maybe she still isn't feeling well." Tom answered a call on his phone. "Hey, Coop, are you guys here? Looks like we're almost ready to start boarding."

Coop sounded exhausted, "We're coming into the concourse now. We just got through security. What a mess. Where the hell is it? Where is our gate?"

A voice on the speaker announced, in Italian, "Flight 0419 now boarding first-class, all first-class passengers for flight 0419, please proceed to gate T."

Coop yelled into the phone, "We're running past gate A! Where is gate T?"

Maddie and Liam rounded the corner, Maddie was holding her carry-on bag. She pointed at the gate, looking at Tom and Levi. "That's us, are you guys coming?"

Tom shook his head. "No, we're waiting for Coop and Ethan."

Maddie either didn't register what Tom said, or she just didn't care. She continued walking toward the gate.

Liam tilted his head looking at Tom. "What? Why are you waiting for them? Did you guys forget something?"

"Nope," Levi said. "But they forgot that they were on this flight. They thought their flight was tomorrow."

Liam chuckled. "Oh, wow. That's so funny." He looked around. "Where are they?" Levi smiled and passed Liam the small plastic bag. "Why are you giving me"—Liam's eyes widened, and he looked up at Levi—"lollipops! Yes, thank you! I ran out last night. This makes me so happy! Thank you, Levi." He quickly put a lollipop in his mouth and smiled.

Maddie boarded the flight, leaving Tom, Levi, and Liam standing by the door.

Coop and Ethan rounded the corner, running at full speed, nearly knocking into a few people. Liam pointed his lollipop at them. "See, now it would've been funnier if Coop had him slung over his shoulder."

Tom walked over and patted Coop and Ethan's backs. "Great timing. Let's go home."

After a pretty uneventful flight and layover, the couples headed their separate ways. Liam stopped Tom and Levi as they headed towards a taxi. "Hey, thank you both for everything. This was a much-needed wake up call for me. I learned a lot from watching you. Now, if I never see you again, it'll be because she killed me and hid my body."

Levi looked at him softly. "Liam, if you ever need anything, just call us."

Tom smiled and patted his shoulder. "Yes, and we'll see you guys at the gala, right?"

"I think so. But if not, I'll see you around." Liam smiled and walked away, hopping into the taxi that Maddie was waiting in.

Chapter 23
Home Sweet Home

Coop and Ethan dropped their bags at the front door of their new home. Ethan inhaled deeply. "I love the smell here. I missed our home. Cooper, lets never leave again."

Coop smiled and walked over to the large kitchen counter, he placed the mail that Sal handed them at the gate onto the counter. He thumbed through, making a pile of junk and important pieces. "Junk, junk, junk, junk…one important…more junk… Why do they waste so much paper on this? Who asked these people to send us mailers about buying a new car, or realtor information?"

Ethan walked around him and turned the lights on. He looked through the sliding panoramic doors, facing the garden and pool. "Garden looks good. The landscapers are doing a good job. Which window was it that Sal said was fixed yesterday?"

Coop pulled his mouth to the side. "I think it was the one next to ours. Let's go see."

They held hands and walked through the long halls. Ethan peeked into a room on the left. "Nope, not this one."

"I think it was the one next to ours upstairs, really. Do you want me to call Sal?" Coop asked.

"Nah, we can figure it out. Let's check the room you're thinking of."

They walked upstairs and found lightly dusted footprints on the gray, wood flooring. Ethan winced at the sight, knowing that Coop was probably going to lose it on the contractors. He shook his head and lightly rubbed Coop's back. They'd moved into their new home just two weeks before the wedding, so everything was still very new. Ethan opened the door to the bedroom that was closest to theirs. There were dark footprints everywhere, and the beautiful seafoam-colored walls that surrounded the window had smudges on them. The window itself was covered in fingerprints and dust.

Coop threw his hands up. "Nope. This is not happening. I'm calling them. They're gonna fix this." He pulled his phone out and called the window installers.

Ethan tapped the glass, then opened and closed the window. The alarm chimed and announced, "Bedroom five, window open." Ethan looked around the room, equally annoyed with the mess.

Coop screamed at the business owner on the phone, "I don't care, this is unacceptable! This is a brand-new house, your guys left footprints and fingerprints everywhere!"

Ethan stood in front of him and rubbed his arms to calm him. Coop pressed their foreheads together and inhaled. Being close to Ethan seemed to calm him. His tone was softer when he spoke again. "Yeah. Just send someone out to clean it up tomorrow, please. We just got home, and I don't want to deal with anyone right now. Thanks."

Coop held Ethan's face in his hands and kissed him deeply. He pulled back and looked at him. "Now, we have a ton of stuff to get ready for: we have the doctor's appointment tomorrow, the gala on Tuesday night, and Arie's party on Friday. There's a lot to do."

Ethan pulled his own shirt off, then removed his pants slowly, teasing Coop. "Yeah, I know…but I'm feeling kind of tense from the last twenty-four hours." He rubbed his bulge through his tight black briefs. "I think I'm gonna soak in the hot tub first."

Coop tossed an underwear-clad Ethan over his shoulder, smacking his ass lightly. "Naughty. Not even home for twenty minutes and you're already teasing me. Now you're gonna get it." He carried him downstairs to the hot tub.

Maddie and Liam stood locked in argument, inside the home that Maddie had shared with Liam's late father. Liam yelled, "What am I supposed to do? You're telling me to leave, just because you don't want to try? Because it's too hard?"

Maddie crossed her arms. "Yes, it's just not worth it, Liam. This isn't going to work. You know it isn't."

Liam shook his head in disbelief and screamed, "This is unbelievable! Where am I supposed to go? I can't go to Kory and Luke's, and I don't want to sleep in a fucking hotel! I've been in a hotel for days. This is bullshit, Maddie!"

"I don't care," Maddie said. "Just go. If I change my mind, I'll let you know."

Liam stormed outside and sat inside his car. Remembering that both Tom and Levi said to reach out if he needed anything, he decided to call Tom, who didn't answer. He dropped his head against the headrest. "Damn it, I really didn't want to call him," he said, as he dialed Kory's phone number.

Kory answered, in a voice lacking any emotion, "Hi, Liam, did you just get back?"

"We got back earlier this morning. Hey, can I stay the night with you guys? Before you say no, I really don't have anywhere else to go, man."

He listened as Kory spoke to Luke. "Do you care if he spends the night?"

Luke asked, "Do I care if who spends the night? I'm texting Maddie. I have no idea who you're talking to."

"I'm talking to Liam; do you care if he spends the night?"

"Of course, he can spend the night. I guess the baker won't be making an appearance tonight, though."

Kory was silent for a moment.

"Hello, Kory, are you there?" Liam asked. "I'm sorry. I really didn't want to have to call you."

Kory answered, "Yeah, it's fine. Come on over."

Liam arrived a few hours later after stopping to grab a bite to eat. Walking up to the door, he knew he was gonna have to answer for his secret relationship with Maddie. He knocked on the door, and Kory let him inside without saying a word, while Toby, their puppy who had grown quite a bit since Liam last came over, seemed excited to see him.

Liam bent down to pet him. "Hi, Tobes, look how big you've gotten. What are they feeding you here?" Liam kissed him on the head. "Hey," Liam said to Kory. "I'm really sorry about this. I don't know what happened. Honestly."

Kory scratched his head and walked toward the guest room, while Liam and Toby followed behind. "Come on, Kory, are you just gonna ignore me? Are really you that pissed?"

Kory walked inside the room without a reply.

Luke came from the other side of the hall and stopped Liam. "Hi, Liam, how…uh…never mind probably not great… Kory made pasta tonight. Do you want me to reheat some for you? Or did you already eat?"

"Nah, thanks, though. I just grabbed a burger from The Pig and The Swan. I'm full."

Luke's face brightened. "I love that place. It's so good. The little pig at the drive thru is so cute."

Liam and Luke joined Kory in the guest room. Liam opened the closet, and his mouth fell open. "Did you throw my stash out?"

Luke made a disgusted face and looked at Kory.

Kory rolled his eyes at Liam. "Yes, I threw your damn lollipops out months ago."

Liam dropped his head back. "That suuuucks." He shut the closet and laid flat on the bed, arms wide. He looked side to side and patted the comforter. "Is this a new bed, too?"

"Yeah, it's a better mattress," Kory answered.

Liam looked up at Luke. "How much did she tell you?"

Luke shrugged. "Oh…not too much."

Toby barked looking at Liam.

"Shh," Luke said rubbing Toby's head. "Don't be a gossip."

Liam knew very well that Maddie had filled him in on everything. His phone rang and he looked down at the screen, it was Tom calling. "Hey, guys, sorry, I need to take this," he said to Luke and Kory. "It's Tom Morgan."

Luke recapped Liam's current situation. "Yes, it is totally normal for you to be on the phone with my stepfather, after getting thrown out by your girlfriend, who was almost your stepmother. This is all very normal."

Kory shook his head, guiding Luke out of the door. "There is nothing normal about any of what you just said."

Liam explained the situation to Tom and Levi. They said they weren't surprised in the least, in fact they'd discussed this very thing on the plane.

Tom said to Liam, "Listen, the side of the estate that Coop and Ethan used to live in is empty. Now, you can't stay there forever, but temporarily, until you get things figured out, you can stay with us."

Liam held a hand on his forehead. "Thanks. But you've only known me for a week, you'd really let me do that?"

Levi joked in the background, "People have been murdered by people they've known for years. Besides, if you do anything stupid, we can both kick your ass."

"Thanks," Liam said. "I'll stay here tonight and call you guys tomorrow if that's okay. Shit, I have to work with her tomorrow, too. Never mind about that. I'll call you in the morning. Thanks, again."

Chapter 24
Unexpected News

The next morning, Coop and Ethan excitedly sat in front of Ethan's laptop inside their office. Their new home office faced the ocean, which was only a few miles away. The custom white bookshelves, nautical décor, and aqua accents made it a very relaxing work environment.

They anxiously awaited the doctor's arrival in their virtual meeting room. Coop wrapped his arm around Ethan's shoulder and squeezed him. "Don't be nervous, pup. It's gonna be great. We'll get to ask him everything that we want and see where things stand."

Coop's phone was face-up on the desk beside the laptop. A call from Liam showed on the display.

Ethan answered the phone on speaker, "Hey, Liam, what's up?"

"Hey, Ethan, I was just calling to see how everything went with the doctor. Was everything okay?"

"We're actually just waiting for the doctor to come on video now. We haven't met with him yet."

"Oh, okay," Liam said. "Do you guys want me to stay on speaker in case anything legal comes up?"

Coop shook his head. Ethan said, "No, I think we're okay, but thanks, Liam."

"Oh, okay, uh, well, listen, I'm going to be staying—"

The doctor appeared on the laptop screen. Coop picked up the phone from the desk. "Liam, sorry, but we gotta go, the doctor's here. We'll talk to you later." He ended the call.

The doctor introduced himself and explained the way that the delivery would work in a perfect scenario. Coop and Ethan asked many questions about the baby's health and movements, which the doctor happily explained. He also shared a sound clip of the baby's heartbeat, bringing tears to both Coop and Ethan's eyes. Those tears were quickly replaced with panic-stricken faces as the doctor said that the carrier's condition was far worse than he anticipated. On top of that, it turns out that she was already around thirty-six–thirty-seven weeks pregnant based on measurements.

Coop wasn't completely sure what all of this meant, but based on the Doctor's disposition, it wasn't good. "Doctor, what does that mean, exactly?"

The doctor pulled up a diagram and shared the image on screen. He explained that normally, this would mean they'd have another three to four weeks before delivery, give or take a few days. However, with the carrier's condition, they'll need to plan for a C-section sometime within the next two to three weeks. He also advised them that she could go into early labor on her own, and they should be prepared for that.

Ethan's eyes went wide as he looked at Coop and held both hands over his mouth.

"Yes, I'm sure this is a shock," the doctor said. "Those free clinics are great, they really are, but it's good that we caught this. I'm not supposed to really discuss this with you, but between the three of us, her odds of her survival are not great. She also doesn't seem to care either way, which is distressing enough on its own. There were several times during the exam, that she asked if I could just take him out, which was alarming. She's one of the most unstable carriers I've ever met."

Coop rubbed Ethan's back, trying to comfort him. He hadn't felt this helpless in so long. "What can we do, Doctor?" Coop asked. "We need to make sure she doesn't do anything to hurt him, or herself."

"At this point I'm considering an in-home nurse for her. Of course, that would be up to you both as well. She wouldn't be able to afford it, and I'm sure she wouldn't want that either. I don't know what kind of language was in your agreement, so I'm not sure if you could legally force the issue or not. You need to consult with your attorney."

Ethan's chin rested on his left palm as he spoke to the doctor through tears, "What about our son? You said he'll be delivered early, from what I read, babies grow the most during the last month. Will he be okay?"

The doctor leaned back in his chair and smiled. "I have confidence that he'll be fine. He may need to stay at the hospital for a couple weeks, but that's going to depend on how soon we have to deliver him and how much he's grown. The timetable is always messy with these situations, but try not to worry. The positive here is that you'll be meeting your baby very soon. Contact my office as soon as you speak with your attorney, so we can decide on a course of action for the nurse."

They thanked him and ended the video. Ethan held back tears as he looked at Coop. "I need to lay down, I-I'm fine. I just need to go lay down for a bit."

Coop held his hand while they walked down the hall and into their bedroom. Ethan got into bed, and Coop laid beside him. Ethan tucked in close, laying his head on Coop's chest and softly started to cry.

Coop rubbed his back. "Shh, don't cry, baby. It's gonna be okay.

I'll call Madeline and we'll get it all straightened out. He's gonna be okay, don't cry."

Ethan fell asleep after a few minutes of Coop consoling him. Coop didn't want to move him, but there was a lot that needed to be done. *If I move him and he wakes up, he's gonna be worried about all this stuff. I have to fix what I can before he wakes up*, he thought.

Coop texted both Madeline and Liam via group message. He turned his phone to silent mode, so Ethan wouldn't be disturbed.

Coop: *I can't talk right now but we have a few problems. Are either of you available to text?*

Liam: *I am. What are the problems?*

Coop: *Carrier will need to deliver within 2–3 weeks. We need to force an in-home nurse because she's unstable.*

Liam: *That changes things as far as the timeline. Unstable in what way?*

Madeline: *Are you their lawyer now? I thought you were just helping when we were abroad.*

Liam: *I told you I wanted to take over their case. Unprofessional to argue in front of a client.*

Liam: *Sorry, guys.*

Coop: *It's just me. Ethan is asleep. Can one of you help, please?*

Madeline: *I certainly can.*

Liam: *I can, too. Don't forget, she left out two crucial things in your agreement.*

Madeline: *Burn on your ex. Very professional.*

Coop: *I'm leaving this chat. I don't care which of you handles it. To answer your question, Liam, she is unstable mentally and physically. The doctor said the safest thing would be a 24-hour in-home nurse. We'll pay whatever it takes to make that happen. Figure it out and get back to me.*

Coop shook his head looking at his phone, he couldn't believe how immature the both of them were acting when he was dealing with something so serious. He rubbed his fingertips on Ethan's back and felt his eyes start to close, but before he could get too comfortable, Ethan's dad texted him.

Coach: *Hi, Coop. I didn't get to talk to Ethan when he called Gina this morning. I just tried calling him, but he didn't answer. Did everything go ok with the doctor's appointment?*

Coop: *Yes and no. Ethan is asleep. I don't want to share anything that he may want to tell you himself.*

Coach: *What's wrong?*

Coop: *There's just a lot happening.*

Coach: *Please have Ethan call me when he wakes up.*

Coop: *I will.*

Coop remembered that he'd cut Kai off before they left Italy, so he texted him too.

Coop: *Hey, sorry about hanging up on you. You saved our asses. We would have missed our flight if it weren't for you.*

Kai replied almost instantaneously.

Kai: *Don't worry about it. I can't believe you guys mixed up your dates. You're both so organized, I'm in shock. How is everything else?*

Coop: *We're adopting a baby, it's kind of a surrogate situation. Long story.*

Kai: *Whoa…that's crazy because I have news, too.*

Coop: *What kind of news?*

Kai: *Sorry, that's amazing and I'm happy for you guys. Remember that I said Ayame had a gig lined up in Hawaii?*

Coop: *Yep.*

Kai: *We leave in a few days. I'm gonna surprise her with a beachside proposal.*

Coop: *Good luck. That's great. I'm sure she'll say yes.*

Coop felt his eyes closing. He couldn't focus on texting anymore. Ethan's body was too warm and comforting beside him.

Kai: *Thanks. I'll let you know when she says yes.*

Coop kissed Ethan's head and closed his eyes. He went over everything else that needed to be done. *Alright, what else can I do? I need to try and find a home for us to rent when we're in Italy... What dates do I use? I hope one of these lawyers gets back to me... I guess they broke up again... I need to call my dad and catch him up on everything, too. Plus, we have the gala tomorrow night...*

Coop fell asleep, his phone dropped silently on the bed.

Chapter 25
Sunbeams And Dragons

Liam stood in front of the Morgan Estate's main entrance and rang the doorbell. He felt incredibly embarrassed to be in the position of asking to temporarily stay with someone. He'd looked at a few houses for rent this morning, but nothing was jumping out at him.

Levi answered the door smiling. "Hi, Liam! Welcome! Tommy will be down in a minute; do you want something to drink before we head out?"

Liam looked around at the huge estate as he walked inside through the foyer. "No, thanks. I'm alright. Thank you for offering to help me grab some stuff. Have you talked to Coop or Ethan?"

Tom answered while coming down the stairs, "No, we haven't. Why? Is something wrong?"

Liam sighed. It definitely wasn't his place to talk about what happened, but he could see the concern on their faces. "There's a lot going on. I'm not sure what they'd want me to say."

"Let me try and call them," Tom said.

Liam shook his head. "Coop said earlier that Ethan was asleep, so he couldn't talk."

The door behind them opened, and rays of sunshine brightened the room. An attractive girl with long brown hair walked inside, headed straight for Tom and Levi. "Hi, dads! How was your trip?" she asked excitedly.

Ah, that must be Coop's sister, Liam thought, looking at her.

She looked at Liam and waved. "Hi, I'm Arie, their amazing daughter."

Liam smiled brightly. "I'm Liam Collins, nice to meet you."

Arie tugged on Tom's shirt. "What did you bring back for me?"

"Such a little princess," Levi said.

Arie scrunched up her nose and gripped tighter on Tom's sleeve. "Did you get permission from the director? Tell me! I can't wait! I'm too excited!"

Levi leaned in close to Liam and whispered, "Her birthday is at the end of the week, he's working on a huge present that she asked for."

"Oh, it's almost your birthday?' Liam asked. "How old are you turning?"

She held up two fingers on her left hand and made a zero with her right hand and held them up proudly.

Liam was confused and looked at Levi, who said, "Arie, that's backwards, we're facing you this way. Are you saying you're turning 02?"

Arie crossed her hands over one another and smiled. "Twenty."

Tom chuckled. "Why didn't you just put the two on the right hand and the zero on the left? You twisted your wrists instead of that."

She tugged on Tom's arm, giggling. "Come on, tell me, please?"

"I'm still working on it. You're gonna have to wait a bit longer. Right now, we have to go get Liam's stuff."

"What stuff?" Arie asked looking at Liam. "Do you guys need help?"

"You're offering to help?" Levi asked. "You don't even know what we're doing. Liam is going to stay on Coop's side of the estate for a bit. We're going to pick up his stuff. I'm sure you wouldn't want to—"

Arie interrupted, "I do. I'll come and help. I don't have practice until later. We'll be back by six, right? It's not gonna take all day, is it?"

Tom tilted an eyebrow looking at her. "No, it shouldn't take long." He turned to Liam. "How much stuff are we talking about?

"Not much. I can leave some stuff there, too. We should be able to do it in one trip. Do you have a decent amount of trunk space?"

"Yeah, and we can pull the backseat down, too."

Arie snapped her fingers. "Liam can ride in my car, and we can use my trunk, too."

Liam was a bit taken aback by her offer. "Uh, I have my car here. You could just…ride with me."

Arie shook her head and pointed towards the front door. "The red Camaro? No. I drive a custom Shelby GT500. I'm not riding in your car."

Levi asked, "Arie, you're going to just let him ride in your car? Don't you normally have to read people the rules first?"

Arie put a hand on her hip. "I will tell him the rules when we get outside."

Liam looked confused at the three people that stood before him. "Rules? Are you joking?"

Arie pulled Liam by the hand. "Come on. Do you know anything about cars? My car costs around $200K…of course I have rules." She smiled over her shoulder as she led him outside.

Arie walked Liam around toward her side of the estate. She looked down at his hand and quickly let go. "Sorry! I was excited to show you my car. I didn't mean to pull you around like that."

Liam hadn't even realized they were still holding hands. He waved it off. "Don't worry about it. Where are we going, by the way?"

"My side of the estate. Which is on the complete opposite side from where you'll be staying. I can give you a tour when we get back. My car is parked over there."

They rounded the corner of the estate and saw Arie's shiny black car.

Liam's mouth dropped. "Holy shit…that's a nice car!"

Arie smiled. "Mmhmm…it's my baby."

Liam walked around looking at it. "These are twenty-inch carbon fiber wheels"—he snapped his fingers at Arie—"I saw this car in a magazine article, the engine, it's a 5.2, right?"

Arie smiled proudly as she opened the driver's side door and started the engine, then popped the hood open.

Liam's face lit up. "Damn! You can feel the power just standing next to it!" He looked under the hood and admired the engine.

Arie nodded. "Yep, that's why I have rules."

"Whatever the rules are; I'll follow them. I just want to go for a ride in it."

"Okay, then we don't need to go over the rules. Get in."

Liam pulled his head back. "I don't know the rules, though."

She smiled over the roof at him. "I think I can trust you."

Ethan slowly opened his eyes, as he lifted his head off Coop's chest. He had no idea what time it was, or how long he'd been asleep for.

Coop squeezed him back down, tight. "Don't get up yet. Let's just stay like this for a little longer."

Ethan laid his head back on Coop's shirt after shifting his body around. He lightly ran his fingers over his abs. "Thanks for letting me sleep. I needed it."

Coop smiled down at him. "Of course. I guess I fell asleep, too. I tried to get some things done, but I must have just passed out."

Ethan held a hand on his forehead. "Cooper, what are we gonna do? I don't even know where to start."

Coop tapped his own mouth with his pointer finger.

Ethan scooched up and kissed him.

Coop smiled. "We start with that, and we'll do the rest one thing at a time." He felt around on the bed, moving the covers around. "Where is my phone? Wait till you see these texts, baby."

Ethan found the phone, it had fallen on the floor. He picked it up and unlocked it. "Which texts did you want me to see? There are five different conversations here."

"Should just be a group text with Maddie and Liam, and a conversation with your dad."

Ethan shook his head. "Nope. You also have texts from Arie, my mom, your dad, and a text from just Liam, that one is separate from the group one."

Ethan hopped back into bed and sat up next to Coop. They leaned against the large headboard and scrolled through the messages together. "Read the most important one first," Coop said. "Go to Maddie and Liam's group text, wait till you see this."

Ethan read through the text, which had a few new additions that Coop hadn't seen yet. The last one was from Maddie asking if they would be comfortable with Liam taking over and having her on standby if needed.

"How do you feel about that?" Ethan asked. "Are we good with Liam taking over?"

Coop held Ethan's hand and kissed it. "I feel like we can trust him."

"I do, too, strange as that is."

They decided to continue reading before replying to anyone.

They scrolled to the texts with Ethan's dad that Gina had jumped in on. Of course, she was just worried and looking for an update on the baby situation.

Ethan smiled. "I'll call my mom and dad in a few minutes. We know my mom is going to make everything so much worse. I just started feeling better. I don't want to deal with her right now."

Coop wrapped his arm around Ethan's body and rubbed his shoulder. "Okay, baby. Whatever you want to do is fine."

Ethan scrolled. "Who's next?"

"Let's see what Arie wants. She's probably asking if we're coming to her party."

Ethan opened the text, attached was a picture of Arie and Liam in the front seat of her car, Arie was holding a peace sign up and making a kissy face at the camera, while Liam smiled next to her in the passenger seat. Ethan slowly turned his head to the left, while wincing, awaiting Coop's reaction.

Coop tilted his head to the right and looked at Ethan. "Why would those two be in Arie's car together? I wasn't expecting to see that. How would that have even happened?"

Ethan shrugged. "Maybe they know each other from college?" He opened a very long string of texts from Liam. He and Coop nodded as they read along, together. The two looked at one another in shock at the influx of information.

"Wow," Coop said. "He really is a good attorney. He did all that stuff for us while we slept."

"Yeah, I feel better now, knowing that there will be a nurse there to make sure the baby is fine. I can't even wrap my mind around what the doctor said." He kissed Coop on the cheek. "Start with a kiss, then move onto the next thing, right?"

"Yes, the kiss always comes first. Puts things into perspective."

Ethan smiled. "I'll remember that."

"Well, at least we know why they were together in Arie's car, had me worried for a minute. My mind just jumped to some crazy places."

"I bet." Ethan patted Coop's thigh. "Alright, onto the next thing, we gotta get up and review everything for tomorrow night."

Coop shook his head. "Nope."

"What do you mean, nope?"

"What did we just agree on, pup?"

Ethan leaned in and gave him a sweet kiss on the mouth.

"There we go. Kiss first, then I'll do whatever you want."

"I love you so much, my Cooper. Thanks for trying to get everything done while I slept. I'm so lucky."

Coop squeezed Ethan's face in close and smooched him on the lips. "I'm the luckiest. I love you, pup."

Chapter 26
Wicked Stepmother

The sound of a car horn honking loudly from behind forced Arie to check her rearview mirror at a red light. She scrunched her nose, as she tried to see if she recognized the people in the car.

Liam turned his head in the passenger seat. "They really want your attention. Do you know them?"

Arie shook her head. "I have no idea, maybe." She readjusted her mirror and looked at Liam. "You know what would be nice?"

"Is this a trick question? I don't know anything about you."

She touched her rearview mirror. "I want something to hang here from my mirror, something that makes me feel good when I look at it. You know? Like makes me feel safe and happy. I haven't been able to find anything, though."

Liam pulled a red lollipop out of his pocket and showed it to her. "Can I eat this in here?"

"A lollipop? I was not expecting you to pull a lollipop out of your pocket…"

"Yeah, I usually always have one in my mouth. I love them."

Arie thought for a moment, then said, "I don't ever let people eat in here. But you wouldn't technically be eating, even though you said eating. It would be more like you're just sucking on it. Not like food that could get in my seats."

Liam started to put it back in his pocket. "Don't worry about it then. I don't want to ask you to break the rules. This is a nice car. I don't blame you, really."

She looked at him as they pulled into the driveway, behind Tom and Levi, at Madeline's. "Alright, you can have it, if you have one for me, too. If there's just one, then we share it."

"What? I don't share lollipops with people. Are you joking? You can have this one," Liam said passing it to her.

Arie pulled the wrapper off and stuck the lollipop in her mouth. "Mmm, this is good. I haven't had a lollipop in forever. Whose house is this by the way? I didn't want to ask you and get all personal, but just so I know what I'm walking into. Is this like your parent's house or something?"

Liam placed a purple lollipop in his mouth. "Actually, it was my dad's house, but now it's not…it's pretty complicated."

"True story, I stopped listening after I saw you put a purple lollipop in your mouth. Why did you give me red? Purple is my favorite color. Wait, I guess my brain was listening, even though I wasn't, did you just say it was your dad's house?"

Liam pulled the remaining three lollipops out of his pocket. "Red, green, and blue. Sorry, I don't have another purple on me."

Arie looked up to see her dad and Levi motioning for them to get out of the car. She and Liam stepped out with lollipops in their mouths.

Tom pointed at the two of them. "You let someone eat in your car?"

She corrected him, "Sucking on a lollipop is not eating, Dad."

Levi looked at the large driveway that wrapped around the home. "Is Maddie still at work? I don't see her car."

Liam pulled his lollipop out. "I have no idea. I used a vacation day, although, with all the work I've done for Coop and Ethan over the past few hours, I won't even need to use vacation time." He put his lollipop back in his mouth.

Arie contemplated whether she should ask who Maddie was but decided to remain quiet. As the conversation continued, she had two possible conclusions in her mind, either Maddie was his stepmother, or she was his ex. She remained quiet as she walked next to Liam.

Levi looked around. "This is a really nice property, Liam. Did your dad build it, or was it previously owned?"

Arie thought to herself, *Okay, Maddie is his stepmother, then.*

Liam answered, "My dad built it after my mom passed away."

Yep, definitely his stepmother, she thought.

Liam opened the door to the home, and they all walked in together.

"Who decorated this?" Levi asked. "It's very nice, calming colors, it's so serene. I like the accent pillows on the couches; that's a nice touch."

Liam pulled his lollipop out of his mouth. "I feel like you should know the answer to that, but I'm honestly flattered that you think I could decorate."

Arie thought, *Why would he decorate his stepmom's house? That's weird.*

"No, I didn't mean you," Levi said. "I meant more along the lines of whether Maddie picked everything out, or if she hired a decorator."

Okay, that makes sense. Definitely his stepmother.

Tom looked around. "Alright what are we grabbing, Liam? I don't want to be here when Maddie comes flying in on her broom."

"Is your stepmom that bad?" Arie asked Liam. All three men

looked at her in confusion. "What, why are you all looking at me like that," she asked.

The door behind them opened and Maddie came in hot, temper already at a ten. She had something in a plastic bag gripped tightly in her hand. She yelled, "Whose car is that in my driveway?"

The group turned to face her from the opposite side of the room. "Hi, Maddie," Tom said. "We just came to pick some of Liam's things up since he'll be staying with us."

Arie didn't like the way her dad had to step in. She could see how uncomfortable Liam looked, too. *Wow, so she's like an abusive stepmother. Must've been a bad situation that he needed to get out of quick. That makes sense. Now, I get it.*

Maddie waved him off. "Shut up, Tom. I know your car. That's not your car"—she turned to Arie—"it's hers. Who might you be?"

Arie pulled the lollipop out of her mouth. "Hi, I'm sorry. Should've introduced myself. I'm Arie Morgan. You have a beautiful home."

Maddie nodded slowly and looked her up and down, then turned her eyes toward Liam.

Levi stepped in front of Arie and pulled Maddie's arm toward the couch. "Maddie, these pillows are genius. I love the color contrast with the blues and grays. Did you decorate this yourself?"

Maddie cocked her head to the side. "I hired a decorator. Do you have any idea how busy I am? Do you really think I have time to decorate? I don't have time for anything." She looked at Liam. "Or anyone, outside of my job."

Liam didn't say anything to Maddie. He motioned for Tom to follow him into a bedroom, while Tom pulled Arie along.

Maddie called out, "Wait, I'm not comfortable with a stranger, even if she is your daughter, going into my bedroom. She can stay out here with me."

Liam came out of the room quickly. "Don't be rude, she's only here to help."

Maddie lifted her eyebrows high. "Well, now look whose sticking up for someone. I noticed her lollipop, too, that's nice."

Levi once again blocked her view of Arie. "Maddie, he's here to get his stuff and get out, like you told him to. Arie is turning twenty years old this week. Do you really feel the need to bully our daughter like this? We haven't seen her since before we left. Her birthday is in a few days, she just wanted to spend time with us and help."

Arie spoke up, looking around Levi at Maddie. "Um, okay, I'm confused. Why does it feel like I'm being targeted here? I came to help your stepson because I felt like it. What's the big deal? You're acting like a jealous ex-girlfriend, not like a stepmother."

Maddie's eyes were fire, looking at Arie then at Liam.

Levi grabbed Arie by the hand and pulled her out of the front door. "Tommy, I'm going to wait out here with Arie. You guys grab whatever you need."

Liam couldn't believe how Maddie was acting. Well, he could believe it, but he was also still processing everything and felt bad that Arie got caught in the crossfire.

Tom closed the door and looked at Maddie. "She's just a kid, what are you acting like that for?"

Maddie rolled her eyes, looking at Liam. "Just a kid…whatever. I need to talk to Liam."

Liam, who held a pile of suits on hangers over his arm, looked up. "About what?"

Maddie shook the object in the tightly wrapped bag in her hand at him.

Liam passed Tom the pile of suits. "Can you please take these for me, along with whatever else is in the closet? Just grab all my clothes and shoes. I'll worry about the rest later. Thanks, Tom."

Tom took the pile of suits from Liam and nodded, then walked outside to the car.

Liam threw a hand up. "What the hell is your problem, Maddie? Why are you waving a bag at me?"

Maddie unrolled the bag to reveal a sealed pregnancy test kit.

Liam stood in disbelief, with a hand on his forehead. "What? You're pregnant? Are you serious?"

She rolled her eyes and held the box up. "It's sealed, genius. I'm late and with the sickness at the airport, I might be."

Liam had both hands on his hips. "Well, go take the test then, please."

"I don't want this, any more than you do. Let me say that before I go in the bathroom."

Liam nodded as she closed the door. *There's no way this is happening,* he thought.

Tom came back inside the house and looked at Liam. "Everything, okay? You don't look so good."

Liam sat on the couch. "Yeah, I just need a few minutes. Sorry. I should be helping, but Maddie's doing something right now. I need to just see what happens."

Tom followed Liam's gaze leading to the bathroom door, then looked back at Liam. He shook his head silently. "Is she doing, what I think she's doing?"

"Yeah. She's taking a pregnancy test."

Tom sat beside him on the couch and looked at him softly. "Do you want me to sit here with you, while you wait?"

Liam rubbed his own face, then put his elbows on his thighs, covering his mouth and closing his eyes. "Yes…please. I'm so confused right now."

Tom patted his back.

Liam raised his head at the sound of Arie's engine starting and then looked at Tom. "Is Arie leaving?"

Levi came in through the front door and saw the two sitting on the couch. "What are you two sitting around for? If you're done packing, let's go."

Tom patted Liam's back again and walked over to Levi. "It's complicated. We have to wait a few minutes."

Levi looked around the room. "What could be complicated? Grab the stuff he wants and let's go. We went for a walk and I'm dying to get into the pool. I'm all sweaty."

Maddie walked out of the bathroom with a scowl on her face. "You can leave. I'm not," she said.

Levi interjected, looking at Maddie, "Why would you leave? Of course Liam's leaving, that's why we're here."

Tom gently pulled Levi toward the bedroom, to grab more of Liam's things. He whispered loudly, "That's not what she was talking about."

Maddie stood with her arms crossed and looked at Liam, in annoyance.

Liam nodded and stood up from the couch. "Alright. Well, that's definitely a relief."

She rolled her eyes. "I know you're just a kid, but try to be civil, okay? We still have to work together. Speaking of work, I really will fire you, if you screw up the surrogacy deal. Do you understand that?"

"Yep. I hear you. Loud and clear." He stood and walked toward the bedroom.

Maddie followed behind. "Did you get in touch with the doctor?"

Liam nodded, while grabbing things out of the large closet.

Tom and Levi walked past Maddie, holding piles of Liam's

things. "Why didn't we bring boxes?" Levi asked Tom, as they left the room.

Maddie asked, "What about a rental home for when they go back? You'll need to make sure the dates are—"

"Already taken care of. You gave me the case, so you can back off, now. I wouldn't do anything that could hurt them. I think you already know that."

Maddie cocked her head to the side. "Oh, I see, the nice guy act, again. Fine. I'll back off, just don't screw them over."

Liam turned to face her. "It's not an act, and I already told you I wouldn't." He grabbed his soccer ball, cleats, and shin guards and left the room.

Arie's phone rang through the car speakers, while she drove back home. She answered the call, "Hey, Aaron, What's up? It's so effing hot out, right?"

Aaron paused before responding, "What's wrong? You're answering a call by talking about the weather. That's not normal for you."

"Pfft…nothing's wrong. Do you wanna come over? I need help with Calculus. Stupid Mr. Smith is giving us a test the week of my birthday."

"Yeah, he's the worst. Nothing bad should happen the week of your birthday. I'll be there in about twenty. I'm gonna grab some stuff from the store on the way over."

They ended the call just as Arie pulled into her side of the estate. She quickly took a shower, then stood in her bra and underwear, while drying her long brown hair, bending forward, as she spritzed it, to give her waves a nice bounce.

Aaron walked into her room carrying two energy drinks. "Well, hello there, Arie's ass."

Arie flipped her hair backwards and righted her posture, smiling. "Oooh you brought me energy! Gimme, gimme!"

She reached for the can, and Aaron pulled it back. "Nope wait a minute. What time is practice?"

"Don't worry, it's not until six."

A few hours later, Tom, Levi, and Liam pulled into the estate after running a few errands on their way back from Maddie's. Tom and Levi waved, as they passed a black 1992 Mustang GT, leaving through the gate. The engine revved loudly, while the driver smiled and waved out the window.

Liam asked, "Who's that guy?"

"That's Aaron," Tom answered.

Levi looked at Tom. "She said she has practice at six. Do you want to stop by and see her before she leaves?"

"No, she's gonna get all moody about it. The dragon was nice to us today. Let's leave her alone. Also, she'll probably start begging for news about her present again."

"That's true," Levi said.

Liam, who was texting with Coop and Ethan over the past few hours, answered a call on his phone, while carrying things upstairs with Tom and Levi, "Hey, Coop."

"Hey, Liam. Ethan and I want to thank you for everything you did today…really. You've helped us out a lot."

"Don't worry about it. It's my job. I was also told if I screwed anything up, I'd be fired, so I have that as an added motivator."

"Well, please don't screw anything up," Coop said. "You're

coming to the gala tomorrow night, right? We added both you and Madeline to the list before everything happened."

Liam dropped the pile of clothes onto the bed. "I don't know, maybe. Hey, how do you work this sauna and shower? It looks complicated."

Ethan shouted in the background, "It really is!"

Chapter 27
Pancakes With A Side Of Jealousy

Arie jogged onto the soccer field with her friend Emma beside her. Her cleats sloshed in the mud, as they made their way toward the rest of the team. Arie shouted toward her coach, "Coach Meg, this is effing gross! Look at my legs, I'm already covered in mud spots."

Arie, was Coach Meg's favorite. She had a soft spot for her, having lost her own mother to cancer around the same age. Besides that, since Arie was the best player on the team, she rarely got yelled at for anything.

The rest of the team followed behind in agreement looking at their legs. Jenna, another teammate, stood on the side of the field by the long aluminum bench. She called out, "I'm not practicing in mud. I'll take the bench today, Coach Meg."

Coach Meg yelled over, "You'll bring your ass over here right now, is what you'll do. Unless you want to take the bench on Saturday, too."

Arie looked at Coach Meg and shook her head. Emma pleaded, "Coach Meg, please, we can't practice in this. You know how long it's going to take Arie to make sure I have no mud on me? Do you even know what I'm going to have to go through before I get in her car?"

Arie scoffed. "Oh, you're already not getting in my car. I'm gonna have Aaron take you home."

Emma turned to face Arie. "What? I'm supposed to sleep over tonight."

Aaron's Mustang pulled into the parking lot. He got out of his car under the watchful eyes of the team. "There he is…fine as all hell," a teammate said.

Coach Meg turned around. "What does fine as all hell mean?"

"Just means he's hot," Emma said.

Aaron smiled brightly, waving at Arie, while he made his way toward the field from the parking lot.

Arie yelled over, "Get back in your car, the field is disgusting. It's all muddy."

Aaron nodded and started walking back to his car.

"Hey, wait! Can you hang out though, and bring Emma back to my place after?"

Aaron yelled back, "Of course. She's not gonna be allowed in your car like that. I can see the mud from here."

Coach Meg looked at Arie. "It's your birthday week number four, and you're the captain. I'll let you decide if we should practice tonight."

Arie looked at the mud and turned her mouth down. "If it's up to me, then no. I want to play, but not in this. We can add extra time to tomorrow's practice."

The rest of the team cheered and headed back to their cars. After getting all the mud off and changing into the spare clothes in her locker, Arie made her way across the parking lot.

Aaron got out of his car and smiled at her. "Of course, you had extra clothes with you. The rest of your team are still in their practice uniforms."

Emma, whose legs were streaked with mud, approached Arie from the side. "Is the dragon all clean, now?"

Arie screamed and ran towards her car, "Don't touch me, Em! You're still all muddy! Aaron, don't let her get me!"

Aaron opened his trunk and pulled out a white towel, then tossed it to Emma, while Arie hopped in her car and quickly shut the door.

Emma wiped her legs down outside the passenger door of Aaron's car, while Arie reversed and pulled her car behind Aaron's. She revved the engine at him and raised her eyebrows, with each push of the pedal.

Aaron chuckled at her. "No. I'm not racing you right now. Come on, let's get back to your place."

Liam finished his shower and stood in the bathroom shirtless, with a pair of slim-fitting navy-blue sweatpants on. He looked outside the bathroom window and saw Arie being carried piggyback style toward the pool area by a man. There was also another woman with her in a soccer uniform. Liam pulled his head back, as he watched the guy toss a fully-clothed Arie into the pool then jump in after her. The friend on the side dove in fully-clothed, too. His phone rang loudly from the nightstand. He tore his gaze away from the window and answered the call. "Hey, Levi, what can I do for you?"

"We weren't sure if you wanted to eat with us, or if you'd already eaten."

Liam walked back toward the window in the bathroom. "I forgot about groceries. Yeah, if you guys don't mind, that would be great. Thanks."

He ended the call and watched, as the man stood up in the water with Arie on his shoulders. *Is he her boyfriend or just a friend?* he wondered.

A few minutes later, Levi and Tom knocked on the open door of his room. "You ready?" Levi asked. "Tommy's making breakfast for dinner tonight."

"Breakfast for dinner? I've never had breakfast for dinner. That sounds fun."

Tom led the way holding Levi's hand walking downstairs. "This way is a shortcut, the pool area is right outside the main kitchen."

Liam stopped at the bottom of the stairs. "So, are we gonna pass by the pool?"

Tom nodded.

Liam turned around. "Hang on, I want to grab something." He quickly jogged back upstairs.

Arie held tightly onto Aaron's hair as he carried her around the pool. She shouted, "I'm the greatest! All others bow before your queen!"

Aaron chuckled. "If I bow, you'll face plant in the water, your highness."

Emma stood on the pool steps and looked at Arie. Using a regal voice she said, "Dearest Queen, might I, a lowly servant, please have a turn on the purple floaty thing that you hold so dear?"

Arie agreed. "Of course, you may use the royal purple float. However, you will be required to give me a very good present on Friday, in return for my kindness."

Emma bowed and got out of the pool walking toward the pile of floats that were stacked neatly behind the lounge chairs.

Tom, Levi, and Liam entered the pool area.

Arie smiled from atop Aaron's shoulders. She waved and greeted them, "Hey, Dads, Liam. What are you guys up to?"

"Hi, Mr. Morgan and Mr. Morgan," Aaron said.

Levi waved him off. "Aaron, I've told you many times to just call me Levi."

Emma stood next to Levi and Tom, while holding the long purple float. She looked at Liam, then at Arie. Her eyes went wide, and she tilted her chin down looking at Arie. "This is Liam?" she asked, while pointing at him.

Aaron looked at Liam, then up at Arie. "Who's Liam?"

"I am," Liam said with a wave.

Emma stuck her hand out for him to kiss it, royalty style. "I'm Emma."

Liam pulled his head back in confusion. "What are you doing with your hand?"

"They're playing Royalty right now," Tom explained. "You need to kiss her hand in respect."

Liam glanced at Arie, then back to Emma. "Yeah, but I heard you a few seconds ago; you said you were a servant. Why would I kiss a servant's hand?"

Arie laughed uproariously. "Em, you tried to steal a kiss, and he called you out! Get back in the pool, servant, before I revoke your floaty privileges!"

Emma picked the purple float up, placed it in the pool and laid on it.

Aaron looked up again at Arie. "Who is Liam, though? I got the name but who is he?"

Arie pushed his head straight. "Don't move your head like that when I'm up here. My dads are right there."

Tom folded his arms. "Yeah, Aaron don't make the queen uncomfortable."

"Yes, sir."

Arie patted his head. "Don't call him, sir; you're the king."

Aaron looked up at her. "I have to, he's your dad."

"I just told you not to move your head like that!"

Levi answered Aaron's question, "Liam is a family friend, Aaron. He's going to be staying with us for a while. He's also Coop and Ethan's attorney for the surrogacy."

"Oh, that makes sense," Aaron said. "Wait, where is he staying? In the main estate?"

"Pftt. Of course not, he's staying in my brother's old place."

Aaron looked at Liam and whispered to Arie, "On the opposite side from you…that's all that matters."

Liam raised his eyebrows at Tom. "So, do you need help making dinner, or I guess I should say, breakfast."

Arie was starving and nearly jumped off Aaron's shoulders. "Ooh! Dad, are you making breakfast for dinner? Please say yes!"

"Yep, and if the three of you want to join us, hurry up and get dried off."

Emma jumped off her float and quickly left the pool. "I'm coming. I call a seat next to Liam!"

Arie, Emma, and Aaron went back to Arie's side of the estate to change out of their wet clothes. Emma pulled her wet uniform off, and looked at Arie, who was changing in her bedroom, "Kiss, marry, kill, come on, Arie. Aaron isn't in here, yet."

Arie looked at her and shook her head. "No, I won't answer that."

Emma threw her pajama top and bottoms on. She tugged at the cotton stretchy pants with little penguins on them as she walked toward Arie. "You have to, those are the rules, babe. If someone says it, you have to answer."

Arie dressed quickly in a baby pink tank top and a matching pair of cotton shorts. She sat on her light lavender comforter and looked at Emma. "Obviously, you're talking about Aaron and Liam, who's meant to be the third?"

Emma thought for a moment, then said, "Julian."

Arie pulled her mouth to the side. "Okay, well if I have to… Wait, you're saying I definitely have to, right?"

"Yes, under the terms of our friendship."

"Well, Julian is a kill. That's too easy."

Emma raised her eyebrows, as she wound up Arie's music box on her dresser. "Yeah, that one was a freebie for your birthday week. You know what I'm really after."

A knock on the door accompanied Aaron's voice. "Is Emma dressed, can I come in?"

"She's dressed, open the door. We're coming out anyway, everyone's waiting for us."

Liam sat at the counter on a stool inside Tom and Levi's kitchen. "Is there anything I can help with?"

Tom stood in front of the stove, while Levi placed various pots, pans, and glass bowls onto the counter. "Do you know how to cook?" Tom asked.

Liam tapped his fingers on the counter and looked around. "Not really. I'm not terrible, though. I can help with whatever you want."

Tom motioned with this hand. "Come on over. You can make the cream for the stuffed French toast."

Liam felt kind of excited that he was going to help with cooking. He had no idea how to make cream, but quickly made his way beside Tom. "Sure, just tell me what I need to do."

Levi looked in the pantry, then inside the fridge. "That's going to be a problem. I don't see any powdered sugar."

"No, that's impossible," Tom said. "I bought a ton of it a few months ago. I haven't even used any of it. There should be two big bags." He pointed to the cabinets above Liam's head. "Check inside those for me, Liam."

Levi, Liam, and Tom searched together through the many cabinets and Levi, once again, double-checked the fridge.

Tom shook his head, with his hands on his hips. "Doesn't make sense. I know I didn't use it for anything. I haven't made any frosting or cream for anything."

All three looked at one another silently. Liam remembered Coop's words at the hotel, *Cannoli was a new thing for us…frosting, now that's a different story.* Based on the look Liam saw on Tom and Levi's faces, they were thinking the same thing.

"Give me your phone," Levi demanded of Tom.

Emma walked through the front door first in her penguin pajamas, while Aaron followed behind, once again carrying Arie piggyback style. All eyes turned toward them, apart from Levi, who was yelling into the phone on speaker, "Now, no one gets stuffed French toast! I hope you two are happy!"

Coop and Ethan were laughing loudly, while the sound of waves crackled through the speaker. "Well, right now we're taking a nighttime walk on the beach, so we're very happy," Ethan said.

Coop added, "Thanks for reminding us that we need more powdered sugar, Levi. See you tomorrow night." They ended the call.

Liam leaned on the counter and asked. "What else can we make? I could also run to the store if you want?"

Tom thought for a minute and looked at Levi. "What else do you want, angel? We have bacon, eggs, sausage, and biscuits. You need a sweet to go with all of that, but what should I make?"

Arie smiled and spoke over Aaron's shoulder, "I want chocolate chip pancakes!" Levi shook his head at her and she stuck her bottom lip out, pouting. "Pleeease, Dad?"

Tom rubbed the small of Levi's back. He knew Levi was a sucker for Arie, and anytime she called him Dad, he'd instantly give in. "You don't stand a chance. Just say yes."

She jumped down from Aaron's back and walked toward the counter. Liam approached her from the side and handed her something. "Thanks for helping me earlier," he said quietly.

Arie looked down and smiled brightly. Emma's eyebrows raised high as she lifted herself in her seat trying to get a look at what Arie held in her hand.

"What do you have there?" Aaron asked while walking around the counter, quickly placing himself between Liam and Arie. Liam could tell that whatever their relationship was, this guy didn't want Arie anywhere near him.

Arie held the purple lollipop at chest level and twirled it in her hand.

Aaron pulled his head back and looked at Liam. "Arie doesn't really eat candy."

Liam nodded slowly. "Hmm…okay. It was just a thanks for helping me earlier. Also, she wouldn't technically be eating it." He winked at Arie.

Arie giggled and Liam shot her a huge smile, despite Aaron standing in between them.

Aaron was obviously confused and looked pretty annoyed. "What's funny about what he said?"

Arie patted him on the shoulder. "Inside joke."

"Who doesn't eat candy?" Emma asked. "Arie? Pfft. Arie eats candy sometimes. Besides, she *just* asked for chocolate chip pancakes, Aaron. Chocolate chips are candy. True story."

Aaron shook his head in annoyance, looking at Emma, then Liam. He took the lollipop from Arie's hand, opened it, and stuck it in his mouth.

"No fair!" Arie shouted. "That was mine!" She pulled the lollipop out of Aaron's mouth and placed it in hers.

Aaron gave Liam a warning glance. *Hmm,* Liam thought. *He seems too guarded to be her boyfriend. His body language is telling me that he's not sure how she feels about him. He's obviously threatened by me being here. Meanwhile, she doesn't seem too interested in him.*

Liam walked around to the other side of the counter and stood beside Tom. "Chocolate chip pancakes sound good. How do we make them?"

Tom passed him a bowl and slid a bag of flour over. "Add two cups of that, along with two eggs, and I'll grab the rest of the ingredients."

Arie sucked happily on her lollipop sitting on her stool, with Aaron on her right and an empty seat on her left.

Tom added the rest of the ingredients into Liam's bowl, and Liam mixed everything together. "Oh, Arie," Tom said. "When is your next game? Levi and I want to try and make it."

"It's Saturday," Emma answered, before Arie could reply. "Coach will be so happy to see you guys. Always goes easier on us when you're around. Especially during Arie's warmups."

Liam looked over at Emma. "Why is that?" He turned to Tom. "Are you friends with their coach?"

"Not exactly friends," Arie said. "Women go crazy over the two of them, Coach Meg is no exception. Just the way it is. They're my dads, so it's weird, but it is what it is."

Liam noticed firsthand while in Italy the way that people stared at both Tom and Levi. "Got it. What's the deal with the warmup?"

"That's when baby girl brings out the purple dragon!" Emma answered. "Coach Meg is cool with it, unless Arie takes it too far, which she usually does."

Arie rolled her eyes at Emma. "I get into my role pregame; listen to music, get the team fired up."

"Taunts our opponents," Emma added.

Liam smiled at Arie. She looked mildly embarrassed at the way Emma explained things. "What position do you play?"

Aaron answered, "Arie's a striker. Best player on the team."

Liam listened, and thought, *Everyone answers for everyone else here. I ask one person something and someone else answers. I can't figure out if it's her friend trying to keep this guy quiet, or if I'm just missing something.*

Emma scoffed. "Where would she be without me? I'm the goalie. I don't care how many flippy bicycle kicks or handsprings she does. If I don't protect, my purple dragon can't attack."

"Okay, you're right," Aaron said. "You're very important."

Arie finished off her lollipop and pointed at Aaron. "Aaron is the captain on the men's team; he's also a striker."

"Nice," Liam said. "I'm a striker, too. Made the all-star team all four years of high school, and in college."

Arie's mouth fell open looking at Liam. "Wow that's amazing! It's hard to even get invited once. Really impressive."

"How old are you?" Aaron asked.

Okay, so he's definitely threatened by me. Maybe he is her boyfriend. "Twenty-three," Liam answered.

Tom added, "Yeah, too bad you weren't there with us in Italy, we played a quick two-on-two match. You should have seen Liam running circles around your brother in the beginning of the game." Tom smiled and nudged Liam with his elbow. "We lost, but it was probably just because Coop was so pissed that Ethan got hurt."

Arie shook her head as she stood up to throw her lollipop stick in the trash. "I would've paid to see that. I'm also kind of jealous, because seeing Coop when he gets all protective is one of my favorite things. Never showed any interest in anyone else, but, man, if someone even looks at Ethan, Coop is gonna take them out. Wait, did you hurt Ethan?" she asked Liam.

"Not exactly. He caught the ball against his chest, and he was shirtless. It was a whole thing."

Tom shook his head. "It definitely was a whole thing." He handed Arie a plate with pancakes on it and announced, "Birthday girl first. Everyone else grab a plate and help yourselves."

Arie took her plate and sat back down. She took a bite of her pancakes and dropped her head back. "Oh my gosh! These are delicious, Liam! Dad…these may be better than yours…probably the best I've ever had."

Aaron sat on her right with his plate, and dropped an eyebrow at her. "I'm sure you're exaggerating. I've made you pancakes plenty of times and you've always liked them."

Levi sat in the empty seat on Arie's left. Tom sat on the right of Liam, on the opposite side of the counter, while Emma, of course, had firmly claimed her seat to Liam's left.

Arie pointed at Aaron's plate with a pancake piece on her fork. "You didn't get any pancakes. How will you know if they're better than yours?"

Liam hadn't noticed that Aaron didn't grab any pancakes, but he was pretty sure it was because he made them. *This guy is really insecure about their relationship. With the way he's trying to let me know that she's off limits, I would have expected him to take her pancakes off her plate.*

Aaron brought his mouth near Arie's fork. "Just feed me some of yours."

So predictable, Liam thought. He ignored the show that Aaron was clearly putting on for him and took a few bites of his food. His phone vibrated in his pocket, and he quickly checked the message, then stood up, looking apologetically at Tom. "Hey, I'm sorry. I gotta go. I need to try and move some stuff around for Coop and Ethan. Thanks for letting me eat with you guys and for the pancake lesson. I'll come back down in a few minutes and help clean everything." He picked his plate up. "Should I put this in this dishwasher for now?"

Tom stood and took Liam's plate from him. "No need for that, just do what you have to do. I have enough helping hands here that can clean up. You did a great job with the pancakes. They really are better than mine."

Levi stood up as well, holding his own plate. "Mmm. I'll eat and walk with you. You won't be able to find your way back around."

Liam waved his hands. "No, that's okay. I got it figured out. It's just out these doors, then straight, left, left again, then I'm there."

"Wow," Levi said. "Usually takes people longer than that to figure their way around this place."

Liam shrugged. "Yeah, I've always been good at finding my way around places." He waved goodbye to the group and left the kitchen.

Emma stood up from her seat. "Maybe I should just make sure that he knows where he's going. Too fine to be wandering around this place by himself."

Arie giggled. "Sit down, Em. He just said he knew how to get back, and if he gets lost, he'll just text one of us."

Aaron asked quietly, "Does he have your phone number?"

Arie picked her plate up. She actually wasn't all that confident that Liam would text anyone if he was lost, so she wanted to do a quick check on the way back to her place. She took Aaron's plate and walked toward the sink. "Of course he has my number, I gave it to him in my car this morning."

Levi and Tom washed the pans and large bowls, while Emma helped load the dishwasher.

Aaron abruptly stood up from his stool. "Wait. You took him somewhere in your car? Why? And how am I just now hearing about this?"

"Take it down a notch," Tom said. "She gave him a ride so we could get some of his stuff from his ex's place. Besides, I don't think your name is on that car title, buddy."

"Right, sorry." Aaron said. "Just not used to Arie keeping things from me. I didn't even know he was staying here until you guys passed by the pool."

"Name isn't on the mortgage to this place, either," Levi added.

Arie wasn't used to the tone that Aaron was using, and she felt slightly uncomfortable. Even after he apologized to her dads, he still looked incredibly bothered by the whole Liam situation.

After cleaning the kitchen, Arie, Emma, and Aaron left and headed toward Arie's side of the estate.

"I don't see Liam," Emma said. "Should I go upstairs and make sure he's tucked into bed?" She held her chest. "Oooh, maybe he's in the shower? I could just walk in and pretend it was on accident."

Arie rolled her eyes. She wasn't sure why, but the thought of Emma flirting with Liam seemed to really bother her…while the thought of Liam *naked* in the shower bothered her in a different kind of way. She shook the thoughts from her head and shoved Emma playfully. "Down, girl. You say the craziest stuff sometimes."

They approached Aaron's car, and Emma put her hands up. "Bye, Aaron," she said. Then she turned to Arie. "I'm going inside. I'll see you in a few. You better not come upstairs, until you're ready to answer my question from earlier. You know what I'm talking about."

Liam sat on the bed with his legs crossed, as he moved Coop and Ethan's schedules around on his laptop. Now that he'd taken over as their attorney, Coop gave him access to the scheduling system that he and Ethan used. This would make things easier when scheduling doctor appointments and arranging the upcoming home visit.

His phone vibrated with a text from Arie. He'd forgotten that earlier she texted him the picture they took in her car to make sure she entered his number correctly in her phone. The picture was the first thing he saw, when he opened the message. He stared at it for a moment, then read the text.

Arie: *Hey*

Liam: *Hi*

Arie: *Ty for the lollipop. U remembered my fav color*

Liam had trouble deciding on a reply. He typed several out and deleted them all, before settling on one.

Liam: ~~*You just told me it was your favorite a few hours ago. I don't forget important things.*~~

Liam: ~~*I just wanted to thank you.*~~

Liam: ~~*I think your boyfriend was mad.*~~

Liam: ~~*Is he your boyfriend?*~~

Liam: *You're welcome. Ofc I remembered your favorite color.*

Arie: *Thought u were leaving me on read*

Liam: *No. I wouldn't do that.*

Arie: *Are you going to the gala 2mrw night?*

Liam: *I'm not sure.*

Arie stared at the phone in her hand, while Emma painted her toenails for her.

Emma looked up. "I think he's into you. I'm kind of pissed to be honest. I thought he might like me… Downside of having a hot best friend. When will I find a Liam? This guy just walked into your life, finer than anything I've ever seen, and he's basically staying in the same house."

"He's not into me. He's just being polite. I'm probably making it awkward for him by texting him."

Emma held her hand out. "Pass me the phone, babe."

Arie held her phone against her chest. "Why? Are you gonna text him if I do?"

"And incur the wrath of King Aaron? Of course not. I just wanna read the texts myself."

Arie reluctantly passed her the phone and Emma read the texts aloud, changing her voice between a deep voice for Liam and a light, squeaky voice when she read Arie's messages. She passed the phone back to Arie, and repeated one of Liam's texts, "Of course, I remembered your favorite color."

Arie pulled her mouth to the side. "Yeah, but he's a lawyer, and they have to remember details... Maybe he just means it like that."

Emma flicked Arie's foot and shook her head. "So pretty, but so dumb. He gave you a lollipop, Arie. A freaking lollipop. He's into you. Trust me."

Chapter 28
Naughty Puppy

The next morning, Liam arrived at the office before anyone else. He headed straight inside and locked his door. He made final adjustments to another case he was working on from before he left for Italy. He stared at the files online and questioned why he got involved in this line of work to begin with. He pulled a purple lollipop out of his pants pocket, smiled at the color, and put it in his mouth. *What do I actually enjoy doing at this job? I like helping Coop and Ethan, and I'm interested in that kind of work. This stuff…dealing with property disputes, trespassing claims…I don't know… Do I even like this?*

An hour later, his office phone rang, it was Madeline. He pressed the speaker button and answered, "Good morning, boss. I'm already closing up the land case with the uncle."

"Good. I was calling to make sure that you saw the notice about the in-home visit for the Morgan's."

Liam sighed. "Of course, I did. I already updated the case notes online and adjusted their schedules.

"The visiting attorney requested that I be there, personally. Are you going to attend, too?"

Liam leaned back in his chair. "I was planning on it, since they're my clients. You're the boss, though."

She abruptly ended the call.

Luke stood behind Kory in his office, rubbing his shoulders. "You're so tense this morning. Are you that nervous about what's going to happen with Liam and Maddie? I'm sure it will be fine, they're both adults."

"Speak of the devil," Kory said.

Madeline walked inside without a greeting as per usual and sat down in the chair across from them.

Luke smiled at her. "Good morning, Madeline. Are we feeling much better this morning?"

"Yes. But I'd feel even better if you'd rub my shoulders like that."

Kory looked at her sideways. "He is not going to do that."

Luke shook his head in agreement with his husband.

Maddie pulled her glasses off the top of her hair and placed them down. "I already know that. I need a favor though…from my best friend."

Luke raised his hand. "I assume, based on the way you're looking at me, that you're talking about me, but I'm really busy this week. I can't take anything else on."

Kory added, "If you're going to ask him to do anything with the surrogacy case, I refuse on his behalf. We don't want to have kids and we're both happy with that. Don't put us in a position that may make us feel differently."

Maddie looked at her glasses. "I forgot these in my office before we left. I think I forgot my mind here too. Phew… Thankfully, as soon as I got back, I realized which way was up. No, I won't put either of you in a position to go against a decision you've already made. It's not about the surrogacy case."

Luke continued rubbing Kory's shoulders and winced while asking, "Then what is it? What's the favor?"

"The Morgan Foundation Gala is tonight. I don't want to go if Liam's going to be there. I also don't want to stop him from going. But I have to make sure someone goes in place of the firm since they're our clients now."

Luke shook his head. "They'll be so busy; they probably won't even realize if you're there or not. It's all over the news. There's supposed to be like a thousand people there or something."

"Yes, I know," Maddie said. "They raised over a million dollars for the charity with ticket sales, so we need representation there. Never know what kind of opportunities you'll find at a big event like that. So, can you just ask Liam if he's going? If I do it, it's going to seem like I'm asking him to go with me."

Kory sighed and looked up at Luke. "I'll handle it," he said. He pressed the speaker button on his desk phone and called Liam's office.

Liam answered, "What can I do for you, Kory and Luke."

"How do you know we're both in here?" Kory asked.

"Because you guys are glued together...just like the others. What's up?"

"Are you planning on going to the gala tonight?"

Liam paused before responding, "Maddie told you to ask me that."

Maddie emphatically shook her head at Kory.

Luke interjected, "Liam, I'm trying to rub your brother's shoulders. He's really tense. Now, we can talk about why his shoulders are so tense this morning, if you want—it involves a mysterious case of a traveler and a baker—or you can just tell us if you're going or not."

"No. I don't want to hear about your role play. I've heard enough about cannoli and frosting…just… No, I'm not going." Liam ended the call.

Maddie looked at the two of them, with her brow furrowed. Luke could tell she was sizing the two of them up. He held up his hand. "Don't. Don't ask which one of us is which. We got you the answer you needed."

"You're right. Thanks, guys." She stood up and walked out of the door, then leaned her head back inside. "Luke is the traveler, you're the baker, Kory." She left the office quickly and got into the elevator, giggling.

Luke leaned down and gave Kory a kiss on the lips. "What was he talking about? Cannoli and frosting?"

Kory made a disgusted face. "I don't want to know."

Liam spoke on the phone to Ethan and Coop, who were running around like crazy trying to get everything ready for tonight's big event.

"No, you don't need to be there, Liam," Coop assured him. "You're good. It'll be fun, but if you can't make it, no sweat."

Ethan asked, "One thing, though, are you not coming because you don't want to, or because Maddie is coming?"

"Honestly, I don't want to be there if she's going. I have some other work I want to do before the at home visit anyway. Do you guys want me there for that? Or are you okay with just Maddie then, too?"

Ethan sighed. "We'd prefer to have you here, since you're the one in charge. If that makes things too uncomfortable, then it's fine if you can't."

"No," Liam said. "That's unprofessional. I want to be there anyway. I'll be there for the visit, but not for the gala. I hope everything goes well tonight. Talk to you later. Thanks, guys."

Liam sat at his desk, deep in thought, as he considered whether he should text Arie. *I'm just being polite. When she asked last night, I didn't know if I was going, and now I know I'm not. It's polite to give an answer to someone when they ask you a question… Yeah…I'm staying at her family's house… I'm just being polite. I'm gonna text her.*

Liam: *Hey, I'm not going to the gala. Just wanted to let you know since you asked.*

Arie: *Oh. Me neither. I have practice. I was thinking of going after but nvm.*

Another text from Arie came through before he could decide if there was anything else to say.

Arie: *I didn't get to give u the tour yesterday. If ur free after my practice, I can show u around.*

Liam: *What time does your practice end?*

Arie: *Tonight, probably around 7:30, normally 7*

Liam: *Yeah. That sounds good.*

Arie: *I'll text u later.*

Following a late afternoon workout in between the sheets, Coop and Ethan showered together upstairs.

Coop squatted down by Ethan's feet and scrubbed the bottom of each one. He looked up at Ethan's backside. "Perfect. Your ass is literally perfect. I wanna go back in." He squeezed Ethan's juicy cheeks together and licked up the center. As he pulled his mouth back, he gave him a light smack on the ass, then stood and whispered in his ear, "Mmm, baby, you taste so sweet. I can't wait to eat you again tonight."

Ethan turned to face him and hung his arms around Coop's neck. "I can't wait either." He brought his mouth near Coop's ear and whispered, "I can't wait for my husband to fuck me even harder when we get home." He ran a finger down Coop's chest, stopping just above his cock. "I'm gonna be thinking about it all night. Any time I put the microphone in my hand tonight, I want you to know that I'm imagining your cock in its place." He playfully pecked Coop on the cheek and quickly hopped out of the shower.

Coop wiped the water from his face. "Tease! My husband is such a tease!" he shouted.

After showering, the two dressed in matching designer black suits and headed to the gala in their Porsche. Ethan rubbed Coop's thigh from the passenger seat. "Thank you for that. I think I would've passed out on stage if we hadn't just done it."

"Me too," Coop said. "I don't know how I'm gonna keep him down when you're holding that microphone, though. I'm gonna have to limit your speeches."

"Yeah, I'm not going to make it easy for you. You look too damn good in that suit."

Coop raised his eyebrows. "I'm gonna be on the lookout for some way to tease you back…nothing is coming to mind yet, though. Also, you've always looked better in a suit than me. You're stunning. I'm so happy we're married now, because no matter what happens tonight, I know I get to take the sexiest man in the room home with me."

Ethan brought Coop's right hand to his mouth and kissed it. "You're perfect. I love you, my Cooper."

Chapter 29
Gina Knows Best

Arie did a bicycle kick, and the ball flew past Emma. She jumped up and high fived Coach Meg, who stood nearby. "Goal! I scored; we get to go home now!"

Coach Meg blew her whistle and yelled, "Alright, that's it… See everyone tomorrow. Drive safe."

Arie and Emma headed for their cars. Arie couldn't wait to get home and give Liam a tour of the entire estate. She unlocked her car and opened the trunk, placing her cleats inside and grabbing out a towel for the driver's seat.

Emma warned her, "Don't do anything I wouldn't do, babe."

Arie giggled. "I would never do anything that you wouldn't."

Emma hugged her and whispered, "And if you do anything with Liam, I need to know how big it is."

Before Arie could shove her and reply, a deep voice called from behind them, "Hey, Arie, can we talk?"

Arie turned to face the voice in annoyance, letting out a long sigh.

Emma raised her eyebrows, seeing the white BMW and devastatingly handsome face inside. "Well, hello there, Julian, how are you on this extremely hot night?"

Julian raised his chin at her. "Sup, Emma, I need to talk to Arie."

Emma whispered in Arie's ear, "You good? Do you want me to leave?"

Arie nodded. "Yeah, it's fine. I'll text you later."

Julian pulled his car into an empty space beside Arie's. He called her through the window, "Come sit inside, let's talk."

Arie walked toward the car in her high black socks and sat inside the passenger seat. "Hate this effing car," she grumbled.

Julian stared at her. "You didn't hate it a few weeks ago."

She sighed and rolled her eyes. "Yes, a great time was had by all…now it's over. What do you want?"

He looked at Arie. "Is it over though? You still haven't told my brother, which makes me think it may *not* be over."

She sat in silence and looked out of the passenger window.

"Arie, I'm into you. I always have been. I'm sorry if it's gonna make things hard with Aaron, but we have something. You guys are just friends, who cares what he thinks?"

"You also have something with the girlfriend that you told me several times you were breaking up with."

He shook his head. "I already broke up with her. It's you. You're the one that I want."

Arie stared at him in silence, then looked back to the passenger window.

Julian turned the AC fan up higher. "You're probably sweaty from practice. Which is incredibly hot to think about, especially since the last time was just like this… Can't believe Emma hasn't said anything to Aaron yet. I'm still surprised by that. She definitely saw the windows fogged up."

"Em doesn't know. Nobody knows."

"But we do."

Arie's phone dinged, with a notification. She read the text from Liam:

Hey. Was I supposed to come meet you, or were you gonna meet me here? I read the text a few times but just in case I misunderstood somehow.

Julian leaned in to see her phone. "Who are you smiling at like that? Aaron can't be done with his game yet."

Arie opened the passenger door, got out and started walking to her car.

Julian quickly followed and jogged after her. "Arie, wait. Is this really your answer? Because, honestly, I'm starting to feel pretty bad for my little brother, getting dragged around by his dick, by someone who doesn't give a shit about him."

She ignored Julian and kept walking, then got into the driver's seat of her car.

Julian stood behind her car and crossed his arms. "I'm not moving until you tell me that you don't want me. You wanted me for so long. Now, what, you're over it?"

Arie stepped back out of her car and stood by the door. "I hate you. That's the truth. I literally hate you. I will run you over with my car and go to jail if you do not move. I'm not joking. Yes, I did like you, but it was more about sex, than it was about a relationship. We have nothing in common. I have zero desire to be in a relationship with you. That's it. I'm getting in my car now." She got inside her car and closed the door. She revved the engine a few times, and Julian finally walked back toward his own car.

She sped off toward home and called Liam. "Hey, Liam, I'm so sorry! I got held up by this effing megabastard. I'll meet you outside of your front door in a few minutes. Oh, wait, I need to shower first."

"You're fine however you are now. You sound a bit on edge... probably from the megabastard. We can kick the ball around if you feel like burning off steam."

"That sounds great."

Arie pulled in beside Liam's Camaro and parked her car. She smiled at the sight of Liam standing on the steps with a ball under his arm. He looked good. She'd seen a lot of guys in soccer shorts, but Liam was sexy without even trying. His black soccer shorts and gray performance shirt hugged him in all the right places.

Arie smiled and got out of her car. She pointed at his legs. "No shin guards? I kick pretty hard."

"Oh, I don't doubt it," Liam said. "I'm not gonna try and block anything though, so as long as you don't fight over the ball with me, I won't need them."

She tilted her head at him. "Get the shin guards."

"No, seriously, I won't need them."

She opened her trunk and took out an extra pair of shin guards. "Seriously, you do."

Liam gave in and put the guards on, as Arie got back into her cleats and strapped her own shin guards on. She tied her hair in a high ponytail and took the ball from him. "This is my favorite brand. They just fly so much further."

"Yeah, I know. This ball is my favorite. I hate when people say the brand doesn't matter."

Arie's phone dinged in her pocket, and she dropped the ball. She read the text quickly and rolled her eyes.

Liam asked, "Everything okay? Was that the megabastard?"

She scrunched up her nose. "Ew, no. It's Aaron, just telling me they won."

Liam pulled the ball over with his foot and bounced it up onto his knees. "So, who is the megabastard, then? I assumed it was Aaron."

"Aaron? No. The megabastard is his older brother, Julian. I effing hate him."

Liam juggled the ball on his knees and asked, "So, why do you hate your boyfriend's older brother?"

She pulled her head back and held a hand up. "Whoa, Liam. Full stop. Back it up, Aaron is not, never has been, and never will be, my boyfriend."

Liam looked at Arie confused, as he placed the ball back on the ground.

"Back up," Arie said. She got a running start and kicked the ball as hard as she could, sending it flying.

Liam watched it land far in the distance. "Daaamn!"

She held her hands on her hips and smiled at him. "You want the whole story, the parts that make me look good, or just whatever comes to mind? I guess hearing none of it, would be an option too."

"I like the truth," Liam said. "I'm a big fan of it."

"Me too."

They walked toward the ball, which was about the distance of a whole soccer field away.

She took a deep breath and started talking, "Aaron has been my best friend since first grade. Always there, through all my ugly cries, all my happy stuff, wins, losses…you get it. Julian, his older brother by two years, is very popular, maybe more than me, but that doesn't matter. What matters is that he was always out of reach when I was younger, so I grew up, like, fantasizing about what it would be like to be with him. I really didn't have that much interaction with him. It was always just Aaron and me. Anyway, Julian had the same girlfriend in middle, high school, and in college. So, for me, I'm thinking I wouldn't have a shot, right? Because they're just this perfect couple. So, the fantasy lives on in my head until one day, Aaron was supposed to pick me up from practice but couldn't make it. Super rare for Aaron by the way; literally, the only time it's ever happened. Also, my car was getting those new seat covers that you sat in installed, if you're wondering why I needed a ride."

Liam shook his head and smiled. "I wasn't wondering that. Keep going."

"So, Julian comes to pick me up, and I'm feeling so effing happy, because I finally get to ride in the car with him. Well, he puts on some music, and is, like, giving me eyes…you know what I mean?"

Liam nodded slowly. "Yeah, I get it."

"Anyway, he made a move, and I let him, he was supposed to break up with his girlfriend, which he didn't. So, I cut him off, I'm not interested in being a side piece. Also, I really didn't like spending time with him. So, now, I don't know, maybe three weeks later, after I've ignored him and told him I wasn't interested, he shows up after practice because that little megabastard knew that Aaron wouldn't be there. He tried to tell me he wanted us to be together…blah… blah…then threatened to tell Aaron. Now, here I am, kicking a ball with you."

Liam stood with his hands on his hips as they finally reached the ball.

"Was that too much?" Arie asked.

Liam shook his head as he bent down and picked the ball up. "No, not too much. I'm just wondering if you purposely left out that Aaron is in love with you, or if you really don't know."

Arie rolled her eyes, smiling. "Aaron is not in love with me. He's been my best friend forever, that's it."

"I'd like to, if I may, recall the events of last night, in which he took the lollipop that I gave you, out of your hand and stuck it in his mouth, then shot me a look and smiled when you put it in your mouth."

"He did? I didn't see that. But, I mean, I share food with all my friends. It's not a big deal."

"I believe that. You were going to share a lollipop with me yesterday, twenty minutes after we met."

Arie tilted her head at him. "You've got him all wrong. Really."

"Okay, from an attorney's perspective, let me ask you a few things. Just answer quickly without thinking."

"Okay."

"How many girlfriends has he had since first grade?"

"None."

"Does he ever sleepover? As a friend?"

"Yes. In the guest room."

"Has he ever made anything resembling a move on you?"

"No."

"Have you ever seen him make a move on anyone?"

"No."

"Have you ever wanted him to make a move on you?"

"Ew. No."

"Does he know that you used to fantasize about his brother?"

"Yes."

"How did he react whenever you said things about Julian?"

"Mostly ignored it."

"Last one, why do you think Julian brought up snitching to him?"

"Because he's a jerk."

"He is a jerk, I can say that without knowing him, but no. He said that because he knows. He knows you're untouchable in Aaron's eyes. He knows it will break him. He knows that his brother is in love with you. Your friends must know, too. I'm sure of it."

Coop and Ethan stood together on stage, thanking the large crowd one final time for their attendance and contributions to the children's charity.

Ethan ever so slightly rubbed and squeezed the microphone, while Coop stood beside him. The two walked off the stage, hoping to make a quick departure.

Ethan's parents, Gina and Paul, waited near the stage exit, clapping loudly, their faces beaming with pride. Ethan hugged his mom, hoping she wouldn't stop them from making a beeline for the door. She whispered in his ear, "Mimmo, where is your charming attorney, Liam? Are he and his girlfriend here? I was hoping to meet them."

Ethan pulled his face back from the whisper and shook his head at his mother. "They broke up. She's here somewhere, but Liam didn't come."

Gina's eyes went meatball with excitement, and she grabbed Coop's forearm. "Ooh, I'm gonna do it. I know exactly who would be perfect for him. A mother always knows."

"Whatever you do, just don't distract him," Coop warned. "His ex is ruthless; she'll destroy him if he screws anything up with our case."

Ethan added, "Yeah, he told us she already threatened to fire him if he does."

Gina tilted her head, with her hand on her hip. "Well, I'll do worse if he screws anything up. This is my grandson we're talking about here...but never mind that. I could tell when I talked to him that he was a catch...and I know who needs to reel him in." She cackled loudly, still holding onto Coop's arm.

Ethan's dad smiled and waved her off. "Just accept whatever she's going to do, boys. It's easier that way."

Ethan's mom gave them both one more hug, then left towards

the bar area with his dad. Ethan overheard her talking about calling someone tomorrow morning. He wasn't sure how she had Liam's phone number but remembered that they gave it to her for any emergencies that may come up.

Coop pulled Ethan's hand toward the exit, while the live orchestra played its final few songs. "We're gonna make it out this time, there's a clear path to the door, baby."

Their escape was quickly halted by Madeline, who stopped them a few feet before they reached the exit. She spoke loudly and quickly, "Hey, guys, this was great. Thanks for inviting me. I'm very impressed with the work you two are responsible for. The crowd just ate the two of you up, too. You're like a PR dream. Anyway, I'll see you guys for the interview in a few days. I'm sure everything will go smooth since Liam won't be there."

Ethan was going to tell Madeline that they requested Liam attend, but decided not to bother with it. He didn't feel like dealing with her, or anyone else right now. He just wanted to get Coop home and in bed with him. Ethan smiled at her. "Yes, well, thanks for coming. We really gotta go."

Coop pulled Ethan another few steps toward the door before a familiar voice stopped them. Brody, the brand manager, stood behind them smiling. "Did that woman say a PR dream? She's right! What a night! You two are such a great team!"

Coop shook Brody's hand, while Ethan tugged on Coop's jacket. He knew that if he started talking to Brody, this would quickly turn into a mini-work meeting, so he decided to stay quiet while Coop talked to him. "Thanks, Brody that means a lot. We really gotta go. We'll see you soon."

Coop grabbed ahold of Ethan's hand again, pulling him within only a few feet of the door. The handle was finally within reach, and

Ethan couldn't contain his excitement. He squeezed Coop's hand. "Finally! Take me home and do unspeakable things to me."

"With pleasure," Coop said, reaching for the handle.

Tom asked from behind, "You guys leaving already? It's only 10:00."

Ethan put a hand on his forehead.

Coop dropped his head forward and muttered the curse that Ethan taught him in Italian.

"Exactly," Ethan said. "We're never leaving here. We should just accept it."

Arie stared into the distance. She hadn't really opened up to anyone about her mom before, but the words were just pouring out. "I don't know, it just feels unfair to have lost her at such a young age. I don't remember her, I can't see her or call her, she was gone before I— before I was even old enough to make memories with her. There's nothing that can replace that for me, even though my dads are amazing, it's just not the same. I won't ever get to sit around and talk to her on the phone and lose track of time, ask her to come over and watch Christmas movies, decorate with her—I can't do any of that, so I think there will always be a part of me that searches for a way to fill that void she left. There's like a sense of safety, that I feel like I'll never have." She held a hand on her head. "Why am I telling you all of this?"

Liam met her gaze with the most understanding look she'd ever seen. "I can relate a little, although it's not the same. My mom passed away when I was young—it was a mess, and my dad died a few years ago from a heart attack. I don't really talk to my brother all that much, I feel like most of the bad stuff that happened, all started because of him and there's a part of me, a big part of me, that knows that's not the truth. But there's a bigger part of me, that sometimes doesn't care, because I want someone to blame. That sense of family is just—gone, there is no family now."

He grabbed the ball off the ground and forced a half-smile looking at Arie. "You can't replace the love of a parent, but you can accept that they're gone and be the best version of yourself that you can be—I don't know, when I think like that, I think I'm doing the wrong things."

Arie found it hard to believe that someone who seemed so composed had so many feelings bottled up inside himself, and despite her own trauma, in this moment, she only wanted to listen. "Do you want to talk a little more about it? Maybe we can help each other?"

"I'd like that," Liam said.

Arie and Liam spent hours talking and kicking the ball, in the open field of the Morgan estate. The two looked up as they heard Tom and Levi's car pull through the main estate gate, bringing them back to reality.

Arie looked at her phone. "Oh eff, Liam! It's 1:30 am. We've been talking for like five hours! I haven't showered or eaten, and I have a Calculus test tomorrow, too. I gotta go."

They quickly sprinted back to the estate. Arie stood by her car and smiled at Liam. "This was really fun. Thanks for listening and for hanging out with me. I'm really grateful that you shared all that stuff about your mom and everything else..."

"You don't need to thank me. I can't remember the last time I had this much fun. Didn't even realize the time, or how hungry I am until right now."

"I know. I'm starving," Arie said. "I'll probably just wait until morning to eat, though. Too late to eat now." Her phone dinged from her pocket.

Liam half smiled at the sound, shaking his head.

She knew it was Aaron, texting again without even looking. She pulled her phone out and ignored it. "I'll tell him… I just don't want to deal with that right now. Especially not, *right* now."

Liam shrugged with a grin. "I didn't say anything."

"True, but after talking to you, I feel like I have to set things straight." She held a hand on her forehead. "No more talk about that because this Calculus test is gonna kill me tomorrow. Luckily, it's my late class, so I can study before then. Anyway, text me tomor…." she giggled. "It's already tomorrow. Text me *later* so we can hang out and do the tour. Sorry we didn't get around to it tonight." She opened the door of her car and sat inside.

Liam came closer to her car door. "If I get done with work early, I can try and help you study before your test. No pressure, though."

Her face beamed, looking up from her seat. "Don't get my hopes up. I hate being disappointed. Also, it's my—"

Liam finished her sentence, "Yes, it's your birthday week. You may have mentioned it."

She knew she needed to leave, but wished she could stay longer and just keep talking to Liam, and if she was reading things right, Liam wasn't ready to call it a night either.

Arie's phone dinged again.

Liam's eyes widened. "Mmm…still not saying anything."

She looked down at the screen. "Eff. It's the megabastard this time."

"They're both texting you at the same time? This is…"

She tilted her head at him, unsure whether to laugh or cry at her current predicament. "I thought you weren't gonna say anything," she said playfully.

Liam shrugged. "Well, now, what choice do I have? You definitely have to deal with that. All of it."

Aaron walked into the kitchen of the apartment that he shared with his brother, Julian. He moved some things around in the fridge, searching for a very late night snack. He pulled out a small container of leftover food from Tagaloa's restaurant. He opened the lid and smelled it, then called out, "Julian, can I have your leftovers?"

Julian walked into the kitchen. "Yeah, go ahead. I'm glad you're up. I wanted to talk to you about something."

Aaron closed the fridge and placed the food in the microwave, covering it with a paper towel. He looked at Julian seriously. "What do you want to talk about? I'm pretty spent from the game and Arie's not texting me back for some reason. If you need a favor, now's not a good time to ask."

Julian leaned against the wall. "Actually, it's about Arie."

Chapter 30
Is This A Date?

Wednesday morning, Arie awoke to Emma shaking her in her bed. "Arie, wake up! We're gonna be late!"

Arie jumped out of bed. "What time is it?!"

Emma ran into Arie's closet and grabbed an outfit for her, then tossed it on the bed. "It's 10:37 we're not gonna make it to Chemistry! Get dressed!"

Arie looked at the outfit that Emma picked out. "What? What the eff is this? Am I going to school dressed as a porn star? My girls will be bouncing all over the place. They won't even be covered!"

Emma dug through Arie's dresser and threw a pair of underwear at her. "Shut up. They're your clothes! Just get dressed! We don't have time!" She walked over toward the door and held it open, stomping her foot. "Arie, come on!"

Arie stepped onto her bed and jumped across it, into the closet. "Just wait. I need something better—I might get to see Liam this afternoon."

A few seconds later, Arie jumped back across her bed dressed in a pair of tiny, ripped denim shorts, with a baby pink sleeveless bodysuit underneath. She held an oversized cream-colored sweater.

"Okay, go, go. I'll put the sweater on while we run downstairs." She shoved Emma into the hallway.

Emma walked back inside the room and closed the door. "Spill it. What happened with Liam?"

Arie opened the door again. "We gotta go! I'll tell you in the car, while you drive. Eff, I still need to do my hair!"

After a short drive and catching Emma up on the events of last night, they pulled into the college parking lot at 10:59 am.

Emma yelled, "Run! We have one minute!" The two sprinted through the people walking and arrived in class three minutes late.

Emma was out of breath sitting in the seat next to Arie. After catching her breath, she elbowed Arie. "All that gymnastics training paid off. You jumped so high over that bench! I thought you were gonna eat it, babe!"

Arie rubbed lotion on her legs and giggled. "I know! True story, I wasn't sure I was gonna clear that. But I was too committed by the time I questioned it."

Emma looked around. "Where's Aaron? I don't see him."

Arie stuck her lotion back inside her oversized tote bag and pulled her phone out. She turned her mouth down. "Oops," she said.

Emma whispered, "Oops what? What did you do, or forget to do?"

"I never texted him back last night… Eff…I just didn't want to deal."

Emma tilted her head at her. "Just to be clear, you don't want to deal with what?"

Arie held her left hand out to Em. "I don't want to deal with any of it. I don't want to hurt anyone…I'm being real with you, Em…I never once considered that Aaron was in love with me. You believe me, right?"

Emma smiled. "True story, babe. You're kinda dumb. Of course, I know that, but does anyone else know that? No. To the rest of the world it looks like you're together."

Arie stared at the floor, feeling frustrated. "I never realized. He's just always been there. What do I even do? Am I supposed to just accuse him of being in love with me? How do I even talk to him about this?"

Arie's phone dinged.

Emma looked over. "Is that Aaron?"

Arie scrunched her nose up in confusion at the text. "No, it's Ethan's mom, Gina. She sent me this picture of Liam." Arie studied the picture. She had so many questions, but one thing was clear—Liam looked good all dressed up. "Wait, she just texted: *This is the one.* What the eff is she talking about right now? Why did she send me this?"

Arie showed the picture to Emma. "Damn…" Emma whispered. "Look at him with a wine glass, he's in a suit, too! Oh, babe… But why is she texting you this? Are you guys close?"

Arie thought for a moment, while looking at Liam's picture. She snapped her fingers, as she remembered something. "At Coop's wedding, she told me she didn't like Aaron for me. I told her we were just friends…she said, 'Good, I'll find someone for you.' Is she saying she thinks I should be with Liam?"

Emma shook her head at her. "I hate you. I really do. I love you, but I hate you. Everything always works out for you like this."

Arie stared at the picture, suddenly feeling tingles all over. She felt the same thing last night when they finally said goodbye. She looked softly at the picture while zooming in on Liam's face. "He's really so…"

All the heads in the classroom suddenly turned to face the door that opened. In walked Aaron, fifteen minutes late. He apologized quickly to the professor and rushed up the classroom stairs toward Arie and Emma in the back. He sat in the seat beside Arie and smiled. "Good morning. Is your phone broken?"

It was the worst of timing, as Arie's phone dinged at the exact moment Aaron finished his question. Arie didn't read the text, she opted to shove the phone inside her bag.

Aaron slowly nodded, and said facetiously, "Great...that's great."

"Sorry about last night." Arie winced. "I totally spaced. That's my fault."

Aaron leaned back in his chair and raised his chin at Arie. "I talked to Julian last night."

Arie was internally freaking out, as a million thoughts raced through her mind, but on the outside, she was calm and collected. "Why is that news? He's your brother, you live together, of course you would talk to him."

Aaron nodded slowly, appearing to challenge her. "So, there's nothing you want to tell me?"

Arie thought, *Fuuuck. That megabastard told him!* She smiled nonchalantly. "Nope, I heard the Foundation's gala went well... I didn't go, though. Also heard that you guys won your game"—she turned to Emma—"Em, you got anything to add? Did I leave anything out?"

Emma leaned over in her seat next to Arie. "We were late today, too, because Arie couldn't her ass out of bed. She even jumped over a bench on the way to class. She was like Olympic gymnast level this morning."

Aaron scoffed. "Wait, you overslept, and you didn't even go to the gala? Why were you so tired?"

Arie held her right hand up at him. "Shh! I can't hear. We can talk after class."

Liam sat behind his desk wrapping up a call with one of his clients on the phone. "I can go there tomorrow and view the property. I don't know what that's going to prove, or how it's going to help, but if you need me to do it. I'll do it. I have a full day tomorrow, though. It's going to be a quick look around. That's all I can commit to. Thank you."

He'd texted Arie about fifteen minutes earlier and hadn't received a reply yet. He read the text again:

Liam: *Hey. Looks like I can help you this afternoon. Still on for the tour, too.*

"Knock, knock," Madeline said, as she walked into his office.

Liam slid his phone into his pocket. "What can I do for you, boss?"

She stood with her arms crossed on the opposite side of his office, leaning against the wall credenza. "I read your notes on the Morgan case. Are you planning to be there tomorrow for the in-home visit? I thought we agreed that I would go, since the visiting attorney requested it."

He twirled a pen in his hand. "My clients asked me to be there."

She narrowed her eyes at him. "I'm going to be crystal clear with you. If you embarrass or provoke me, I will fire you. Do not make me look bad in front of this attorney."

"I have no interest in doing either of those things. I'll be there to make sure my clients get what they need. That's it."

When Arie's class ended, she gathered her things and stood up from her seat. Aaron walked down the stairs in front of her, and she quickly pulled her phone out to see who the missed text was from earlier. She read Liam's message and hoped it wasn't too late to reply to him.

Emma whispered, "What do you think Julian said to Aaron, that's got him so pissed off?"

Arie turned to face her and pleaded with her quietly. "I need your help. Let's go talk in your car really quick. Come up with something to get rid of Aaron. Anything."

Emma pulled her head back and threw her hands up.

Once they stepped outside of the classroom, Aaron turned to Emma. "Hey, I need to talk to Arie alone before the next class."

Arie widened her eyes in panic at Emma.

Emma grabbed her hand. "No. Um, I need to um…I have… I got kicked in the biscuit with a cleat last night at practice, and I need Arie to check and make sure it looks okay." She quickly pulled Arie away, and they ran toward her car. "Don't look back! I can't believe I just effing said that!"

They hopped inside of Emma's blue crossover and laughed hysterically for several minutes. Arie's face turned serious as she patted Emma's leg. "You're my best friend, you know that, right?"

Emma held her hand softly. "Of course. I love you, babe. You're my ride or die, true story."

Arie fidgeted with the straps on her bag, avoiding eye contact. "The thing is, that I may have had sex with Julian."

"I know. Did you really think that I didn't? Wait, for real? I thought you knew that I knew, but you just didn't want to talk about it… Did I say that right?"

Arie sighed. "Thought you might have known, but I didn't want you to have to lie to Aaron, so I avoided talking about it. I mean, I was also embarrassed because that megabastard said he was gonna break up with his girlfriend and then didn't. Made me feel like a homewrecker."

"Don't feel bad, babe. He sucks. Also, you said he was an instakill when we played KMK the other night. I thought that was our moment of understanding."

"I'm such an idiot." Arie ran a hand down her face. "I'm sorry."

Emma squeezed her into a hug. "You're my girl. I'll lie to anyone for you. But listen, now that we're talking about this; how big was it?"

Arie waved her off. "I deleted that from my memory. I have no idea."

"How big and how good? Spill."

"Average size, and, eh, it was okay. The fantasy was better than the reality, so that probably had something to do with it."

"What about the other stuff, was he good at that?"

Arie tilted her head. "That, he was good at. But no more questions. We need to move on to the problem. He threatened to tell Aaron, and I think he actually did."

"So, last night after practice when Julian stopped by, he came to threaten you?"

"Not exactly. He came for sex and when I refused, he threatened to tell Aaron. Effing megabastard." Arie's phone dinged with a text from Aaron, which she didn't open. "I gotta call Liam. I hope I didn't miss my chance to meet up with him. Damn it, why didn't I drive today?"

Emma pulled her mouth to the side and opened her car door. "I'll go feel out Aaron, you stay and call Liam. We still have about thirteen minutes before our next class. I'm leaving you the keys if you need to go home."

Arie called Liam, who answered on the first ring. "Hey, I'm sooo sorry. Are you still free this afternoon? My Calc test is at 4:00."

"Hey, yeah, that works out. I can leave here and meet you wherever works best. Are you hungry, do you want to grab lunch, or do you have a class now?"

Arie couldn't contain her excitement. "Yes!" she shouted. "I mean yeah, that sounds great, Liam. I can skip the class I have right now, but I don't have my car. Emma left me her keys, but she's gonna need her car because she doesn't take the 4:00 class."

Liam's smile could be heard in his reply. "That's fine. I'll come and pick you up from school, then drop you off after. I'll pick you up by Building A, in about twenty minutes. Does that work?"

"Yeah, that works, but why Building A?"

"I only go there for lectures every once in a while, so Building A is the only one I can remember."

Arie giggled. "Building A is great. I'll head that way in a few minutes." She grabbed her bag and headed toward the classroom, where she saw Aaron and Emma locked in an argument.

Emma stepped closer to Aaron, crowding his space. "I don't care what you believe. It's none of your business."

Arie placed herself between the two of them. "Hey, everyone, just take a step back." She turned to face Emma. "I have to go. Here are your keys. Take notes for me and I'll see you at practice." She gave her a hug, then turned to Aaron. "I know you want to talk, but there's just a lot going on right now. I'll catch up with you later."

She turned to leave, and Aaron lightly tugged on her bag. "No hug for me? That's a little weird."

Arie turned and gave him a quick half-hug. "Sorry, buddy," she said, then sprinted off towards Building A.

Liam arrived at the college with Arie nowhere in sight. He did a quick lap around the parking lot then parked in a spot close to the sidewalk facing the main building. He checked his hair in the mirror and straightened his black tie, feeling a bit worried that he may be overdressed for a quick lunch, but since he came from the office, there wasn't much he could do about it. He had no idea which building Arie was coming from, so he decided to wait outside near the front of his car.

He reached into his pocket and pulled a lollipop out. Seeing that it was a purple one, he slid it back in his pocket, planning to save it for Arie, and pulled out another, which was purple, too. Digging deep, he pulled out three lollipops; all purple and for some reason that made him smile. He stuck one in his mouth and looked around for Arie. *I did say Building A…maybe she changed her mind? I should just call her.* As he pulled his phone out of his pocket, Arie came around the corner. Once they locked eyes, she sprinted towards him smiling.

"Hey! Sorry, I got here as fast as I could. I didn't realize how far away the building was."

Liam pulled his lollipop out of his mouth. "Don't be sorry. It's my fault. I didn't even think to ask which building was closest to where you were."

"Is that a purple lollipop?" she asked.

Liam nodded. "Yeah, I have one for you, too. Do you want it now or after lunch?"

From the side of the building, Aaron saw Liam hold the passenger door open for Arie, as she smiled and got inside. "Fuck! How is this happening right now?" he shouted, as he leaned against the side of the brick building. "I have to do something."

Someone wearing a baseball jersey walked by, and Aaron quickly came up with a plan. He walked to his car in the other parking lot and sat inside, leaning his head on the steering wheel. *Let me think before I do this. Arie will probably be really pissed at me, but I can't lose her to this guy…I can't lose her to anyone. I've waited too long… It's always been us… It can't be anyone else. I won't let this happen.*

"Ooooh, can we eat at the Pig and The Swan?" Arie asked from the passenger seat.

"Yeah, if that's what you want. I could also take you to a nicer place. It's your birthday week, so you get to choose."

Arie pulled her mouth to the side. "In the spirit of truth telling, and honesty, is this…like, a date?"

Liam's eyebrows raised as he stopped at a red light. "Do you want it to be?"

"No fair," Arie said. "You answered my question with a question. What's that about?"

"Lawyer tactic."

"Oh yeah? When is it necessary to use that tactic?"

Liam grinned. "When you don't know what someone wants you to say, or you don't understand a question…also we use it to derive motives."

"I see. Very interesting. So which reason did you use it for?"

Liam tilted his head back as they stopped at another red light. The smell of Arie's perfume overwhelmed him, and the way she made him feel was something he wasn't sure he'd ever felt before. In the past twenty-four hours, he'd already told her more about himself than he'd told any other person. She was just that easy to talk to…but, still, he felt hesitant. "You have a lot going on and I have a lot going on too, especially at work with Coop and Ethan. I guess I'm not sure what my answer is. But I think you look really pretty today, and I'm happy that you're letting me spend time with you. I worked extra hard all morning, so I'd be able to make it. My brother thought something was wrong with me. He'd never seen me finish things so quickly."

Arie gave him a warm smile. "That's really sweet. Thanks for doing that." She tucked her hair behind her ear and looked out the passenger window. "Also, I think you look really good in your work clothes."

Liam was flattered and thought it was pretty cute that she looked out the window when she complimented him. "So, birthday week girl, how about this, you get to pick the lunch spot, and I'll pick where we eat dinner after the tour, tonight. Unless you want me to make you pancakes?"

Chapter 31
Do We Know You?

Coop and Ethan sat on their bed reviewing tomorrow's interview questions on Ethan's laptop. Ethan scrolled through the document. "These are all easy for us. I'm still not sure why they insist on knowing what his name will be. Don't parents name their babies after they're born? Madeline insisted from day one, too. Why is this different?"

"I'm pretty sure Madeline said it was for the pre-birth certificate. We can ask Liam to explain it a bit more."

Ethan leaned his head on Coop's shoulder. "We still haven't picked his middle name. I like both options. Are you leaning toward one?"

"No, I feel the same. They're both good, but one comes with more of a risk than the other."

Coop's phone rang; he held the screen toward Ethan. "Unknown number?" He pulled an eyebrow down and declined the call. "We don't do unknown numbers here, pup."

"No, we don't. Oh, but hopefully it wasn't something about the baby."

Coop kissed him on the cheek. "Don't worry, they'll call back if it's important." His phone rang again from an unknown number, and he accepted it on speaker, holding it toward Ethan.

"Hello?" Ethan said.

"Hey, uh, Coop, this is Aaron."

Coop turned his mouth down and shrugged, looking at Ethan.

"Hi, Aaron, this is Ethan Morgan. Uh…do we know you?"

"Oh, hi, Ethan. I'm sorry, I thought you were Coop. Yeah, I was at your wedding with Arie. I'm her best friend; don't you remember me?"

Coop rolled his eyes. "Hey, Aaron, we don't normally answer calls from people who block their numbers. I didn't realize you had my phone number. Is there something wrong with Arie?"

"Arie gave me your number a long time ago in case of an emergency."

"What's the emergency, then?" Ethan asked. "You sound pretty calm for an emergency."

Aaron explained his very long, distorted view of what was happening with Liam staying at the estate.

Ethan pulled his mouth to the side, looking at Coop. "Aaron, we try not to judge…"

Coop chuckled, unable to keep quiet. "That's not true."

"Ahem, let me start over," Ethan said. "Aaron, we judge everyone. Constantly. You sound really jealous right now. Liam just moved in there, what, two days ago? You're making it sound like she's in danger. Liam's a good guy."

"I'm not saying he's a bad guy. I've been her best friend for thirteen years… I'm just worried. I don't want anyone to take advantage of her. Coop, you know what I mean, right?"

"I agree with my husband. It's been obvious to everyone for a while now, that you're in love with her. Our whole family knows it."

Ethan cut in. "With just one exception: Arie. Unless I'm wrong, you've never told her that you see her as more than just your best friend, right?"

"Obviously, she knows how I feel. Best friends can be couples, too."

Ethan pinched Coop's cheek and replied, "Of course they can. I'm married to my best friend. That's not what I'm talking about, though."

"Aaron, I don't think Arie knows," Coop said. "She sees you as a friend, a part of the family, same as Emma."

Ethan was torn in between telling him that he was pretty sure Arie wasn't into him, and flat out asking him why he thought calling Coop was a good idea. "Listen, we're not trying to push you into saying something to her that you don't want to. I don't really think it's your place to do what you're doing, though. I can understand that you're worried, but if you called my husband to try and get him to interfere with whatever you're imagining is happening with Liam, then you and I have a problem."

Coop added, "You're the only one who's worried here, Aaron. Also, it's her birthday week and you know how seriously she takes that."

Aaron paused before replying, "I'm sorry. I just care so much about her. He's a guy living in the house. I guess I may have overreacted. Can we just pretend this didn't happen?"

"Oof…I can't," Ethan said.

Coop agreed, "Me neither. You said a lot of things earlier…"

"So many things…" Ethan added.

Arie and Liam sat across from one another in a swan-shaped booth inside the restaurant. Liam wasn't someone that normally got nervous, but he was generally cautious of strangers and found himself constantly trying to figure out people's motives. His trip to Italy was the first time he'd been around people who seemed to have no other motive aside from love—not including Madeline, of course. Sitting across from Arie, felt comfortable, she was like a warm breeze on a sunny day, refreshing his soul in the gentlest way. He wasn't sure exactly what he was feeling, but he wanted to know more about her. "So, you want to be a nurse that specializes in geriatric care? How did you decide on that?"

"Well, when my mom was in hospice, I was pretty young, but I still remember all the nurses taking really good care of me when I came to see her. Not just me, but my mom, and all of the patients there, too. I just thought that was really special. They reminded me of angels, taking care of people before they passed away. I do a lot of volunteer work at a retirement home, too. I could also see myself working there. I just feel like the elderly are so vulnerable, and it breaks my heart. They all have such amazing stories. You should go with me sometime. They would like that, especially Ms. Doris. She's wild."

Liam couldn't help but smile at the warmth he felt from her words. He hadn't yet met a woman that seemed so focused on making a career of helping people. "That's really sweet. I'd like to meet the people there. What do you mean by wild, though?"

Arie raised her eyebrows. "Let me just say this, some people do not stop seeking out certain types of *comfort* just because they're advancing in age… You get what I'm saying?"

Liam's mouth turned down. "You don't mean…" He raised his eyebrows at her.

"I do mean that. Yes. They're wild and they are not ashamed of it. Why should they be, anyway? Let them have their fun."

The two shared a giggle and Arie shrugged. "So, yeah, either one of those for a career. I just want to help people."

"Your whole family is really into charity work, that's nice," Liam said. "Your dad talked a lot about it on the trip. Plus, that gala was just an insane amount of money that Coop and Ethan raised for the children's charity. After working closely with them over the past week, I've just started to feel like I want to do more of that kind of work. I like convincing people that I'm right, but I'm not really into fighting—which is most of my job, honestly."

"Well, I love being right, too, but I don't like fighting either. Unless I'm on the field, then forget it. The dragon takes over."

"The dragon… I can't wait to see it one day."

Arie shrugged. "Well, any videos that get posted get taken immediately down by Brody. I don't know if you know him, but he's the brand manager for my dad's company. He's always yelling at me about getting too rough on the field. I can't win with him. Oh, yeah, I help out at the animal shelter, too. I get yelled at for the opposite reason for that, though."

Liam pulled his head back in reply. "He yells at you for volunteering?"

"No, of course not. He yells because I won't let him post pictures of it. I volunteer because I care, not to make myself look good, or to bring attention to my dad's company."

Liam took a sip of his water. "I like that about you."

Arie shook her head lightly, her cheeks turned a light shade of pink, which Liam thought was pretty cute for a girl who seemed to have so much confidence. "Thanks. So, what do you think you'll do about your job? Do you think you really want to do something else?"

Liam shrugged, leaning back against the hard white booth. "I have to think about it. For now, I have my hands full with the surrogacy situation and a few other small cases."

Arie snapped her fingers. "You should talk to Coop and Ethan about it. Maybe they can use you in some legal capacity for the foundation. I have no idea, but maybe?"

"Yeah, when the baby's home and they're settled, maybe I will. Right now, I just want to make things as easy possible for them."

A server quickly grabbed the order tag off their table and placed their food in front of them, then headed back behind the counter without a word.

Arie munched happily on grilled Cajun chicken fingers. "These are so good! They're the only place that makes them."

Liam took a bite of a French fry and eyed her plate. "I've never had them before. No breading, huh?"

Arie cut a small piece with the side of her fork and poked it. She held it up to Liam. "Say ahhh…"

Liam hesitated to open his mouth, trying quickly to decide whether he should allow himself to give in to those gorgeous aqua eyes and beautiful smile. He knew based on the last twenty-four hours that she didn't see sharing food as a big deal, but he did. Before he could decide, his phone rang loudly in his pocket, at the same time as Arie's sounded from her bag.

Liam held a finger up to her. "Hold that chicken. It's Ethan. I'm sorry, I have to take this."

Arie placed the forked chicken bite down on her plate and grabbed her phone out. "That's funny, it's Coop calling me."

Liam answered, "Hey, Ethan, what can I do for you?"

The sounds of giggling and shushing were heard before Ethan replied, "Hey, Liam, what, uh, what are you doing right now?"

Arie accepted Coop's call. "Loser Morgan, why are you calling me in the middle of the day? I'm having lunch."

Arie and Liam looked at one another across the small table.

Liam replied, "I'm having lunch at the Pig and the Swan."

"I'm with Liam," Arie said.

Liam's eyes widened across the table.

Ethan asked, "Are you with Arie?"

"Yeah. I took her out for lunch before I help her study for Calculus."

"Oof, Liam…you better be careful. Coop is real protective of Arie." Liam heard Coop laughing in the background.

Arie scrunched up her forehead. "I know you two are together, you're both laughing really loud. What do you actually want?"

Liam was not yet relaxed; he knew the inner thoughts that ran wild in his head and found it hard to push past them. The last thing he needed was to get fired.

Arie was no longer smiling. "Aaron called you? How does he even… Oh, I gave him your number like years ago, before we went on that trip."

Ethan said, "Liam, I'm gonna hang up since Coop's talking to Arie."

Aside from a few giggles, which after spending days with Coop and Ethan, Liam knew could mean anything, his brief conversation with Ethan and what he just heard Arie say, made him more than a little nervous.

He thought to himself, *Coop's gonna kill me. I watched him lift Ethan up like he was a feather. I'm so dead… Wait…why am I freaking out? I didn't do anything wrong. My thoughts are my thoughts…they don't know what I'm thinking…I don't even know what I'm thinking… how could they?*

Arie held a hand on her forehead, while she continued her conversation with Coop. She scoffed. "What did he hope to gain by calling you? Like what were you supposed to do? Kick Liam's ass or something?"

Liam's eyes widened across the table, he pointed at himself, "Me? I don't want that. No, thank you."

Arie appeared to realize something. Her mouth dropped open and she snapped her fingers, then looked up at Liam. "Hey, I'm gonna step outside really quick. I'll be right back. I need to talk to Ethan."

Liam was even more nervous than before, as he watched Arie talk to Ethan outside the restaurant window. He decided to call Luke to see if he could get a better picture of things.

Luke answered cheerfully, "Hi, Liam, what's going on?"

"Hey, don't get any crazy ideas when I ask you this, okay?"

"I can't wait. Go ahead."

"How protective is Coop over Arie?"

Arie stood just outside the window, beside the booth that she left Liam in, talking to Ethan on the phone. "So, Ethan, your mom sent me a picture today."

"Of what?" Ethan asked.

Arie corrected him, "Not of what, of who."

Coop asked, "Who?"

Arie tapped on the glass and waved at Liam, who was on a phone call of his own. He smiled and waved back. Arie was quickly distracted by the sounds of talking from the parking lot. Approaching from the left were a group of soccer players from the men's team.

"Aaarieee! What up?" Duncan yelled over, cupping his hands to be sure she heard.

She smiled and waved. "Hey, guys, heard you won last night. Nice."

Ethan asked, "Arie, who was the picture of?"

Duncan pressed on Scott's back bending him over in the parking lot and looked at Arie. "This was us last night—especially Aaron." He smacked Scott's ass several times, while thrusting for emphasis. Arie was too distracted by the soccer team to pay attention to the phone call. "Ethan, I'll try to call you guys later. I gotta go."

The group of four soccer players had made their way around her. Travis asked, "Is Aaron here, or are you here with your friends? Please say it's Emma."

She pulled her head back. "Travis, are you into Emma?"

"Maybe… I'm still deciding."

Duncan stepped forward. "Listen, there were three girls last night from South Port, smoking hot, that stayed after the game and waited just to talk to Aaron."

She held her palms out. "So?"

Duncan scoffed and folded his arms. "So? What do you mean? You don't care that other girls try to hook up with him? They were begging for it. All of us saw it. No one else would have turned them down."

Arie shook her head. "No, Duncan. Why the eff would I? I gotta go." Arie turned to walk back inside.

Another teammate, Brian, called out as she walked away, "Arie, don't worry about Duncan. He's just jealous. Aaron's not interested in anyone else. How could he be? Right?"

Arie opened the door and walked back to the booth with Liam. She sat down and touched his hand that rested on the table lightly. "Sorry. I wanted to talk to Ethan about something weird. Then those guys from the soccer team started talking."

Liam smiled at her and waved it off. "Don't worry about it. I should tell you, though. I didn't hear your conversation with Ethan, but I heard the rest of it. All the stuff with the team." He knocked on the window. "Cheap glass."

Arie rolled her eyes. "They're idiots."

Liam leaned back against the booth and sipped his water. "Sounds like his friends think you're together too."

"I don't even know what to say," Arie said, rubbing her temples. "I'm so embarrassed." She covered her face with both hands together.

The soccer group from outside came in and stood in line at the counter. Liam gestured over Arie's shoulder since Arie's back was facing them. "Soccer team is in line now. Do you wanna go?"

Duncan got out of line, leaving the rest of the group behind, staring Liam up and down as he approached. Arie nearly tripped him as she slid out of the bench to leave with Liam.

Duncan scoffed. "Who do we have here, Arie?"

Arie stepped around him. "Back up. You're in my space, and who I hang out with is none of your business."

She was so embarrassed that Liam heard and saw everything that happened outside. All she wanted to do was grab his hand, but realized she didn't have the right to. They left the restaurant quickly, without saying anything else to Duncan, or the rest of the team.

Liam opened the passenger door for her, then walked around to the driver's side. He leaned back in his seat and dug into his pocket. "Here," he said as he handed her a purple lollipop, then put one in his own mouth.

Her face brightened. "Thank you. See, now I'm glad I waited until after lunch for it."

"I find that waiting for something, makes it that much sweeter. Now, it's time to study for that test," he said, while reversing out of the spot.

Aaron's phone vibrated while he sat in the school parking lot after his class.

He opened a message from Duncan, which included a picture of Arie and Liam in a swan booth. *Arie was over here with some guy. They looked pretty close. She got pissed when I asked who he was.*

He decided he would try and call her. He squeezed the steering wheel tight as the phone went to voicemail. *I can't believe she's ignoring me.* He leaned back in his seat and stared at the picture of Arie and Liam. "This is not happening." He straightened his posture and pulled out of the school parking lot.

Liam followed Arie upstairs toward her bedroom. She smiled over her shoulder at him. "Okay, this is not the official tour, so we're only going in my room. Don't look at anything else yet."

"Well, we're walking upstairs, so I can't exactly keep my eyes closed."

Arie giggled. "You don't have to; my room is right here."

Liam walked inside the large bedroom. He smiled at the mess of sheets on her bed.

She looked around nervously. "Oops, I didn't have time to make it this morning, ha ha. Good thing it was Em's turn to pick me up, or I might've slept all morning." She quickly pulled the sheet and comforter tight and tossed several throw pillows onto the bed.

Liam looked around with his hands behind his back. "This is nice. Is there anything I shouldn't look at?"

"What?" she asked. "Why would there be?"

"Just want to respect your space." He walked near one of Arie's dressers and picked up the purple music box. He opened the latch and raised his eyebrows, looking at Arie. "I have never seen a music box with a little king and queen inside. I was not expecting that. Where did you even find something like this?"

Arie pulled her textbook off her nightstand and sat on the bed. She looked up at Liam. "Oh, Aaron got me that last year for Christmas. It's like an inside thing, about the game we made up called Royalty."

Liam tilted his head and furrowed his brow. "Royalty? What's that about?"

"We were playing it the other day, when you passed by the pool, remember?"

"Oh yeah, when your friend Emma tried to get me to kiss her hand."

"Yes, that's Royalty. Basically, I'm the queen and Aaron's the king, just because we made the game up together when we were younger. Anyway, a bunch of people play at once and I get to tell them what to do, they also have to ask me before they do anything. If they refuse to do what I say, or they do something without permission, they're out. The last person gets the honor of being the Royal Servant; as their prize they can ask the Queen for one thing. The rules dictate that I have to do whatever they say or give them whatever they ask for. There's also a super obscure rule we created for Aaron, he can force a Kings edict and stop something from happening. He's never done it though; we just added it because he was whining."

Liam looked at the music box and then at Arie. "So, this queen and king are you guys, then?"

Arie shrugged. "Well, I guess. I just took it as a picture of our game, though.

Liam nodded slowly. "What do people usually ask for when they win?"

Arie pulled her mouth to the side, as she flipped her Calculus book open. "Well, Em asks to use my favorite purple float every time. My other friends ask for money, or something from my room, guys phone numbers…silly stuff."

She flipped her TV on and pulled up her playlist. "I gotta get loose before we study." She stood on her bed while Liam looked on, standing next to her dresser on the right. "This might be loud, but it's my routine, I gotta get into it." She started shaking her hips and sang into her closed fist along with the singer on screen, pointing at Liam, while bouncing around on her bed.

She finished the first song and Liam clapped. "That's quite a routine to get ready for Calculus.

Arie plopped on her bed. "Alright I'm amped, lets study." She patted the spot next to her on the bed, and Liam sat beside her.

"What are we working on?"

Arie turned her laptop to face Liam and scooted in close. She placed her book on her lap and sighed. "Improper integrals."

"Easy stuff. You came to the right guy." Liam felt a little hot sitting so close to Arie. The smell of her perfume and her smiling face near his quickly overwhelmed him. He mentally reminded himself that he was there to help her study and now was not the time to think about the fact that he was sitting on her bed alone with her. He leaned in toward the computer and felt Arie's gaze on him. She was so close that Liam wondered if she was actually going to try and kiss him. He looked over at her face, which was only a mere inch or two away from his.

Suddenly she sprang off the bed. "I'm thirsty. Are you thirsty?"

"A little."

Arie walked to the far corner of her room, toward her mini fridge, bending down to look inside.

Liam looked up from Arie's bed to see Aaron standing in the entrance to her room. Arie was still bent over at the waist, in her tiny denim shorts, reaching inside her mini fridge.

Aaron locked eyes with Liam but spoke to Arie. "Well, this is the second time this week I've been greeted by your ass bent over. At least this time you aren't in a thong."

Classy, Liam thought, looking down at the laptop, ignoring him.

Arie stood up with one water bottle. "Nice…that's a nice way to say hi," she said facetiously.

"I'm just messing around," Aaron said, handing her an energy drink. "Look I brought you energy for our Calc test."

She turned to Liam. "Do you want the water or the energy drink?"

Aaron's mouth dropped open, and he held his arms wide. "I bought that for you. He can have mine if he wants one."

"Well, he *should* take it, since you snatched the lollipop that he gave me the other night."

Aaron looked at Liam, then Arie. "Did I? I thought we shared it?"

Liam was getting pretty heated inside. *This mother… Is he serious right now? He's just trying to bait me. I can't give in…* Liam smiled at Arie. "I'll have whichever you want least. I'd rather you have the one that makes you happy."

Arie pulled her mouth to the side in thought, looking down at the drinks in her hands. "I'd rather have the water. Thanks." She passed him the energy drink and sat beside him on the bed.

Aaron walked closer to her. "You already started studying? What about your warmup?"

"I already did it."

Liam could feel Aaron staring at him. He popped the tab on the energy drink and took a sip, looking intently at Aaron. He made a sour face. "Too strong. It's kind of like this drink is trying too hard. The label says it all: *The one and only.* You can't force that on someone."

Arie smiled with her mouth open and patted Liam's thigh. "Yes! I've said that before! Like don't try to brainwash me with your labels! I'll tell you if you're the best. Just because I drink it doesn't mean it's the best. True story."

Aaron looked at Liam. "Yeah, every once in a while another brand comes around—they're all the same cheap garbage. They can never replace the original."

"What do you think about that?" Liam asked Arie.

Arie, not realizing the indirect verbal sparring between Liam and Aaron, thought Liam was actually asking about the drink. "I think the original usually isn't the best. How would you know if the original was the best if you didn't try other flavors?"

Liam nodded. "Well said."

Aaron scoffed, shaking his head. "Arie, I need to talk to you before Calculus about what Julian said. I can help you study after."

She whispered to Liam, "Help me."

Liam really didn't want to get in the middle, but with Arie asking for his help, he couldn't stay quiet. He gestured at the computer and looked at Aaron. "Hey, I came to help her study because she asked me to. I know you're her best friend, but she's entitled to time away from you. You can't force her to spend time with you."

Aaron smiled softly looking at Arie. "Arie, is that how you feel? Really? I would never force you to do something you didn't want to."

Arie rubbed her arms.

Liam looked up at Aaron. "Can't you see that you're making her uncomfortable?"

"Aaron, just—" Arie started. "I don't wanna talk right now. I can't believe that you called my brother and Ethan."

Aaron approached the side of the bed that Arie sat on and leaned in toward her. "We both have a lot to get off our chests. Let's talk after soccer, okay?"

Arie shook her head. "I have plans with Liam after practice."

Aaron stood up straight and walked toward Arie's dresser. He picked the king and queen music box up and wound it. As the music played, he smiled and placed it down. "Alright. I'll see you in class then," he said, as he walked out of the room.

Liam stood up and closed the box, silencing the music that came from it. "That was a crazy thing to do. Winding this box up, then walking out."

Arie shook her head. "I just need to tell him about everything, just totally come clean, but I have plans with you tonight. I don't want to cancel."

Liam smiled softly at her. "I don't want you to cancel either."

"What time do you need to go back to work?"

Liam pulled his phone out, standing near Arie's dresser. "I should probably start heading back in a few minutes." He walked near her bed and pointed to her computer screen, then quickly gave her some tips to help with the exam.

Liam's phone rang in his hand. "It's my brother. He's calling from his office phone, so it's probably important."

Arie smiled and nodded.

Liam walked near the door and answered his phone, "What's going on, Kory?"

Kory answered, "Are you coming back to the office or are you out for the day?"

"I should be there in about twenty minutes. Do you need me for something?"

Kory sighed. "Yeah. I do. Come see me as soon as you get back."

Liam looked at Arie softly. "I have to go, I'm sorry. I feel like I didn't even get to help you."

Arie shook her head, sitting on her bed. "No, don't be crazy. You helped me a ton. Honestly. I'm not even nervous anymore."

Liam pulled his keys out of his pocket. "Alright. Well, I had a nice time. I'm looking forward to the tour tonight."

Arie smiled brightly. "Me too. I'll call you after practice. Drive safe."

Liam left Arie's place and headed back to the office. While waiting in the firm's elevator, he patted his pocket in search of a lollipop. Even though there weren't any left, he felt incredibly giddy, remembering how happy Arie was with her purple lollipop earlier.

Kory's office door was open, so Liam went straight inside. Luke was sitting at Kory's desk, while Kory was on his cell phone, seemingly in a bad mood. Liam raised his chin at Luke and whispered, "What do you guys need?"

Luke tilted his head and stood up. "Come with me to my office. He's going to be on this call for a while."

Liam walked inside the small office and looked around. "This is the first time I've been in your office. This is nice. You have a good view, too."

"Thank you. Now, why were you asking me about Arie earlier?"

Liam shook his head. "What's the deal with this guy, Aaron?"

"Can't stand him," Luke said. "He's a nice guy, though."

Not getting an answer to his question, which was pretty common when talking to Luke, Liam started over. "Let me ask again, what is the deal with him? He's in love with Arie, right?"

Luke dropped an eyebrow, standing beside the window. "Obviously. Arie's not interested in him like that, though. You should've seen him at the wedding. It was awful. I had secondhand embarrassment, really. Wait…why am I telling you all of this?"

"I'm just curious," Liam said. "Had a few awkward run-ins with him when we were hanging out. I guess he called Coop today, to try and get him pissed at me, I don't really understand what he was trying to do."

Kory entered the room and sat in Luke's chair.

"Well, Liam," Luke said taking a seat on Kory's lap. "I can tell you that Coop and Ethan both don't like him, so if he did that, I'm sure Ethan put him in his place."

Kory rubbed Luke's arm, wrapping him in a hug from behind. "Who are we talking about?"

Luke leaned back into Kory's embrace. "Aaron, remember? He was the guy that Arie brought to the wedding, the one that followed her around the whole time."

"How could I forget? I can still hear Ethan's mom talking way too loudly about setting Arie up with someone else. It was hilarious."

Luke added, "Aaron definitely heard her. That was the secondhand embarrassment I was talking about. She sat down and said to Arie, 'I don't like him for you.' Arie told her they weren't a couple, and Ethan's mom stayed near her, talking for a bit. It was uncomfortable. I think he walked down to the water after that for a few minutes."

Liam asked, "Do you know if he heard Arie say that they weren't together?"

Luke looked at Kory. "Do you remember? Was that before or after?"

"Why does that matter?" Kory asked, looking at Liam.

Liam stood near the window in Luke's office. "I'm just trying to figure this guy out."

Kory squeezed the sides of Luke's ass and kissed the back of his neck. "Let's go in my office, Liam. I need another set of eyes on something."

Chapter 32
Don't You Dare Insult Anime

After arriving on time and sitting in the seat closest to the professor, Arie finished her Calculus exam with confidence. Aaron was about ten rows behind her. She planned to make a quick dash for the door once the professor allowed her to leave.

Arie thought to herself looking around the room, *I really hope Em is standing outside that door. She said she'd try to make it in time. I don't want to get dragged into an argument before practice.*

The classroom door opened, and Emma entered. She walked quickly over to the professor and whispered. The professor pointed to Arie and motioned for her to come over. "Are you done with your exam?" he asked her.

Arie nodded. "Yes, I already finished it."

The teacher gestured toward the door. "Your soccer coach needs you for something urgent."

"Oh, okay. Thank you." Arie grabbed her bag from her desk and avoided looking toward Aaron's seat in the back. She and Emma walked quickly out of the classroom together. Arie hugged her tightly. "You just saved me again. What do I owe you? What do you want? Anything…"

Emma squeezed her. "I'll think about it."

Arie and Emma drove to the soccer field in separate cars, then parked, walking quickly inside the locker room. Coach Meg called around the corner. "Arie, Emma, get in my office."

Arie looked confused at Emma. "Wait, that was for real? I thought you made it up to get me out of class before Aaron?"

"I did," Emma said, wincing.

"Then, what did we do? Sounds like we're in trouble."

Emma pushed her on the shoulder. "Yeah, right. You're never in trouble with her. Me? Definitely. You? Doubtful."

They walked into Coach Meg's office and sat down in the two seats across from her desk.

Coach Meg said, "For the scrimmage today, I'm thinking of swapping Jenna out for Maya, what do you think about that, Arie?"

Arie and Emma looked at one another, mouths wide.

"My captain didn't forget, did she?" Coach Meg asked.

Arie put her hand on her head. "Maybe… Damn it."

Coach Meg was floored. "Arie, how could you, of all people, forget a scrimmage against the Predators?"

Emma smacked Arie on the arm. "Yeah, we forgot, but who cares? We're playing the Predators, babe. You get to stick it to Alex before your birthday. Like an extra present."

"Listen," Coach Meg said. "I know you and Alex have your little dragon rivalry going on, but just keep it under a ten, okay? I can't afford for you to get into trouble. If you get a card tonight, you're riding the bench, don't care if it's your birthday week."

For Arie, keeping the taunting under a ten, wouldn't be possible. She was already envisioning the beatdown she would deliver to her rival tonight. In her mind, one of her favorite songs played loudly. "I'll try, but I'm a hunter, Coach Meg."

Emma giggled. "I actually love when we play them, aside from watching Alex eat it, the song Arie uses in warmups fits perfect."

Arie gave her a big smile. "You know it, babe." She snapped her fingers as she recalled Coach Meg's initial question, "Let's stick with Jenna. I can get her in the zone. I'll pull them all in with me... We're all hunters tonight."

Coach Meg gestured toward the door. "Alright, get outta here. Don't forget what I said, keep the taunting under a ten, Arie."

Emma corrected her as they stood to leave, "Coach, you mentioned Alex... Arie's already in dragon mode now. I believe you mean she needs to keep the flames to a minimum."

"Oooh yeah," Arie said. "That's better. I'll try, Coach Meg."

Leaning against her locker with Emma beside her, Arie called Liam.

He answered the call, "Hey, how'd the test go?"

"Super easy! You were a big help. But, hey, about tonight..."

"Ahh... You're not calling to disappoint me, are you?"

"Pssh, no. Definitely not. It's just that I forgot that we have a scrimmage tonight. We don't always get started right at six. So, I may be just a few minutes later than we planned."

Liam was quiet for a moment, then asked, "Do they let people watch your scrimmages?"

Arie's eyes went wide. "Do they let people watch my scrimmages?" She imagined herself staring blindly at Liam, and the ball hitting her square in the face, while Alex laughed above her. She couldn't let that happen.

Emma seemed to know exactly what Arie was thinking. She took the phone from Arie's hand. "Hi, Liam, this is Emma. I heard what you just asked her, but listen, I can't have you here tonight. Arie's playing her arch nemesis, Alex. It gets ugly real fast, and I love it...but if you're here, I'm not gonna see any purple flames. You feel me?"

Liam sounded a bit confused. "I think so..."

Arie took the phone from her. "Sorry about that, Liam. Yeah, as much as I'd love to see you before the tour tonight… I gotta focus. This practice sets up the beatdown for Saturday's match. Now, that one you can come to, if you're free."

"Alright. I'll check my schedule and let you know tonight. Let me know when you finish up and good luck with the purple flames."

Arie and Emma readied themselves for the scrimmage in the locker room. Emma put her purple Vipers jersey on and shook her head at Arie. "Babe, good thing Coach makes us leave our practice unis here. We would've been late if we had to go grab them."

Arie nodded in agreement, as she turned her music on. Her favorite artist blasted through the small portable speaker, the same song on repeat. Several teammates walked in and got dressed by their lockers.

Jenna pointed at Arie, as she heard Arie's music. "Purple dragon time, baby! Alex and Dana are gonna eat cleats tonight."

Arie nodded. "That's right!"

Jenna came closer and stood beside Arie's locker. "I'm kinda nervous that Coach might not let me play today, has she said anything to you?"

Arie put both hands on Jenna's shoulders as Emma looked on from behind. Arie asked, "What are we tonight?"

Emma pointed at the speaker.

"Hunters," Jenna replied.

Arie patted Jenna's shoulders. "You're damn right. Now, you keep Dana off me, so I can cover Alex in flames. If you do that for the first half, she'll keep you in tonight."

Arie called out, "Alright, let's go! Time for the show, ladies."

The team jogged onto the field for warmups. Emma set the speaker up, and Arie bounced around through her stretches. She sang loudly and danced with her teammates, getting everyone involved.

She had a very contagious energy, and her confidence shattered the spirits of the strongest competitors. "Sing with me, babe," she said, holding her air microphone near Emma.

Emma sang along and thrusted her bottom half forward.

Arie smiled dancing beside her. "You're gonna kick ass today, Em. Alex isn't gonna get a single one past you."

Emma rolled her eyes and lifted her chin over Arie's shoulder. "Ohhh, here they come…"

The Predators jogged onto the other half of the field for warmups. Alex was flanked by her best friend, Dana, an equally horrible girl. Arie and Emma hated them both. The rivalry ran deep, all the way back to their elementary school days. Arie was always first, and Alex was always second. In truth, the girls were very similar, they had the same taste in most things, but there was no common ground in their eyes, only deep disdain.

Alex and Dana looked over and gave smirks toward Arie and Emma.

Arie checked over her shoulder to see if Coach Meg was within earshot. Emma gave her a thumbs up after seeing Coach Meg in conversation with someone in the distance.

Arie yelled over, "Sup, whores? Ready for another beatdown? It's my birthday in a few days. If you bow now, I might not embarrass you too much"—she looked at her nails—"I have something I wanna do tonight, and I really don't feel like pulling your hair out of my nails again."

Dana scoffed. "No one here is bowing, and we're not interested in what you do with Aaron."

Alex pulled her head back and looked at Dana. "She's not dating Aaron. What are you talking about?"

Arie threw her hands up. "Yes. Thank you. Wow…can't believe you said something smart."

"Wait, for real?" Dana asked Arie. "He's always here and you're always around each other. His socials are flooded with pictures of you."

Emma replied, "They're best friends…some people have more than one friend, Dana."

Coach Meg yelled over, "Captains, you have ten minutes, finish your warmups."

Arie jogged over to restart her song. She was really feeling it now; she danced and sang to the small crowd that sat in the bleachers. The crowd cheered her on and danced along.

The sound of one of Arie's favorite songs came from the Predators' bench. Arie paused her song and ran over with Emma behind her.

Alex was dancing and smirked at Arie as she approached. Arie screamed at her, "Oh, hell no! This is my song. I'm the dragon. Shut this off!"

Alex rolled her eyes. "You can't have every song about dragons, Arie."

Arie's head started banging to the music, as she looked at Emma.

Emma grabbed her shoulder. "Focus, babe."

Arie snapped back to reality. "Bullshit. Shut it off. I'm the dragon. You're a cheap imitation. Kill it now."

Alex, who was still dancing, shook her boobs at Arie, and turned to Dana. "Hey, D, tell me, what color is Arie's dragon?"

Dana answered as she played the air guitar looking at Emma, "Purple."

Arie's head started lightly banging again, against her will.

"I'm the gold dragon," Alex reminded her. "This song is about a gold dragon. You lose. This is my song."

Arie put a hand on her hip. "Shut the hell up, Alex, purple is better than gold."

Arie winced at her own words and whispered over her shoulder to Emma, "Eff…even I don't believe that. Gold is better. Shit."

Emma elbowed her. "Blow past it."

Arie said, "Switch to track four. We both wear number four, so I'll give you that one…since you'll be crawling in my flames, soon. Peace."

Arie and Emma turned and walked back toward their bench. Arie stopped walking and looked at Emma. "Wait, I really love that song, she can't have that one either. The shredding is next level, and his voice is so good. Let's go back and tell her she can't have it."

Emma shoved Arie forward. "No, that was badass what you said to her. Leave it. You won that round."

Arie pulled the girls into a huddle. "They are not predators. You hear me? Their jerseys are bullshit. We are Vipers and they're our prey! Now what are we gonna do?"

They all put their hands in the middle and yelled, "Win!"

Arie and Alex stood across from one another in the middle of the field as the ref showed them their coin for the toss. Arie's team won the toss, and Arie, of course, chose to receive.

Alex and Arie stood very close to one another in a stare down after the toss.

The tall female referee looked at both girls, who stood at five-foot-four, "You two, don't make me separate you already. It's a scrimmage, for crying out loud."

Alex taunted Arie as she backed up. "You know what, Arie? Anime is stupid."

Arie loved few things more than anime. Her mouth dropped open and her eyes narrowed. "I'll kill you."

The ref gave them both one more look of warning with her whistle in her mouth.

Following the kickoff, Arie gained possession quickly, thanks to handy footwork and defense from Jenna. She and Alex were locked up tight, as per usual. "Get off me, Alex, you're so obsessed with me. Copying my warmup routine."

Alex elbowed Arie. "Shut up. You think you're so much better than everyone."

Arie grunted at the elbow to the gut, cut around and said, "Because I am." She stole the ball and flew downfield, easily scoring on the goalie, who dropped to her knees.

Arie got down on all fours, and shouted at Alex, "Crawl, Alex! Crawl through my flames…"

The ref looked at Arie and shook her head. Arie winced, well aware that she pushed it with that one. She jumped up and was greeted with ass slaps from her teammates.

Alex immediately went on the attack, knowing that Arie was almost carded. She came straight at her. "You know how I knew you weren't with Aaron, right?"

Arie focused only on Alex's feet, she herself was a master of this tactic and would not be distracted.

Alex continued, "You need a challenge. He's too easy…I'd bet you're interested in his brother, now, that's who I'd be interested in."

"You can have the brother," Arie said. "Or both. I'm not interested in either." Arie stole the ball and flew back the other way, she passed to Jenna, who lost the ball to Dana.

Arie skirted back around and cut inside, she stole the ball back and kicked it as hard as she could, sending it straight into the goal! Arie jumped in the air. "You're sinking, Alex! You're burning! Bow before the one true dragon!"

Alex charged at Arie, and Arie met her head on.

Their foreheads pushed together, while the ref blew her whistle, issuing them both yellow cards.

Both coaches ran over as their teammates pulled Alex and Arie apart. No punches were thrown, but they both refused to move.

Coach Meg yelled as she approached, "Arie get on the bench! Now!"

The girls stared each other down as their coaches forced them both to their benches.

Arie sat on the far side of the bench for just a moment and kicked a chunk of grass up. She stood and watched Alyssa get subbed in for her.

Arie shouted to Coach Meg, "How long are you keeping me here for?"

Coach Meg shook her head, walking toward her. "I asked you to keep it under a ten. What would happen to the team if they didn't have you on Saturday?"

Arie put her hands on her hips. "I know. I just hate her. She stole my song and said anime was stupid."

"What the hell does that matter?"

Arie shrugged. "I love both of those things. She pissed me off."

"You two gotta work your crap out. You'll never make the national team like this."

"So? I don't want to play for the national team. I'm gonna take care of elderlies and rescue all the dogs."

Coach Meg playfully pushed her. "I'm mad at you and don't even think of reminding me that it's your birthday week."

Arie tried to make her laugh, while walking back toward the bench. "I can't help it. I'm a dragon and they're all my prey."

Coach Meg shook her head. "Shut up. Or I'm not letting you out."

Arie tightened her ponytail and looked behind, hearing a whistle.

Duncan, sitting beside Aaron, yelled over, "Arie, you're making Aaron nervous. Calm the hell down!"

Arie rolled her eyes and walked back beside Coach Meg. "Let me out Coach Meg, Aaron's here. I don't want him to talk to me from the bleachers."

Coach Meg looked confused but didn't move her eyes from the match. She asked Arie while looking forward, "Did you guys break up? Or is it just a fight?"

Arie dropped her head backwards, hands on her hips. "Damn it. I'm so tired of this. We're not together. It's a complicated mess that I need to clear up. Can you just keep him away from me, somehow?"

Coach Meg still hadn't looked at her, but replied, "Score for me again, and I'll keep him off you after the match."

"Deal. Can I go out now?"

Coach Meg shook her head. "No. Five more minutes."

At minute four, Arie was screaming, "Put me in, Coach! Alex is eating her alive!"

Coach Meg signaled for a substitution and put Arie back in.

Arie and Alex were locked up again, as soon as Arie hit the field.

Alex asked Arie, "Hey, real talk, who is the guy with Aaron?"

"Don't know. Don't care. You're not gonna distract me."

Alex elbowed her in the gut, again, forcing Arie to pass out wide to Jenna.

Arie jogged near the far side of the goal, Alex was not going to leave her alone, while Dana chased Jenna down.

Jenna kicked the ball over Arie's head, right to Arie's sweet spot, and Arie flipped backwards sending a bicycle kick into the goal!

Arie screamed, "Burn!" She blew pretend flames toward the other team! "I've burned it down! This is my throne!"

She held her arms wide as the team swarmed her, and the practice match ended.

Coach Meg called Arie over, and whispered in her ear, "I can keep him off you long enough for you to get to your car, after that you're on your own."

Arie nodded and pulled Emma quickly toward the opposite exit with her.

"You are just next level," Emma said.

"You too, Em. You shut them down. I'm nothing without you."

They high fived and jogged toward the parking lot. Arie told Emma about her deal with Coach Meg.

Emma shoved her. "Go, have fun. I'll stay and help keep Aaron off you."

After taking off her dirty cleats and gear, Arie got in her car and headed home. She called Liam, "Hey, I'm all done... Whooo!"

Liam answered, "Hi there, you sound happy. Guess the practice match went well."

"I'll tell you all about it, but yeah, I'm happy. Just gonna grab a shower, then I'll meet you at the entrance to my place."

"Great. I'll see you soon."

Chapter 33
How'd That Get Up There?

Arie quickly showered and braided her hair into two Dutch braids. She dressed in a comfy baby pink, long-sleeved, ribbed cropped top, with matching high-rise cotton sweats and cream-colored slippers.

She opened the door for Liam, who looked exceptionally gorgeous in a pair of dark jeans, a khaki green button-down shirt, rolled up to the elbows, with the top two buttons open.

The two silently looked one another over.

"Wow, you look really cute, Liam."

Liam shook his head smiling. "That's what I was going to say."

Arie held the door open, and Liam walked inside. "Alright, show me your place."

Arie happily walked Liam around her side of the estate, which was decorated with blush pinks and dusty rose colors.

She showed him her home gym, which had standard exercise equipment, colored in pinks and grays.

Liam raised his eyebrows. "I've never seen a pink treadmill, or weights—I've never seen any of this stuff in pink."

"Yeah, my dad can find anything. He's the best. I rarely use any of it, though, I'm usually too busy, plus you know with soccer, I already have a pretty solid schedule for workouts."

"Yeah, that makes sense." Liam nodded. "I used the gym on the other side this morning. It's nice."

Standing in the hallway, Arie received a text from Emma and shook her head, looking at her phone.

"Something wrong?" Liam asked.

"You wanted to see the dragon, right?"

"Of course, I do."

"Alright, fine, but please don't let it change the way you see me. I've already told you that I go crazy out there."

"Oh, is there a video?"

Arie nodded. "Yes, soon to be taken down, for sure." She passed her phone to Liam.

The video titled: *Dragon's clash, Arie vs Alex,* showed all Arie's highlights, as well as her taunting and dancing.

Liam's mouth dropped open in a big smile as Arie crawled on the ground after scoring. "Oooh! Nice goal! Definitely both should've been carded there, though."

Arie rubbed her side. "She elbowed me hard."

His eyes widened watching the video. "Look at you two going at it. Damn! You shook her! Nice! Wow, this is crazy!" His face went serious for a moment, as Arie and Alex's heads were pushed together. He paused the video and asked, "Are you guys actually gonna fight?"

Arie turned her mouth down and shook her head. "We don't."

Liam pointed at the screen. "This is the girl you told me about last night, right?"

"Yeah...that's Alex."

"There's the card," Liam said. "Took that ref long enough."

Arie shrugged, with a smile.

"Oh my God, look at you on the bench. You're not even sitting down... Unbelievable."

The clip showed the bicycle kick and Arie's last bit of taunting before ending.

"That was intense for a scrimmage. You're amazing, Arie. I liked the dragon stuff too, it was funny."

Arie sighed. "I can't help myself. She knows exactly how to piss me off."

"I know why you hate her, but what did she do in the match that set you off?"

Arie looked at the floor. "Well today, she stole my favorite dragon song, then said anime was stupid."

"Alright. I was not expecting those to be the things that set you off."

Arie put a hand on his shoulder. "Liam, we're enemies, she could say almost anything, and I'd want to punch her. It's just the way it is."

Liam locked eyes with Arie, who still had her hand on his shoulder. Arie was frozen, she really didn't want to move her hand but couldn't keep it there.

Mercifully, her phone rang. She released his shoulder and took the phone from his hand.

She showed the screen to Liam and sighed. "I told you, this always happens. Now, Brody's calling to yell at me."

Arie led Liam into her bedroom, so she could take her lecture from Brody. He started shouting as soon as she answered the phone. She sat on her bed and patted for Liam to sit beside her.

Liam didn't move from the doorway. *Why is he hesitating?* Arie wondered. *Did I make it awkward when I touched his shoulder?*

Arie was still being yelled at by Brody, but tilted her head at Liam and patted the bed again.

Liam placed his hands in his pockets and shook his head at her softly.

"Brody, hold on," she said, looking up at Liam. "Sit with me, what's wrong?"

Liam smiled. "You said you wanted pancakes earlier, aren't you hungry?"

"Yeah, let's go do that. We can use the main kitchen. I don't have anything for pancakes"—she pointed to the phone—"he's still yelling. Let's just walk there."

"Wait," Liam said. "I brought the stuff, it's in my car. I called your dad earlier and he told me what I needed."

Arie smiled big. "You did? That's so sweet. Well, let's grab the ingredients, then use the main kitchen anyway. My dad's griddle is the best." She hopped off her bed.

Brody continued his rant in Arie's ear, while the two walked to Liam's car. They grabbed the ingredients that Liam bought and headed to the main estate. Arie showed him a new shortcut, and they reached the kitchen quickly.

She looked at the phone and said, "Brody, please, I can't take any more. You've been yelling for seventeen minutes and thirty-five seconds. I'm hungry. I haven't eaten dinner yet."

Brody finally relented and ended the call.

"Sorry, Liam. It's always like that with him."

Liam had already begun mixing up the ingredients while she was on the phone. "Doesn't your dad get upset that he yells at you like that?"

Arie shook her head softly. "No. It's not like he's being mean about it. It's a bad look, I understand. My dad would get mad if it upset me, but it doesn't. I know Brody really cares about our family and the company. I don't take it too personally. I know I shouldn't do it, but I just can't help it. I like having fun."

Liam poured the pancake batter on the griddle. "Seems like a lot of pressure for a twenty-year-old. Doesn't seem fair that you have to act a certain way, based on your dad's company."

Arie pulled her mouth to the side. "Yeah, I used to think that too, but, I mean, I'd do anything for my dad…and Levi too. They suffered for a long time. There was a time before Levi came into the picture, when it felt like a lot of pressure, but not anymore. It was during all of that stuff with Alex in middle school, not the high school stuff. My family really helped me during that time… I think our whole family dynamic is pretty unique, sure, all families are unique, but we don't really get overly involved unless someone is reaching out."

Liam sighed, shaking his head. "I understand. Kory and I really only talk about work anymore. Like I told you last night, I talk to Luke, more than I talk to him."

Arie's eyebrows raised. "Well, that's because Luke is amazing! I only met Kory at Coop and Ethan's wedding, so I don't really know him. I did love the way he catered to Luke, though. They're really cute together. I was pissed about their wedding…I hated that I wasn't invited."

"Well, don't be too pissed. No one was invited, it was just at City Hall. I know my brother liked Luke for a while, but stayed back until he ended things with Coop. I don't think that was easy for him. I think Luke felt the same, so they just wanted to get married as soon as possible."

Arie looked at him softly. "Maybe you should try talking to your brother, about all the stuff we talked about last night. He's been married for a while now. I'd say he's probably in a better place than the last time you tried."

Liam watched over the pancakes, smiling. "He's definitely in a better place, but I don't know. Talking to you is easy, talking to him is not the same."

Arie playfully wagged her finger at him. "You don't know unless you try. Someone's gotta take the first step. You said you wished you had a better relationship with him, so I think you should be the one. Gotta tell him how you feel." She dropped her head and covered her mouth. "Oh my God. I'm an idiot."

Liam lifted the edge of a pancake checking it. "You're not an idiot. But why are you saying that? You just basically convinced me—do you think it's a bad idea now?"

Arie shook her head. "No. I just need to clear things up with Aaron. I shouldn't be giving you advice when I have a best friend that's apparently been in love with me for thirteen years, without me knowing. Kinda makes me sound like an idiot. I wouldn't take advice from me. I have to deal with this before my party on Friday... Wait, you're coming to my party, right? I just assumed you were."

Liam placed a large pancake on a plate for Arie and handed it to her. "Hopefully, I made it right. And, of course, if you want me there, then I'll be there."

Arie clapped with a bright smile. "Yay! Thanks for the pancake and I definitely want you to be there with me."

As Arie took her first bite, Liam winced.

Arie dropped her fork on her plate, making a loud clang.

"What happened, was it too hot, or just bad?"

Arie shook her head. "Liam, this one is even better than the one from Monday! I wish I could eat these every day."

Liam's mouth dropped into a big smile, and he held his chest. "I'm so glad. Scared me with that fork drop." He sat across from her and tried his own pancake, turning his mouth down after a bite. "This doesn't even taste good."

Arie poked a piece of her pancake and held it up to Liam. "I didn't get to feed you the chicken earlier. Maybe the pancake will taste better if we share."

Liam leaned forward and the two locked eyes, as Arie held the bite halfway across the granite counter.

Arie's dad's voice interrupted the almost sensual moment, "Arie, Liam! Did we miss the pancakes?"

Arie dropped her head, and her fork, in disappointment, while Liam sat back in his seat.

Tom and Levi came downstairs smiling. "You got Brody all upset with your routine, didn't you?" Tom asked.

"Nope. I got Brody upset because I was taunting and got carded for almost fighting."

Levi joked, "Dragons can't be carded, they'd just burn the card with fire."

"I'd get tossed for sure if I blew fire at the ref," Arie said with a giggle.

Tom tugged on the bottom of one of Arie's braids. "The taunting doesn't surprise me. But who did you almost fight with?"

Arie looked at her phone to see if the link was active. She slid the phone to her dad. "Here, Brody didn't get it taken down yet. He said he was working on it."

Tom held the phone in between himself and Levi. "Oh, it was Alex. I didn't know you had a match tonight."

"It was a scrimmage. I totally forgot about it."

Tom and Levi watched the highlights. They were both pretty unfazed; they'd seen Arie like this plenty of times.

Levi chuckled, pointing out the contrast between the Arie who stood beside him and the one in the video. "This was a few hours ago, now look at you! Perfect braids, all in pink, smiling. You really do transform, Arie!"

Arie leaned across the counter to grab her phone back. "Yeah, what can I say? She copied me during warmups and tried to steal my favorite dragon song. And she said anime was stupid. I know she doesn't believe that, since she bases her whole effing existence on whatever I like."

Tom nodded. "You two…I guess some things can't be forgiven."

"Nope. I tried, Dad. You know that I did."

Liam pulled his phone out and stepped to the side of the counter. He held a finger up to Arie. "Excuse me for a sec. It's my brother calling." He answered, "Hey Kory, what do you need?"

Arie didn't want to listen but was able to hear what Liam said.

"I'm just finishing up dinner with Arie," he said to Kory. "Tom and Levi are here talking to us. Can I call you when we're finished?" After a few seconds he ended the call and walked back toward Arie.

"Everything okay?" she asked Liam, while pulling the dishwasher open.

Liam nodded, and grabbed the griddle, bringing it to the sink, so he could clean it. "He said he wants to talk. I don't know about what, though."

Arie stood beside him smiling, as she loaded the last few things into the dishwasher. "You should go talk to him. I'm pretty tired, and you have a busy day tomorrow, anyway."

"You don't mind, really?"

She shook her head emphatically. "Absolutely not. We just talked about this. It's like really amazing that he called. Maybe he's been feeling the same way as you."

"You have a way of making me believe you, without even trying." Liam smiled, shaking his head softly. "He's probably just going to yell about some case."

Tom and Levi were quiet as they watched their conversation from the other side of the counter.

Liam finished cleaning the griddle and dried it off. "Hey, before I forget, tomorrow morning I have to run out to this restaurant that my client is having built. They want me to see something for myself.

Normally, I'd try and drag another lawyer with me, but I thought you might want to come, since you don't have class tomorrow morning."

Arie's face brightened, she answered excitedly, "Yes, for sure I do!" She playfully tapped Liam's stomach with the dishtowel in her hand.

Levi called over, "I'd like to remind everyone that we're here. Just in case either of you forgot."

Arie rolled her eyes at him, then smiled at Liam. "Alright, thanks again for the pancake, text me later with the details for tomorrow."

Liam waved goodbye and headed toward his room.

Tom's demeanor turned serious once Liam left. "Coop told me that Aaron called him today. He and Ethan weren't happy about it. I'm not too happy about it myself. He's never acted this way before, at least not that you've told me."

Arie pulled her braids out and ran her fingers through her hair. "Sooo much better. I put them in too tight."

Tom waved in front of her face. "Hello, did you hear what I said?" He and Levi chuckled looking at her.

"I did but you didn't ask me anything. What did you want me to say?"

Levi put his hand on Tom's shoulder and spoke to Arie. "We want to understand what's happening. We try to stay out of the way, but that was a weird thing for Aaron to do. We saw how he acted the other night; he certainly fired a few warning shots at Liam. We're trying to find out why he would be bothered by him so much."

"Exactly," Tom said. "It's always been my understanding that you two were best friends. A best friend wouldn't act like that. A jealous boyfriend, or maybe an ex would, though. Couple everything he's done with him calling Coop, and that paints a worrisome picture for us."

Arie sighed. "I don't know. But if you saw him in my room with

Liam today, he was like a different person. He's never acted like this before. Some stuff happened with his brother not too long ago, before I met Liam, and I think he just found out about it. Maybe that pushed him into this state of…I don't even know what to call it. He's like territorial or something."

Levi and Tom looked at one another.

"Hmm," Levi said. "Why did you need to make the distinction that it was before you met Liam?"

Arie pulled her mouth to the side. "Did I?"

Tom and Levi nodded.

"Huh." Arie folded her arms looking at the two. "I don't know why. It just came out."

Levi stepped closer to her. "Arie, before we decide whether to dive into…whatever the stuff with Liam is, have you ever told Aaron that you only see him as a friend?"

"No. I didn't see a reason to. But with everything that's happened, I'm going to tell him tomorrow."

"We're not going to lecture you," Tom said. "Just make sure you listen to your heart. Don't feel bad about being honest with people, even if it may hurt them."

"It's the only way," Levi added.

Inside his room, Liam threw a pair of cotton lounge pants on, brushed his teeth, then sat in bed.

He called Kory, who answered after one ring, "Hey, Liam, that was fast. I thought it would be later when you called back."

"No, I was actually going to call you tonight anyway. I wanted to talk to you. But you go first. Did you need something?"

Kory replied, "No. I don't need anything. What did you want to talk about?"

"Oh come on," Liam huffed. "You didn't need anything, but you called me; that doesn't sound like you."

Kory sounded nervous, "I, uh, I didn't get to talk to you about what happened with Maddie or...well...I haven't talked much to you...about anything in a while. I felt like it was time for us to try and clear the air, if you're up for it."

Liam smiled, thinking of Arie. "Yeah, I'd like that. Arie thought I should reach out to do the same."

"Wait, before we start in on Arie, are you already over the whole Maddie situation? By the time I tried to process you guys being together, you'd already broken up."

Liam looked up at the unmoving fan in his room. "What am I seeing on this ceiling fan, it's like white something? What is that?"

Kory asked, "What are you talking about? I asked you about Madeline. Is this your way of saying you don't want to talk about her?"

Liam stood on the bed, looking at the fan blades. "No, it's not that...just...give me a minute."

Liam flipped his flashlight on and shined it on the blade in question. It was definitely dried up frosting. He sighed. "Man...these two... Hang on, Kory." He dropped the phone on the bed and grabbed a few disinfectant wipes from the bathroom, then wiped the blades down. After washing his hands, he got back into bed. "Hey, I'm back. Sorry. Coop and Ethan with their damn food sex. I hope there isn't anything anywhere else. This place is so clean, I didn't think to check anything over."

"I don't even want to know what you're talking about."

Liam agreed, "I don't want to know the things I know either, but here we are. Anyway, with Maddie, I can say a few things for sure. I'm definitely over it...whatever veil I was looking through was definitely lifted. I mean, it just happened one night, then it became a normal thing. I felt at the time that it was what was supposed to happen. Then in Italy, after being around the other four, it just became obvious that this wasn't what I wanted…well, what either of us wanted. I actually tried to break up with her, but after sleeping on it, I felt like maybe if we changed a few things and didn't keep it a secret, then it would be fine. We had this huge fight with sauce and flour…it was crazy. We made up and then I just started feeling the same again. I found myself caring more about spending time with the guys there than Maddie. It was really confusing. Tom and Levi helped me a lot. They're both really amazing, they're just always willing to listen, and they care so much."

Kory was silent for a moment. Liam heard him sigh before he spoke. "Liam, I haven't been a very good brother. I should've been able to see what was happening and I didn't. It's my fault that you feel this way. I know that."

"How is any of what I said your fault? I didn't say anything about you."

"It's all my fault, Liam… All of it… I'm the reason mom's gone… dad's heart attack…everything that made you feel so vulnerable…it was all because of me."

Liam tried to process what Kory just said and heard Luke comforting him. He tried desperately to make the right words come out. Finally, he spoke softly, "Yeah. I thought that too until I talked to Arie. But people aren't perfect, Kory. What Mom did…I mean as an adult, we have to question her and dad's relationship, right? If there was a solid support system, then would she have done that? Think about it, she was *that* embarrassed over what happened that she did that? That's…I mean, it's possible, but it doesn't seem like that was the whole story. Think about it, really. With Dad and his heart attack… Well, I dated Maddie, so if anyone's at fault there, it was probably her. I'm playing, but also serious. Arie really helped me see things differently."

"Luke said something similar to me before. Still, though, I should have been the support system for you, and I wasn't. I failed in that regard. I'm surprised to hear that you talked to Arie about all of this. You haven't known her very long, have you?"

"No, but she's just…really special. She listens to me and shares with me…we talked for five hours the other night. I've never talked for five hours straight with anyone. She's that amazing."

"You've been different in just the few days you've been back. I'm inclined to believe that she is *that* amazing."

Luke added, "She is amazing, but Liam, she does have a dragon mode that she goes into. You should prepare yourself for that."

"Dragon mode? What does that mean?" Kory asked.

Liam chuckled. "I got to see it tonight. She had a scrim against Alex. Her friend sent her a video, and she showed it to me. It was intense, but, Kory, you have to see her play. I only got the highlights, but she did a few cuts and ended the game with a bicycle kick that was absolutely ridiculous!"

"You got to see her against Alex?" Luke asked. "That girl…she's the worst."

"Where can I see this video?" Kory asked.

Luke scoffed. "It's definitely been taken down by now. I'm surprised you even got to see it, Liam. Brody's been all over her since the incident in middle school."

"Yeah. I don't want to talk about that, though. Makes me upset even though I didn't know her when that happened. But Brody did call and yell at her for a good portion of the night."

"I bet," Luke said.

"If she had a scrimmage, when is the next official match between her and this other girl?" Kory asked.

"On Saturday. I'll definitely be there. I think Levi and Tom are going, too. Oh, Kory, listen to this, she's so amazing that do you know what she asked her dad to get her for her birthday?"

Kory and Luke both asked, "What?"

"Well, she didn't tell me, Tom did, when I called him today. She asked him to throw a night in Italy event for the seniors at the retirement home. Told him it has to have everything that they could ever think of doing in Italy. I guess there are a few people there that she's really close with. She wanted to make them feel special. She's got the biggest heart I've ever seen. When have you ever heard of anyone asking for something like that, for their twentieth birthday? Tom said he's still working on an artificial gondola that they can sit in… They're a really amazing family… I've never seen so many selfless people."

"That's definitely not the norm for a birthday wish. My question is, what are you getting for her? Can't be anything too big. You just met and you're not together yet…even if by some chance that happens before—"

Liam interrupted him, "I already found something. It should be here tomorrow."

"Wow. Already? With confidence, too?"

Liam smiled. "She's gonna love it."

After a bit more conversation, the brothers ended the call. Liam felt much better about his relationship with Kory than he had in a long time.

Liam texted Arie before he fell asleep:

Liam: *Hey, I just got done talking to Kory. I'll tell you about it tomorrow.*

Arie: *I can talk now if u want. Is everything okay?*

Liam: *No, you should rest. BTW Tomorrow you'll need to wear pants, the restaurant is still technically under construction. Also, you'll have to follow behind in your car. I won't have time to get you back home, with everything else going on. Does that work?*

Arie: *Wait. You didn't answer me. Is everything okay?*

Liam: *Yes, better than okay. Sorry. I missed that question.*

Arie *Then yeah. I'm good w/everything else.*

Liam: *I'll meet you at your place at 9:00.*

Arie: *Can't wait. Goodnight Liam.*

Liam: *Me too. Goodnight Arie.*

Chapter 34
That's How It's Supposed To Feel

The next morning, Arie got dressed and stood by her car, waiting for Liam.

He arrived a few minutes early and pulled in next to her. He rolled down his passenger window, as Arie leaned down to see him. "Good morning, you look really beautiful for 9:00 am."

Arie smiled. "Thanks, it's just jeans and a shirt, though. I don't feel very cute."

Liam tilted his head at her. "You'd look cute in anything."

Arie's covered her face with her right hand and peeked at him through her fingers. "Thanks. You look really good all the time, Liam."

"Thanks... Alright, I'll meet you there. You're sure you know where it is?"

"Yep. Got the address. I'll follow behind."

They arrived at the restaurant about twenty minutes later. The inside was mostly complete, except for the ceiling, which was still being painted. As they entered, they were greeted by large wooden scaffolding across the restaurant.

Arie looked up in awe. "Oh wow, that's stunning. This is what they're fighting over, right? The paintings on the ceiling?"

"Yeah, that's the problem we're here for at least. They're fighting over the land, and the restaurant name, too, but the nephew says these are his designs and the uncle didn't have the right to use them."

There were two piles of clean and dirty rags near the painting supplies. Liam grabbed one from the clean pile and the two walked up the makeshift stairs, toward the highest platform. "Arie, please be careful. This is kind of high off the ground."

Arie giggled at Liam beside her. "I've flipped around on higher bars than this when I did gymnastics. I have great balance, don't worry."

"Still…just be careful." As they reached the highest platform, Liam extended his hand toward her, and she held tightly onto it.

Standing on the top platform, Arie reached up toward the ceiling. "I'm confused, how can he paint this from here. True, we're high up, but he can't reach the ceiling to paint those little details."

Liam pointed to the switch on the side of the platform and smiled. "It moves. That's why I asked you to be careful. Only this top one moves."

"Oh, okay. I didn't know that. I'll be extra careful."

Liam wiped a spot on the platform for Arie to sit on with the clean rag, then wiped a much larger one for himself. Arie joked, "Why did you clean such a big space for yourself? It's not like you have a huge ass!"

Liam tilted his head at her and then laid down on the boards.

"Ohhh…. You're gonna lay down and take the pics. I get it."

Liam pulled his phone out. "Yeah, I need to really see the details."

Arie reached beside Liam and took the rag off the board next to him. She wiped a body-length spot clean for herself and laid next to him. "I'll help," too, she said, while pulling her phone out. "Ethan would've probably loved to help with this if it weren't for the interview today."

Liam looked through his phone lens with the camera, zooming in on the various depictions of knights, horses, lances, and other medieval themed paintings on the ceiling. "Yeah, I think so, too. I wanted to bring you with me, though. Never crossed my mind to even mention it to him."

Arie smiled and took some pictures on her phone. "Everything will be fine with their surrogacy interview today, right?"

"Of course. Everything will work out. The lawyer that's coming was really the only nice one in Italy. They're going to be great parents, and this lawyer already knows that. They have nothing to worry about."

Arie turned her head to the left and watched Liam as he continued taking pictures. She had a very strong urge to do something. Something that normally she wouldn't even consider to be that big of a deal, but she decided not to and resumed taking pictures alongside him.

"Arie, move your camera over here, Look, there's a tiny dragon!"

Arie held her phone up and looked through the lens, zooming all the way in. She squinted and asked, "Where? Are you messing with me? I don't see a dragon."

Arie leaned onto her left elbow over Liam looking through his phone. He suddenly turned his head to the left, seemingly pulling his face away, but held his phone in the same position. "It's there. I promise."

Arie noticed the way he turned his head away from her and felt like she shouldn't have moved toward him so quickly. She laid back down and said, "Yeah. I think I saw it."

Liam remained looking toward the left, while Arie lay on his right. She watched completely still, unsure of what might happen next, while Liam rubbed his eyes with his hand.

I am such an idiot. Why did I think he was into me? I really have no idea how to read people. He's probably gonna say we should leave now. Then, I'll never see him again. He'll tell the story of the girl who threw herself at him, against his will, as a cautionary tale to his grandkids one day. I am so dumb.

Liam sat up, as Arie still lay beside him, she turned to the right, unwilling to meet his gaze and possible rejection. Liam looked down at her and said, "We should probably get going. I think I got enough pictures…but…"

Arie nodded, still looking to the right. *I blew it.* She felt Liam's hand cup her cheek turning her face gently toward him. Arie, realizing that he was moving in, moved toward him. He leaned down and softly kissed her. Arie held his face through the softest, sweetest kiss she'd ever received.

Liam pulled back and looked into her eyes, stroking her cheek lightly. "Wow…"

Arie nodded, staring up into Liam's eyes, feeling completely overwhelmed. "Wow…" That connection between them ignited a spark that awoke every sense in her body. *That's what a kiss is supposed to feel like.*

Liam's phone alarm sounded, he'd set it earlier, so they wouldn't lose track of time. "Ah, we gotta go." He held his hand out to Arie and helped her stand, but this time, he didn't let go. They held hands tightly, while walking slowly across the rickety platform, and down the stairs.

Liam still held Arie's hand as they stood in between their cars. "I don't want to leave right now, but I really have to get to the office."

Arie blushed and sucked her lips in, then smiled. "Liam, that was…that kiss was…"

Liam pulled her into his arms and said softly, "I know. I think so too. I'll call you as soon as I have a few minutes. It's gonna be awhile though, so please don't sit around waiting or anything. I have so much to do before the at home visit."

Arie nodded, as Liam let go and opened her driver's side door for her. She sat inside and looked up at him smiling.

He sighed. "I can't do that again right now, as much as I want to."

Arie smiled brightly and nodded, while Liam closed her door.

He quickly got into his car, and they both headed out of the parking lot. She decided to stop at the gas station for a drink following her kiss with Liam. Before she could head inside, her phone rang with a call from Tony. "Hey, Tony, what's up?"

"Hey, Arie, I got a flower delivery here for you. Guy says he won't leave it with me. I told him to just leave them, but he says Aaron said he was to deliver them only to you."

Arie rolled her eyes. "What? Why would… Tell the guy I'll give him a hundred dollars, to rip the card up and take the arrangement to the Flowering Palms Retirement Home."

"Why would you want to do that? I know you like the people there, but these are beautiful flowers. They're from Aaron, too. Did you miss that part?"

Arie replied frustrated, "Tony. I heard you. I don't want them. Ask him what I told you to, please?"

"Alright." After a few moments, Tony came back on the line. "He says he'll do it for two hundred. But Arie, why do that? Just bring them yourself."

Arie shook her head. "Please pay him the two hundred for me, I'll pay you back when I get home. Tell him to send them to Ms. Doris. He doesn't need her last name."

"Got it," Tony said.

She thanked him and ended the call.

Aaron sat in his apartment on the couch and answered a call from Duncan. "Hey, did she like the flowers? What did her face look like when you gave them to her?"

"Man, I tried. She wasn't home. I told the guy I'd wait, too."

Aaron leaned back on the couch. "So, what did the security guard say? Did you tell him you were supposed to deliver them to her, personally?"

"Yeah, and he called her. She offered to pay me a hundred dollars to take them to the retirement home, said she didn't want them."

Aaron stood up with a hand on his forehead. "What? Did she know they were from me?"

Duncan sighed. "Bro…I don't know what to tell you. That's why she didn't want them. Long story short, she got him to pay me two hundred to rip the card up and drop them off at the retirement home."

Aaron was silent as he leaned against the wall in his apartment.

"I'm sorry, man. Maybe she's going through something right now. You just need to talk to her. I'm going to drop these flowers off… Unless you want them and the two hundred. I'd actually feel bad taking flowers from an old lady named Ms. Doris, though."

Aaron sighed "No. She's a really sweet woman that Arie and I visit a lot. Bring her the flowers, I don't care about the money."

Arie stopped at Tony's favorite cookie shop after grabbing money from the ATM. She picked up a box of treats for him to make up for the trouble she felt like she'd caused. Afterward, she pulled up to the gate and passed them out of the window.

Tony's face lit up in excitement. "This is why you're my favorite Morgan…of all the Morgans! Don't tell Levi, though. He brings me treats, too." He winked at Arie and smiled.

"Sorry for getting you in the middle of that. I can't accept flowers from him right now. There's just so much—"

Tony waved it off. "No problem. That guy was determined, though. Didn't seem like a normal delivery guy. He was adamant, I'll give him that. You ready for your party tomorrow night?"

"Yeah, but I need you to do something for me."

Tony lifted his chin at her. "Anything for you, what do you need?"

"I'm going to have a very uncomfortable conversation with Aaron at some point today. I need you to give me a call if he comes in."

"That's easy. Your dad already put him on the call list. Is that what you want, too? Just a call? Or do you want me to stop him?"

Arie shook her head. "No, you can let him in, just call me. I'll be at home."

"Alright," Tony said. "I call your dad first, then you. Your dad's gotta know first, kiddo."

Arie smiled at him. "I understand. Thanks, Tony."

Liam waltzed into his office, in quite possibly the best mood he'd ever been in. He grabbed a lollipop out of his desk and popped it into his mouth, then turned his computer on, so he could upload his case notes.

Luke stuck his head inside Liam's office. "Good morning, did everything go okay with your field trip?"

Liam tried to keep his smile under control. "Well, which are you asking about? The case or Arie?"

"Both," he said, walking inside the office.

Liam avoided eye contact and looked at his computer. "Yeah, everything went really well."

"Okay, good to know. I'm glad."

Liam kept his lollipop in his mouth and continued looking at his computer. "Yep. Thanks for checking in."

Luke walked out of the office with a look that Liam didn't miss. He knew Luke was going to run straight to Kory and recap everything.

Liam happily entered notes on his case, while uploading the pictures he took. His entire body felt lighter than it had in a long time, and he couldn't stop himself from smiling. Even though he and Arie didn't talk about anything—he knew this was different. There was a silent understanding in that kiss, and the moments after, the tenderness of it washed over him, warming him from the inside out.

A few minutes later, Kory walked inside Liam's office holding hands with Luke.

As soon as Liam saw the two, he righted his posture and muted his large grin, well, he tried to, at least.

Kory and Luke exchanged a glance. "Hey," Kory said. "There are cameras all over that restaurant, did you know that?"

Liam's mouth dropped open, and his lollipop nearly fell out.

Luke's eyes almost fell out of his head, while Kory's mouth dropped open at Liam's reaction. "Well, we have our answer!" Luke said.

"Are there really cameras?" Liam asked.

Kory tilted his head at him. "Liam! Think! You already know there aren't! Just what did you two do there, that would make you forget that?"

Kory and Luke continued laughing at Liam's expense.

Liam leaned back in his chair, relieved. He looked at the two of them with an enormous grin, and said, "Nothing happened."

Kory rolled his eyes. "Okay, sure."

"Liam, we don't believe that. Not for a second. Besides the fact that we caught you with the camera thing, your smile is out of control."

Liam looked up from his desk and sighed softly. "We kissed… and it was the best kiss I've ever had."

Luke and Kory's eyes went wide as Maddie came quickly into the office. She went right into boss mode. "What are you two standing around for? Best friend or not, Luke, if you two have time to visit with Liam, then you can use another case or two. Is that what your presence here indicates? That you need more work?" She didn't wait for an answer and turned to Liam. "You look happy, are you ready for the interview? Wait, before you answer, I was not asking if you *are* happy, or *why* you are happy. It was an observation. So, are you ready for the interview?"

Kory and Luke quietly left the office, while Maddie's attention was diverted.

Liam nodded. "Yes, and I took some more pictures for the Uncle case this morning."

"Okay, don't embarrass me tonight, please? Mario is the lawyer that I really hit it off with. The one that you were all pissy about."

Liam shook his head. "Listen, boss… Actually, never mind. I understand."

"I'm going to pick Mario up from his hotel and show him around a bit. I'll meet you at the Morgan house later. Also, whatever you're smiling about…don't let it distract you. He may be the nicest of the group we met, but he's still here to do a job." She quickly left the room and headed toward Kory's office.

Chapter 35
Take It Easy On The Cupcakes

The sounds of Italian crooners played loudly as Ethan's mom cleaned the kitchen of Coop and Ethan's home, while his dad stood by the large sliding back patio doors. His mom's hair was tied in a messy bun, and she was visibly sweating as she rigorously wiped down the counter with a special granite polish.

Ethan stood with his arms crossed, looking at her from beside the stairs. He huffed. "Mom. It's already clean. Our home is spotless. You are literally doing everything that we've already done."

She stopped her aggressive rubbing and looked up at him. "Mimmo, sweetie, there were leftover cleaning swirls all over this counter. Do you think I want my grandson's fate to be decided by a few foggy marks?"

Coop walked down the stairs and kissed Ethan on the cheek, then stood beside him. Ethan's mom had been re-cleaning everything they'd already done since early in the morning.

His dad shook his head and turned around. "Gina, his fate is not going to be decided by marks on a counter. That may be the most ridiculous thing a person has ever said before a home visit."

She tilted her head at him, with a bit of attitude. "You think so, Paul? Because I don't. Besides, who would take that chance?" She pointed toward the kitchen window. "The light comes in through there, it looked terrible."

"Seriously? Mom, I cleaned it right before you got here," Ethan said.

She smiled at him. "And you did a great job, sweetie."

Coop and Ethan chuckled.

Ethan asked her through laughter, "How can it be both? You just said it was terrible."

She put the cloth down and walked over to him. She held his face in her hands. "It was terrible. But because you did it, it was perfect. I'm just helping, sweetie." She patted his cheeks and walked over toward the refrigerator and began wiping it down.

Coop pulled Ethan into a hug and kissed him on the cheek. "She's right about that. Everything you do is perfect."

"And yet here she is scrubbing away."

Ethan's dad gestured for the guys to join him outside and slid the door open.

"Before you go out there," his mom shouted to him, "is Liam is coming for the visit, or will it only be the other one?"

"Liam is coming, too. Why?"

Gina smiled big and her mouth opened wide. Paul held a hand up to her. "Stop. I need to talk to them before you start in on that."

"Alright, I'll wait," she said. "Boys, I'm going to your bedroom next, should I wash the sheets?"

Ethan turned around and looked at her. "Mom, no. Don't touch the sheets. Our room is clean, you don't need to worry about that."

She raised her eyebrows and tilted her head, looking between the counter and Ethan. "I'm going to check it anyway, sweetie. Also"—she opened a cabinet, and pointed inside—"what in the name of sweet spumoni do you have so much powdered sugar for? You boys need to take it easy on the cupcakes."

Coop shook his head. "That's not for—"

Ethan covered Coop's mouth. "Got it, Mom, we'll take it easy. No more cupcakes." The three men walked outside onto the patio, leaving Ethan's mom inside the kitchen.

Emma ran into Arie's room, flopping on the bottom of her bed, out of breath.

Arie giggled. "You have the best entrances and exits, Em, I swear! Wait, entrances, that gives me an idea. Do you think Coach will let me bring a smoke machine for Saturday? That would be so cool, right? I could like, come in first with you next to me and everyone else behind? Or you and I could come in last? What do you think? Ooooh, wait, even better would be if we could get the music to play loud enough for the whole field to hear, then the smoke. I bet my dad would do it for me."

Emma leaned up on her elbows. "Babe, none of that will happen. Delete it, defragment it, erase it, just no. None of that can happen. Well, we could walk in first or last, whichever you want, but the smoke and whatever other hot nonsense you just spit out are a definite no."

Arie pulled her mouth to the side in thought.

Emma sat up patting Arie's leg. "What if we could get your dad to get a big fake dragon float and roll it onto the field with the smoke?"

Arie's eyes widened in excitement. "Do you think we could?"

"No!" Emma whacked her with a throw pillow. "I was kidding! Come on! None of that will happen! Not even the smoke machine and that was the least crazy thing you said."

The two giggled together, each clutching a throw pillow on their laps.

"Alright, for real. You said this was important, I know this isn't why you called me over. What's up?"

Arie held the fuzzy pink pillow in front of her face. "Liam kissed me."

Emma pulled the pillow down. "What? When? How? Tell me everything!"

"We were just laying down and…"

Emma interrupted her, "Laying down? What? I thought you were going to a construction thing?"

Arie explained the scene, setup, and the lead-up to the kiss. "I still don't know why he turned away from me."

Emma pointed to Arie's chest. "Okay, well, you were wearing that shirt, right? Or did you change?"

"Yeah, same shirt, but I was wearing jeans at the time. Not these." She tugged on the bottom of her tiny cotton shorts.

Emma appeared to figure it out easily. "Oh…I see what happened when he turned away at first."

"What? How could you possibly know?"

Emma pointed to the large mirror on Arie's wall that hung beside her TV. "Lean to the side like you did over lawyer guy, earlier."

Arie leaned over, and Emma pointed at the mirror. "Boom baby! He saw your girls!"

Arie looked in the mirror, mortified. "Oh my God! Em, no!" She covered her mouth in embarrassment.

Emma shrugged. "Who cares? You have great boobs, look at them. They're perfect. But yeah, I think he turned to the side because he probably felt guilty looking."

"That is something he would do," Arie said with a smile.

Emma recrossed her legs, putting the throw pillow back on her lap. She clapped her hands and said, "Tell me more, what kind of a kiss was it? Your eyes are all dreamy like a damn glossy filter or something. It must've been a good one."

Arie nodded holding her chest. "Em, it was so soft and sweet, kind of sexy but not like it was trying to be. It was perfect. I felt like I was floating, especially because I was up so high."

Emma stuck her face in the pillow on her lap. "I am so jealous of you. It's been so long since I kissed someone. I don't think I've ever had a kiss like that, though. Wait, was there tongue?"

"Barely, just like a tiny tap. Uggghhh. It was delicious. I'm gonna die, Em!"

Emma shook her head. "Party is gonna be interesting tomorrow. When do you plan on talking to Aaron? You're gonna have to do it before then."

Arie sighed. "Yeah, I'm gonna do it today. I thought I'd call him in a little and try and talk to him.

Emma thought for a moment. "Well, it's Thursday so he has early practice, you're gonna eff him up if you do that first. You shouldn't do that, babe."

Arie held her palms up, "Well, what am I supposed to do then?"

"I don't know but we gotta come up with something," Emma said looking around the room. "You already rejected his flowers...oh, but Aaron probably doesn't know that. I'm sure that shady delivery guy just lied and said he delivered them to you."

"Yeah, he made an extra two hundred dollars. I actually should call and make sure Ms. Doris got the flowers."

Arie looked at her phone, and it started to ring in her hand. Her eyes widened and a smile covered her face. "Hi, Liam! Are you on a break?"

"Hey, no, not really. I wanted to talk to you about something, then I have to get back to it."

"What did you want to talk about? Is something wrong?"

Liam sighed. "No, nothing is really wrong. I'm just worried about how your conversation with Aaron is going to go down. I'll be tied up with Coop and Ethan till…I don't even know what time, actually." He sighed again. "I would just… It's not really my place… But…"

Arie heard the worry and struggle in his voice. "It's okay, just be honest and tell me how you're feeling."

"I really wish I could at least be at the estate when you do it. I'm afraid that this is going to upset you more than you think it will. I can't stand the thought of you being sad or upset. We're not even, I mean, we haven't even talked about anything yet and I already feel very protective over you."

Arie stuck her bottom lip out and looked at Emma.

She said to Liam, "Hey, listen. Everything you just said was very sweet and I'm grateful that you care that much about me, but I'll be okay. Emma and I were just talking about how I was gonna handle this. Wait, I got it. Em can sleep over and hang out in the bathroom, while I talk to Aaron."

Emma looked at her and nodded, she and Arie high-fived each other.

"Ahh. That makes me feel better. But Arie, if you need me, just let me know and I'll be there, okay?"

"Thank you. But really don't worry. It's gonna be fine."

"Okay, I'll call you later."

"Thanks, Liam. Talk to you soon."

Emma and Arie smiled at one another. Arie's phone rang, and she looked down at it. "I get so many phone calls these days. It's the retirement home this time.

"Hello?" Arie answered.

"Hello, Arie, darling. It's Ms. Tamara, I'm Doris' nurse today. She wanted you to know that she's not feeling well, but she received the flowers, and she loves them. That young man that dropped them off, sure kicked up a fit when we asked him who they were from. Almost had to beat it out of him."

"Oh, really? I'm sorry about that. I don't know who the driver was, it's a long story, but thanks for letting me know. I should be by sometime tomorrow to visit Ms. Doris."

"Alright, doll, we'll see you soon."

"Thanks, Ms. Tamara."

Emma grabbed her keys off the bed. "Hey, I'll be back in a bit, I'm gonna run home and grab my stuff for tonight."

"Okay, see you when you get back," Arie said, while hugging her. "Drive safe."

Tom and Levi sat outside at the bar on their patio. Levi sipped a frozen coconut drink through a straw. He winced at the bitter taste. "Tommy, this one is no good, too much coconut milk, maybe?"

Tom stood up, took the drink and dumped it down the sink behind the bar. He was trying to come up with a new drink for Arie's birthday. The main party would be catered, but beforehand they normally had a quick family gathering inside the estate. This year would, of course, be different because Levi would be there, and based on their limited interaction with the two last night, they assumed that Liam would be joining them, too.

Tom grabbed an empty glass. "Well, what about the one earlier that you said was okay, just a bit too sweet? Should I try that again? It's hard to neutralize the sweetness without any alcohol."

"Well, what if you mix a little of everything together that's left on the counter, Tommy? Use the frozen fruit and the juice. Try the lime juice with the pineapple, coconut, and strawberry."

Tom dumped the ingredients into the blender, and the two watched the colors swirl around.

"This is gonna be the one, I know it." Tom poured the drink into a glass, popped a straw in and handed it to Levi.

Levi took a sip and his face brightened. "Yes! This is it! Delicious, fruity, but not too sweet." He handed Tom the glass. "Try it, you'll love it!"

Tom took a long sip from the straw. "Oh, that is good!" He sighed and leaned across the bar on his elbows. "What are we going to do with this kid?"

Levi tilted his head. "Be more specific. Which one?"

"You know what, any of them. They've all got stuff going on that I'm nervous about. I thought that the hard stuff was over."

Levi smiled softly and placed his hand on Tom's across the bar. He repeated Angelo's words from the cooking class, "Tommy, kids are terrible, and we shouldn't have had them."

Tom loved Levi's impersonation, he thought it was spot on. "Oh wow! Angelo? When did you get here?"

Levi giggled. "I thought you'd like that. I loved how Ethan and Coop were feeling so confident too, right? Angelo's hair was falling out…guy was probably only thirty-years-old, and those two were so oblivious to the trials that come with raising children."

"That was a fun time, though. I'm sure everything will go okay for them. They have each other." Tom lifted Levi's hand to his mouth and lightly kissed it. "Right now, I'm worried about Arie. I don't know what she's gonna do with Aaron."

Levi rubbed Tom's hand. "You just called Tony and told him to let you know when Aaron gets here. We can hover around for the rest of the day. Also, like we talked about last night, she's going to rip that kids heart out, no matter how nice she is. I'd be more worried about him being upset than her. Hopefully, she doesn't just come flat out and tell him she's interested in Liam and make matters worse. I don't think she would, though. Judging from their interaction last night, I'd say they haven't gotten any further than talking. There probably wouldn't be any need for her to mention that to Aaron."

Tom raised his eyebrows. "Is it okay, that we're just watching this happen, though? With both situations?"

"I think so. Interfering won't do anything. No one knows that better than us. We're lucky that she lives here, saves us a lot of worrying. But with Aaron, I'd say he should have known by now. What twenty-year-old doesn't make a move on someone they've liked for this long? It's really not Arie's fault. If he didn't make any advances, why would she have seen him differently? Meanwhile, Liam with those eyes last night leaning across for that bite. There was no mistaking what he was thinking. Now, if Arie said she didn't think Liam was interested, then I'd be worried about her judgement."

Aaron dressed for practice in the locker room with his teammates, feeling more than annoyed that Arie didn't want his flowers.

Travis called over, "Hey, can you ask Arie if Emma is into me? We've been texting, but I'm not sure if she is. She seems to be distracted a lot. One second, she's texting me, flirty, then the next she just ghosts me."

Aaron slammed his locker shut. "No, I'm not gonna do that. Ask Emma your damn self. Arie's not answering my texts anyway."

He sat on the locker room bench and sighed looking up at Travis. "Sorry, man. Shit's been crazy with her lately. I don't know what's going on. It's always been us. Arie and Aaron. Now, there's this guy living there and it's just all fucked up. I have to talk to her before her party. I should have skipped practice."

Travis sat beside him. "Listen, I saw her with that guy yesterday, but only for a minute and Arie's back was toward us, but Duncan said—"

Aaron stood up shaking his head. "I already know what Duncan saw. I don't need to hear it again. I'm going to talk to Coach and see if I can skip practice."

"I wouldn't do that, man. He's in a bad mood."

Aaron shrugged. "These days no one is happy to see me. I don't really care what kind of mood he's in."

Aaron knocked on the door of his coach's office and entered after he waved him in.

Coach Rick leaned back in his chair. "We hit the field in five minutes, what can I do for you, Captain?"

Aaron's phone sounded from inside his pocket. He knew it was a text from Arie, since her notification sound was different than all the others. He looked at his coach. "One second, I've been waiting for this text all day."

Arie: *Hey, can u come over tonight? We really need to talk.*

Aaron sighed and said aloud, "Not what I wanted to see, but at least she's not ignoring me."

Aaron: *Yeah. I'll be there.*

He slid his phone in his pocket and looked at his coach. "Never mind. Let's hit the field."

Arie had just finished painting her nails and was waiting in her bedroom for Emma when her phone rang. Her face instantly brightened seeing Liam's name. "Hi, Liam."

"Hey, I just got in my car. I'm on my way to your brother's. How is everything going?"

"All good. I just texted Aaron, he's gonna come over after

practice. Hey, but forget about that. How is everything going with you? Did the client like the pictures?"

"You're always thinking about other people. I'm great. I mean, I'd be even better if I was coming there to see you, but I'm happy that I get to be with Coop and Ethan for the interview. As for the pictures, the client is a pain. It's too complicated to get into. We don't have that much time to talk, but I got a notification that your present was delivered."

"What present? From who?"

"From who?" Liam asked. "From me, of course. Did you think I wasn't going to get you anything?"

"I didn't expect it... I really didn't. That's really sweet. You didn't have to do that, though. I just want to spend time with you. But I'm really excited about the present, now."

"Well, don't get too excited about it. I haven't seen it in person yet. I'm going to hedge my bet here a little, in case you don't like it. If you like it, I'll say it was exactly what I planned, but if not, I'm going with, it looked different online."

Arie giggled. "I appreciate your honesty so much. Please never stop. Oh, wait, did Luke mention if he and Kory are coming to my family party tomorrow?"

"Is that different than the night party?"

"Yeah, before my friends come over, we usually get together and eat pizza, and my dad makes me a special birthday drink. Last year Luke wasn't there, but normally he is."

"He didn't mention it to me, but wouldn't it be awkward for Luke and Kory, being around Coop and Ethan? I just spent almost a week with them, and they're really not into being around other people. Luke and Kory are constantly together too…I can't picture all four of them hanging out. Plus, that was also before your dads got back together, right? There's a lot going on inside this picture in my mind."

Arie thought for a moment. "Hmm, well, they were fine at the wedding. I don't think it's awkward for them. Either way, as long as you're there, I'll be happy."

"You said a few minutes ago that you wanted me to keep being honest, right?" Liam asked.

"Absolutely. I never want anything but honesty."

Liam sighed. "Okay, well, I was thinking that with the stuff with Aaron tonight, that you should really focus on explaining your feelings for him. Don't let him steer the conversation toward me, which I have a strong feeling will happen… Truthfully, if he brings me up, then that's your sign that the brother didn't tell him everything…not that I want to think about that either. If he steers your rejection toward me, you need to make it clear that this is the way *you* feel, not because of me, but because it's how you've always felt. If he gets it in his head that you're just feeling this way because of me, he's going to think he has a shot if he can convince you that he's the better option…or he's going to just try and wait it out."

Arie was silent.

"I'm sorry, was that too much?" Liam asked. "I went into exploration mode there. But do you understand what I'm saying?"

"I do. It makes a lot of sense, but what do I do if he brings you up? I can't deny my feelings for you."

"That's really sweet, Arie. In my opinion, and I want to be clear here, I am absolutely not telling you to lie or deny your feelings for me—I'm telling you that they are irrelevant to the way you feel for him. You have to steer him back toward your feelings for him if he brings it up. Maybe he won't, but I seriously doubt that."

Arie held her forehead. "I seriously doubt it, too. Not based on what he's been acting like. Ugh, I don't wanna talk about him anymore."

"I don't particularly want to either, but if you're upset afterward, it's okay. I want you to know that I'll understand. The honesty thing works both ways, I want you to tell me what happened, and how you're feeling as soon as you're up for it. If that's tomorrow and not tonight, I would be okay with that. Just promise me that you'll text or call as soon as you're done. If you want to talk, then I'll listen, and if not, that's okay, too."

"I promise to let you know," Arie said.

Emma rushed inside Arie's room wearing her backpack on her shoulders, holding purple fuzzy slippers in her hand, with her arms wrapped tightly around her favorite pillow, which blocked most of her face. Arie laughed loudly, as Emma nearly tripped, but regained her footing, landing face first on her bed. She peeked up from the pillow. "Babe, my flip flop just broke, I almost ate your floor."

Arie laughed again as Emma pulled off the broken sandal, showing it to her. The connecting piece had popped right out of the glittery sandal.

Emma shook her head. "This would never happen to you. Not in a million years. But me? Every time. I have the worst luck."

Liam chuckled overhearing their conversation. "I'm really glad she's going to be there with you tonight."

"I'm glad she'll be here, too," Arie said with a smile.

Liam pulled up to the stone guardhouse outside the entrance of Coop and Ethan's home. "Arie, hang on a sec. I'm at your brother's gate."

Sal, the security guard approached. "Hello, name please?" he asked, in a very thick Brooklyn accent.

Liam smiled up at the giant man. "Liam Collins. I'm the Morgans attorney."

"Oh, very nice to meet you. I need your ID, pal." Liam pulled his ID out of his wallet and showed it to him. Sal checked the license over and gave him a nod. "Alright, you check out. You're good to go. Just follow this long driveway to the left, it wraps around. Don't go to the right, that's the entrance for landscapers, garbage pickup, or anyone they don't like that comes to visit."

"Thank you. I'm glad they told you to let me go in through the left then."

Sal looked left to right. "Yeah, they did. Now, she ain't here yet, but the other lawyer, Madeline, she's going to the right entrance, C and E's orders."

Liam chuckled. He knew they didn't like Maddie, since they'd already told him that several times. "That's funny. Those two are something else."

Sal lightly tapped the roof of Liam's car. "Yeah, they're a riot. Alright, buddy, I have to get back inside. It's too hot out here."

Liam picked the phone up from his lap and drove through the large black iron gates as they opened. "Hey, Arie, I'm back. Sorry. Sal had to let me through. How long is this driveway to your brother's house?"

Arie giggled. "Honestly, I think their driveways are longer than my dad's. But before you go, is it okay if I mention the fact that we kissed to my dads? Like, if it comes up?"

"Well, I'm not going to bring it up to Coop and Ethan, but if they asked about it, I'd tell them. With your dads I'd feel bad not saying anything if I saw them. It would feel like I was hiding something. I couldn't do that. Ideally, we should talk first."

"You're such a nice guy, Liam. I doubt it will come up, though. They don't pay attention to stuff like that."

Liam remembered the look that both Tom and Levi had on their faces when they came downstairs last night. He could still picture it now, almost twenty-four hours later. "Oh, I don't know about that... But I have to go inside now. I just pulled in the driveway. I'll be thinking about you."

"Me too. Bye, Liam."

Liam was a little nervous as he approached the large double glass doors. The home was gorgeous, and although it wasn't as big as the Morgan estate, it was still a massive property. He rang the doorbell and took a deep breath, straightening his navy tie.

Coop and Ethan answered the door smiling.

"Hi, Liam," Coop said, stepping to the side.

Ethan held the door open. "Welcome to our home."

Coop patted Liam on the shoulder. "How was the drive from the gate? Did Sal send you to the left, or the right?"

Liam, in an attempt to see if the two really did like him, said, "He sent me on the one for people you don't like."

Ethan and Coop looked at one another. "Wait," Coop said. "He sent you on the right?"

Liam shook his head. "No, I'm just kidding. He sent me on the left." He walked around the first floor of the home checking out the kitchen and living room spaces with Coop and Ethan. "It smells good in here, like fresh lemons, and clean laundry. I don't know what I expected your house to smell like, but it wasn't this."

Ethan stepped on the bottom stair and turned to look at Liam. "You thought our house would smell bad?"

"No, definitely not. I think I was expecting some typical cologne smell or something. This is better than that."

He followed Ethan and Coop upstairs and tried to remind himself that he had nothing to worry about. *I'm their attorney, and I've done a good job for them... so what if I kissed Coop's sister? Coop probably wouldn't even care. Besides, I can't help who I like. Either way, hopefully, it won't come up.*

Ethan opened a door on the left side of the long hallway, and the group stepped inside. "This will be the baby's room. It's right next to ours."

Liam looked around at the empty space. "Uhhh. You guys have to get some baby stuff in here. What are you going to do if you get a call saying she's going to deliver tomorrow? You'd have to hop on a plane right away."

"We plan on going shopping this weekend for his room," Ethan said. We wanted to make sure everything was completely finalized before we did that. Besides, if they have to deliver him unexpectedly, we can always order furniture and pay to have the room set up. If my mom comes to supervise, there wouldn't be a need to worry."

Coop added, "Yeah, she was here all day, cleaning and asking us the craziest questions."

Ethan shrugged, looking at Coop. "Yeah, pretty normal day for her."

The two chuckled, while Liam smiled, remembering the few interactions he'd had with Gina, which led him to thinking about Arie.

Ethan crossed his arms and looked at Liam. "What's this breezy, happy air you have coming off you? We noticed it when you were walking up the driveway, you looked nervous for a minute, but then you had a huge grin on your face."

Coop stood beside Ethan and puffed his chest out while crossing his arms. "Yeah, what's that about? You're asking us questions, but I think we should be the ones asking the questions."

"Mmmhmm…I agree," Ethan said, looking Liam over.

Liam avoided their gazes and their questions. He walked to the window and tapped the glass. "These windows are really thick. When we were in Italy, you said they were hurricane windows, right? They're nice."

Coop and Ethan were silent. Liam turned around to see them raising their eyebrows at one another. *Oh God. Don't ask me about Arie. Please don't ask me about Arie.*

Ethan pulled his mouth to the side, narrowing his eyes at Liam. "So, we didn't get to finish our talk about Arie yesterday."

Coop held a straight face and eyed Liam.

"What time is it?" Liam asked, pulling his phone from his pocket. He figured his best course of action was to pretend he didn't hear Ethan. He stared down at his phone, fumbling between apps. "Okay, you should probably show me the backyard. The other lawyer will want to see that, too." He continued looking at his phone, waiting for one of the others to move toward the door. As he stared down, two pairs of feet in black socks moved very close in front of him. He really didn't want to look up.

Coop's voice was serious, "Liam, why are you avoiding talking about my sister?"

"Yeah," Ethan said. "You just went out to lunch before studying, right?"

Liam finally looked up. "I um…uh…guys, we should really get downstairs and finish up before the others get here. You may have missed something."

Ethan put a hand on Liam's shoulder, and Coop put a hand on the other. They stared at him silently for a moment.

Ethan moved in closer. "Liam. We're not going anywhere until you tell us what happened."

Coop exploded with laughter and Ethan followed, hysterically laughing beside him. "Cooper!" he playfully scolded him. "You were doing so good. He almost told us!"

Coop was in stitches, hunched over. "I couldn't take it. Your face was too much! You looked so serious, puppy!"

"Well, I'm proud of you. You lasted longer than I thought you would." He kissed Coop on the cheek.

Liam was a bit confused but feeling far better since they were laughing.

Coop stood up and wiped the tears from the corners of his eyes. "We're just messing with you. We're not really interested in whether you're into Arie or not."

"That's between you two," Ethan said rubbing Coop's back.

Liam let out a loud exhale in relief. "You guys are always screwing around! Scared the shit out of me." Liam held a hand on his chest. "I'm not playing…my heart is beating so fast right now."

Ethan gave him a pat on the shoulder. "Liam, we like you. Relax."

Coop pulled Ethan by the hand outside of the room. He looked over his shoulder at Liam. "Yeah, you really gotta chill. You're good. We'll show you the backyard."

Liam followed them outside and was completely astonished at the massive fenced-in property. "This is a big yard, and the pool is really nice, but you guys need to get—"

Ethan interrupted, "We already special ordered a security fence for the pool and the hot tub. It will be here next week. The lawyer can't complain about that, right?"

Liam shook his head. "No, he can't. You knew exactly what I was going to say, too." He crossed his arms looking around. "Did you make the money for all of this from the foundation? Or is this inheritance money?"

Ethan's mouth dropped open, and he tilted his head at Liam. "Wow, we told you we liked you ten minutes ago, and now you're asking us rude questions."

"Tsk, tsk," Coop said. "You already changed our minds once. If we throw you over the fence, there's no coming back from that."

Liam rolled his eyes and waved them off. He wasn't about to fall for the same set up again. "I don't believe that you're actually offended."

"You should," Ethan said, looking seriously at Liam. As soon he finished the words, he and Coop immediately broke into laughter. "I'm sorry. I'll stop."

Coop through laughter said to Ethan, "No you won't. I don't think I can stop either."

Liam held a hand on his forehead. "Well, you both should stop. These agencies don't like shenanigans."

Ethan and Coop looked at one another and laughed even harder.

"Shenanigans?" Ethan asked. "Did you just say shenanigans?"

Coop was hysterical. "My dad doesn't even say shenanigans. Liam, who says that to someone?"

Liam joined them in laughter, "What else could I say? Hijinks, tomfoolery, asinine behavior? Shenanigans was the first thing that came to mind."

Coop and Ethan were really in a giggle fit; they truly couldn't stop, both hunched over. Ethan begged, "Please, Liam, we'll do whatever you need us to, just don't say shenan...shenani..." He couldn't even get the word shenanigans out.

Coop tried to help him get the words out. "Liam, just don't say shenan...shenanig..." He couldn't stop the laughter either.

Liam chuckled watching the two. He really enjoyed being around them, and for just a moment he wondered how amazing it would be if he was actually part of their family. He shook that thought from his mind. *What the hell am I thinking? I'm here to do a job, not imagine scenarios that won't happen in a million years. It was one kiss.* "Okay, guys, I won't say it, but we should go inside before the others get here."

Coop and Ethan slid the door open and straightened each other's ties, when they stepped inside. They offered Liam water, tea, or homemade lemonade, that Ethan's mom made this morning.

Liam opted for the lemonade, and happily drank it, sitting at the large counter. "Oh, so what is the baby going to call you? Are you both going to be dad? Or are you going with something else?"

Ethan's face lit up and he rubbed Coop's arm. "I'm gonna be Babbo, it's Italian for dad, and Coop will be Dad or Daddy, whichever the baby decides, since Coop likes both. We just can't wait to have him here."

Coop kissed Ethan on the cheek. "Soon. Really soon, pup."

The doorbell rang, and all three men turned their heads toward the sound, but the front door was not within eyeline. Coop pulled the security feed up on his phone. "They're here," he said showing the group that Madeline and Mario were standing outside the front door.

Chapter 36
Not My King

Earlier in the evening, Alex had tagged Arie in a social media post with a picture of herself wearing headphones, looking at a laptop. The caption read: *Working on my playlist for Saturday.*

Arie sat on her bed with Emma watching videos, trying to decide which songs she would use in warmups. "She really can't help but copy me. She thinks she's gonna get in my head. It's not gonna happen."

Emma patted Arie's leg. "She's already in your head, babe, but yeah, she won't get the best of you. That's what you mean."

"Yeah, well…I can't let her get to me. Can't believe she would even say anything after last night."

"You said it yourself; she's just like you, and you're kinda dumb, babe, you know this."

"She's a different kind of dumb, though."

"If you say so, but she's definitely mean. You've never been mean to anyone without reason. She's just cruel, that's the difference."

Arie tilted her head side to side. "They're all good songs, but damn, I can't give up on my original for the Predators. Also, I claimed the dragon song on Saturday to Alex's face. I feel like I should just use those two in warmups." The next song played, and Arie was hit with an unpleasant realization. She held her forehead and shook her head silently.

Okay, I knew this was gonna hit you sooner or later, It's fine." Emma grabbed her hands. "I'm sure you and Aaron can still be friends, even after you break his heart. I'll be right behind that door if things get too intense, though."

Arie pulled her hands back and pointed to the TV. "What the eff are you talking about right now? I'm pissed because I gave her this song."

Emma shoved her. "You're too damn much. She's probably having nightmares about it. You literally lived this song in her face. You crawled and screamed; you burned it all down. She's not gonna use it," Emma assured her.

Arie's head bopped to the music. "Yeah, that would be…"

Emma stood up from the bed and walked toward Arie's fridge. "Yeah, but next time think before you just throw a track out. Luckily, the only fire out there was yours, otherwise this song could've been really bad. She would've been feasting on you, instead."

Aaron took a deep breath pulling up to the gate at the Morgan estate. Tony flagged him down, then headed inside the security gatehouse before speaking with him. Although the windows were tinted, Aaron was able to see that Tony was on the phone, after stopping him. He sighed, unsure of what was happening. He'd never been stopped at the gate before.

"Hey, sorry about that, Aaron," Tony said, as he approached the window. "Had to do something quick. How you doing tonight?"

Aaron looked ahead at the closed gate in front of him. Then looked up at Tony. "That's okay, Tony. I'm good, just here to see Arie. Can I go through now?"

Tony put his hands on top of the car. "How's soccer going? How about your classes? You guys never stop in and see me anymore."

Aaron nodded slowly. Tony was far bigger than him and over the years, he'd seen Tony take down a few trespassers. He didn't want to get on his bad side, but he was also anxious to see Arie. He gave him a false smile. "Classes and soccer are good. Arie wants to talk though, so I really want to try and get in to see her."

"Alright, you can head in. I'm glad you're good. Have a nice night." Tony opened the gate, and Aaron pulled through toward Arie's side of the estate.

"What the hell is Emma doing here?" He parked his car beside hers, then leaned his head back in his seat and closed his eyes. He seriously considered everything that just happened. *So, I was stopped at the gate for the first time ever, then Tony takes the time to talk to me for no reason at all, and now Emma's here. I thought she wanted to talk to me alone. Damn it. I have way too much to say in front of Emma.*

Arie had quickly thrown on a pair of loose-fitting sweatpants and a sweatshirt as soon as Tony called her. She opened the bathroom door for Emma. "Just go in there and stay by the door. He won't even know you're here."

Arie's phone rang, and she quickly answered it, "Hey, are you coming up?"

"Why is Emma here?" Aaron's voice was firm, he clearly sounded annoyed. "I thought we were gonna talk, just the two of us?"

Arie's eyes went wide looking at Emma. "We are, she's spending the night, though, so she's gonna just hang out in another room until you leave."

"Is there anyone else up there that I should know about?"

"Nope, just me and Em."

He sighed into the phone. "Alright, I'm heading up."

Arie tossed her phone on her bed and chuckled, looking at Emma. "Your car gave away our secret plan."

"Damn, we're both dumb. How did we forget about my car?"

"Who knows? Thanks for doing this, though." Hearing footsteps coming upstairs, she shoved Emma into the bathroom and closed the door.

Arie quickly sat on her bed with a pillow on her lap and waited.

Aaron walked in and immediately put the pressure on, as he approached her from the side and went in for a hug, which she lightly returned. He squeezed her tight and said, "I feel like I haven't seen you in days… I missed you."

Arie half-smiled. "I saw you yesterday. What are you even talking about?" She watched uncomfortably, while Aaron sat on the floral embroidered chair across from her bed.

Arie rubbed the pillow on her lap and looked at him silently, trying to process her thoughts. *How do I even start this conversation? I can't just ask him if he's been in love with me this whole time. Do I start with the Julian stuff? What do I do?*

Aaron gave her a nervous smile. "That was a great scrimmage last night. But you ran off, and I didn't get to see you before you left. You've never done that before."

"Yeah…I just didn't want to argue with you, and I told you I had plans."

Aaron nodded slowly. "Why would we argue? When have we ever argued, Arie?"

"You've just been acting different lately."

"What have I done that's different, than what I normally do?"

Arie thought, *Shit, how do I even say all the things he's been doing without bringing up Liam? Everything he's done has been toward him…* "I feel like you know."

Aaron let out a groan of disapproval, leaning forward on his elbows. "No. I don't. Here's what I do know though, ever since that guy moved in, you've been treating me differently. It's complete bullshit, Arie. We've been together for a long time; it's always been you and me."

"We've been best friends for a very long time, yes. I don't feel like I've treated you any different."

Aaron shook his head in disbelief and looked at Arie. "Really?"

Arie didn't respond. She didn't really know what to say. She had been treating him differently, but it was really hard to explain why, without just coming out and saying everything.

"Arie, I don't like this guy living here in the same house as you. Yes, I acted jealous because I don't want him near you. My brother told me that he stopped by the other night after practice just to be sure you didn't need anything, since I wouldn't be there. He said that you were smiling at someone on your phone, texting, or something… he said there was no mistaking the look in your eyes, that you were definitely texting a guy. He obviously knew it wasn't me, since I was in the middle of a match. So, you ghosted me all night for the first time ever, then the next morning, you ran off for the day and went out to lunch with the guy that's living here. Why wouldn't you just tell me? Why would you feel like all of a sudden you needed to block me out?"

Arie scoffed. "Julian said he came to check on me? Wow."

Aaron threw his arms up. "That's what you're focusing on? All the stuff I just said and that's what you're coming back around for?"

"I don't know, Aaron. I felt uncomfortable. Your behavior was making me uncomfortable."

Aaron got up from his chair and sat on the side of the bed, while Arie sat in the middle leaning against the headboard. He looked at her softly. "I really need you to tell me exactly what I did wrong. I've always been protective of you. Is that what you're talking about? How could I be anything else?"

Arie shook her head looking down. "I don't know. Maybe I'm the problem. I guess I never noticed."

"How could you ever be a problem? You're…you're my Arie… You're perfect."

"You shouldn't call me your Arie. You'll give people the wrong idea about us."

"What kind of wrong idea? You've always been my Arie. Everyone knows that."

Arie shook her head. "What does that mean to you, though?"

Aaron blew air from his mouth and dropped his head forward. "You're gonna force it out of me, aren't you?"

"I need to know. I can't be honest with you if I don't understand how you're feeling."

Aaron looked seriously at her. "Do you really want me to be honest? I have to be real with you, if I'm honest—I'm not even sure what I'll say."

"Have you really been holding that much in?"

He nodded silently.

"Then of course, please be honest with me. I'll listen."

Aaron closed his eyes and exhaled. "To me, you have always been the only one. The only girl I've ever wanted or needed. You're perfect. We've been through everything together… I wake up every day and wonder what hilarious or cute thing you're going to do. I have held your hand through everything because…I love you, Arie. I always have…and not just as your best friend but as someone I truly want to be with, forever."

Arie had tears in her eyes and sat unmoving, while Aaron moved closer toward her on the bed. "How can you say that to me?" she asked. "Why? What did I do to make you feel this way? We're friends, Aaron. We've always been friends."

"That's true, we've always been friends. It takes a strong friendship to build a relationship. Do you really mean to tell me that you feel nothing for me outside of friendship? What about cheerleading? Remember when we went to high school, you didn't want us to go to tryouts because you didn't want me picking other girls up. Same with college, you didn't want that for college either."

Arie pulled her head back. "No. Definitely not. I didn't want it for *you* because I knew you'd follow me and do whatever I did. We both played soccer since we were kids, it was the thing we both wanted most. I never thought about you picking other girls up." She grabbed her phone off the bed and held it. "Aaron, I have like five people I can think of right now that I would set you up with. That's how much of a friend I think of you as."

Aaron challenged her for the first time tonight. "Then why haven't you done it? Why haven't you tried to get me to go out with anyone else?"

"I have definitely told you that there were girls asking for your number before."

Aaron scoffed. "Yeah, and what does that matter? Girls hit on me all the time. It happens at least five times a day, more on game days. I reject every single one…because they're not you."

"There hasn't been another girl that you've wanted to be with? Ever?"

Aaron said resolutely, "No. It's always been you. You're worth the wait. That's what I've always told myself. My buddies always give me shit about it, but they know how I feel. It's you, Arie. You're the one I've always belonged with."

Arie buried her face in her hands and nearly started to sob. She was so frustrated and felt really bad. She wished that she could make this all better for him, but she knew how she felt and couldn't hold back. If she was anything less than direct, she'd only hurt him more in the long run. "Aaron, I don't feel the same. I'm sorry. I really don't. If I had known you were waiting for me, I would've told you sooner."

"What are you saying? You're saying that you had no idea? You had no idea how I felt?"

"How could I? How could I have known?"

The look on Aaron's face was clear, he was starting to feel the sting of rejection and was obviously getting a little frustrated. "That doesn't matter. I can't control how you perceive things any more than you can control how I do. But I *can* say that I had Duncan bring flowers here for you and you paid him two hundred dollars to send them away. I can also say that I watched you drive away in a car with that guy yesterday and it felt like my heart was being ripped out of my chest. I could say that all of these things have been the worst things you've ever done to me. But would any of that matter? No. It wouldn't matter because you've already decided that you like this guy. So, now, I have to sit around and wait… Wait this one out just like the others. It's really unfair. Can't we just skip this part? You're going to realize that you're in love with me. You just admitted that you'd never even considered it. So how can you say you don't, so resolutely? You don't know how you feel."

Arie was thrown by the fact that Duncan was the one who attempted to deliver the flowers, but remembered Liam's words from earlier, and tried to regain control of the conversation. "This has nothing to do with Liam. It's true that I never considered us being together, but how could I? Why would I do that? You never gave any romantic signals whatsoever. I'm sorry that this hurts… It sucks… But, Aaron, I won't change my mind. I don't see you that way."

Aaron sat silently on the bed, and the two stared at one another. A few tears fell from Arie's eyes as she looked at him. Aaron reached over with his right hand and softly wiped them with his thumb. He moved in slowly, leaning in, he brought his face close to hers.

Arie jumped off the bed in shock. "What the eff are you doing? Were you really about to try and kiss me? Aaron, I said I don't see you that way. I will *never* see you that way."

Aaron rubbed his hand down his face. "I'm gonna go…you need time to think things through." He stood up from the bed and walked toward the door, glancing at the music box on Arie's dresser, long enough for her to meet his gaze. "The queen had no idea the king was in love with her…that's a twist."

Arie shrugged. "I don't know what else to say. I told you how I feel."

Aaron pulled his keys out of his pocket and gave her an uncomfortable smile. "Don't worry about it. We're best friends, Arie. I'm not worried. I'm fine. But, hey, before I go, why did you have Tony stop me at the gate?"

"I didn't have Tony stop you at the gate. I asked him to call me before you got here, so I wasn't standing in my underwear again."

Aaron nodded, seemingly trying to piece things together. "So, you realized just a few days ago that I was in love with you, or at least you thought so. Yeah, you still need time to process." He walked back toward her door, then turned before leaving. "I'm sorry. I want us to be best friends and I'm sorry if I made you uncomfortable. I know how you process things, and I just need to be supportive."

Arie nodded rubbing her arms. "Okay, but if you're thinking I'm gonna change my mind, I'm not."

"I understand. I'll see you tomorrow."

After Aaron left, Emma charged through the door and embraced Arie, who was sitting on the edge of her bed sobbing. Emma rubbed her hair. "It's okay. You said everything that needed to be said. It's all out now. What do you need, babe?"

Arie softly cried, mumbling through tears. "I just…I want Liam… I want him to hold me. I haven't even gotten to tell him how I feel. I just—I want him here with me."

"Well, he's busy, he's a working man, babe—something you and I don't know anything about, but you did promise to call or text him. So, text him and tell him you're done, or whatever you want to say."

Chapter 37
I Want To Kiss You Again

Liam sat beside Coop at the large round dining room table, with Ethan on Coop's right. To Liam's left was the other lawyer, Mario, who sat next to Maddie. The interview had mostly concluded, and they were just finishing up the few remaining items.

Liam received a text from Arie and looked at his phone under the table.

Arie: *Hey. Aaron just left.*

Liam: *Thanks for letting me know. I'm almost done here.*

He let out a sigh of relief and quickly shoved his phone in his pocket.

Maddie laughed loudly at something Mario said that the rest of the group couldn't hear. She playfully pushed against his shoulder. "I still can't believe he's your brother! His whole 'Boo, Peter' shtick was a lot of fun. You're funny too, that's the only similarity I see."

Ethan and Coop looked at one another, confused. "The wine tour driver is your brother?" Ethan asked.

Mario nodded. "Yes. He is. There are five in my family. I'm the only one who didn't get into the family business."

"He told us about the vans and the wine tours that your family operates. He was a very nice guy," Coop said.

Mario sipped from his glass, raising his eyebrows at Coop. "Definitely depends on which day you catch him on. Larry does get the best reviews, which Peter hates. My parents had to hire outside of the family recently, because my brother and his partner just had a little girl. She's beautiful, looks like my brother. Gestational surrogacy is a remarkable thing. They've been at home having the time of their lives. I'm not sure if they'll come back to do the tours or not, which is rough, because my parents also added gondola tours to the offerings recently. My dad loves doing the tours, but my mom is always offering unsolicited advice to tourists. My father calls me every night and asks if they got any bad reviews. My mom can't help it, she just builds immediate connections with people."

Ethan looked at Coop, then Mario. "Hey, I think we went on their gondola ride. What are their names?"

"Ronnie and JoAnn. You'd know it if you did. She would've said something inappropriate at least once."

Coop wrapped his arm around Ethan and chuckled. "It was definitely them. They were both really nice."

"We had a great time with them," Ethan said. "Reminded me of my parents' relationship."

Liam read the text from Arie again in his mind and realized that he didn't ask her how things went. It was clear that his part in the meeting was already over, so he quickly excused himself. He made his way inside one of the bathrooms on the opposite side of the home and called her. He whispered, "Hey, Arie, I don't want to push you to talk, but I just…I needed to check on you. Are you okay?"

"Hi, Liam, I'm fine," she replied softly. "You're working…it's okay…I'm okay…" Arie sniffled.

"Are you crying?"

Arie paused, letting out a small sniffle. "Yeah…but it's…it's my fault anyway… Don't worry about me. My brother and Ethan need you…but can you just come over as soon as you're done? Would…would that be okay?"

Liam put a hand on his head and leaned against the bathroom door. He'd never felt the need to protect and care for someone the way that he seemed to with Arie. The urge to rush to her side overcame him, he couldn't stand the thought of her hurting. He spoke calmly, "Arie, don't think about anything else, just answer me honestly, do you need me to come there now?"

"I can't ask you to do that…I… Yes…I need you…but I don't want you to get—"

Liam interrupted her, "I'm leaving. I'll be there as soon as I can."

His body was moving all on its own, as he walked down the long hallway toward the table. Once he heard Arie say that she needed him, nothing else mattered. He needed to be there for her.

Before he rounded the corner, he caught Ethan's gaze. He couldn't force himself to smile, he needed to pull Coop and Ethan aside and quickly explain what happened.

Ethan patted Coop on the shoulder and whispered something to him, and the two made their way toward Liam. "What happened, Liam?" Ethan asked. "I'm not going to ask if you're okay, because you definitely aren't."

Liam shook his head and looked at both of them. "I really need to go be with Arie, Aaron just left."

Coop asked, "Did Arie ask you to go there? Or are you just thinking that's what she needs?"

Liam didn't want to explain that both of those things were accurate, he knew she needed him before she said it, but he wouldn't have left so suddenly if she didn't ask. "She was crying, and I asked her if she needed me—she said yes, but she was worried about you two. I really need to go, we're done here, everything went well. If there was anything you guys needed, I'd tell you, but everything is signed, it's all good."

"Well," Coop said, "if she said she needs you, that may be a first for Arie. She's more about making sure everyone else has what they need. You should go."

The group looked down the hall toward the table at Maddie who was whispering in Mario's ear. Ethan shuddered. "Can we ask them to leave? Or is that a bad look for us in front of Mario?"

Coop shrugged. "Let's just get them out of here. If Liam says we're good, I trust him."

Ethan squeezed Coop's hand, looking at Liam. "I trust him, too."

Liam exhaled, he felt like he was holding in a breath this whole time. "Thanks, guys, that really means a lot to me."

Ethan and Coop patted him on each shoulder and smiled, then walked him to the front door.

Liam stood nervously outside Arie's place and rang the doorbell.

Arie's voice came through the speaker, "Hey, Liam, the door is open. Come on up."

Liam walked inside and headed upstairs. The door to Arie's room was open, and he approached it cautiously. Arie was standing near her dresser in her sweats with her hair tied in a messy knot. Liam could tell she'd definitely been crying. He stepped into the room and pulled her into his arms. She tucked her face into his chest, and sniffled, while he rubbed her hair softly. He was at a loss for words holding her like this. She felt like she belonged here, his heart beat faster, just the same as when he kissed her earlier, and he wondered if just maybe this was the girl his heart was supposed to beat for.

"Liam, are you gonna get in trouble for leaving?" she asked.

He looked down at her. "How is it that you're worried about me, right now?"

Arie shook her head but didn't look up. "I just…I like you so much… I don't want you to get in trouble."

Liam continued to hold her tightly against his chest. "You don't need to worry about me. Everything was fine. Now, they just wait for the baby to be born."

Arie looked up, slightly pulling back from his arms. She asked softly, "Do you like me too, Liam? It's not just me, right? Because after everything that just happened, it turns out"—she began to cry again—"I am not good at reading people."

Liam grabbed a tissue from the box on her nightstand and wiped her tears. He tilted her chin up and looked into her eyes. "Arie, listen to me. You don't need to read me. I'll make it easy for you. I like you. I want to be with you. I want to be your boyfriend. I want to kiss you again—"

"Oh, hot damn!" Emma's voice came from the bathroom, interrupting the moment.

Arie and Liam looked at the bathroom door. Liam chuckled. "Hi, Emma, sorry. I knew you were here, but I didn't know you were in the bathroom."

Arie giggled looking at the bathroom door. "You can come out, Em."

Emma opened the door and covered her smile with her hand. "Sorry. I'm so sorry. I didn't mean to interrupt. I can leave."

"No," Liam said. "You don't need to leave because of me. You guys had plans, you don't need to change them. I can go."

Arie took Liam's hand in hers. "Why don't we all just hang out together?"

Liam looked down at their clasped hands and smiled. "Whatever makes you happy. It's your birthday eve."

"Yeah, I'd like that. I'm gonna just get into my pajamas, since Em already did." She tugged at her sweatshirt. "I'm also sweating in this."

"Okay," Liam said. "I'm gonna run over to the other side and get out of my work clothes. I feel kind of hot myself."

Emma eyed Liam. "You *are* hot."

Arie raised her eyebrows at Liam, looking him up and down. "Well, she isn't wrong."

Liam looked at the floor, feeling mildly embarrassed. He squeezed Arie's hand lightly. "I'll be back in a few minutes, but before I go, are you two hungry? Do you want me to order something?"

Emma raised her hand.

"I'm a little hungry, too," Arie said. "But do you think you could—"

Emma interrupted, "Arie, babe, do not ask this man to make you pancakes. That's all you've been talking about every time we eat anything. Please. I don't really want pancakes right now." She patted Arie on the backside. "Also, your ass is gonna start getting real jiggly, if he keeps making them for you."

Arie playfully shoved Emma. "How did you know what I was gonna ask?"

"I don't mind making pancakes for you," Liam said."I can always order something else for Emma. Whatever you want, Arie."

"Nah. Em had to hide in the bathroom earlier. She deserves to pick."

Emma nodded. "Oooh! Let's order some crab rangoon, fried rice, and Szechuan chicken, and maybe some General Tso's."

"That sounds so good," Arie said. "But, I mean, will my ass not get jiggly from that?"

Liam gave Arie his debit card. "Here, take this, and order whatever you both want. I'll be back in a few minutes."

Arie looked at the card then up at him. "You don't need to do this. I can get it."

"Yeah, her dads are like super rich. Arie doesn't have to pay for anything. They don't want her working till after college, they give her tons of money."

"I see," Liam said. "Well, if it's for you, I'd rather pay for it myself."

Emma shooed him playfully toward the door. "Damn, okay, you're perfect, stop rubbing it in. Go get changed."

"Alright, I'll be back in a bit," Liam said, stepping out of the room.

Before his foot hit the stairs, Arie shouted from behind, "Liam, wait!" She quickly closed the distance between them and pulled Liam's face in, pressing her lips against his softly. "Sorry. I couldn't wait anymore. I've been thinking about that all day."

A huge grin covered Liam's face, and he pulled her in for a hug. "Me too. I was really worried about you. I felt so stupid, but I just didn't know how things were gonna go down. I'm so happy to see your smile."

Arie blushed and took a few steps back toward her room. "What do you want me to order for you?"

Liam chuckled. He'd completely forgotten to order anything for himself. "Thanks for realizing that I didn't order anything. General Tso's chicken for me, but with white rice. Thanks."

"Almost the same as what I get," Arie said with a smile, "but I like it with fried rice."

"Hmm…I've always gotten the steamed rice. Does it really taste better with fried rice?"

Arie crossed her arms. "You know, I'm not really—"

Emma shouted from the room, "Okay. Damn, you guys like each other…great! Of course, it tastes better with fried rice, Liam. It's fried! She also eats her rice with a spoon, please don't get started on that next. I'm starving!"

"Alright, I'll see you when you get back," Arie said. "Oh, and bring your cards, so you can show me how to play. Just come upstairs when you're done."

Liam left Arie's place feeling better than he'd ever felt before. In the past week, he'd made up with his brother, finally stepped out of his dad's shadow, and found a girl that seemed almost too good to be true. Even though life had made him a bit pessimistic over the years, he wasn't willing to think about anything going wrong, not when holding Arie felt so right.

He unlocked the door to the side of the estate that he was staying in and his phone rang, just as he stepped inside. *Shit…* He dropped his head back seeing that it was Tom calling. *I have no idea how he and Levi are gonna feel about me going out with their daughter.* He took a deep breath and answered the call, while grabbing the package off the table in the foyer.

"Hi, Tom, what can I do for you?"

"I'm glad you answered. We saw your car at Arie's and were wondering how things went with Aaron. Is Arie okay?"

"She's good. Really good. She and Emma are ordering food right now. I'm gonna change and head back over in a few minutes. I didn't get the play-by-play, but she's fine."

Tom's voice deepened as he spoke, "Ah…I see… Liam, let me ask you, just how far do you plan on taking things with Arie tonight with Emma in the room?"

"What? I don't even know how to answer that. I'm just planning on hanging out."

"Give me that phone!" Levi said. "Don't listen to him, Liam. He talked to Coop and Ethan and thought it would be funny if he messed with you, too."

Tom shouted in the background, "No! I really mean it! Liam, don't even think of doing anything like that with our baby girl!" Tom laughed loudly. "I'm out. How do people do that with a straight face?"

Levi giggled. "If Arie's happy, it's none of our business. But please, for the love of all things, don't accidentally call us. Got a very awkward voicemail a little bit ago. Never want to hear that again."

Liam had honestly stopped listening once he knew that Tom was kidding. He held the present he bought for Arie in his hands and got an idea. "Okay, Levi, I won't… or I will… whichever was the appropriate response to whatever you just said. Sorry."

"Alright, behave," Levi said. "We'll see you tomorrow at the family party if we don't see you before then."

Liam smiled. The way that Levi said that, made him feel so welcome. He wasn't sure how everyone in this family made him feel like he belonged, but he was grateful for it. "Thanks. See you tomorrow." He grabbed his laptop and quickly navigated to the website that he ordered Arie's present from and placed a second order with next-day shipping.

He looked inside the dresser, where he'd put most of his clothes. *This isn't really a date, so I think I can just dress comfortably.* He settled on a pair of dark gray gym shorts and a slim-fitting black T-shirt and quickly spritzed himself with cologne. He wasn't planning on staying the night, but he grabbed his travel toothbrush, floss, three lollipops, and his card box remembering that Arie asked him to bring it.

Arie was still deciding on her own comfortable outfit, she'd been through around five already. "How about this?" She wore a white racerback top, along with a pair of tiny black and white gingham pajama shorts. "Well, good or no?"

Emma tilted her head looking her up and down. "Good for what?"

"Good for hanging out."

"Well, your ass is hanging out, so it's good for hanging out, yeah."

Arie looked at her ass in the mirror. "No, it's not. You can't even see it. It cuts off right at the bottom."

Emma smiled at her. "You're perfect. No more fashion show. I promise he's gonna think you look cute. Why are you worrying so much?"

"I just really like him. I've been so worried that the way I was feeling was one-sided, and I felt like I overshared by being so open, and then all the stuff with Aaron, plus he's so hot, Em, so, so hot. The hot ones are never good listeners…he's both."

Emma tossed a throw pillow at her. "Don't rub it in! I'm glad you like him, especially when it was painfully obvious from day one that he was into you. Don't ever feel bad about being open, though, you've done like nothing wrong—ever."

Arie heard the sound of her front door opening and quickly jumped on her bed. "Emma, sit here, let's put *Haikyu!* on."

"I'm back," Liam said, walking inside the room.

"Ooh you brought your cards!" Arie smiled brightly at him. "I'm so excited. You can put them there on my dresser." She hoped he'd notice that the music box that Aaron got her was no longer there.

Liam looked at the empty dresser, and smiled, placing his card box in the empty space. "Yeah, we can try and play at some point tonight if you feel like it. I'm also fine to just watch"—he looked at the TV—"whichever anime this is. Looks like the volleyball one, you were telling me about."

Arie patted the left side of the bed, looking at Liam. "This *is* the one I was telling you about! It's *Haikyu!* My absolute favorite."

Liam slid his shoes off and sat beside her, while Emma scooted down the bed, lying across the bottom. Emma playfully chided him, "It's our favorite, that means no more talking, even for hot guys. And we don't watch dubs, so you need to read the subtitles."

"Got it," Liam said.

Arie moved in closer to him, until their shoulders were touching. *Can I just hold his hand now? He said he wanted to be my boyfriend, we're good, right? I can't be worried about this…gosh how can someone make me feel so nervous and yet so at peace at the same time?* Before she could decide whether to hold his hand or not, she got a good whiff of Liam's cologne, thanks to the ceiling fan. "You smell so good," she said under her breath.

Liam's eyes were glued to the TV, while Arie's eyes were drawn to the toned muscles on his legs, and his hands that were resting on his thighs. She'd held his hand before, and he didn't pull away… all she had to do was take his hand in hers, but she sat there frozen staring at him, too afraid to move.

Her phone vibrated on her nightstand, and she quickly checked the notification. "That was a text from Tony. Food should be here in a sec."

"About time," Emma said.

Arie turned toward Liam. "Also, Tony wants me to ask if you got the package he left in the foyer that was delivered for you."

Liam playfully dropped his mouth open. "Yes. I got it. It's your present, but it's not ready yet. You might have to wait until tomorrow night for it."

"Oooh, mysterious," Arie said.

"Damn!" Liam said, pointing at the tv. "That little guy can jump! He's so much smaller than the others and he just spiked that ball down!"

Arie sighed lovingly. "He's the best. The best everything. Just a little ball of sunshine."

Emma agreed, "The best character, and this is the best sports anime. *Blue Lock* is a close second. Two totally different types of sports anime, though."

A few minutes later, the food was delivered, and they went downstairs so they could eat. The three sat comfortably at Arie's small round dining room table, with Liam and Arie sitting beside one another, and Emma across from them.

"I've never seen anyone eat rice with a spoon before," Liam said, looking at Arie.

She ate another spoonful and smiled at him. "But look how much more fits on the spoon. It's so much easier. Try it." She held the spoon near Liam's mouth and fed him a spoonful of fried rice.

Liam nodded. "Hmm…yeah, I get it. Also, the fried rice is definitely better."

"Tch…please. This boy doesn't know when to quit," Emma said, looking at her phone.

"Who is it?" Arie asked.

Emma passed her phone across the table, showing her a text from Aaron.

Aaron: *Hey, sorry if that was awkward earlier. I hope she isn't too upset about everything. BTW Travis asked me if you were into him.*

Arie rolled her eyes and shook her head, while passing the phone back.

"Everything okay?" Liam asked.

Arie waved him off. "Yeah, it's nothing, just Aaron."

Emma grabbed a crab rangoon from the bag in the middle of the table. "Shouldn't have tried to kiss you. Now he wants to say sorry, and he had the nerve to bring up Travis."

Liam looked at Arie, confused. "Did he try to kiss you tonight?"

Arie really didn't want to think about it. She considered Aaron to be like a brother, and the fact that he tried to kiss her still wasn't sitting well with her. She nodded. "Yeah, it was stupid. He didn't get too close. I jumped off the bed as soon as I saw what he was trying to do."

"Such a waste," Emma said. "Should've been trying to kiss me. Everyone's always trying to kiss Arie. Damn, I would've done it. Let him try to kiss me after all this time…bet I'll do it."

"Really?" Arie asked. "I thought you liked Travis."

"A kiss is just a kiss, nothing more. I'm not saying anything you don't already know. I've told you plenty of times that I think Aaron is hot, so does every other girl we know. Doesn't mean I want to date him. I would sleep with him, though. Wait…" Emma's eyes widened. "I just realized, it's super-hot that he's just been saving himself for you all this time. Damn. Whoever gets it, is gonna get it good."

Arie giggled but noticed that Liam had stopped eating his food. "She's just messing around," Arie said.

Emma scoffed. "Oh, I hope you're not feeling jealous already. Arie doesn't like jealousy. I think it's hot, though. Aaron brought that sweet fire tonight, too."

Arie held a hand over her mouth and shook her head. "Em…you

gotta stop. You're saying the craziest stuff. True story." She turned to Liam and touched his hand softly. "Don't worry about it. It was alright, he acted the way you thought he would. He didn't get aggressive or anything."

Arie proceeded to give Liam a full recap of the entire conversation with Aaron, along with commentary from Emma.

"So, he basically just said he was waiting for you to realize you were in love with him. Now, what crazy thing will he try to do? Because he's definitely gonna do something…"

Arie shrugged. "I have no idea."

"Is the party going to be here on your side of the estate, or over at the main?" Liam asked.

"Oh, it's a pool party, so it's at my dads' place.

Emma added, "Yeah, there's usually a lot of people here. Sometimes people we don't even know just show up. Usually gets crazy."

Arie could tell the whole thing was making Liam uneasy. "It's not that bad. We have enough room for everyone out there. Usually, things get a little crazy and Tony hates it. He's gotta just let people in and take copies of their IDs, so it's extra work for him. I usually send him his favorite cookies the day after, then he's happy again."

Liam asked, "Why don't you have a list of people, instead of him letting anyone in? Seems dangerous."

"Pftt," Arie said. "What's anyone gonna do? Try to steal or vandalize? My dads have so many security cameras on the property. They wouldn't make it very far."

"I was talking more about your safety, than the house," Liam said.

She patted his hand. "That's even more ridiculous. If anyone tried anything…it would end very badly for them. I told you; my dad and Coop usually hover inside the kitchen, they mind their own business, but neither my brother nor my dads are gonna just sit by while someone bothers me."

"Oh, are Coop and Ethan coming, too?" Liam asked.

Arie finished the last bite of her rice. "I don't know. I'm sure we'll see them at the family party, but I don't know about the nighttime one."

Emma grabbed another crab rangoon and squeezed it between her fingers, pointing it at Arie. "Don't you tell me that Liam is going to the family party… No, ma'am…I have been trying to get into that party for years. How is that fair?"

"It's not up to me," Arie said. "You know my dad likes to keep it only to immediate family. He's always like that, he likes it to be special with just a few of us. I can't control it. But…yes, I did invite Liam."

Emma's mouth dropped open, and she shook her head. "Your dads love me. I know they do. We have a special bond. I thought this was gonna be the year." She forcefully shook the crab rangoon at Liam. "This is your fault. I bet I was gonna get an invite."

"Sorry. I guess?" Liam said with a shrug.

Arie smiled at him. "She's just being silly. She wasn't getting one. I've never invited anyone to come before. Kinda surprised my dads didn't mind, actually."

Liam whispered to her, "Your dads already assumed I was coming anyway. They told me earlier they'd see me at the family party."

Arie's mouth dropped open, and her eyebrows raised. "Oh wow! That's huge! That makes me so happy!"

Liam squeezed her hand, bringing it under the table onto his lap. "Me too."

Emma was too busy looking at her phone to notice the shared

moment of joy between them. "You two ready to go back upstairs?" she asked, looking down.

"Ready," Arie said. The group stood up from the table, cleared off the food and went back up to Arie's room.

Liam pulled his travel toothbrush out of his pocket, showing it to Arie. "Hey, I have a thing about my oral hygiene, I like to brush as soon as I can after eating, it's why I've never had a cavity."

Arie smiled broadly, showing off her pearly whites. "That makes sense, your teeth are as white as mine. I'll brush mine now, too."

Arie felt strangely comfortable brushing her teeth beside Liam. Standing next to him at the double sinks, Arie couldn't help but imagine what it would be like to wake up beside him in the morning. She imagined a sleepy-eyed, shirtless Liam, pulling her close. *That would be the best way to wake up in the morning. I've never woken up next to a guy. I bet his sleepy face is so cute, too.*

"Hey!" Emma shouted. "I'm starting another episode. If you want to watch, hurry up and get out here! You guys have been brushing your teeth for like ten minutes."

Arie tugged on Liam's shirt. "Come on, you can show me how to play your game." She grabbed the card box off her dresser, as they walked back into her room.

Emma turned around and looked at the two. "Not me. I'm watching my boys fly right now." She laid on Arie's bed sideways across the bottom and started another episode of the show they were watching earlier.

Liam tapped the top of the large wooden box of Magic the Gathering cards. "We should try this another night. There are a lot of rules, it's easy once you learn it, but it can definitely seem overwhelming at first."

Arie put the box back on her dresser and gave him a smile. "Okay, well at least let me see the mobile version, that has to be easier, right?” She sat on her bed, and scooted to the side, making room for Liam, who sat beside her, leaning against the headboard.

He pulled up his game profile and held his phone in between himself and Arie. “This is it. These are all my stats, matches, other stuff like that.”

Arie leaned in closer to get a better look. “I love that you worked lollipop into your username, that’s so funny. Hey, speaking of lollipops, did you bring any?”

Liam pumped his eyebrows at her and reached into his pocket, pulling out three lollipops, two purple and one blue.

“Lollipops?” Emma asked, turning around.

Arie pulled the blue one out of Liam’s hand and passed it to Emma. “I can’t believe that you even remembered me saying Em’s favorite color is blue, Liam. It’s so sweet that you remembered that.”

Emma smiled. “Thank you, Liam.” She narrowed her eyes looking at Arie. “Babe, it’s nice that you told him my favorite color, but I’m still pissed about the family party.” She popped the lollipop in her mouth and turned back toward the TV.

Liam whispered, “I don’t feel right about taking credit when I didn’t do something. I had no idea her favorite color was blue. I grabbed purples for you and me, then threw in an extra one for her. Just worked out that it was her favorite color.”

Since they just brushed their teeth, Arie put the two purple lollipops on her nightstand. “Never mind, Em. It was just a coincidence. He didn’t remember your favorite color.”

Emma held the lollipop over her head. “That’s okay…tastes the same.”

Liam’s body was so warm beside Arie, and she was so tired from the day that she naturally just moved closer, lifting Liam’s arm and tucking herself under it. She slipped her legs underneath her blanket and pulled it up snugly.

Liam rubbed her arm, pulling her in closer. He gave her a soft kiss on top of her head. "Let's look at the game later. I really want to watch the show."

"Don't be doing anything behind me," Emma warned them. "I can see you guys in the tv reflection."

Arie wouldn't try anything with anyone else in the room, besides, now that she'd snuggled up next to Liam, her eyes were already closing. "I'm way too tired. You don't have to worry about that."

Liam looked down at Arie. "Oh, I'm not tired at all. I'll probably head back after another episode since you're sleepy."

"Why don't you just stay the night?" she asked.

"I'll stay until you're ready for me to leave." He kissed the top of her head. "I can't stay the night, because I have that hearing first thing tomorrow morning."

Within a few minutes, both Arie and Liam were fast asleep sitting up, locked in an embrace. Emma also fell asleep, lying across the foot of the bed.

Chapter 38
My Pillow Smells Like You

The next morning at 8:00 am, Tom and Levi walked over to Arie's, carrying a jumbo birthday cupcake from Arie's favorite bakery. They saw Emma's car there, which was no surprise, and headed inside.

Arie's bedroom door was open, and they were greeted with the sight of Arie and Liam asleep in bed. Liam was flat on his back and Arie's head was on his chest, with his arm wrapped tightly around her.

Levi was speechless at the sight; he had no idea how Tom was going to react. He winced looking at him over his shoulder.

Tom took a step inside the room and nearly tripped over Emma who was asleep on the floor near the foot of the bed.

Levi figured she must have rolled off, since her pillow and blanket were still on the bottom of the bed.

Tom whispered, "There are so many possibilities for fun here. Which should we choose? I don't know who to mess with."

"You're pretty calm for seeing Arie sleeping in bed with Liam," Levi whispered.

"Well, they're wearing clothes, so that makes me feel better. It's obvious that all three fell asleep while watching TV. Look, it's still on."

Levi smiled and clutched Tom's arm. "They look cute, Tommy. Look how they slept."

"Yeah, they do," Tom whispered. "Hey, remember all those times the boys told us we were bad at whispering. Look at us now." He gave Levi a kiss on the cheek. "I'm going for Liam, unless you think Arie would be funnier."

Levi shook his head. "I agree, Liam would be the funniest option."

The two tiptoed around Emma and over to the side of the bed that Liam was on. Tom passed the cupcake to Levi and gave him a nod, they both leaned in close to Liam's face. Tom whispered, "Liam, what did you do with our daughter?"

Liam jolted and shouted loudly, "Aaah!"

Arie's head sprung up and she screamed, "Aaah! What is happening?!"

Levi jumped at the unexpected screams, and lost control of the cupcake, causing it to land squarely atop Emma's head.

Arie was still rubbing her eyes seemingly trying to figure out what happened, as Liam's eyes nearly fell out of his head.

Emma's head popped into view, as she sat up from the floor. The cupcake had fallen off, but there was a large portion of purple butter cream still atop her head. There was also a blue lollipop hanging from the side of her long hair. She wiped her eyes. "Whoa. Am I dreaming? Arie's two dads…and me… Alright…I'm down."

Levi initially felt bad about the cupcake, but not anymore. He made a disgusted face and shouted, "Ugh, Emma. You're not dreaming! You have cupcake in your hair and a damn lollipop stuck on the side! Go clean yourself up!"

She squinted looking at Levi. "Wait, what did you say?" She touched the top of her head reaching the frosting in her hair. "What the hell is happening? Why is there frosting in my hair? Why is there a cupcake on the floor? And my lollipop is just hanging here?" She tried to untwist the lollipop from her hair.

Liam sat up, rubbing his temples. "Nothing happened. I uh, didn't mean to sleep over. I must have just fallen asleep."

Tom and Levi crossed their arms and stared at him silently.

Emma now stood at the foot of the bed, still trying to pull the lollipop out of her hair. "True story," she said. "We all fell asleep watching TV. That's how this lollipop got stuck in here."

Arie sat up looking at her dads. "Wait, why are you in my room? What's even happening?" she asked.

Tom said, "We came to wish you a happy birthday. We weren't expecting to see Liam here."

Levi added, "We brought you a cupcake from the bakery you like. But it's on the floor and in Emma's hair. I lost my grip on it when Liam screamed."

Liam lifted his face from his hands, and looked at Arie, smiling softly. "Happy birthday, Arie."

Arie leaned her head on his shoulder. "Thanks, Liam… I can't believe we fell asleep. You were just so snuggly."

Levi thought the two looked quite comfortable with each other and was kind of in awe of the tenderness he could see in Liam's eyes when he looked at Arie.

Liam's facial expression shifted as he looked up at Levi and Tom looming over his side. "Honestly, I really meant to go back last night… Wait…what time is it?"

Tom looked at his phone. "8:17."

Liam jumped out of bed. "Oh no. I'm sorry, I have to go, I'll be late for court. Bye, everyone."

The group watched him rush out of the room for just a second, then he immediately re-entered and walked quickly toward Arie. He gave her a kiss on the cheek and hugged her tightly. "Thank you for last night. I'm really happy that I got to see you this morning." He kissed her one more time on the cheek.

"I'm glad I got to wake up next to you on my birthday."

Liam smiled and pulled back from the embrace. "Alright, I have to go for real, still not even dressed. I'll call you when I'm in my car."

Emma tossed the cupcake in Arie's trash bin and checked the front of her hair in the mirror, after Liam rushed out the door. "That was a good exit. Damn, that man is swoon-worthy... Did I get it all?" she asked, lifting sections of her hair.

Arie pointed to the back of Emma's head. "Nope. There is way more frosting in your hair than you think. You should get in the shower."

Emma looked across the room at Levi. "No invite to the family party, and you threw a cupcake at me when I was sleeping on the floor... I need a new best friend."

Arie reached her arms out for a hug. "You love me."

"I do love you," Emma said hugging her from the side. "Happy b-day."

Arie sniffed Emma's hair as she hugged her. "It smells so good though...too bad they don't make a cupcake scented shampoo."

"Ooh, that would be so good," Emma said. "I'm gonna take a quick shower."

Once Emma was in the bathroom, Tom and Levi gave Arie a joint hug from beside the bed. Levi chuckled. "I'm sorry about the cupcake. Liam's scream was so loud and unexpected."

"I think it was more the way his body jerked, than it was his scream. That cupcake really got some air," Tom joked. He rubbed his hands together, looking at Arie. "Alright, you ready, kiddo?"

Arie looked around the room. "For what? Am I ready for what?"

Tom smiled proudly. "To go tell Ms. Doris all about your birthday present."

Arie jumped off her bed excitedly, eyes wide, mouth open, she asked, "They're gonna let us do it?"

Tom and Levi nodded, and Arie hugged them both together. "You guys are the best dads! I'm so lucky! Ms. Doris is gonna be so excited!"

Levi agreed, "Too true, we really are. Saw Liam sleeping in here and didn't even yell at anyone."

Arie smiled brightly at them both.

"Well, get dressed," Tom said. "We're going to go tell her all about it. We have a meeting with the director in about forty-five minutes, and we can see Ms. Doris afterward."

Arie pulled her mouth to the side looking at Levi.

Levi looked down at himself. He was dressed nicely, and didn't see any cupcake on his clothes. "What? Why are you looking at me like that?"

"Mmm…your pants are kind of tight, and Ms. Doris is pretty frisky, you may want to change into something else."

Levi hadn't been to the retirement center before, so he thought Arie was just kidding around. He waved her off. "Oh, stop…don't be silly."

"Alright, don't say I didn't warn you," Arie said walking to her dresser.

Tom patted Levi on the ass. "Meet us in the kitchen when you're ready."

Arie stood by her dresser looking at Liam's card box. She rubbed the custom wooden designs atop it and let out a little "Eeee" in excitement, thinking of Liam holding her while she slept. She dove onto her bed and smelled her pillow, inhaling deeply. "Oh my God…my pillow smells like him! This is the best birthday morning ever!" she squealed, kicking her feet.

Arie's phone rang on her nightstand. When she saw it was Liam calling, she grabbed it and lay back onto her pillow. "Hey, Liam, are you gonna make it to court on time? I hope I didn't make you late."

"You didn't make me late. I fell asleep. I didn't even have an alarm set. I'm lucky I made it back in time for a fast shower. But, in the spirit of honesty, I took my shirt off, and it smelled like your perfume…I really didn't want to leave that shirt behind."

Arie giggled. "That's so cute. My pillow smells like you. I may never wash this pillowcase again."

"Aww. I don't feel like going to court today. I wish we could spend your birthday together."

"I know. Me too. But I have exciting news! Like best news ever. Second only to you saying you wanted to be my boyfriend."

"Oh yeah? What is it?"

Arie answered excitedly, "My dads got approval for the Night in Italy for the seniors at the retirement home! We're gonna go meet with the director. I can't wait to tell Ms. Doris!"

"That's amazing! I'm so happy to hear that."

"I know, right? My dads can convince anyone of anything. I bet Levi was all sass with the director, and my dad probably just let him go to town until the guy relented. That's usually how it goes."

"Oh, I have a funny story to tell you later. There was a kind of a reverse situation with them in Italy. It was hilarious. I kinda pretended your dads were my dads, it was so much fun."

Arie giggled. "I don't even need to hear the story, they're always acting crazy together. Can't believe Levi got Emma with the cupcake earlier."

"Yeah, that was my fault. I'm pretty sure I screamed way louder than I needed to. But waking up to both of their faces hovering over me was kind of crazy."

"Agreed. What time will you be done with work? Or is it kind of a floating end time when you have court?"

"It just depends. I'll be done in plenty of time for the family party at five. I'm just not sure exactly what time I'll finish up."

"Then you'll come be with me?"

"Of course. I'd be with you right now if I could."

Emma walked out of the bathroom and placed her backpack on the bed.

Arie said, "Liam, give me one sec." She looked at Emma. "My dads got the Night in Italy approved. We're gonna go meet with the director in a few minutes!"

Emma clapped. "Yes! Oh, babe, that's gonna be so cute for those old people!"

Arie shook her head at her. "Don't call them old people!"

"Fine. That's gonna be so lit for those amorous elderlies." She put her backpack on and grabbed her keys.

"Alright, I'll see you tonight," Arie said, standing to hug her.

Emma squeezed her. "Can't wait for the party. See you later."

Arie lay back on her bed and held her pillow to her chest, taking a whiff of Liam's cologne. "Hey, sorry, Liam. She was taking a shower and didn't hear the news."

"No, that's fine. But hey, I have to go. I just pulled in. Listen, my phone has to be on silent mode, not allowed to even vibrate when I'm in there. I'm just telling you in case you text or call and I don't reply. I can try and look at it every once in a while, or when we go on break but it's sporadic."

"Oh, okay. Thanks for letting me know. Good luck today, I'm sure it's gonna go great."

"Thanks. I'll be thinking about you."

"Me too. Bye, Liam."

Arie sat in the back seat of the car with her dad driving and Levi in the passenger seat. As soon as they'd gotten in the car, Levi asked for a rundown of what happened with Aaron last night. Arie gave them a recap, making sure not to leave out any details.

Levi looked at Tom and said, "I agree with Liam. That kid is gonna do something stupid."

Arie had thought about the same thing, but since Aaron wasn't ever really mean to her, it was hard for her to imagine him doing anything that would upset her. "What could he do? Also, like, why? I didn't say anything mean to him. I was honest. It's not like I yelled at him."

Her dad glanced at her in the rearview mirror. "I think it would have less to do with how you reacted, and more to do with the fact that you rejected him after all this time."

Arie looked out the window. "I don't know. I'm just kinda effing pissed about it, though. Like, okay, I get I'm not good at reading people, sure, fine, but, like, he was staying by my side just waiting for me to sleep with him? While, like, silently sabotaging my relationships? Also, I've changed clothes in front of him...a lot. That feels just wrong to me. I wouldn't have done that."

"Well, I think we know why he was sabotaging your relationships then," Levi said.

Tom shook his head. "I had no idea that you did that. He shouldn't have looked, though, not if he had those feelings for you."

"Exactly!" Arie said. "Yesterday when I leaned across Liam, my girls were accidentally on full display, and you know what he did? Turned to the side, didn't even look. They were right in his face."

"We did not need to know that," her dad said.

"No, we did not," Levi added.

Arie rolled her eyes. "I said accidentally, and besides, I told you he was being all polite and didn't even look."

"Still," Tom said. "I'm going to see if Coop and Ethan can stay for the night party. I'd feel better with a few extra bodies watching over in case Aaron does do something stupid."

Chapter 39
A Good Boy, A Greek God, & A Pool Man

Coop sat on the couch while Ethan knelt between his legs, licking freshly made frosting off his thick, hard cock. He rubbed Ethan's hair and watched as he licked and sucked slowly while maintaining eye contact. Coop moaned, "Mmm—such a good mouth—get it nice and clean—then I want you to ride me."

Ethan shook his head, looking up at him, moving his tongue left to right on the head of his cock.

Coop softly grasped a hand full of Ethan's shaggy brown hair, tilting his head back. "Did you just say no?"

Ethan smiled and wrapped his hand around his husband's massive cock and stroked it, while flicking his tongue across the tip. "I did—because I want your cum in my mouth." He stuck his tongue out flat and licked the underside slowly, cleaning off the rest of the frosting.

"Ungh—Fuck—Ethan—I want to be inside—mmm—" He tightened his grip on Ethan's hair, as Ethan worked him up and down with his wet little tongue. Coop begged, "Please—mmm—let me fuck you—" He leaned his head further back against the couch and closed his eyes. Ethan's mouth felt so good, and if he watched him suck any longer, he was gonna come, and he really wanted to fuck him. "Baby, come on, get up here and let me touch you."

Ethan gave the head of Coop's cock one final kiss, then straddled across him.

Coop grabbed the lube from the cushion, and squeezed some onto his fingers, then slid them around Ethan's hole. "Mmm—I love the way you feel." He teased Ethan, gently prodding at the center before finally pressing a finger inside. Ethan's head dropped onto Coop's shoulder, while Coop fingered him slowly.

"Cooper, fuck me, I don't want it soft right now. Come in my mouth or fuck me hard."

Coop passed Ethan the lube and picked him up. He carried him into the spare bedroom down the hall, then pushed the door open with his foot. "Haven't fucked you in here yet, Mr. Morgan," he said, placing Ethan on his back near the edge of the bed. He spread Ethan's legs wide and pressed the head of his dick against Ethan's slippery hole, rubbing it around the rim. "How bad do you want it?"

Ethan passed him the lube. "So fucking bad. Don't tease me."

Coop squirted the lube generously into his palm, then rubbed his cock around Ethan's rim. "I like when you get bossy, but you're not in control, puppy."

Ethan moaned in anticipation and reached for his own dick.

"No," Coop said, pinning Ethan's strong arms above his head. "Lay there and get fucked. That's what you wanted. You didn't want me to play with you, so lay there like a good boy."

Precum leaked from the top of Ethan's fat cock, making Coop even harder. "Look at you, leaking for me already. So fucking good."

Coop grabbed Ethan's legs, tossing them over his shoulders and started pressing inside. "Tight—still so tight—"

Ethan winced, turning his face to the side. "Do it—make it hurt."

Coop shoved his dick further inside until he was tightly sealed against Ethan. His hips moved back and forth, fiercely pounding into him. The slapping of their bodies only turned Coop on even more, sending him into a complete frenzy. He thrusted harder and faster, while Ethan begged for more.

"Fuck yes, harder, harder."

Coop leaned down and sucked Ethan's neck, biting hard into it, he moaned and sucked the soft skin, lost in the feeling of Ethan's warmth. "Mmm—mmm—your ass—baby—so fucking good." He released one of Ethan's legs and worked him at the perfect angle, driving into his prostate.

Ethan's nails raked down Coop's back, while his orgasm erupted between them. "Mmm—Cooper—ungh—I'm coming—"

Coop shoved their mouths together, rolling his tongue around Ethan's, in a hot passionate kiss. He gripped Ethan's sides tighter. "Mmm—so fucking good—you taste like frosting—"

Ethan brought his mouth next to Coop's ear and sucked his earlobe in, then released it. He whispered, "My cum is all over us—it's so hot—now—give me what I want—come deep inside me, Cooper—I want all of it."

Coop slammed into Ethan's ass repeatedly, watching his cock, wet and slippery between them. "Fuck—mmm—I'm gonna—" He closed his eyes, releasing inside. "Ungh—hah—there you go, baby—"

Coop's body relaxed and Ethan pulled him close, kissing him on the cheek. "My Cooper," he whispered.

Coop smooched him on the mouth. "My puppy."

After a quick shower, the two threw on a pair of their comfy track pants and sat in bed. Ethan placed the laptop on Coop's thighs and scooched in close, while Coop wrapped an arm around him.

"What should we look for first?" Ethan asked.

"Crib, definitely that, or the bassinet? I think that's what your mom called it."

"We're not calling to ask her. She'll take over this whole operation."

Coop grabbed his phone off the nightstand and noticed a missed call from Levi. "Ugh. You know, right after hot sex, I really do not feel like interacting with other people."

Ethan giggled. "Yeah, but we never feel like interacting with other people."

"That's cause you're the only person I like," Coop said nuzzling against Ethan's cheek.

Ethan kissed him. "You're the only person I like, too."

Coop's phone rang from beside him. "Well, it's Levi again, might as well answer it." He put the phone on speaker and answered, "Hey, Levi."

Levi scolded them, "What if this were an emergency? Aren't you two supposed to be at the ready in case the baby has to be delivered? Really irresponsible to miss a phone call at a time like this."

Coop and Ethan's eyebrows raised, and they looked at one another.

"I'm kidding," Levi said "Sorry. You guys messed with poor Liam, then you got your dad in on it last night. Poor Liam nearly had a heart attack when we found him in Arie's bed this morning."

"Wait, he was in Arie's bed this morning?" Coop asked.

Levi sassed him, "Oh, what do you care? You two were probably knocking one out thirty minutes ago when I called."

"Oh, Levi, you know us too well," Ethan said.

Coop rubbed Ethan's arm. "So, what are you calling about?"

Levi sighed. "Hang on, let me walk outside. I'm at the retirement home with your dad and Arie. Oooh, there's a spot. I found a pretty bench in a flower garden…ugh, but it's so hot. I feel like a puddle already. Anyway, your dad and I think it would be a good idea if you two could come and hang out in the kitchen, during Arie's party tonight."

Ethan and Coop made disagreeable faces at the suggestion.

"Why do you both think we need to be there?" Ethan asked.

"We'll be there for the family party," Coop added, "but we don't really want to stay for the pool party."

Levi huffed. "Well, Liam and your dad are afraid that Aaron might do something stupid at the party tonight that could upset your sister. So, your dad just wants extra bodies if he does. You're both big guys…"

Ethan and Coop looked at one another. Coop whispered, "People say the craziest shit to us, right?"

"Every day."

Coop shook his head. "Why do you guys think that little remora is gonna do something crazy? He knows Arie doesn't like fighting. If you're worried about Liam, I'm sure Liam could take him. He's smaller than us, but he's still cut. I wouldn't worry about that."

"Yeah," Ethan said. "I wouldn't worry about Liam…he's scrappy."

Levi groaned. "Guys, it's not that we're worried about Liam, but you both just said the reasons you should be there. Aaron is a remora that's latched on to someone he can't have, Liam is scrappy, and Arie doesn't like fighting. So, if the remora goes after the dragon, the scrappy is going to want to fight, making your sister very unhappy."

"Be serious, Levi," Coop said. "I don't think Liam would actually fight him. He's an attorney."

Ethan agreed, "Yeah, he probably wouldn't, but I'm still a little confused. Are you and Tom saying you'd expect us to fight the fish?"

"No!" Levi shouted. "Why are you two being so difficult? We just need you to be there. Can you do it or not?"

Ethan and Coop looked at one another.

"Let us talk about it," Coop said. "We're really not trying to be difficult. Of course, we care about Arie's happiness and safety, but we also just got our surrogacy agreement approved last night. We're just trying to think through this as parents."

Ethan added, "Yeah, let us talk about it. We can't get involved in something that could jeopardize our agreement. We can ask Liam what he thinks, since he's our attorney."

"I'm sorry, guys," Levi said. I didn't even think about that. You're right. But to answer your question, Ethan, we would not expect anyone to fight…except for Tony, maybe. We just meant that we'd like you there as a deterrent. If you can do it, great, if not, that's okay, too. Now, I have to go back inside and be harassed by a very feisty ninety-two-year-old. I'll have your dad call when we're done here. See you both later."

As Levi walked into the room with Ms. Doris and Tom, Arie stepped outside to answer a call from Liam. "Hi, Liam, how is everything going? Are you winning?"

Liam chuckled. "Hmmm, hard to say for sure, but I should win, so yes."

Arie was happy to hear that. "That's great! Well, I think that the party is gonna be the biggest one ever tonight. Oh, and my dads are trying to get Coop and Ethan to come because they think that Aaron may do something stupid. But he texted me and seemed normal."

"What did he text you? Not asking from jealousy, at all, just trying to figure out his next move."

"He just said happy birthday and that he'd see me tonight. Em said that he asked her if I meant what I said about not caring if he had a girlfriend or something? Or would I really not care and set him up with someone…I wasn't super focused when she told me. But that's good, right? It sounds like he's thinking about getting a girlfriend."

Liam was silent for a moment, then said, "I think I know what he's gonna do. But let's not let him ruin your day or take any more time talking about it. You said you'd be happy if Luke and Kory came, right?"

"Oh, definitely! Do you think they'll do it?"

"I'm not sure. I'll try and call them on my next break and find out. How are things going at the retirement home? Was Ms. Doris excited?"

"My dads are very popular here," Arie said. "Ms. Doris has been all over them all morning. She's so bad, she's pretending that Levi is her lover and my dad is her husband. She keeps winking at me to play along. They're both too nice to stop it. I think Levi might be reaching his limit soon, though. My dad's role is easy, she's mostly just pretending he's at work."

"Before I react to everything you just told me, does she have any type of condition that makes her feel this way? Or is she actually just playing?"

"No, she's fine," Arie giggled. "She's only here because she's fallen a few times and her family didn't want her at home alone. Let me tell you, at ninety-two, Ms. Doris still gets down. She has no problem with her memory. I have heard things that no person should hear about her nighttime escapades in this place."

"Well, then it's hilarious that she's pretending Levi is her lover, and your dad is her husband. I wish I could be there to see it."

"I don't know. I'm kinda scared to bring you near her now."

Liam chuckled. "Nah, I'm sure it would be fine. But, hey, I have to get back inside. I'll talk to you the next time I have a break. Bye, Arie."

"Good luck. Talk to you later."

Arie skipped back inside Ms. Doris' room, smiling brightly. Tom stood over by the bouquet of red and white roses on the small nightstand to the right of Ms. Doris.

Their game of pretend continued, as Ms. Doris fanned herself with a magazine feigning worry that her husband may return home from work to find her lover, Levi, with her.

The magazine slipped from her hand, and Levi bent over to pick it up for her. Levi gasped. "Oh my God…Um…Tommy. A word, please." He whispered quite loudly, into Tom's ear, "No more! She grabbed my ass! She grabbed my ass, Tommy! No more!"

Ms. Doris giggled in her bed.

Arie covered her mouth, holding in a laugh.

Tom looked at the flowers seriously. "Who sent you these flowers while I was working? Have you taken a lover, Doris?"

Ms. Doris fluttered her lashes and looked around.

Levi whispered loudly to Tom again, "I'm done playing. She grabbed my ass! Can you hear me?"

Tom patted him on the tush and looked at Ms. Doris. "I can't blame you for taking a lover while I've been at work, and such a handsome one." He rubbed Levi's cheek. "Face of an angel, tush like a marshmallow."

Ms. Doris shrugged. "Well, it is your fault, dear. You've ignored me for so long. I was far too lonely, and a woman has needs."

Levi blushed as Tom playfully patted his bottom again, and lifted his chin at him, encouraging him to play for just a bit longer. Levi moved back beside Ms. Doris. "But I'm afraid, darling, how can I, a mere lover, compete with your husband, whose looks rival a Greek God?"

Tom laughed loudly, looking at Levi.

From the door on the right, an elder gentleman, Mr. Robert Finch, came in smiling. He was Ms. Doris' special nighttime friend.

He waved both hands at the parties in the room. He was quite familiar with the games Ms. Doris liked to play. "Alright, the pool man is here," he said. "And I'm taking the lady for myself. The rest of you cats can hit the road." He leaned down and gave Ms. Doris a kiss on the cheek.

Arie, Tom, and Levi laughed and waved goodbye, giving the two their private space.

As the group walked out of the retirement home, Levi gave Tom a playful whack on the arm. "My ass, Tommy! She actually grabbed my ass!"

Tom opened Levi's door for him and patted his ass before he sat inside. "I'm sorry, angel, but the more you scream about your ass, the funnier it is. Come on, let's get lunch."

Arie hopped into the back seat. "Yes, I'm starving! Let's go somewhere nice by the water."

Tom drove them to a nice, dolphin-themed outdoor café on the beach. The hostess quickly sat them at a table facing the ocean. "Welcome, your server should be with you shortly," she said, passing them their menus. "We've hired a few new ones, so please be patient. They're doing the best they can."

Levi pulled an eyebrow down and looked at Tom next to him. "I don't feel good about a pre-apology. I don't know about you two. Maybe we should go somewhere else. He looked at Arie. "It's your birthday, what do you think?"

Arie shrugged with a smile. "It's fine. Liam's gonna be in court all day. I'm good hanging with you guys until later. Doesn't matter how long it takes."

"Are you ready for your party?" Levi asked. "The event planner said she'll be there extra early to set things up."

"Yes!' Arie said, doing a little dance in her chair. "I can't wait!

Gonna be so fun! Oh, Liam said he's gonna see if Luke and Kory can come! I hope they can make it."

Tom asked, "Aren't you the slightest bit nervous that Aaron may try and ruin your party?"

"No, and I'll tell you why. Because he can't. There is nothing he could do to ruin my party. Honestly, as long as I have Liam and Em there, and no one is fighting, I don't care. It's gonna be fine."

"I agree," Levi said. "It will be fine. I'm looking forward to your match tomorrow. We've barely made it to any games this season. I feel bad about that."

"Don't feel bad. It's okay, you guys are busy. Liam's gonna come tomorrow, too."

Tom chuckled. "He's gonna see the dragon in all her glory. That video was just a teaser. He has no idea what he's in for."

Arie wasn't worried about it. She'd already shared the most embarrassing parts of her personality with Liam. She waved her dad's comment off. "It will be fine. Besides, he played soccer, he understands."

Levi tilted his head at her. "You won't be worried about what he thinks and take it easy on Alex out there, will you?"

"Ha! Never. I physically can't control myself on the field. Besides, I can't worry about who's watching, even if it's him."

Levi spoke animatedly with his hands. "Picture this, you versus Alex, fighting for the ball, you lock eyes with Liam, and you lose the ball, falling and getting humiliated as she laughs in your face."

"What is this a nightmare?" Tom asked, "Why are you putting this out there?"

"Not gonna happen," Arie said confidently. "You know that I don't really notice people unless Coach throws me on the bench. I'll know he's there, but I won't focus on him."

"Still no waiter?" Levi looked around annoyed. "I'm going to try and call Luke about tonight and see where this waiter is. If someone comes before I'm back, you know what I want, Tommy." He stood and walked toward the hostess stand, then gave a thumbs up to Arie and Tom before walking toward the dock to call Luke.

Arie's friend and one of Emma's many love interests, Travis, came to serve them. "Hey, Travis!" Arie said. "I didn't know you worked here."

Travis nodded, and held his small notepad in his hand. "Yeah, I just started, but it's crazy busy. I took an afternoon shift today, so I could make it to your party tonight. Happy birthday, by the way."

"Thanks! I can't wait."

"Do you already know what you want to order? Or I can go over the specials."

Tom pointed at Arie. "Birthday girl first."

Arie ordered a grilled chicken sandwich, with sweet potato fries, while Tom ordered fish sandwiches and regular fries for himself and Levi.

Travis wrote the order down, then looked concernedly at Arie. "Hey, I feel like I should tell you that Aaron…"

Arie held her palm outward and shook her head. "Whatever you're about to say. Don't. Whatever it is. It's cool."

Travis nodded. "Yeah…it's just…"

Arie waved her hand this time. "I don't care. Seriously."

"Alright," Travis said. "I'll get the order put in. But for your birthday, I'll put everything in the system as an appetizer, so it gets done faster."

Tom rolled his eyes. "Well, we've been here for thirty minutes, not really doing us a favor at this point, buddy."

"Fair enough," Travis said, turning on his heel. "I'll be back."

Arie pulled her phone out so she could text Emma, and Tom

tapped the table in front of her. "Should've at least let the kid say what he needed to."

"Nah, it was something dumb. I could tell."

Chapter 40
Peacocking

Luke stood pinned against Kory's office wall, while Kory unbuckled his belt and kissed the side of his neck during their lunch break. They'd gotten used to sex in the office at lunch, while Madeline was in Italy, and Kory wasn't ready to give up their new lunchtime tradition yet.

Luke squirmed, pressing his hands on his husband's firm chest. "Mmm…that feels so good, but you know Madeline's back in the office."

Kory unbuttoned Luke's pants and whispered beside his ear, "You didn't say you didn't want to…" He licked the side of Luke's neck and reached down his pants.

The feeling of Kory's hand on his dick made Luke weak in the knees. He pulled his face in and kissed him deeply, fully expecting Kory would pick him up and move him to the desk, as he normally did.

Just as Kory grabbed ahold of Luke's ass, the elevator sounded outside their office. Kory dropped his head on Luke's shoulder, in defeat and re-buckled Luke's belt.

"Open this. Now," Madeline said, knocking on the door.

Luke adjusted his shirt, and Kory gave him a quick kiss on the cheek.

Kory opened the door, just enough to peek his head through, since Luke wasn't done fixing his shirt. He raised his chin at Madeline nonchalantly. "What's going on, boss?"

Madeline tilted her head to the side. "I said open it, not stare with your damn head peeking out. Open the door."

Kory peeked over his shoulder and saw that Luke was already done with his readjustments and finally opened the door.

Madeline entered and sat down immediately. She was a rumpled mess. Her normally bouncy curls were tied in a high unbrushed ponytail, and she wore a very thick pair of glasses, even her skirt and top were wrinkled. Madeline had never come into the office looking like this before. Luke was pretty sure she was actually wearing the same outfit she'd worn yesterday. She leaned back in the chair across from Kory's desk and held a file against her chest. She closed her eyes and sighed. "That man is an animal. What a lay."

Luke and Kory both grimaced at her words.

She let out a laugh and pulled the thick glasses off, staring at them in her hand. "We broke my glasses last night, or this morning. I don't know when last night ended at this point."

Luke raised his hand.

"Yes? What?" she asked him.

Luke said, "Well, we don't know who you're talking about, or why…mostly why…why are you talking about this?"

Madeline giggled. "Best friend talk, of course. Kory, you can leave. Your presence isn't needed," she said, pointing to the door.

Kory sat down at his desk, rubbing his temples, and Luke sat in a chair beside him. "Few things," Kory started. "You're not his best friend, we're working, and also this is my office, so I'm not leaving."

Madeline shifted in her chair, grinning from ear to ear. "Fine,

fine, you can stay. I'm talking about Mario, the lawyer from Italy. Holy stromboli. I can't remember the last time someone satisfied me like this. I feel great." She rolled her shoulders in circles and smiled.

Luke's phone rang, giving him an easy excuse to leave this uncomfortable meeting. "Oh, it's my dad calling, I should take this in my office," he said, standing up from his chair.

Kory looked up at him and said, "You will not see the professor tonight, if you leave me in here with her."

Roleplay was one of their favorite things, and Kory knew the one way to get Luke to bend was to threaten him with taking away his favorite persona for the night. Luke pulled his mouth to the side and looked down. "What about the baker?"

Kory's head dropped forward, and he blew air from his mouth. "Don't bring him into this."

Luke rubbed his shoulder and sat back down in his chair. "Fine, I'll take it in here." He answered the phone, "Hey, Dad, what's up?"

"Do you two have plans tonight?"

Luke turned to Kory and smiled. Thoughts of their roleplay ran wildly through his head. "Yeah, I think so. Why?"

His dad sighed. "It's a long story." He gave Luke a quick rundown of everything that happened with Aaron and Arie. After finishing he asked, "So, can you guys do it?"

Luke pulled his mouth to the side in thought, and Madeline let out a loud laugh.

"Was that Maddie?" his dad asked.

"Yeah, she's been in here for probably fifteen minutes staring at her phone. She's out of it today."

"Put me on speaker," his dad demanded "I need to tell her something."

Luke put the phone on speaker and placed it on the desk in between himself and Kory.

His father cleared his throat and shouted, "Maddie Parson!"

Madeline's head shot up from her phone.

He continued, "The next time you accidentally call my husband during one of your nighttime affairs, I will personally drive to your home and throw up on your car! That was absolutely disgusting! Never again, Maddie."

Maddie looked confused, and she turned her mouth down. "What are you talking about? And you're on speaker, you don't need to shout. Thank God, Ms. Martin's out today, she could've heard that."

Kory and Luke faced one another, they each covered the other's ears, wincing.

Levi huffed. "I don't care. Really, Maddie. We can't unhear that."

"I'm actually sorry about that," she said. "Don't even know how that happened." She stood up from her chair and started walking toward the door. "I have to go, guys. I'm going back to the hotel for another round. I just stopped in to make sure everything was okay here." She smiled and left the office looking at her phone.

Luke's dad ended the call without another word.

"That was pretty rude," Luke said, looking at his phone. "Neither of them even said goodbye to us."

Kory shrugged and pulled him in for a hug. "At least she's gone. What do you want to do about the party?"

"I don't know. Sounds like Liam and Arie are together now. So maybe we should ask him what he thinks."

Liam walked outside of the courtroom, following a win for his client. He was ready to call Arie, but saw a text from Kory asking him to call him as soon as he was out. He quickly texted Arie to let her know that he was done, and that he'd call her soon. He still needed to stop by the office before he could leave for the day, and there were a few other things he needed to do before Arie's party.

Once he got in his car, he pulled out of the courthouse parking lot and called Kory. "Hey, why did you text me when I was in court?"

Kory answered, "Your new phone number sometimes says your name, and other times it doesn't."

Liam repeated his question, "Why did you text me when I was in court?"

"How'd the Uncle case end? Did you get a W?"

"Of course, I did. Did you doubt me?"

Kory and Luke both laughed, and Liam's mouth dropped open. "Am I on speaker? You guys really shouldn't do that to people, you know? What if I said something I shouldn't about someone else and they walked in the office?"

"Alright, alright," Kory said. "You're on speaker because we both need to talk to you about this party tonight."

Liam stopped at a red light and pulled a lollipop out of his pocket and stuck it in his mouth. *Oh wow, this one is purple too. I feel like I've only been pulling purples lately.* "Well, I'm almost at the office. I was gonna call you about that anyway. Let's talk when I get there."

A few minutes later, Liam walked into Kory's office and sat down. "What's up?" he asked, looking at Luke and Kory.

Kory turned his large monitor to face Liam. "This kid's gonna make a scene tonight."

Aaron's profile was shown on the monitor, with various pictures of him flexing while trying on different outfits including swim shorts.

Liam rolled his eyes. "Why are you looking at this? I don't want to see that. Guy got rejected last night and now he's trying to peacock for my girl?"

"Peacocking? You're so funny!" Luke said.

Liam looked at the screen and shook his head, while Kory and Luke scrolled through posts. He sighed after reading all the captions. "I know exactly what he's gonna do."

Kory crossed his arms. "Yep. Me too."

"What?" Luke asked confused. "Somebody tell me. I don't know what he's gonna do."

Kory, ever the professor, wrapped an arm around his husband and pointed at the monitor. "Take a look at this like it's a case; lets predict his next move based on what we see here on his profile and what Liam told us."

Luke nodded. "Riiight…I get it."

Liam narrowed his eyes and pointed his lollipop at Luke. "Tell me what you think he's gonna do."

"Start a fight, probably with you."

Liam hit a pretend button on Kory's desk, "Eeeeeh. Wrong!"

"No, he won't do that," Kory said.

Luke threw his hands up in frustration. "Well, what the fuck is he gonna do then?"

Liam pulled his head back at Luke's reaction. "Damn, what are you, pent up? Little bit of an overreaction."

Kory rubbed Luke's back. "He's not pent up, it's just been a frustrating morning."

Luke held his hand on his forehead. "Sorry. Listen, Liam. I think we're gonna go to the party. My dad and Tom think it would be a good idea to have extra people around."

"Sweet. I agree. My question is, why the hell do they just let anyone in? That estate is impossible to get into, but on the night of her party they just throw the gates open and let the whole world in?"

"I think you're underestimating how many people will be at this party," Luke said. "Arie is insanely popular, she has a lot of friends. If they stopped every car, the private two-mile road that leads to the gate would be backed up all the way onto the boulevard. Seriously. So, Tony has everyone park their cars along the road, then he copies their IDs and lets them in. A list would never work, too many people know about it. Also, since everyone is on foot, they wouldn't get very far in that place. Security inside the estate is no joke."

Liam shook his head. "How does Tony keep people out that she doesn't like, or even know, for that matter?"

"Don't know. I don't think he can," Luke said with a shrug.

"This sucks." Liam groaned and leaned his head back in his chair. "I don't want this guy ruining her party."

"The only way her party would be ruined is if you fight with him. Verbally or physically," Luke said. "Arie hates fighting. So, if you remain calm no matter what he does—which I still have no idea what that will be—then she's gonna be fine. I promise."

Liam stood up. "Alright, well, yeah, if you guys can come hang out, that would be good. Coop and Ethan texted me asking if they should go or not, for the same reason."

"Well, I think they should," Kory said. "But I don't know them that well. If they aren't easily provoked, then I'd say yes, but if not, they shouldn't. Just because of the surrogacy agreement."

Liam walked over toward the door. "Yeah, I agree."

"Alright," Luke said. "We'll see you tonight. Remember, Arie doesn't like him, she had that option for thirteen years, but you, she likes, don't let him get to you."

Chapter 41
Flowers And Cannoli

Liam entered the main estate and saw Arie, Tom, Levi, Coop, and Ethan sitting in the kitchen at the long granite counter. The inside of the kitchen was decorated with purple, pink, and gold balloon garland, which was elegantly draped around the expansive glass doors, along with a large gold glitter happy birthday sign that hung from the right side of the balloon display.

The five sat on the same side of the counter, facing the back doors. They appeared to be watching a woman outside who was wearing a tight fitting short black dress and high heels, placing various tables and decorations around the pool area.

Levi gestured toward her from his seat. "She almost fell in the pool! Can she sue us if she falls in and gets hurt? Why is she wearing heels? I don't understand. She's an event planner! She's here to decorate!"

Liam came in from behind unnoticed, and answered Levi's question, "Yes, she can sue you."

Arie beamed brightly, seeing Liam holding a gorgeous, wrapped bouquet of lavender roses. She stood up from her stool and kissed him on the cheek.

"Happy birthday, again." he said, passing her the flowers. He felt a little weird knowing that everyone was watching the two of them but was too focused on Arie to worry about it.

"Thank you so much, Liam," she said, smelling the flowers. She dug through the cabinets to find a vase, quickly pulling one out.

Liam couldn't help but stare at her, while she filled the vase with water. *How does someone so perfect even exist, and actually want to be with me?*

Her eyes sparkled looking at the flowers. "They're so beautiful, Liam. The prettiest flowers I've ever seen. Oooh, they're freshly cut, too," she said, looking at the stems. "They're my favorite shade of purple. Absolutely perfect."

Levi, Tom, Ethan, and Coop all gave Liam nods of approval. Liam smiled and approached the opposite side of the counter. "Why are you all sitting on the same side?"

Tom pointed toward the back doors. "We're watching them set up for Arie's party."

Levi stood and shook his head agitated and walked near the doors. "I told her to block the bar off out there. Ugh, I'll be back," he said stepping outside.

Liam sat on a stool facing the rest of the group, and Arie sat beside him after placing her flowers on the counter. Liam pulled his phone out and looked at Arie. "The second part of your present isn't here yet. It says it will be here by 8:00."

"Don't worry about it," Arie said. "Having you here is already the best present you could give me. Plus, you gave me the prettiest flowers I've ever seen."

Tom stood up from his seat after the group noticed Levi gesturing wildly toward the bar. "He's not happy with her at all. I have to get out there. You guys order the pizzas. I'll make the drinks when I get back."

Arie got up from her seat and pulled out the drawer that held the old paper menus. "Liam, you said that Kory and Luke are coming, right?"

Ethan whispered to Coop and Coop laughed. Coop whispered back into Ethan's ear, drawing an even louder laugh from Ethan.

Liam pointed at them smiling. "Talking shit about my brother and Luke, right?"

Ethan and Coop pulled their heads back and furrowed their brows.

Arie looked up confused. "What did you just ask them?"

Liam said confidently, "I know the secret about their whispers now. That was definitely a whisper of smack talk."

"That most certainly was not," Ethan said.

Coop shook his head. "Nope."

"Yeah, right," Liam said. "I don't believe you."

Ethan shrugged with a smile. "Tell him, I don't care."

Tom and Levi walked back inside.

Coop said to Liam, "We were wondering if the Italian place we're ordering from makes cannoli."

Tom and Levi chuckled loudly as they walked toward the refrigerator.

"I'll never understand you guys," Liam said.

Arie brought the menu over beside Coop and Ethan. "They do have cannoli. Says so right here. Do you guys want me to order you some?"

Coop and Ethan winced.

"Ha!" Liam said. "She ruined cannoli for you now, right? Nice."

Coop shook his head at Liam. "Arie, just order a dozen and however many you guys want."

Arie looked around at the men in the room, who were all giggling. "I am so effing confused right now. Coop, you want twelve just for you two? Or like twelve for all of us? And what are you all laughing about?"

"Order some for us, too," Levi said. "How many do you want, Tommy?"

Tom looked confused at Levi, then to Arie, then back to Levi. "Are you asking me what I think you're asking me?"

Levi held his arms out and shrugged. "I'm talking about food play, what else?"

Ethan and Coop waved their hands. "Okay, forget it. That did it," Coop said.

"Yeah, never mind," Ethan said. "Forget the cannoli."

Arie was obviously still out of the loop. "I have no idea what's going on, but I'm just gonna place the order. I'm starving and you're all being super weird. I'll get the cannoli, and whoever wants it can have it." She looked at Liam. "Oh, wait, unless you want cannoli? I care what you want."

Liam shook his head side to side resolutely. "Never. These two completely ruined cannoli for me."

Tom and Levi pulled the frozen fruit and other ingredients out for Arie's birthday drink. Together they dumped the ingredients that they had settled on into the blender. They waited until Arie finished ordering the food, then made the drinks.

Once everyone else had a glass in their hand, Tom said a few sweet words, as did Levi, and the group tapped their colorfully swirled drinks together.

Tom watched as Arie took her first sip. Her eyes widened. "Dad, this is so good! The best one ever!"

Liam took a sip of the drink, which he found a bit too sweet, but was more concerned with positioning during Arie's party. He faced Coop and Ethan and said, "This is too far away. Can you guys come out there with me for a minute?"

He turned to Arie. "Hey, I'll be right back. I need to talk to them real fast. I'll fill you in after." He kissed Arie's forehead, then looked around at everyone staring at him. *I just kissed her forehead in front of everyone. Why am I like this with her? I feel so protective over her.*

She smiled up at him sweetly. "Okay."

Liam walked outside with Coop and Ethan while Arie, Tom, and Levi stayed inside.

Liam explained animatedly what he expected Aaron would do and where he would enter from. He gestured toward the side entrance to the pool. "If Aaron comes in here like this, and we're over here in the kitchen, he's already got his way. He can make her cry, or at least ruin her night. He needs to be able to see that you guys, and the other four, are out here."

Ethan shook his head in disagreement, looking at Liam. "In my opinion you're planning only for one half of what he's going to do."

Liam shrugged. "What else could he possibly do?"

"Bring his brother," Coop said.

Liam's hands were on his hips, and he leaned his head backwards. "Shit…the megabastard. I forgot about him."

Ethan nodded. "Yeah. Arie told us about that. I think the brother's got a big play to make tonight, too."

"The brother is a punk," Coop said. "Got a real big mouth."

Liam crossed his arms and sighed. "How am I supposed to be calm with all this going on tonight? Everyone has told me repeatedly that she hates fighting and jealousy, but what am I supposed to do? Let these two assholes ruin her party?"

Ethan and Coop patted him on opposite shoulders.

"Just ignore whatever they do," Coop said.

Ethan pointed at the bar. "The six of us will sit over here at the bar, which thankfully Levi got roped off, and we can intervene if either of them does anything stupid."

Coop added, "Just have fun with Arie."

Arie slid one of the doors open and stuck her head out. "Pizza will be here in a few minutes."

Once the pizza was finished, it was almost time for Arie's party to start. Liam was still a bit nervous as he held Arie's hand and walked her over to her side of the estate. "Looks like Emma is here," he said lifting his chin toward her car.

"Yes! She said she'd be here in ten, probably just got here a few minutes ago. I'm so excited, Liam."

Liam held both of her hands in his and kissed them softly. He wanted to kiss her, but peeked back at Emma's car first, to be sure she wasn't sitting inside.

Arie looked over her shoulder. "We're alone out here," she said, while hanging her arms around Liam's neck.

Liam, with his hands on her waist, pulled her into their deepest kiss yet. It was the first time he'd allowed himself to give into the passion he'd felt for her, and he really didn't want to stop. Arie's hand lightly stroked the back of his neck, while they kissed, bringing with it an almost tender affection that he hadn't felt before. After a few moments, Liam forced himself to pull back. "Okay, you should really go upstairs and get ready."

Arie's gaze shifted toward Liam's lower half. "Are you sleeping over tonight?" she asked with a mischievous grin.

Liam's mouth dropped and his eyebrows raised. "What?"

She turned and opened her door. "I hope so," she said before walking inside.

Liam put his hands on his thighs and hunched over, exhaling deeply. *What the hell am I supposed to do now? Got me all worked up,*

I'm so hard, and now I have to go back there with her entire family…
Damn it. I need a cold shower first.

Chapter 42
Your Everything Is Out

The outdoor bar was covered in platters of food and Liam's Magic the Gathering cards. Liam, Kory, Luke, Ethan, Coop, Tom, and Levi all sat around the bar, while Liam explained the many rules of the game. Kory was somewhat familiar, as was Luke, so those two also did their best to teach the others.

Coop looked confused at the cards in his hand. "I don't get it."

"Me neither," Ethan said. "But let's just play and see what happens. We have nothing else to do out here."

Kory took his turn. "I can't believe we're all sitting here because of this one guy. Hopefully he doesn't even do anything."

"Now that would be funny," Luke said. "We're all out here because of this little twerp and then he doesn't even do anything."

"I think you mean that it would be great, if that happens," Levi said. "I personally don't feel like sitting out here, with a bunch of loud, half-naked young adults."

Liam's stomach was in knots, worried about what he should or shouldn't do if Aaron did something to upset Arie, and her flirtatious invitation only made matters worse for him.

Tom held a card up. "This guy looks like you, Coop."

"No, it does not," Ethan said.

Liam looked at the card from the other side of the bar. "Nah. Coop is bigger than that Warrior. Hey, wait, that reminds me…" Liam placed the cards in his hand down. He looked at the rest of the group. "Respectfully, I have to ask that none of you, with the exception of Levi and Luke, take your shirts off tonight while we're out here."

Coop and Ethan laughed, while Tom and Kory rubbed their husband's backs.

Levi cocked his head to the side with sass, looking at Liam. "Excuse me. I have to ask, why were the two of us singled out?"

Luke added, "It better not be what I'm thinking."

"Easy," Liam said. "I'm bigger than both of you. I won't look bad if you two take your shirts off. The other four are too jacked, they'll make me look less cut."

Ethan said, "Neither of our shirts are coming off."

"Especially not Ethan's," Coop said, pulling him close.

Levi grabbed a grape off the tray and threw it at Liam. "Little asshole."

"I can't believe I'm sitting here with you right now and you are still just as stupid as ever," Kory said to Liam.

Liam held his palms open on the counter. "You don't know, okay? I played soccer with them, shirtless…and, and Coop fucking bench pressed Ethan like he was a damn paper doll! I can't compete with muscles like that."

Levi, still visibly annoyed, looked doubtfully at Coop. "You can bench press Ethan?"

Ethan closed his eyes and covered his face.

"Yeah," Coop said. "But it's not a party trick. I just did it because—" He looked at Ethan. "Wait, why did I do that?"

Tom answered, "Liam wanted to see how much you could lift, remember?"

"Yeah," Liam said. "And you had the video of the four-forty, then you lifted Ethan just for fun."

"What?" Kory asked Coop. "Four hundred forty what? pounds?"

Coop leaned his head against Ethan's and shrugged.

"Yes, his max is four hundred forty pounds," Ethan said. "Yes, he can easily press me." He held a hand up. "Before you even ask, no, we won't show you. Cooper is not laying on this hard-ass ground."

"But," Levi said, "we could go inside and do it in the gym."

Liam's mouth dropped open. "No! No! You're all out here to help in case there's a problem. Guys, don't do this right now."

Kory waved off Levi's suggestion and rubbed Luke's arm. "I won't believe it unless I see it. But it's fine, I don't need to."

Levi stood up. "Speak for yourself, I want to see it. I don't want the video. I want to see Coop bench him. I missed it in Italy."

Coop pinched Ethan's chin and gave him a quick smooch. "Do you want me to do it, baby?"

Levi urged Ethan. "Come on, everyone shows up late anyway. Arie's not even out here yet. We have a good fifteen to thirty minutes before anyone gets here. Tell him to do it, Ethan."

"Only if you want to," Ethan said to Coop.

Tom stretched his arms over head. "I think I can get to three-eighty tonight, I'm feeling good."

Kory stood up and reached his hand for Luke to join him. "Okay, now I don't believe anything that any of you have said. We're coming, too."

Luke shook his head, sizing up Liam. "No, you guys go. Liam and I are going to have a little chat about my lack of muscle definition."

Kory sat back down. "If you're not going, I'll stay, too."

Tom, Levi, Ethan, and Coop walked toward the kitchen doors.

Luke kissed Kory on the cheek. "Go. I'll stay with Liam. I won't beat him up."

"Really? You don't mind?" Kory asked. "I want to see if he can do it. Ethan's a big guy." He gave Luke a quick kiss and joined the group on their way inside.

"You're wasting your time," Liam shouted. "I told you I saw it."

Arie came into view from the opposite entrance, wearing a tiny purple bikini, leaving very little to the imagination. Luke saw her and looked at Liam. "Yeah… I'm gonna go with them. We'll be back." He quickly jogged after the rest of the group and headed inside.

Arie and Liam locked eyes, as Arie showed off her suit, turning to the side and back so Liam could get a good view.

Liam covered his mouth. "Holy shit," he said inside of his cupped hands.

Arie asked, "Do you like it?"

Liam's hands still covered his mouth, and he nodded slowly at her.

Arie stood next to Liam and looked at the bar. "Where is everyone else? They left you out here all alone with your cards?"

"They wanted to see Coop bench press Ethan. They're all in the gym. I don't know which gym, though."

Arie leaned down and brought her face close to his. "Good, then I get to kiss you again."

Liam re-covered his mouth and shook his head.

Arie pulled her face back, shocked. "No? Why not?"

Liam slowly looked her up and down. "Arie, I'm a man. I'm wearing swim shorts…your…everything is out. I need you to try and think of how uncomfortable this will be for me if I kiss you right now. Especially given the kiss we had about an hour ago."

Emma came into view in her own tiny black bikini. She called over, "Yeah, babe, look at my birthday girl! Shake it for me, Arie!"

Arie turned her ass toward Emma and gave a little shake.

Liam bit his bottom lip, trying to calm himself. *You can't get jealous, don't think of all the guys that will be here looking at her, don't think about it, don't look at her ass, don't look at her boobs, don't look at her…shit, where can I look? Even her mouth turns me on.*

Ethan carried weights over toward the bench Coop was lying on, while Tom lay on a bench beside him. Tom's gym was far larger than the other gyms at the estate, but, more importantly, there were two weight benches side by side, making it a perfect place for their competition.

As Ethan placed the weights on the bar, Tom said to Coop, "This time don't skip straight to four hundred, okay? Just get there slowly. Give me some face here," he chuckled.

"This is a big gym," Kory said, looking around. He asked Luke, "How many gyms do they have here?"

"Hmm, three in total, unless they added more. Coop's place has one, Arie's place has one, and then this one."

Kory shook his head. "It's sometimes strange to think that you grew up here, and that Liam is staying in Coop's old place."

"What do you mean? This is all very normal. I'm standing here with my dad and stepdad, watching my ex-boyfriend, who is *now* my stepbrother, bench press his husband, while your brother, my brother-in-law, sits outside waiting for his girlfriend, my stepsister's, birthday to start."

"None of that was normal," Kory said.

Luke shrugged. "What family is normal? Also, you pick me up all the time, what's the difference in him bench pressing Ethan?"

"It's not the same, maybe I could do it. I could try, but not here."

Luke's eyes widened in excitement. He rubbed Kory's bicep.

"Maybe tonight I can be your personal trainer, and you can be the down on his luck soccer player, who's looking to get back into the game."

Kory chuckled. "Why does the soccer player bench press you? What's my motivation for doing that? I need the character straight in my head for it to work."

"You could be…you know, lifting weights and I'll just fall on you…accidentally… How about that?"

Kory rubbed his chin deep in thought, nodding. "That can work. Let's do it tonight."

Levi's mouth hung open looking at Luke and Kory.

Ethan said to Tom and Levi, "See, that's what you two sound like, when you think you're whispering. Oblivious."

"Yep, every time," Coop said.

Top gripped the bar above his head and looked over at Coop. "Oh, yeah? We whispered so good this morning in Arie's room. You should've seen us. You don't even know. Isn't that right, angel?"

Levi nodded. "That's right. We sure did."

Ethan put his hands atop Coop's on the bar, stopping him from lifting. "Wait, he either lifts the four-forty, or he lifts me. He's not doing both."

Coop looked over at Levi. "What's it gonna be, Levi?"

Kory called out, "Lift Ethan. Come on. I want to see it. Four-forty is truly an insane amount, but lifting him—if you can do it, I'll really be shocked."

Ethan held a hand out for Coop. "Alright, come on, Cooper."

Tom sighed and sat up. "*Again* this is happening? I wanted to show off my new best. This sucks."

Levi bent down and gave Tom a quick kiss. "You can show me tomorrow. I'll get up early and watch you work out."

Chapter 43
The King And His Queen

Back at the pool, the sun was going down, and the party was in full swing. There were already around seventy-five people there, and it was only 8:00.

Liam sat on a lounge chair off to the side, while Arie bounced around from person to person. Every few minutes she came back over and gave Liam a few hugs and light pecks on the cheek. He decided to stay in his chair instead of walking around with her, so he could keep an eye on the entrance, since he'd been abandoned by the rest of the guys.

A group of Arie's friends started chanting, "Royalty, Royalty, Royalty!"

Arie smiled walking towards Liam. It was obvious from where Liam sat that a lot of the people at her party had no idea they were together based on the things he could hear. "Where's Aaron?" one person asked.

"She can't play until her king gets here. I can't believe he's late to Arie's party," another said.

Emma shouted over, "Babe, let's do it! Let's play! Give the people what they want!"

"Come on, I need my king," she said pulling Liam up by the

hand. "I require your shoulders for my throne. And don't forget, you have to talk royalty style."

Liam pulled his shirt off, revealing his finely toned chest and abs.

Arie's eyes widened in excitement as she took in the sight of him. "Sweet mother of all things holy," she said, sliding a finger down his chest, stopping just below his navel.

Liam bit his lip looking at her, trying his best to think of anything else to distract himself from the feeling of her touch.

Oh my God, this girl, she's gonna kill me. I cannot get turned on right now.

The chatter around them continued as Arie pulled him behind her, and they walked into the water together.

Arie announced, "I present King Liam, my royal subjects."

The crowd clapped and cheered, gathering closer to the pool. Liam smiled even though he was still a bit confused. Arie did explain the game to him, but he wasn't really sure how much he was supposed to do, aside from being her personal throne. He ducked under the water, and Arie sat on his shoulders. He resurfaced a few seconds later, with Arie's tanned thighs firmly in his grasp. *Don't think about her body, don't think about anything. Just keep calm*, he told himself.

Arie announced loudly to the crowd, which had grown to well over a hundred people, "Now, all those wishing to be my royal servant, bow! Bow before your queen!" She giggled as her friends bowed.

The crowd collectively looked to the right, as did Liam, who instantly regretted it.

Into the pool area walked Aaron, standing very close to none other than Alex, along with who had to be his brother Julian, with his arm draped around Dana.

Aaron locked eyes with Arie who was atop Liam's shoulders, he then looked at Alex, as if he was making sure Arie noticed her.

Liam thought, *I fucking knew he would bring that girl. I knew this little bastard was gonna do this. Where the hell is everyone? I guess that's his brother with the other girl… Shit. I have to keep calm.* Liam looked up at Arie. "Do you wanna get down, honey?"

Arie looked down at him. "Ooh that tickles. Your hair…it's tickling my… Wait, did you just call me honey?"

Liam nodded, smiling up at her. "Yeah, I guess I did."

Arie rubbed Liam's hair. "I'm not worried about it. Let's play. Just ignore whatever they do. Alex just wants to get into my head before tomorrow's game."

Liam found it funny that out of everything facing Arie, she was only concerned with Alex, she seemed completely unphased by Aaron and his brother.

Aaron pulled his shirt off and called over to Arie, "I've never gotten to play for a servant spot before, this should be fun." He bowed to Arie outside of the pool along with everyone else.

Alex rolled her eyes. "Tch. I'm not bowing. Not here and not tomorrow either."

"That's right," Dana added.

"Oh, shut up!" Emma shouted. "We don't need you to bow. You were crawling in Arie's flames last time. Can't believe you two would even show your faces here. Gonna be real bad for you tomorrow."

Arie held a hand up. "Em, don't, they're not worth it." She looked at Alex and smiled. "Thanks for coming to my party, Alex. I'm looking forward to our match tomorrow."

"Oh, me too," Alex said, giving Arie a fake smile.

Julian pulled his shirt off and stepped inside the pool. "I'll play, too. I have something I want from the queen."

Liam tried to remain calm despite Aaron and his brother. His attention was quickly diverted, thanks to Alex and Dana who were talking extra loudly beside the pool.

Alex rolled her eyes. "Pacifist off the field, catastrophist on the field…ridiculous."

Dana shook her head in annoyance. "She doesn't even care that we came in with them. This was a huge waste of time."

"She cares, trust me," Alex said. "But she's really comfortable on that hot guy's shoulders. Who is he? Must be her boyfriend. That's probably why Aaron called me after all these years. Eh, it doesn't matter. I'm in her head now."

Arie repeated the rules of the game aloud, for anyone who was unfamiliar and began issuing royal orders. More and more people continued to join, as the party size grew.

Liam still didn't see any of the other guys, and he was getting pretty heated over the looks that Aaron kept tossing his way. Between Aaron and his brother, Liam wasn't sure which of them was going to act like the bigger asshole if either of them won. He started imagining the things they might ask Arie for, and that only aggravated him even more.

After several rounds, there were only a handful of people left vying for the royal servant position. They played another three rounds, and it came down to Julian, Emma, and Aaron who stood in the pool, about seven feet away from Arie and Liam.

Finally, backup had arrived. Liam saw the muscle crew out of his peripheral vision. He felt incredibly relieved watching as Coop, Ethan, Kory, and Luke stood near the side of the pool.

Arie was completely at a loss for what command she should call out. She couldn't focus, because right now, her main concern was that her biscuit—as she and Emma liked to call it—was pressed right against

Liam's neck. Every time Liam moved, she felt a hint of pleasure, which was something she'd never experienced while playing Royalty. She normally just felt uncomfortable whenever Aaron moved his head around. But now was not the time to focus on her sexy boyfriend's head in between her legs, because she needed both Julian and Aaron to lose, fast. Knowing how full of himself Julian was, she declared, "Julian and Emma must kiss!"

"Oh, hell yes, my queen!" Emma shouted.

Julian took one look at Emma, then glanced at Arie and shook his head. "I'm out. I kiss who I want." He stepped out of the pool, removing himself from the game. He was quickly surrounded by several girls, who held towels and offered to help dry him off.

Emma gave a little pout and looked at Arie.

Arie suddenly remembered what Emma said about Aaron last night and declared loudly, "Emma and Aaron must kiss! Queen's orders."

Aaron looked at Liam, then up at Arie "You really want to see me do this, Arie? You really think you won't care?"

Arie didn't see Alex or Dana anymore, she assumed they'd served their purpose in their eyes and left. She ignored Aaron's question and rubbed Liam's head purposefully.

Aaron turned toward Emma, who stood somewhat frozen beside him. He licked his lips slowly, looking up at Arie, prompting a very tight squeeze of Arie's thighs from Liam.

Aaron placed both hands on the sides of Emma's face and moved in with his mouth open.

Emma ducked out at the very last second. "Nope, no. I can't." She quickly got out of the pool, leaving Aaron as the victor.

The crowd clapped and cheered; it was time for Aaron's royal request to the queen. Aaron walked about three feet toward Arie and Liam, as Coop, Ethan, Kory, and Luke also moved closer.

Arie sighed. "I hereby name you the official royal servant to the queen. What does the royal servant wish for?"

Aaron looked around at the large crowd that had gathered. He extended a hand up to Arie. "My queen, would you please come down from your throne? So that I may request this, to thine beautiful ear only?"

Arie shook her head. "No. That's two things. One thing. You get one thing. That's the rule. If you want me to get down, that counts as the one thing." She thought to herself, *Why didn't I just get down and tell him he wasted his request? Stupid, Arie, stupid.*

Aaron smirked at Liam then looked up at Arie. "This humble, wholly devoted, royal servant wishes for only one thing, your majesty. It is but a kiss from thy beautiful lips."

Liam said quietly to Aaron, "This is a bad idea, man."

"We'll see about that," Aaron replied.

Arie remained on top of Liam's shoulders, running her fingers through his hair, trying to think of a peaceful way out. Knowing full well that she would never kiss Aaron, but didn't want Liam, or anyone else, to get into a fight.

Julian shouted over, "Rules are rules, Arie. You always do what's fair, isn't that right?"

Kory and Luke moved quietly behind Julian, and Ethan and Coop stood beside them. There was so much chatter, and the music was so loud, that Julian obviously didn't hear the four of them plotting to take him out if he said one more stupid thing.

"It's me," Luke said. "I'm gonna punch that bastard."

Ethan corrected him, "Arie calls him the Megabastard."

Luke twisted his hips. "Yeah, I'm gonna punch that mega-bastard. My husband is the best lawyer in the world, my brother-in-law is also an attorney, and my best friend runs the practice and makes people cry for a living. I'm untouchable. What's gonna happen if I punch him? Nothing," he said while stretching his arms out.

Kory ran a hand down his own face. "You absolutely can't punch him. Yes, I can get you out of trouble, but you'll still get in trouble. I can't have that."

Luke tilted his head. "Riiight, but I could be a convict, and you could be a prison guard. Just saying. We could make that work."

Kory put a hand on his back. "I need you to calm down. I know you're all worked up, but let's just see how this plays out. I'm more worried about Liam at this point. Can't believe he hasn't punched this guy. Liam takes no shit from anyone." He turned to Coop. "He must really like your sister. I've never seen him keep his cool like this. That guy is basically taunting him."

The crowd chanted, "Kiss him, kiss him, kiss him!"

Aaron smiled up at her. "Come on down, Arie, I've waited a long time for this."

Liam shouted, "Kings edict! Kings edict! I declare that the queen's lips shall never touch another's, for we have already declared our feelings for one another, and this is my queen."

"Oh, damn!" Emma yelled. "How'd he know about that rule?"

Aaron nodded slowly, staring fiercely at Liam.

Julian called over, "Hey, bro, come over here for a minute. I need to tell you something. Don't worry about that guy."

Luke held his arms wide, looking at Kory. "Do I go? Do I punch him?"

Ethan and Coop had already moved directly behind Julian.

Aaron got out of the water and walked over toward his brother. "What? What's so important?"

Julian said loud enough for all to hear, "See, I've been meaning to tell you that I slept with Arie. Isn't that right, Arie?"

Liam shook his head. "Arie, I can't do this anymore. Please get down."

Arie rubbed his hair and smiled down at him. "Ignore it. It's in the past."

"Is that true, Arie?" Aaron asked. "Did you really?" He looked at his brother. "And you, you slept with her knowing how I felt?"

Julian shrugged. "Sorry, bro."

Aaron nodded and gave a hard right-handed punch to his brother's face.

Kory looked at Luke and laughed. "The brother beat you to it!"

Ethan and Coop watched as Aaron walked quickly towards the property gate. A few girls chased after him as he left. "One down," Ethan said.

Julian was also quickly surrounded by girls who were eager to help him.

Luke was so upset that he didn't get to punch him. He said from behind him, "Hey, you little megabastard, get the hell out of here. Be happy your brother punched you because—"

Kory covered Luke's mouth, and spoke to Julian, "Listen, me and my brother over there with Arie are attorneys, so I'm gonna threaten you a tiny bit, because you pissed both my husband and my brother off. You either leave now, or I let him loose and he makes that punch from your brother look like a love tap. You understand?"

Julian who stood at five-foot-ten looked at the four much larger men in front of him, as he held the side of his already swollen jaw.

Coop crossed his arms, staring him down. "You don't want it."

Ethan added, "Yeah…you're gonna want to leave now."

Tom and Levi walked out from the kitchen, having missed everything that happened.

Julian's eyes shifted to Tom, and suddenly he walked away without saying a word.

Kory scoffed. "That guy just looked at all four of us and really thought he stood a chance, then he saw Tom and dipped. What the hell was that about?"

"I have no idea," Coop said. "But please don't tell him."

"Oof…" Ethan added. "We'll never hear the end of it."

Liam ducked under the water, so Arie could swim off his shoulders. He scooped her up from the side and carried her out of the pool princess style, then placed her down, grabbing her towel from the chair and hugging her tightly while wrapping it around her. He really wanted to take her back to her place, but the DJ was still playing music, and Arie's guests were still dancing and having a great time.

Arie looked around at all the people. "I had fun, Liam, but…"

Liam tilted her chin up with his finger. "But what?"

"I want anime, cake, and you."

"Done," Liam said taking her hand in his.

Liam and Arie walked over to Tom and Levi holding hands.

"Thank you for my party, Dads. I had so much fun. But I'm really tired and I just want to go to my room now. We can just let everyone stay, no one will even know I'm gone."

"That's cute," Levi said. "But no. Tommy, handle it."

Tom whistled loudly, and shouted, "Party's over, you have ten minutes to vacate the property!"

Arie and Liam thanked Coop, Ethan, Kory, and Luke for their help, and Kory pulled Liam aside. "Hey, I'm proud of your for not losing it in the pool. I've never seen you so composed outside of court. Luke actually almost punched him, so I can't imagine how hard it was for you."

"Thanks," Liam said making eye contact with Arie. "She means a lot to me. I just didn't want her to be upset. What a prick he was, though."

Kory pulled him into a hug, and Liam froze. Kory hadn't hugged him in years, maybe ever? He couldn't remember it ever happening before. He hugged him back and soaked in the feeling of love he felt from his older unmovable brother.

Kory whispered beside his head. "Liam, I love you, but you shouldn't have sex with her in this house. Tom can lift almost four hundred pounds and he's itching to show his husband how strong he is. I've already seen him eyeing you up a few times. Don't do it." He patted Liam on the back and pulled back from the hug. "Just kidding. You have fun tonight."

"What is wrong with you?" Liam asked. "You hug me for the first time ever and you say that? You're such a dick." Liam said, shoving him.

Kory smiled as he walked backwards toward Luke. "Your funeral," he said with a smirk. "Maybe?"

"I can't find Emma," Arie said to Liam. "She wouldn't leave without saying bye. I'll have to text her when we get back to my place."

Liam kissed her hand and held it tightly in his. "I just want to change into actual clothes, then we can go hang out. I need to grab something, too."

Chapter 44
Let Me See It

Liam opened the entrance door and looked around inside the foyer. His posture dropped and he sighed.

"What's wrong?" Arie asked.

Liam sighed as they walked up the stairs. "I told you I needed to grab something. The other part of your present isn't here. I was hoping it would be. They said it would be here by 8:00."

Arie giggled as they walked into Liam's room and released one another's hands. "Well, I definitely thought you meant you were grabbing something else for tonight. But Tony wouldn't have been able to bring it over. It's probably at the gatehouse with him. We can go get it if you want. We should just wait until everyone clears out."

What did she think I meant? Liam asked himself. Kory's words echoed in his mind, when he caught a glimpse of Arie shivering from the shift in temperature while standing by his bed. *No. Don't touch her.*

Liam tossed his clothes over his shoulder, and shook the worry away, wrapping her tightly in a hug. Arie breathed a sigh of relief. "That's better, thank you."

Liam rubbed her arms softly, trying to warm her.

"You didn't answer me earlier," Arie said.

Liam put his nighttime clothes on the bed and looked at her. "What didn't I answer you about?"

Arie stared intently at Liam's naked chest, while lightly biting her bottom lip. She replied, "About sleeping over. Are you gonna?"

Liam had never felt so conflicted in his whole life. He sat on the edge of the bed and looked at Arie, who was still in her very skimpy bikini, with just a light pink towel draped over her shoulders. She stood in front of him looking down at his face, her gorgeous body directly in his line of sight.

Liam sighed. "Honesty, right?"

She nodded and moved slowly toward him, now extremely close, standing in between his legs, while he sat on the edge of the bed.

He looked at the floor. "Arie, I told you this before, but I've never been in a true functioning relationship…they've all been bad. And I want to do things right with you. I don't want to screw up by rushing into—"

Arie dropped her towel on the floor. "Okay, honesty time for me, I don't care about your other relationships. I care about you, and right now"—she climbed atop his lap, facing him—"I want you."

Liam couldn't resist, he been staring at her perfectly round ass all night, the feeling of it on his neck earlier had driven him to near insanity. He squeezed it tightly in his hands and brought their mouths together in a hot, wet kiss.

She pushed his shoulders down onto the bed, and Liam looked up… He looked up and saw the fan…which reminded him of Coop and Ethan and what they'd done in this bed.

He sat back up and shook his head at Arie. "I can't do this in here."

Arie, obviously confused, stood up from the bed. "What? Why not?"

Liam covered his mouth with his hand. "This is your brother's old bed. I can't."

Arie pulled Liam's hand into the guest room beside the bedroom. She shut the door quickly and approached Liam, who was standing still, trying to get the image of Coop and Ethan out of his head.

She stood close against him and took his hands, placing them on both sides of her ass. "Squeeze it again. It's my birthday. You're supposed to do whatever I say."

Liam tilted his head and moved back in for another kiss while squeezing tightly, as requested. They stood pressed together kissing deeply.

Arie whispered, "Liam…I want you."

The sounds of multiple footsteps coming upstairs could be heard. Liam quickly let go of Arie and pressed his ear against the door. His eyes widened as Arie, unfazed, adjusted her bikini bottom.

He whispered, "Oh my God. It's your dads. What the hell am I gonna do?"

Arie walked near him, and whispered, "Why are you freaking out? They already know we're together."

Liam pointed down to his shorts; he couldn't have been any harder.

Arie's eyes widened. "Oh, that is very, very nice, and, like, pleasing for me to see. Take it out."

He whispered harshly, "Are you crazy? No!"

She stared at his dick a bit longer, then sighed and smiled at him. "Here, I got it. Give me a minute."

Liam backed away from the door, completely terrified of what she would do next.

Arie opened the door and stuck just her head outside. She called down the hall, "Hey, Dads?"

Tom and Levi both answered, "Yes?"

Arie giggled. "Have you guys seen the package that Liam was waiting for? We can't find it." She put a hand behind her back, and Liam gave her a low five.

Tom and Levi came into view from the gym. Levi held the package in his hand, walking toward her. He extended it to her, then pulled it back toward himself. "Are you dressed?"

Arie, still in her bikini, opened the door fully, while Levi winced. "So, no, you're not dressed. Here. Tell Liam we're leaving, he doesn't need to be afraid."

"Oh, yes he does!" Tom shouted.

Levi rolled his eyes at his husband, elbowing him. "Stop it," he said, pulling him toward the stairs.

Arie closed the door, and Liam held his chest. "This family is gonna kill me. One of you, I just know it."

Arie laughed and tapped him with the large, padded envelope. She shook her head. "I give up. I won't try anything else. Let's just go back to my place. I really have to get out of this suit. I'm seriously freezing."

Liam was disappointed in himself, as they walked back into his room so he could change. "I'm sorry. I feel like I messed that up."

Arie shook her head. "No. You didn't. I'm not upset. I'm just freezing. Grab whatever you need and let's go."

"I'm gonna bring your present with me and I'll give it to you later, okay? I may have to explain it. It's not something I want to wrap."

Arie shivered and rubbed her arms standing by the door. "Oooh, mysterious. Sounds good. Can't wait."

Liam picked his clothes up from the bed. "I should really take a shower first."

"My place, use my shower. It's too cold over here. Pleeeeease."

Liam tossed all his nighttime essentials, and Arie's present into backpack and held her hand. They quickly headed outside into the warm night air.

"Oh, I have never been so happy for humidity," Arie said. "It's like a sauna."

Liam smiled at Arie's beautiful face in the moonlight as they walked toward her side of the estate. He still wasn't sure what he was going to do. He knew he wanted to do things right with Arie, but he wasn't sure if there really was a *right* way? Things already felt so perfect between them, so wouldn't doing whatever feels right in the moment, be the best thing?

"Awww, boo," Arie said with a pout. "I didn't get to have any cake. I really wanted you to try it."

Liam looked at the main estate door to the left and headed toward it. "Let's fix that. We'll bring it with us. I'm sure your dads put it away."

No one else was in the kitchen, as Arie and Liam quickly looked inside the refrigerator. The tiered lavender colored cake was separated into four boxes.

Arie grabbed one of the boxes, along with two plastic forks, and they headed toward her place, forgoing a shortcut in favor of the warm night air again.

As they rounded the corner, Arie noticed Emma's parked car, she looked up towards her bedroom window from the outside of the estate. "Maybe she left with someone? My lights are off, so she's not in my room. I need to grab my phone and text her."

"Wait, where is your phone? You said you were gonna text her earlier, I just assumed you had it."

Arie opened the front door. "It's inside my dresser. I wouldn't have been able to keep track of it if I kept it with me." She gestured to her body. "No pockets."

They walked upstairs and into her room together. Arie flipped the light on, and Liam walked toward the bathroom door. "So, can I take a shower? I smell like chlorine."

"Of course, go ahead. I'm gonna go through the hundred texts I have. No joke." She turned her phone to show him.

He smiled and kissed her on the forehead, then walked into the large bathroom. He pulled his shower supplies out and slid the glass door open, quickly stepping inside. He washed his hair, then lathered up his bath pouf and scrubbed himself down. *What am I gonna do? She's so gorgeous; if I stay the night, can I really not have sex with her? When we both want it so bad?* His dick began to harden at the remembrance of their kisses in his bedroom. He pulled the handheld sprayer down and rinsed himself off, resisting the urge to take care of his quickly hardening situation below. Liam spoke to his dick, "I'm gonna need you to keep it together, we can't rush this." He stepped out of the shower, onto the plush pink bathmat and reached for his towel on the counter. From the opposite entrance of the bathroom, two bodies locked in an intense kiss bounded inside.

"Aaahhh!" Liam screamed.

Emma stood eyes-wide, looking at Liam's full package for the second that it was exposed. The man beside her covered her eyes, while Liam quickly shielded himself with his towel and left the bathroom.

Arie was on her way into the bathroom after hearing the scream and bumped into him. "Why are you screaming?" She touched his chest. "Holy shit, your body, it's all wet and sexy."

Liam shook his head, clenching his towel tight around his waist. "No. No. Your friend and her friend are in there. She saw my"—he gestured to his dick—"all of it!"

Arie's mouth dropped, and she flung the door open.

Emma was leaning on the counter shaking her head. "I'm sorry, babe. I didn't mean to peek. I really didn't. Travis and I were gonna shower and we didn't think anyone was in here. I texted you; I thought you had your phone."

"We just got here. I can't believe you saw it. I haven't even seen it yet."

Emma's eyes were wide. "I feel bad for Travis now. I know he saw it too."

"What?" Arie asked. "Why would you feel bad for Travis? Wait? Did you guys have sex in the guest room?"

"No, but we were gonna. We were coming in to shower first." She shook her head. "But after seeing that, I don't know if Travis can impress me."

Arie's eyes widened, and her mouth opened into a large grin. "That big?"

Emma nodded silently.

Arie shoved her. "Don't picture it anymore!" She held a hand over her mouth. "Damn…you guys gotta go."

Emma playfully pushed her. "Tch, we'll use the other shower. But we may stay the night. I promise, we won't come over here."

"Fine. But for real, use the other bathroom. I'm locking this door from the inside."

"Thanks. You're the best. Don't get too rough with that thing, we have a big game tomorrow," Emma joked, as she left.

Arie tried to compose herself. She really did want to have sex with Liam, but even more than that, she couldn't wait to wake up to him lying beside her on game day.

She walked out of the bathroom and looked at Liam who was lying on her bed, now dressed in black gym shorts and a tight navy-blue compression shirt. *Holy shit, he's so hot.* "Hey, I'm really sorry about that. I hope you're not too embarrassed. I guess they're gonna stay in the guest room, but don't worry I locked the bathroom door from the inside. We can forget they're here."

Liam shook his head. "It's not your fault. You don't have to apologize. I'm not really excited that your friend and her friend saw my dick, but it's okay. Just gonna pretend it didn't happen."

"Well, still, I feel bad. Are you sure you're good? Can I hop in the shower?"

"Yeah, I'm good. Do you care if I watch more of that volleyball anime?"

"No, of course not," Arie said. "But just maybe like one more episode, you're almost at one of my favorite parts. Anime, cake, and you... In that order, as soon as I get out."

Liam smiled and turned the TV on. His phone vibrated with a text from Tom.

Tom: *You did good today. Guys told me about what happened. Levi and I are proud of you for keeping your cool.*

Liam: *Thanks. That means a lot.*

Tom: *Levi grabbed your card box from under the bar. I'll leave it in the main kitchen.*

Liam: *Oh, thanks. I can't believe I forgot that I put it there.*

Tom: *See you tomorrow for the game.*

Liam: *Looking forward to it.*

Several minutes later, Arie came out wearing a tiny pair of cotton lavender shorts and a thin white lace camisole. She grabbed the box of cake and forks off her dresser and sat beside Liam on the bed. "One for you," she said, passing him a fork.

Arie took a bite and leaned her head back. "So goood! I'm

starving." She looked at Liam and motioned with her fork. "Eat some, there's like a whole big piece here."

"Wow," Liam said after taking a bite. "That *is* good cake. Is this your favorite?"

"Yep. Vanilla with buttercream, from my absolute favorite bakery. They make the best treats. But for cookies, I use a different place. Oh, that reminds me, I have to go to the bakery after the game to get Tony his thank you cookies."

Liam nodded and took another bite of the cake. "Gotta be honest, I was pretty surprised with your ability to stay calm in awkward situations tonight. Those people did their best to get you rattled and you were just calm, completely unfazed."

Arie tilted her head side to side and started another episode of the anime. "I wouldn't say I was unfazed, but, I mean, Alex has done stuff like that before. She can't beat me physically, so she tries to do it mentally. I may suck at reading some people, but not her. If I had let her see that she bothered me, she'd have one upped me before we even hit the field. I couldn't have that. If I'm being honest, I wasn't really surprised that she showed up. I *was* surprised that she showed up with Aaron, but for real, I think they would be good for each other. Both conniving little schemers. Unbelievable."

"Well, they've both tried to kiss you, and you didn't want either of them, so they both acted like assholes afterward—yeah, they seem like the same person. I mean, you were best friends with her before that happened, so I guess there's no difference."

"Nope, only I was really upset and felt lost and embarrassed, when she lied and told people that it was me who tried to kiss her, people started talking so bad about me, but we were younger then. If Aaron did that, no one would believe him, and I definitely wouldn't be depressed about it. I'd just feel bad for him. Her—she deserves whatever she gets. Brought me to my lowest point. I won't ever forgive her for that."

Liam rubbed her back lightly. This was the second time she'd talked to him about what happened, and thinking about Arie, who is so full of happiness, being at her lowest point really upset him.

"I don't think you need to always forgive people," he said. "But I'm kind of an asshole. There are people I won't forgive, but I don't let them affect me. If she doesn't upset you in a way that makes you sad, then it probably only helps you play better against her. A fierce rivalry can bring out the best in some players. But if she makes you sad, which I don't think is the case, maybe someday you should talk to her. Before you say anything, I'm not advocating for that. I hate her and I don't even know her, so as far as I'm concerned, keep on hating her, as long as it's not hurting you in a different way."

"Nah, I'm unaffected by it. I was sad about our friendship for a while, but now I couldn't be friends with her, and I don't want to be. If it's not about soccer, I don't care what she's doing."

Liam shook his head. "I can't believe he really thought that bringing her here would somehow win you over."

"Me neither. Just goes to show you he doesn't know me as well as he thought he did."

Liam took another bite of cake and nodded his head. "You're not sad?"

She pulled her head back. "Sad? Why would I be sad?"

"Never mind. If you're not sad then you don't need to worry about it."

Arie took another bite of cake. "Nope, and I wasn't sad during the party. I was feeling pretty juicy."

"Juicy? What does that mean?"

Arie lightly choked on her bite of cake and held a finger up, so she could finish chewing. "Emma and I say juicy because we don't like the word horny. It's just too ick, so we say juicy. My biscuit was pressed against your neck, and I was feeling…juicy things."

"That wasn't easy for me either. Very tempting, and your thighs were just right there. I was distracted pretty quickly, though. If it were just the two of us…" He blew air from his mouth.

Liam stood and placed his fork in the trash can, then walked over toward the bathroom. "I'm going to brush my teeth. I'm all done with the cake."

Arie winced as she looked down at the remaining cake in the box. "Oooch, just one more bite, then I'll be done too." She took another bite, then one more. "So good. Okay. I'm done." She placed the box in the trash can, then joined Liam to brush her teeth.

Liam washed his hands, looking at Arie after he finished brushing his teeth. "You guys crack me up—biscuit, juicy, and the whole dragon thing."

Arie smiled. "She's a good friend, we've made up lots of words for things. She speaks my language. A lot of times I just talk in song lyrics, or lines from shows, and she always knows what I mean. One of my favorite things about Em is that she's always there for me, she's just as excited about the Night in Italy for the seniors as I am, and she initially had no interest in it, but since it was important to me, it became important to her. That's my definition of a real friend."

"Everything you care about will be important to me," Liam said. He placed his hand on the small of her back while she did a final rinse of her mouth. "Just so I know, your dads don't normally come into your room in the morning, right?"

Arie giggled. "No, that was only because it was my birthday. The cupcake for breakfast must have been Levi's idea. He's always thinking up cute stuff, they were so funny about it today, though. They reminded me several times that they were cool dads, said they didn't yell because we both had clothes on when they came in."

Chapter 45
Sorry I Saw Your Schlong

The next morning, when Liam opened his eyes there was no one else there to greet them, and there were no clothes on, aside from his underwear, and Arie's tiny thong.

He pulled the top cover up higher, covering Arie's chest and kissed her on the cheek. "Good morning, beautiful."

She opened one eye and stretched. "Good morning, you just covered me. That was so sweet."

Liam leaned on his elbow as he faced her on his left. "That was a little bit for both of us. I thought you might be cold, but also, we have to get you ready for your game."

Arie looked up at the fan then turned to face him. "Liam, last night was really amazing."

Liam nodded and kissed her on the cheek. "Mmmhmm…so amazing…"

He squeezed his eyes shut.

"What?" Arie asked. "Why are you closing your eyes? Do I have morning breath?" She blew into her hand, checking for herself.

Liam shook his head and kissed her lightly on the mouth. As he pulled back, he said, "No, you don't. We just need to get out of this bed and get dressed. You can't be late, and my brain is remembering things, positions…feelings." He rubbed her forehead and smiled. "So, let's get up."

Arie stood and wrapped herself in a lilac satin kimono that hung beside her bed. She walked toward the window and moved the curtains to the side. "Em is already gone. I guess she's gonna drive herself to the game. Are you riding with me, or going with my dads?"

Liam stood up from the bed and looked at his phone. "Ha, your dads just texted and asked me the same thing. Which would you rather I do?"

Arie without hesitation replied, "With me. You go with me." She smiled and approached him, wrapping her arms around his neck.

Liam embraced her and they shared a soft, sweet kiss. "Okay," Liam said, backing up. "I'm gonna run and get ready and then I'll be back. Make sure you eat. Sometimes, I'd be so pumped for an early game that I'd forget to eat breakfast. Don't let that happen."

Arie's eyes went wide. "True story, I was about to forget to eat. So, thank you."

Liam grabbed his bag and approached the door. Arie smiled brightly at him, forcing him to come around for one more quick kiss. Liam smiled and shook his head at himself. "I can't help myself with you. You're too enticing." He walked back toward her door. "Okay, I'll be back. I'm not gonna look at you, because I'm leaving for real this time."

He walked out of the room, then quickly came back inside smiling and shaking his head. "This is gonna sound weird, but can I have your car keys? I promise I won't lose them, and I'm not gonna drive your car."

Arie smiled and dug inside of her purse, she tossed the key fob to him without question.

Liam caught it. "Oh, this is cool. There's a cobra on it."

Arie smiled at him. 'Yeah, it is cool," she said, opening her dresser drawer.

"Aren't you curious why I asked for them? You're not afraid I'll drive it or something?"

"Nah. I've trusted you from the moment I met you. I'm not worried." She pulled out two long black socks and threw them on her bed.

Liam still held the fob in his hand looking at her. The implicit trust of another person was something Liam never had, and with Arie he hadn't even asked for it. He remembered how he felt the moment she took him by the hand and led him out to her car and their long conversation in the backyard. *Trust. I trusted her from the beginning. She trusts me, the same way that I trust her. How did I get so lucky?* He walked over and kissed her on the cheek, drawing a giggle from Arie. "Alright, for real. I'm going to get ready. I'll be back."

Liam sprinted from Arie's, over toward the side of the estate that he was staying on. Tom and Levi were loading their trunk and noticed him.

Levi said loudly to Tom, "Don't mess with him this morning. Look how happy he looks running over. Don't crush the poor guy."

Tom smiled looking over at Liam. "Good morning, Liam, are you riding with us? You didn't reply to the text."

Liam stopped near them, smiling, and shook his head. "No. Arie wants me to ride with her. Thanks, though."

"Okay, well, we have a chair for you, and we already packed the cooler. Do you need sunscreen? We have some if you do."

Liam shook his head. "No, thanks. I'm good. Do we not sit in the bleachers?"

Tom placed the cooler into the trunk. "No way. The parents there are crazy…the students are crazy…it's all crazy. Also, when these two schools play, it's a big deal. We're leaving in a few minutes so we can get a spot."

"The game doesn't start for another two hours. There's that many people?"

"Most definitely," Levi said. "Don't worry, we have our pop-up canopy and our chairs; we'll make a space and hopefully be left alone. I can't be harassed again today. Did Arie tell you that Ms. Doris grabbed my ass yesterday?"

Tom laughed loudly.

Liam shook his head and chuckled. "No, but she did tell me that Ms. Doris had fun with you two yesterday."

Levi walked toward the passenger door. "Not fun for me…I can tell you that."

"Alright, we'll see you over there in a bit," Tom said closing the trunk.

Arie just finished her hair and was tying the bottom of her left braid as her phone rang loudly beside her. She looked at the phone in confusion. *Why is Ethan's mom calling me? Oh, maybe it's something about the baby?* She answered, "Hi, Ms. Gina, how are you?"

"Hello, Arie, darling! I'm calling to see how you're doing. Ethan told me about Liam. Now, before you think anything, Mimmo is no gossip. He called this morning to ask a question about a pack and play, and I did what any good mother would do—I withheld the information until he told me what I wanted to know!" She cackled loudly at herself. "I'm so excited! I couldn't wait to call you for girl talk!"

Arie sat on her bed and giggled. "It's so nice of you to call. Everything is great. Had my party last night, which I guess you know about, but, yeah, Liam is just…great…he's just, like, amazing."

"Ooooh!" Gina squealed. "I'm so happy! You know, I knew about Coop and Ethan before they did, too. Always had a feeling. Same feeling with you two. That's why I texted you that picture, as soon as I heard he was single. I told the boys right away that I knew who would be perfect for him! Oh, sweetie, can you even imagine how beautiful your kids will be? Models. Definitely."

Arie loved talking to her. Since she couldn't remember conversations with her own mom, conversations with Gina felt like a warm motherly hug. "Well, we've only been together a short time, I don't even know if Liam wants kids. Probably way too soon for that type of conversation."

"Nope. Never too soon to talk about that, and if you don't want kids, fine, and if you do, start early. You two are gonna be together forever. I can already guarantee it. I'm never wrong about these things."

Arie stood and zipped her soccer bag, she grabbed her ball and tucked the phone in between her neck and shoulder. "I think so, too. He makes me feel so safe…and Ms. Gina last night…I can't even say, but… Wow."

Gina squealed in excitement. "You can tell me anything, I'm here to listen and support. But you two should come over soon, maybe tomorrow for gravy. You let me know."

Arie smiled and flipped her light off, heading downstairs. "Thank you. I'm headed out to a match right now, though, so I'll have to call you and let you know about the gravy."

"Oh, alright, well, you have fun and be safe, and call me if you need anything…anything at all."

As Arie closed her front door, she saw Liam sitting in the passenger seat of her car. He looked like he was adjusting her rearview mirror, repeatedly. She walked over and looked inside from the open passenger door.

Liam covered the mirror with his arms, playfully. "No, no, don't look until you get in your seat."

Arie giggled unsure of what he was doing to her mirror. "Okay, just hit the trunk button for me."

Liam got out and took her bag, he placed it in the trunk and said, "Wow, you have a lot of brand-new gear in here."

"Yeah, you never know if someone forgets something, or if I break something. I like to be prepared."

Liam closed the trunk and walked Arie over to the driver's side door. He opened the door and held her hand. "Okay, wait until I get inside before you do," he said jogging around the car.

Arie dropped an eyebrow at him. "Did you break my mirror?"

"Pftt. Of course not. I just want to see your face when I show you something." He quickly got into the passenger seat. "Alright, you can get in."

Arie looked at what dangled from the rearview mirror, her mouth hung open. "I love it," she said. She hugged Liam tightly and gave him a kiss on the lips.

Liam smiled. "You like it? Really?"

Arie nodded and touched the gold cursive "L" that hung from her mirror, she rubbed the tiny purple amethyst that was attached to it. "How did you even know I wanted something like this?"

"You told me yourself. Five minutes into our first car ride, don't you remember? You said you wanted something that made you feel safe and happy."

Arie was completely in shock that Liam remembered something she'd said in passing on their first outing together. "And you remembered?"

"Of course." He pulled a matching letter "A" in the same style, with the same stone, out of his pocket. "Well, to be honest, I bought this one for you first, but then it got here right after I told you how

I felt. When I came back to get changed, before I went back to your place, I ordered that one. I thought it would be better if we both had each other's initials. Took a chance that you liked me as much as I liked you, but I had the A as a backup."

Arie smiled and shook her head softly. "So sweet. I love it. It's perfect." Arie kissed him on the cheek then kissed the letter L that hung from the mirror. "Now, I feel safe and happy." She drove them out of the estate and headed toward the soccer field, blasting her pre-game playlist.

Liam stuck his charm in his pocket and lightly bopped his head to the music.

Arie pulled her mouth to the side not liking the song that was on.

"What's wrong?" Liam asked.

Arie switched to another song on her playlist. She scrunched up her nose and shook her head, still not feeling it. She switched to yet another song, still unable to get into pregame mode. The screaming in the songs wasn't doing it for her this morning.

Liam asked again, "What is it? What's wrong? Are you looking for a certain song?"

Arie's phone rang through the speakers, and the screen showed that Emma was calling. Arie answered it, in hands free mode, "Hey, Em! You on your way to the field?"

"Yeah, baby girl! Hey, thanks for letting us stay over last night. That was a wild end to your party," Emma said with a laugh.

"Yeah, it was fun. So, are you and Travis, like, together now, or what?"

Emma's voice dropped, "Did you hear us last night?"

Arie glanced quickly at Liam who shook his head. Arie answered, "No, we didn't hear you. Thank God."

Emma yelled incredulously, "Thank God? Thank God? Do you

have any idea how many times you screamed last night? The moans, Arie, the fucking moans, I was trying to keep my screams louder, gave Travis way more credit than he deserved."

Arie bit her lip in embarrassment.

Liam looked out of the passenger window, covering his smile.

"Here's my question," Emma started. "After you had such mind-blowing dick last night, how the hell are you gonna get into dragon mode this morning? I bet you're just smiling driving by yourself. Not even thinking about Alex…just thinking about that big, sweet D."

Arie shook her head, in embarrassment. "Em, Liam is in the car with me."

Emma was silent then asked, "Oh, and you got me coming through the speakers?"

Arie nodded and gripped her steering wheel tightly. "Yep."

Emma laughed heartily. "Ho ho ho, well, hello, Liam, and a good morning to you."

"Hi, Emma."

Emma cleared her throat. "Listen, Liam, I'm real sorry that I saw your schlong last night, didn't mean to. I've basically deleted it from memory, though."

Liam shook his head silently.

Arie decided to change the subject. "Em, Liam got us matching initial charms for our cars, like to hang from our mirrors. So cute, right?"

"Oh, that is cute! Yes! Tch, see you got a smart guy. Travis is dumb, he wouldn't think of something like that."

"You can't call him dumb after you guys just got together," Arie said.

"Yes, I can," Emma said. "That boy is dumb, hot but dumb. I'm okay with it. Alright. Let me go. I'm stopping to grab gas. I'll see you in a few."

Arie pulled into the parking lot behind the soccer field, and Liam gestured at the cars lined up outside the gate. "Wow. Your dads weren't kidding. There are a lot of people here. They're probably all here for you. You look so cute in your uniform."

"Thanks, and, yeah, a lot of them are here for me…and I have a problem."

Liam looked at her with concern. "What's wrong? Do you feel sick?"

"No. It's just like Em said, I'm too happy to go into dragon mode. I don't know what I'm gonna do." She smiled at Liam and shook her head, covering her mouth. "I can't even get into my playlist. This has never happened before."

Liam smiled broadly. "That makes me happy, though. To know that you're the happiest you've ever been, makes me feel really good."

Arie brought her face near his, and they shared a soft sensual kiss.

Liam held her face in his hands as he finished the kiss.

"I don't even care about Alex, or the game. Let's just stay here and make out." She went back in for more, which Liam happily gave her. She was completely lost in the taste and feel of Liam's mouth. Not even soccer could compete with the rush she felt kissing him.

A light knock on the driver's side window made them break apart. Emma stood tapping her wrist. Arie wiped her mouth and sighed, "Alright. More make-out time after the game."

Chapter 46
Arie In Waves

Arie greeted Emma with a hug and a high five as she and Liam stepped out of the car. She quickly grabbed her bag out of her trunk and threw it over her shoulder, then extended her hand to Liam, who held it and gave it a quick kiss.

Emma with her hands on her hips, leaned her head back in frustration looking at them. "Daaamn it. I knew this would happen if Liam came. Look at you, babe! Alex is gonna be here soon, where is my dragon?"

Arie shook her head and looked at Liam. "I'll be alright, Em. Don't worry."

Liam squeezed Arie's hand. "I'm sure as soon as you hit the field, you'll be fine."

They walked toward the field, which was already packed, even though warm-ups hadn't begun. Liam couldn't believe how many people were there.

"Oh, good, your dads are here," Emma said. She ran quickly over to Tom and Levi, leaving Arie and Liam walking slowly behind. Emma spoke wildly, her arms flying all over the place, as Levi casually glanced over his shoulder at the two, then leaned back in his chair.

Arie and Liam stepped under the canopy with her dads and Emma. Liam wasn't sure if it was okay for him to sit, or if he should wait until Arie hit the field.

"You good?" Tom asked, looking at Arie.

"I'm fine." She gave Liam a quick kiss, then grabbed a bottle of water out of the cooler.

Emma threw her arms up and pulled Arie by the hand, toward the field entrance, while Arie blew Liam a kiss with her free hand, beaming brightly over her shoulder.

Levi looked at her, pulled his sunglasses down and turned to Liam. "You broke the dragon. Her coach is gonna kill you."

"You should hide," Tom said.

Liam chuckled. "I didn't do anything, she said she wasn't feeling it this morning. She's happy, isn't that a good thing?"

"Of course, that's a good thing," Levi said. "But not right now."

Tom turned the portable fan toward Levi and looked at Liam. "You better hope Alex really pisses her off in warmups."

Liam watched Emma pull Arie onto the field, to the sounds of cheers from the bleachers. He remembered how incredible her skills were and how fierce she looked when he watched the clips of her scrimmage a few nights ago. Suddenly, he felt incredibly nervous thinking that he could have possibly set Arie up for a loss. "That's a lot of people calling her name at one time. I wasn't expecting that."

"Of course, there are a lot of people calling her name," Levi said, "everyone is here for Arie or Alex."

Tom stood and looked toward the opposite end of the field. "Oh shit, her coach looks mad already."

"Well, should we go say hi to Coach Meg?" Levi asked. "I don't want her to yell at her."

Liam felt really bad, he didn't want Arie to get in trouble. "I feel like I should leave, but she wants me here. I can't do that. What do you guys think I should do?"

Tom patted him on the shoulder. "Her coach is calling her over. Let's just see how this plays out. Maybe have a lollipop or something."

Liam tilted his head in thought. It was only in this moment, that he'd realized he hadn't had a lollipop all day, and now that he was thinking about it, since he started hanging out with Arie, he'd been eating fewer and fewer of them.

"I don't think I saw a lollipop in your mouth at all at the party," Levi said. "Did you give them up?"

Liam shook his head. "No, I'm not sure why. I just haven't wanted one."

Levi nodded at him. "Well, in Italy, you said they calmed you. Maybe you were using them as a sort of soothing device, and now that you've got Arie, you aren't as stressed out."

"I think you're right," Liam said.

Coach Meg yelled, "Number four, get over here! Taking your sweet time this morning."

Arie smiled big, and she patted Coach Meg's arm. "Good morning, Coach Meg. You look really pretty today."

Coach Meg looked confused at Arie, then eyeballed Emma. "What's wrong with my dragon?"

Arie giggled. "Nothing is wrong with me. I'm good. Let's do it. I'm ready."

Emma motioned with her head toward the tent where Arie's family sat.

Coach Meg saw Liam, she held her forehead and sighed. "Oh, no, not today."

Arie smiled like an idiot in love. "What? What's wrong?"

Coach Meg shook her head looking at Arie. "Emma, go put her music on and start warming up. I can't believe this is happening."

Emma and Arie were quickly joined by the rest of the team as they made their way to the bench in front of the bleachers. Arie's playlist blared much louder than normal through the portable speaker. The refs weren't there yet, so they were able to get away with it. Before warming up, Jenna pulled Arie aside and apologized for losing the ball to Dana the other night. Arie patted Jenna's head and smiled. "Don't worry about it. You did your best."

Jenna's eyes looked up, as Arie continued patting the top of her head, while staring at Liam.

"Look, babe, your song is on, let's go stretch it, out," Emma said. A glimmer of hope appeared, as Arie's head started moving to the music.

The fire within Arie's eyes rekindled, as Alex and the Predators entered the field. Alex was walking with two referees and her coach beside her.

Arie turned and looked at Alex's feet. "She's wearing new cleats, what is she? Stupid?"

Emma tightened her fist, and said under her breath, "Yes, my dragon is coming back."

The two referees and the Predators coach walked over to Coach Meg.

Arie started her arm stretches and bopped her head lightly, while looking over at their conversation.

Coach Meg yelled, "Four! Get over here!"

Arie quickly jogged over and put her hands behind her back. She listened, as the referees warned both her and Alex. The lead referee said, "This is your only warning. I'm not giving out any others. All these people here want to watch you play. "You," she said pointing at Arie, "keep the taunting to a minimum, and you"—she pointed to Alex—"play a clean game."

Alex rolled her eyes and stared at her nails, while Arie looked at Alex's feet, noticing her squishing her toes around in what were obviously new cleats, as Arie suspected.

"Arie, do you understand?" Coach Meg asked.

Arie nodded. "Yeah, I'm not gonna do anything to her. If she doesn't elbow me again." Arie's arms remained behind her back as she looked at the referee.

Alex said, "But the thing is, I just want to warm up with my music. The other night Arie came over and yelled that I couldn't use the song that I was playing." Alex put a hand on her own chest. "I did nothing. I was just trying to warm up and she came at me."

Alex's coach spoke to Coach Meg, "Can we just agree that neither tells the other what music they can listen to. Absolutely ridiculous that we're even having this conversation. Alex expressed to me earlier that her playlist is very special to her, so if we can just keep them on their own sides, we shouldn't have a problem."

"So stupid." Arie put a hand on her head. "Yeah, that's fine. I won't say anything."

Alex gave Arie an obviously fake smile. "I really just need my music to get me into it. So, I appreciate that, Arie."

"Are we done?" Arie asked. "I need to stretch."

The meeting ended, and Arie ran to the right as Alex ran to the left.

Emma flipped on Arie's favorite song. "You get yelled at?" she asked, looking over at Alex and Dana.

Arie nodded. "She's gonna try to piss me off with a song. Don't let me go at her. Ref said she'd toss me instantly. Just throw me to the ground if I try to do something."

"Are you back?' Emma asked. "Are you good?"

"Yeah, I'm just blocking Liam out, so I can stay mad. Don't mention him, okay?"

Emma pointed at the speaker. "Let's go, baby girl!"

Arie bounced to the music and pointed to the crowd, drawing cheers. She swayed her hips and rolled her head while Emma played air guitar. Arie danced around to her teammates giving ass smacks all around. She was in full dragon mode now, she screamed, "This is Viper territory, we're the predators, not them!"

The crowd roared loudly with her.

She stood and faced Emma, and they sang together, "Taaaake it!!" The first song ended and Arie's favorite dragon song started, she lifted her right knee up, stretching, while bobbing her head. Emma grabbed ahold of Arie's cleat and walked toward her stretching Arie's leg completely straight in the air, and then did the same to the other leg.

Arie's song ended, and Alex purposely turned her music up. Arie lunged to the side, listening. She'd seen Alex's message earlier in the week and with the meeting earlier, she understood that Alex was coming for her, with whatever was on this playlist she put together.

Emma pushed Arie's shoulders to the side as she did her lunges. "What is this?" Arie asked. "She's playing my song again. Mother eff... Nope, I'm not gonna say anything."

"Just listen and sing along," Emma said. "We love this song anyway."

Arie looked around for any refs then yelled over just loud enough for Alex to hear, "I did burn everything you've known…but I don't think even the vultures want you."

Alex and Dana stretched smirking over.

Arie added, "I'm not atoning for any sins. Why would you pick this song? Sitting there smirking at me, too. Stupid…"

One of the side refs heard Arie yelling over. She pointed at Arie and called to Coach Meg, "Number four is chirping already."

Arie dropped her head and reached for her cleat as she stretched in a sitting position.

"Babe, shush," Emma said.

The next song came on from Alex's playlist, and Arie listened while looking at Alex.

Emma said, "What the eff? Why would she pick this song?"

Arie looked at Alex, then up at the ref who was only ten feet away. Arie rolled her eyes, then smiled wide, realizing she had a way to trash talk without getting into trouble. She called loudly, "Hey, Jenna! Can you hear this song? Alex is telling me she's in love with me and she's sorry for ruining our friendship! Isn't this too good of a song for someone two-faced to play?"

Alex's mouth dropped open, and she ran over to a ref.

Arie laughed and looked at Emma. "She can't get me in trouble for that. I didn't say anything to her."

Coach Meg stood behind Arie. "Get up," she said.

Arie stood up and smiled nervously. "Hi, Coach Meg, did you, uh, go say hi to my dads?"

Coach Meg had her hands on her hips and shook her head at Arie. She wagged her finger at her, "Listen, I'm not mad at you, but I have to look like I'm yelling at you. So, pretend you're getting yelled at."

Arie threw her hands up and rolled her eyes, she kicked the grass, playing along.

Coach Meg said, "I don't care what they say. But you are not to let the ref hear you. You can't get tossed; you hear me?"

Arie nodded.

Coach Meg, feigning frustration, walked away.

"Alright, let's go hunters one more time, Em," Arie called out.

Emma ran back over to the bench and flipped Arie's song on. Arie gathered the team into a huddle, and they talked over strategy.

Arie heard the song that Alex put on, which definitely played louder than the others.

Arie's face changed instantly, she looked at Emma and said, "No. No. Em, No. This is too far."

Arie charged over to the ref standing by Alex, while Alex smiled and laughed. Arie screamed, "She can't play this song!" She turned while yelling. "Coach Meg, come over here!"

Coach Meg jogged over, as did the other refs and Alex's coach.

Arie screamed, "She knows this song is personal to me! This was from a very bad point in my life, and she knows that!"

Alex's coach threw her hands up, while Coach Meg held a hand on her own head.

Arie felt like she was going to cry. "No. This song brought me out of my darkest moment… It's a very meaningful, emotional song for a lot of people. Listen to the words…" Arie sniffled.

Alex put a hand on her own chest. "Oh my gosh! I had no idea. I'm so sorry. But you know songs can mean different things to different people. Couldn't it also just be about waves? Or maybe people in water?"

Arie inhaled deeply and looked at Coach Meg, she whispered, "Make her shut it off. Please? She got what she wanted. She got in my head. I can't take it. I love this song, but damn it, she took me right back there."

Alex agreed to shut the song off with a smile, as Arie walked over to Emma shaking her head. Emma put a hand on Arie's shoulder, and her teammates gave her a big group hug. Emma said, "Shake it off. We're gonna destroy her. She messed up doing that. Arie, look around you. You're not alone. Pick your head up and look behind you."

Arie lifted her head to see Liam leaning against the fence, looking over, he looked incredibly concerned. Arie left the group and ran over to him. She quickly kissed him, and said, "I'm fine. She did something stupid. I'll tell you later."

Liam pulled the charm out of his pocket and kissed it, drawing the biggest smile from Arie. She gave him a crisp kiss on the cheek and ran back to the group, still smiling.

Emma pointed over to Liam and nodded approvingly.

The match began and Arie was amped, gone were the feelings of self-doubt and loneliness that she briefly remembered. She went hard after the ball, as Alex came straight at her. "Gonna show off now for your boyfriend, Arie?"

Arie ignored her and focused on the ball, she passed to Jenna on the outside and ran quickly up the field. Alex tripped and bumped her from behind, she let out a genuine, "Sorry."

Alex's brief sincerity broke Arie's concentration, allowing Dana to steal the ball from Jenna, and clear it down field. Arie charged back toward the ball. The rest of the first half went much the same, with neither team scoring at the end of the first half.

During the halftime break Arie noticed Alex sitting in her socks on the bench. It looked like she was trying on other people's cleats.

Coach Meg motioned for Arie.

"What's up?" Arie asked.

"What size cleats do you wear?" Coach Meg asked.

"Eight and a half, why?"

Coach Meg sighed. "Listen, this is totally up to you. But Alex's coach said her cleat broke, and she may not be able to play in the second half."

Arie looked over her shoulder at Alex's disappointed face. Her posture dropped, and she rolled her eyes.

Coach Meg said, "She won't wear anyone's old cleats, but I know you normally have extra stuff. She also wears an 8.5. I think she deserves to sit on the bench, so I can just tell her coach that we don't have any spare ones. She'll never know. But I wanted to ask you, because I know how badly you want to finish this one. I know you too well. If you come out here and wipe the field with the rest of them, you're not gonna be happy. You won't be happy unless you destroy her and unless you loan her some cleats, that's not gonna happen. But it's your call."

Arie put her hands on her hips, "Efff. This isn't some kind of a movie where I give her my cleats and we become friends, okay? I hate her and I always will." She held a hand on her forehead. "Why is this happening? You know she's the worst human being on the planet, right?"

Coach Meg smiled. "I do. But I also know that you are the most compassionate person on this field right now. It's up to you. What do you wanna do?"

Arie sighed and dropped her head. "I'll be right back. But, wait, don't tell her coach that they're mine, or she probably won't take them. Just tell her I'm grabbing them out of the locker room because I'm the fastest. It's only a half lie."

Coach Meg smiled. "You got it."

Arie ran off the field, to the parking lot. She quickly popped her trunk and grabbed out the pair of custom-made, brand name cleats, that she'd yet to wear herself. She ran back to the field and handed the box to her coach, who brought it over to Alex.

The second half began, and Arie and Alex were knotted together like a pretzel, fighting over the ball. Arie cut to the side then reversed and flew down field, she kicked hard, and the ball flew past the goalie into the net. Arie dropped to her knees, as she scored! She screamed, "Yeahhh!"

The crowd roared, and her teammates swarmed her.

Dana quickly gained possession after the point and ran down the field with Alex beside her. Jenna stole the ball and passed to Arie, who advanced down the field quickly. Time was running out, and Arie knew if she scored just one more time, the game would be over.

Dana yelled to Alex, "Come on, do something!"

Alex cut inside, and Arie started smack talking, "I'm unbreakable, Alex… You will never break me…not like those cheap-ass cleats you had."

Arie kicked the ball toward the goal, but the goalie saved it. Arie sighed with her hands on her hips. "Would've been so cool if that went in, too."

The goalie cleared the ball, and Arie stayed behind for just a minute, quickly catching her breath.

"Those were custom cleats that broke," Alex said to Arie. "They weren't cheap."

Arie panted heavily with her hands on her hips. "Well, what the hell were you thinking wearing new cleats to a game?"

Alex tightened her ponytail. "They had tiny gold dragons airbrushed on them." Alex looked down at her cleats. "Thanks for letting me use these. They're obviously yours, the purple dragons gave it away."

Arie rolled her eyes and ran toward the ball without a reply. There were only two minutes remaining. Arie tried to get the ball away from Dana and couldn't shake it, Alex came in between the two and elbowed Arie hard, which of course the ref didn't notice.

Arie screamed, holding her stomach, "Everyone in, just block! Just fucking block!"

Jenna tried to regain possession from Dana, and screamed, "Get off me!"

Arie quickly pulled back in case of a clearance, then ran back in the mix to block after realizing there were only fifteen seconds left.

Emma came out of the net, Arie screamed, "No! Get back in the net, Em! Get back in!"

Dana took her shot as Emma dove—bam! Dana's cleat connected clean and hard with Emma's biscuit.

The ball landed outside the goal and time expired with the Vipers winning 1–0, as Emma lay on the ground screaming in pain, "Ouch! My biscuit, my biscuit!"

Liam's phone rang, as Arie ran toward him smiling, he answered, "Hey, Coop, what can I do for you?"

Coop screamed into the phone excitedly, "It's baby time! We're getting on a plane!"

Epilogue

Two years later

Arie screamed as Liam held her left hand, "My biscuit! Ouch! Liam! Get them out!

Liam rubbed her hair, encouraging her, "You're doing so good, Arie. I love you so much. You're almost done. We're gonna meet our boys soon. Just a little more, honey."

Arie was in the final stages of delivering twins and was currently in excruciating pain. Gina, stood on the right side, reminding Arie to breathe, the two had grown close after the birth of Coop and Ethan's son, Aiden Liam Morgan, in Italy two years earlier.

Coop answered a call from Levi, who was at the hospital. "Hey, guys, you can head over now. Liam said the doctor told him they'll be born any minute," Levi said.

Coop smiled. "Alright, we're on our way. Aiden's grumpy though, fair warning."

Tom laughed in the background. "Tell him that I'm here and I'll take him to get cookies."

"Aiden, you wanna go see the babies?" Coop asked him.

"No, thank you," his small voice replied.

Ethan laughed and held his arms wide. "Come here, you wanna go get cookies with Grandpa Tom?"

"No, thank you," Aiden said softly.

"What do you wanna do, big guy?" Coop asked.

Aiden jumped into Ethan's arms and said loudly, "Grandpa Levi!"

"I'm gonna pretend my heart isn't broken," Tom said.

Levi giggled. "Put him on the phone. I want to talk to him."

Coop held the phone to his ear. "Say hello, Aiden. It's Grandpa Levi."

Levi spoke loudly, "You want to come hang out with Grandpa Levi and I'll get you some cookies, buddy?"

Aiden smiled and nodded. "Yes, please."

Coop ruffled his hair as Ethan kissed him on the cheek.

"Alright, that did it," Coop said. "We'll head that way."

After packing up a bag for Aiden, the family hopped into their car. Ethan flipped the in-seat monitor on for Aiden, so he could watch his favorite show. He fell asleep inside his car seat within five minutes.

Coop shook his head. "I don't know how our office staff is going to function without Liam there for three months."

"Well, he only asked us for eight weeks, we're the ones that told him he could have twelve," Ethan reminded him.

"I can't help it when it comes to Liam," Coop said. "He does so much for the Foundation. He deserves the time off."

"I agree. I'm honestly more worried about what names he and Arie came up with for the twins. Can't believe they kept it a secret. I mean, we kept Aiden's middle name a secret, just because we wanted to surprise Liam."

"Levi said that Liam keeps coming in and out, saying our names together. Levi thinks he's going to name one of them Cooper, just so he can say Cooper whenever he wants."

After arriving at the hospital, Ethan carefully took Aiden out of his car seat and held his sleeping body on his shoulder. Coop kissed Ethan's cheek and the top of Aiden's head. "You guys are so cute. I love seeing him asleep like that on your shoulder."

Ethan smiled. "I love it when he's asleep like this, too. He's just out. I could run around the parking lot, and he wouldn't even bat an eye."

They walked up to the labor and delivery floor and saw Levi and Tom hugging one another, with happy tear-streaked faces.

Coop asked excitedly, "Are they here? What are their names?"

Levi and Tom looked over at them and nodded, smiling brightly.

"Can we go in?" Coop asked, pointing at the door.

"Yeah, just knock first," Tom said. "It's just Liam, Arie, and the babies in there, Gina just ran down to the cafeteria."

Levi asked Ethan, "Do you want me to take Aiden before you go in?"

"Nah, he's out," Ethan said. "If he wakes up and we aren't there, he won't be happy."

"Okay," Levi said. "Oh, and Kory and Luke should be on their way. Luke said something about a baker, or that they were stopping at a bakery… I don't know."

Coop and Ethan knocked on the door, and Liam opened it, smiling big. He hugged Coop tightly then rubbed Ethan's back in lieu of a hug, since Aiden was asleep on his shoulder. They both congratulated him and stepped inside. They walked over to Arie and congratulated her quietly.

Arie smiled, half asleep with the babies in their own tiny hospital bassinettes beside her. She said softly, "Hey, guys. Thanks for coming. Did Liam already tell you their names?"

Ethan and Coop shook their heads. They gazed in adoration at the two perfect little babies.

Liam walked over to Arie and kissed her head. "Do you need anything?"

Arie shook her head. "Just you."

"I love you so much. Look at our babies, honey." He kissed her again on the forehead.

Arie smiled softly. "I love you with all my heart, Liam. They're perfect, just like you."

Liam looked at Coop and Ethan, then pointed at the bassinettes. "Bet you can't guess which one I named."

The crib tag on the left read:
<u>Baby Name</u>: Matthew Jonathan Collins
<u>Birthdate</u>: 9/30/2024
<u>Time</u>: 3:49pm
<u>Weight</u>: 5 lbs 10 oz
<u>Mother</u>: Ariel Lynn Collins <u>Father</u>: Liam Ruel Collins

The crib tag on the right read:
<u>Baby Name</u>: Cethan Morgan Collins
<u>Birthdate</u>: 9/30/2024
<u>Time</u>: 3:52pm
<u>Weight</u>: 5lbs 1 oz
<u>Mother</u>: Ariel Lynn Collins <u>Father</u>: Liam Ruel Collins

Ethan and Coop read the twins crib cards. They were both honored and shocked that Liam chose a mix of their names for one of the babies.

Coop asked, "How did you know our ship name? We've only said it once or twice in our entire lives."

Ethan smiled and rubbed Aiden's back.

"Your ship name?" Liam asked. "I didn't do it because of that. I just couldn't decide which one of you to name him after. I mixed your names up until I found one that Arie and I both liked. I feel a little bad because it's mostly Ethan's name, but it didn't work any other way. But your letter is the most important one, Coop."

Ethan and Coop smiled and thanked him, as Liam came in for another teary-eyed hug.

Ethan hugged Liam from the side, which made Aiden move around a bit. He lifted his sleepy head; his thick black hair hung in his face. He looked around through half-lidded eyes, then laid his head back down. "Aaand he's out again," Ethan said. "He's gonna be up all night."

Tom and Levi joined them inside of the room. Tom came around and gave Liam a big hug. "We're so proud of you, both."

Levi pushed Arie's hair out of her face, as she fell asleep from exhaustion.

Gina came inside the room, smiling. She hugged Coop, then Ethan, and kissed Aiden on the head and pouted at his adorable sleeping face. "Your father is on his way," she told Ethan, as she passed Liam a container with a chicken sandwich and fries from the cafeteria. Noticing that Arie was asleep, Gina said, "Oh, I got Arie the dessert she wanted. I'll just leave it here for her, Liam." She placed the container on the nightstand and looked at Coop and Ethan. "Don't you just love their names? Such dolls, look at them, absolutely adorable. I told Arie they would make beautiful babies together, one day. I'm never wrong."

Liam quickly devoured his sandwich, while the others stared down at the babies. They had a very large private room, so there was no lack of space within it.

Ethan looked at his mother. "Don't forget tomorrow we need you to watch Aiden during our game."

Gina cocked her head to the side. "How would I ever forget that? Like I would ever forget. Your father can't stop bragging every time he sees you two on TV, he takes full credit for you guys getting signed on the same team."

Tom rolled his eyes and laughed. "Oh, Paul, he takes credit for everything."

Gina giggled and looked at Ethan. "You tell Aiden that Nonna and Papa will be there bright and early tomorrow morning to play."

Levi sassed, "He definitely would've rather played with his much cooler grandpas if given a choice. Everyone knows he likes me best."

Aiden lifted his head hearing Levi's voice, his eyes remained closed, as Ethan looked at him on his shoulder. Aiden slowly laid his head back down. Ethan rubbed his back and kissed his head.

Coop shook his head and rubbed Aiden's back. "He really is gonna be up all night. I will say, if we're talking about who he'd really rather play with, it would be Anya, but you two can argue over which of you he likes best."

"Well, it's really no competition," Tom said. "Anya is adorable. She looks just like Kai's wife but has the same personality as Kai. It's great that they're only a year apart."

Levi waved him off. "He likes me better than Anya, because I can give him cookies."

Ethan and Coop walked over to Liam who lay on a pull-out bed that was beside Arie's hospital bed. Ethan said, "Liam, we're both really thankful for all that you've done, for us and for the Foundation. We're even happier that you're a part of our family. Thank you, really, for everything. We'll always be grateful to you. We'd do anything for you guys."

Coop added, "You're gonna be a great dad, Liam. Whatever you guys need, you just let us know. And thank you for naming a baby after us. Really."

Liam's bottom lip shook, and his eyes teared up. "I really love being a part of this family."

Tom with his arm wrapped around Levi, said, "We love that you're a part of the family too, Liam."

The next day

Following a win earlier in the afternoon, Ethan sat on the floor, shirtless, his jeans rolled at the ankle. He held a pencil in his mouth and stared at the family picture he finished drawing on the large canvas. It was the same one he'd started sketching on their honeymoon.

"Babbo!" Aiden called. Ethan pulled the pencil out of his mouth. Aiden ran in and gave him a big kiss on the cheek. He turned toward Ethan's drawing. "That's me!" he said pointing to the canvas. "And Babbo, and Daddyyyy!"

"That's right," Ethan said, pulling him into a hug. Ethan giggled noticing that his shoulder-length black hair had blue paint in it.

"Ahh, you got into my paint. Aiden, where is Daddy?"

Aiden smiled and showed Ethan his blue hands then laughed. "Daddy sleep."

Coop came rushing through the door, his face had a small blue handprint on it, there were several other smudged prints on his shirt. He smiled at Ethan. "I swear, I closed my eyes for only a second and then…this…" Coop gestured to the handprints on his body.

Ethan pulled Aiden in from the side. "Daddy is silly, huh?"

Aiden grabbed a dry paintbrush from the floor beside Ethan.

"Babbo's turn," he said, holding the paintbrush near Ethan's smiling face.

"You want to paint me, too?" Ethan asked.

Aiden nodded and ran the dry brush on Ethan's cheeks, then his arms.

"You're doing a great job, I can tell," Ethan said.

Coop squatted down and tilted his head. "Hmmm. I don't know, Aiden. Something is missing from Babbo."

Aiden's big brown eyes looked at Ethan. "Babbo needs blue!"

Coop nodded and ruffled Aiden's hair.

Aiden ran out of the room, and Coop quickly smooched Ethan then chased after him.

A few seconds later, Coop came back in, holding Aiden, his brush now dipped in blue paint. He sat on the floor next to Ethan and placed Aiden down.

"Now, Babbo's turn," Aiden said.

Ethan smiled as Aiden painted blue lines on his face and arms.

"Done!" he said dropping the brush onto the floor.

Ethan pulled their son's tiny body into a family hug. "Who does Aiden love?"

Aiden looked at both of his dads and pointed. "Babbo and Daddy!"

Coop frowned. "Why is Babbo always first, why not Daddy and Babbo?"

Aiden tilted his head. "Aiden loves Daddy and Babbo!"

Coop turned Aiden's body around. The small replica jersey he wore matched Coop's from their new team. The name Morgan and the number 1 were both covered in blue smudges and swirls. He asked, "How did you get blue paint on the back?"

Ethan giggled at the sight. "Aiden, tomorrow you wear Babbo's jersey, so I can hit a homerun like Daddy!" He stood and lifted Aiden up high.

"Babbo steal!" Aiden said.

"What? Who taught you that?" Ethan asked.

Aiden laughed uproariously. "Babbo steal! Babbo steal!"

Coop stood up chuckling. "He got it from me. When we watched the replay earlier, his eyes were glued to you. I told him, 'Aiden, watch, Babbo's gonna steal!' He was jumping up and down watching you steal second base. It was so cute. Then I hit a home run, and he just walked away...he was not impressed with that."

Aiden played with the number 1 charm that hung from Ethan's neck, then reached toward Coop. Ethan passed him over. Coop asked him, "You think daddy's homerun was awesome, too, right?"

Aiden didn't answer, he played with the number 2 charm that hung from Coop's neck. "This is Babbo's," he said.

Coop smiled. "Yes, Daddy is Babbo's, and Babbo is Daddy's."

Ethan gave them both a kiss on the cheek, "You two are the most adorable."

Coop placed Aiden down and hugged Ethan tightly.

"I love you so much, my Cooper. I'm so happy."

"You are my everything. I love you, puppy. There's nothing I wouldn't do for the both of you."

They shared a quick smooch.

Aiden walked beside them and looked up. "Aiden wants a puppy..."

About Cali Kitsu

Cali Kitsu lives in a very sunny state with her amazing husband and daughters, and she enjoys making people smile. She tries to bring a little bit of her Cali sunshine and energy wherever she goes. Cali believes that love is for everyone, and she's found the perfect way to express that in her writing. Cali absolutely loves writing—she's having so much fun telling steamy boy love stories, with a bit of her Cali sense of humor!

Aside from co-hosting the *Cali & Craig Talk…* podcast with her bestie Craig, Cali is also assistant to Craig Gibb, publisher at Story Perfect Books and its family of imprints, and author of the MM YA romance books *You Can Call Me Cooper* (2024) and *Froderick, Gay Son of Dracula* (2024), and the MM adult romance books *Cookies, Candles, and Cute Butts For Christmas* (2024), *Vincent & Sivan: Book 1: Rum-Soaked Awakenings* (2025), *You Can Call Me Cooper: Author's Cut* (2025), and *Only My Husband Calls Me Cooper* (2025).

Cali's other hobbies include watching Anime, reading Manga, baking, going to the beach, and she's an avid gamer in all forms: console, tabletop, strategy card games…*Magic the Gathering* is probably her favorite strategy card game.

YA Romance Books by Cali Kitsu
You Can Call Me Cooper
Froderick, Gay Son of Dracula

Adult Romance Books by Cali Kitsu
Cookies, Candles, and Cute Butts for Christmas
Vincent & Sivan: Book 1: Rum-Soaked Awakenings
You Can Call Me Cooper: Author's Cut
Only My Husband Calls Me Cooper

More Books by Cali Kitsu

Vincent & Sivan
Book 1: Rum-Soaked Awakenings
Cali Kitsu

Vincent & Sivan is an explicit, best-friends-to-lovers, dual gay awakening, adult MM romance novel.

Vincent and Sivan, sons of the world's most powerful pirates, are to be named captains this year, an honor for when they turn twenty-one. Under their fathers, they will rule in the modern age of pirates where the seas are at peace and long gone are the days of pillaging and plundering.

Best friends since childhood, they couldn't have more opposite views on love. Vincent wants to settle down with the right person, despite pressure from his father to marry once he's named captain. Sivan, however, finds the idea of love and marriage laughable.

Reunited after months apart as their fathers' ships patrolled opposite ends of the seas, Vincent and Sivan share a bottle of rum in the ship's storage room. A moment of curiosity steeped in hidden desire, filthy with lust, leads to a very hot and heavy night of rum-soaked awakenings…

But no one can know about this, no one can find out, or their promotions as captains, and the trust of their fathers, may be altogether shattered.

Vincent and Sivan are thrust into a world of secrets and betrayal, as their crews now face a long-buried threat when those determined to bring back the old ways of pirates emerge from the shadows.

More Books by Cali Kitsu

**Cookies, Candles, and Cute Butts
for Christmas
Cameron D. James & Cali Kitsu**

It's gonna be a hot Christmas in Frosty Bottoms, when Braden, the new hunky veterinarian strolls into town, but this gorgeous man is no stranger, and he's no longer a vet. He's coming back to Frosty Bottoms to bake cookies and dip his wick in Kellan, the local candlemaker, who happens to be his childhood best friend.

Kellan knows Braden is coming back to town and taking over BJ's Cookies and he's unsure how to feel about it. They have a past; Kellan felt something but then Braden moved away.

Sparks soon fly when Braden reunites with Kellan, but they want different things. Braden is only interested in a relationship, while Kellan is only looking for hookups. With mishaps galore, including over-excited family, unrecognizable otters, and motorboating a muscle chest, everyone and everything seems to be pushing the two men together.

When the initial ice between them melts, it's not long before more than cookie dough is being rolled out on Braden's counters…and a certain bottom is getting frosted.